Playing to the Gods

TOR BOOKS BY MELANIE RAWN

Spellbinder
Fire Raiser

THE GLASS THORNS SERIES
Touchstone
Elsewhens
Thornlost
Window Wall
Playing to the Gods

Playing to the Gods

MELANIE RAWN

TOR

A TOM DOHERTY ASSOCIATES BOOK
NEW YORK

PLAYING TO THE GODS

Copyright © 2017 by Melanie Rawn

A Tor Book
Published by Tom Doherty Associates
175 Fifth Avenue
New York, NY 10010

www.tor-forge.com

Tor® is a registered trademark of Macmillan Publishing Group, LLC.

The Library of Congress Cataloging-in-Publication Data is available upon request.

ISBN 978-0-7653-7736-4 (hardcover)
ISBN 978-1-4668-5517-5 (ebook)

Our books may be purchased in bulk for promotional, educational, or business use. Please contact your local bookseller or the Macmillan Corporate and Premium Sales Department at 1-800-221-7945, extension 5442, or by email at MacmillanSpecialMarkets@macmillan.com.

First Edition: August 2017

Printed in the United States of America

0 9 8 7 6 5 4 3 2 1

for
MARY ANNE FORD
and
PHIL DION

Playing to the Gods

Covered from toes to chest by a quilt that not so long ago had reached to his nose, Derien Silversun lay absolutely still in bed, waiting to hear Mistress Mirdley's weighty footfalls fade downstairs into silence. He knew just how long it took her to descend the staircase, and just how many short, sharp paces it took to walk to the kitchen. He knew the specific noises of each door (the one into the back hallway creaked; the one into the kitchen whined). He could judge her mood by the swiftness of her steps and how emphatic they might be. Tonight she was worried, but not overly so, and very tired. This correlated perfectly with what he had seen in her face and her eyes when she'd told him Cayden would be all right and his hand was not permanently damaged. Had she been afraid, he would have heard it in quickened footsteps or a slammed door.

He was tired, too. But he had a task to complete before he slept. He counted to one hundred, and again, then called blue Wizardfire to a candle and reached under his mattress for a folded-up parchment. He spread it out on the sky-blue velvet counterpane and gently smoothed the creases.

He had always loved maps. Though he'd never been farther out of Gallantrybanks proper than Mieka's house at Hilldrop, he could look at the markings on a map and instantly envision cobblestone streets or dirt roads, forests or rivers or plowed fields, lofty mountains or green-ferned valleys. Maps spoke to him as charted music spoke to a lutenist, and he read them with the suppleness Alaen Blackpath brought to his strings—or had, before thornful after thornful of dragon tears began to obliterate his talent.

This was a different sort of map. It was of his own making and not contiguous; its five sections bore no relationship to one another. The sole common point of reference was the Gally River. That, and the substantial wealth of the neighborhoods depicted. There was the odd anomaly—Wistly Hall, for example, situated in one of the most exclusive areas of the city but inhabited by a chronically impecunious family (though with the successes of several of the younger generation, the Windthistles weren't so skint as they'd been when first Dery had visited there). Some of the houses belonged to the parents of his schoolfellows. All were neatly labeled with the name of the family who lived there.

His work tonight was to add a few notes while everything was clear in his mind. He hadn't his older brother's remarkable memory. It was an effort to memorize his lessons at the King's College when the learning involved listening to a lecture or reading a text. He was at his best with drawings. Any mention of a country or town or district, and a map of it seemed to conjure itself before his eyes. It was simply a quirk of his brain, and by no means the most important. *That* one was what he had used at intervals today, roaming about Gallybanks with his friends to watch the celebrations of the King's twenty-fifth year on the throne. He'd nearly burst with pride during Touchstone's display in Amberwall Square, laughing and cheering with everyone else at the scenes displayed on the outside wall of the Kiral Kellari. Afterwards, he and six friends had somehow managed to scurry through the crowded streets in time to see the Shadowshapers' tribute on the newly renamed King Meredan Bridge. He'd been looking forward to telling Cade all about it, but that would have to wait.

Derien shoved aside anxious wonderings about what exactly had happened to the withie that exploded and injured Cade's hand, and who had done it, and why, annoyingly aware that everyone would think him too young to understand or even to hear the ominous details. Cade would tell him, eventually. Or mayhap he could persuade Mieka. But that was for later. Right now, he had work to do.

After rising from the bed, he retrieved a box of watercolors and a brush from his desk. A little water from the pitcher on his bedside table went into a small glass bowl. Seating himself cross-legged with the map before him, he coaxed the Wizardfire a trifle brighter and mixed a brushful of yellow paint. And then he began to carefully mark certain houses on his map.

*   *   *

Shortly before dawn, four young men descended the grand staircase of Archduke Cyed Henick's mansion at Great Welkin. They managed this descent in various ways. One of them, tall and thin and dark and intense, leaped down with light, purposeful steps, head high and eyes glittering. The man who followed him moved with the same lithe assurance, though he was the first man's opposite to look at: blond and fair-skinned, with the type of limpid-eyed golden handsomeness that inexperienced girls wanted simply to stare at, and daring women wanted to see distort with lust. The third young man, nondescript in every way, had a shoulder wedged under the armpit of the fourth, who staggered and stumbled, small whimpers escaping his lips with every step.

"Oh, for fuck's sake, Pirro!" the first man snarled. "Shut it, would you?"

"I think he's gonna be sick again," said the blond.

"If he is, he'll lick it up off the floor himself. Come on. I want to be back in Gallybanks for breakfast."

The word caused the unfortunate Pirro to groan mightily and slip from his companion's support to the marble floor.

"You have to keep it down this time, old son," was his friend's advice as he looked up with bleary, bloodshot eyes. "Yark it up again, and we'll just have to go back."

The main door opened on the feeble beginnings of the day. The light, murky though it was, seemed to make the dark young man pause, but after a moment he laughed—a bit high-pitched, a bit nervous—and strode outside. The blond hesitated, glancing uncertainly from the door to the other two men, then shrugged and went to help them.

"Mind the drink and the thorn from now on," he said as he helped Pirro to his feet. "Until we're certain of what the changes will mean, we all have to have a care to that sort of thing. How are you feeling, Herris?"

"Fine. Up you come, Pirro, there's a good lad. We'll take you home and you can sleep it all off, and wake up fit for anything."

Between them, they managed to get him across the marble entry hall and out the door. They shoved him into the waiting carriage, where the dark young man received him with an exclamation of disgust. Once they were all four inside and the door shut behind them, enclosing them in wood and leather and black tapestry curtains, Kaj drew a square of green silk from a pocket and handed it to Pirro, who had curled miserably into a corner.

"Here. You've blood on your chin."

Even in the dimness of the closed carriage, with curtains shutting out all exterior light, the other three clearly saw him wipe feebly at the smear, and then pause, and then slide the silk into his mouth and suck at it: eagerly, hungrily, with a grin spreading across his face.

"Anticipating in advance of the plot, are we, old lad?" Thierin Knottinger laughed and patted his glisker on the knee. "Have patience. It's still sunlight by day and stew at dinner for us, until that theater is finished."

*   *   *

She finished scraping her hair into a knot at her nape and didn't bother glancing into the mirror to make sure she was tidy; at this hour, and after last night's events, nobody she was likely to see would care. Neither, nearly always, did she.

About to turn towards the warm anarchy of her bed, a scratching sound at her door swung her round in the other direction. "Vren?" she whispered. "Is that you?"

A young woman of about her own age peeked in. "Good Gods, Megs! You're already dressed!"

"Well, until about five minutes ago, I wasn't—I promise!"

The two women laughed silently as they shut the bedchamber door behind them. No one stirred in the long hallway that led to Princess Miriuzca's apartments, but the place would soon be swarming with servants. Though there would be no fires to lay and light in this mild weather, wake-up cups of tea or mocah would be coming from the kitchens within the half hour. There were no guards here. Not only had Miriuzca charmingly, politely, and adamantly refused them on the day she moved into the chambers, but there was also no need. Someone had once asked Lady Vrennerie who guarded the Princess when she went outside the Palace to do some shopping or visiting, and Vrennerie, somewhat surprised, had replied, "Everyone does." And she was right:

Miriuzca was adored in Albeyn only slightly less than the King himself. No one so much as criticized her—not even Princess Iamina, not in public. No one would even dream of harming her—except her younger half brother, and he was halfway across the Flood by now.

Miriuzca was already awake in bed, with little Princess Levenie at her breast. This was another matter on which she had insisted: She fed her children herself for the first year of their lives. By the time she asserted this maternal prerogative with her firstborn, Prince Roshlin, her husband had seen that delicate jawline harden to stubbornness often enough to know that she meant what she said. It wasn't the first time he simply shrugged and avoided the matter. They both knew it would not be the last.

Forget-me-never blue eyes glanced up and brightened at the sight of Megs and Vrennerie. "And so?" she asked eagerly.

Megs waited until Vrennerie had closed the bedchamber door. Then, with elaborate casualness, she replied, "Not half bad."

"Even one-handed?" Vrennerie teased.

"Even so. Though I doubt he'll remember much, poor dear. His eyes kept glazing over like fog on a lake."

"He does have lovely eyes," Miriuzca commented. Levenie stirred and whined fretfully. Megs went to the bed, frowned slightly with concentration, and the child quieted while Miriuzca guided her back to feed. "I wish I knew how to do that," the Princess sighed. "Especially when Roshlin is shrieking the roof tiles loose. But tell me everything, Megs. *Everything*," she emphasized with a muffled, deep-throated laugh.

"Ah, if others only knew what we know about you!" Vrennerie said with the ease of long friendship.

"Look at that face!" Megs scoffed. "Who'd believe it?"

Miriuzca batted long golden eyelashes, then chuckled again. "I want to know everything, Megueris. Gentlemen might not tell, but we ladies have a duty to each other."

"Absolutely," Vrennerie seconded, seating herself on the other side of the bed. "I have to know whether he liked that thing I told you about, the one Kelinn taught me, where you—"

"He liked *everything*." Megs looked bemused. "As if he'd never done it before. We all know he has, and quite often, too. But he was so sweet about it all, and sort of . . . I don't know, *grateful*."

*   *   *

She was roused from sleep by the sound of her husband's mutterings. It was barely dawn; he couldn't possibly be awake; and yet there he was, hunched in a chair to pull on his boots.

"Silly git," he grumbled, "coulda blown his fingers off—or his whole hand—everybody saying how brave he was—*brave* being another word for *stupid*!"

"Mieka? Where are you going? Why are you awake so early?"

He gave a start and looked over at her. "Didn't sleep much. I have to go see Cayden."

Always Cayden. The thought was there in her eyes, and the sudden twist at the corner of his mouth meant he had seen and understood. He stamped his right foot into his boot and started work on the other one.

"I have to make sure he's all right."

"But didn't you say Mistress Mirdley and the Court physicker and—and *everyone* said he wasn't permanently damaged?"

"Won't know that until his hand heals, will we?" A second thunk of a bootheel on the carpet, and he got to his feet.

Propping herself on one elbow, she stifled a yawn and then said, "Be sure to give our best wishes to the Princess. She's been so kind."

"I'm not going to the Palace to pay a social call."

"Of course not. I didn't mean it that way. I just thought that if you happened to see her—or Princess Iamina, or anyone like that—"

"Anyone *important?*" he snapped.

She flinched and lifted a hand to her cheek.

"Stop that! I'm bloody sick and tired of it!"

But when her huge, iris-blue eyes filled with tears, he came to her and sat beside her and took her into his arms.

"I'm sorry, darlin'—forgive me, I didn't mean it."

She snuggled into the warmth of his body to show that she accepted the apology. Rubbing her cheek to his shoulder, she frowned on feeling the plainness of his linen shirt. Couldn't he wear something more appropriate? Something grander, more expensive? Didn't he understand?

Of course not. She had always had to do that sort of planning. And though on any other day she might have pleaded with him to put on a nicer shirt, this morning she said nothing, for those plans, intricately set by her mother, were on the verge of fruition.

She drew back and smiled. "Go carefully, love."

*   *   *

Of course Cayden knew about none of these occurrences. He wasn't there to witness any of them. Neither had he seen them in Elsewhens. The decisions that led to them had never been his to make.

He woke to full morning sunlight. He felt fine—remarkably fine, really, but for a tingling sensation in his right hand. His fingers were curiously stiff. He looked at the bandages and the pale greenish ooze staining them here and there, and remembered last night all of a piece, as if he'd turned a corner to confront a huge magical painting that moved and spoke and changed with every second, showing him exactly what had occurred. The performance, the back hallway, the withie, Mieka's horror-stricken face and swift movements, Blye's glass basket shattering inside the cushioned crate. Princess Miriuzca, her physicker, Mistress Mirdley, and everyone's assurances that there would be no permanent damage to his hand. And then the thorn: no idea what kind it had been, trying to communicate that most thorn didn't work on him the way it did other people, feeling it spread through his body, looking up at Megs's green eyes—

Oh, shit.

Cade wasn't dismayed that he and she had made love. What worried him was how little of it he remembered. With every other girl he'd bedded, it mattered little what they'd done or how often, what had been said or left unspoken. Megs mattered. He knew this because he wanted so much to remember all of it.

Whatever thorn he had been given left him with only disconnected flashes, scenes like fleetingly glimpsed Elsewhens. He retained impressions of wonderfully smooth skin and satisfying laughter, and he had awakened feeling very happy, but anything that might have been said and most of what had been done eluded his memory.

And that was a real shame, he thought as he studied the morning sunlight dappling the sheets and the smears of ointments and blood dappling the bandages on his right hand. Megs would be well worth remembering. But the thorn that had deadened pain while allowing him the full use of the rest of his anatomy evidently worked oddly on the brain—or maybe just *his* brain, quirky and unpredictable (Mieka would have said *weird* and *wobbly*) as it was. For all he knew, the stuff ought to have sent him right to sleep until noon today.

In which case, he would have missed even those few lovely remnants of memory, fragmented though they were.

When the door opened, he sat up in bed, ready with a smile (but no words; he'd have to wait and hear what she said before he could frame an appropriate reply). It wasn't Megs who came in; it was Princess Miriuzca.

"Ah! You're awake! They said you were still sleeping a little while ago. How are you feeling?" She bustled over to the bedside and picked up his right hand, turning it this way and that to examine it, chattering all the while. "It doesn't hurt when you move? Good! I've been so worried! But you mustn't be fretting about anything, everyone says you'll heal quite nicely, with only a few scars." She gave him her wide, wonderful smile and sat down on the bed beside him. Folding her hands in her lap, she looked at him with sudden seriousness. "Now. Who could have done such a thing? For I am believing it was deliberate. None of you is careless with magic."

"I—I don't know."

Arching brows told him she knew he was lying. "You need not spare my feelings," she said softly. "It was someone working for my brother, wasn't it? Someone who believes what he believes, and wants what he wants. To me, it is a sign that the Lord and the Lady do *not* look with favor on his way of believing, that nothing these foolish people have tried is succeeding. But how angry it makes me that they try anyway!"

He could never tell her that but for him, they would have succeeded all too well. Sobering thought, that: *If not for me* . . . Sobering, and quite disgustingly conceited. And frightening. It was too much responsibility, too unwieldy a burden for scrawny shoulders such as his. Of course, he could always refuse to see the Elsewhens again, as he'd done for almost two years. If he'd continued rejecting the visions, the woman seated beside him might be dead right now.

It wasn't so much a question of *If not for me;* the more honest version was *If not for the Elsewhens.* They weren't him—they were just something that happened to him. But that wasn't right either, because the things that happened to other people—a talent for music, say, or making lutes—went a long way towards defining those people. Briuly and Alaen Blackpath. Hadden Windthistle. Blye. Jeska and Mieka and Rafe and everybody else with the abilities of masquer or glisker or fettler—and what about him, the tregetour, with his writing? Mieka had been right, the damned little Elf: Without the Elsewhens, Cade wasn't completely who he was, and refusing them crippled who he could become.

So in fact it was true: If not for him and only him, and the Elsewhens that were a part of him, Miriuzca and her children and Megs and countless others might be dead now in the destruction of the North Keep.

But he could never tell her that.

Miriuzca's temper had cooled. She reached into a pocket of her gown and brought out a small velvet pouch stuffed so full of coins that it barely chinked at all as she handed it to him. "You'll be needing a new glass basket, yes?"

Under any other circumstances, his first impulse, childish and haughty, would have been to refuse the gift with words along the lines of, *Is this from you, or is Lady Megueris paying for stud service?* But that faintest of sounds, gold-on-gold, sent an icy tremor through his guts. Money was a thing he and Touchstone had precious little of these days. All other thoughts and feelings scurried into oblivion with that soft metallic ringing. His only emotion was fear.

He accepted the pouch. It was worth more than his pride. But before he could get even the most paltry phrase of gratitude past his dry throat, the outer hallway echoed to a bellow of Cade's name.

"Out of my way or I'll give you ears like a rabbit and a face like a goat! Not that either wouldn't be an improvement! *Move!*"

Miriuzca's blue eyes widened. "He couldn't really do that, could he? The ears and the face, I mean."

"Not without a withie to hand." With an effort at a smile, he added, "But he threatens convincingly, doesn't he?"

The door burst open and there stood Mieka, jut-jawed with determination. At the sight of Cayden, he relaxed visibly. When he approached the bed, it was with his usual easy saunter, all the menace vanishing as if it had never been.

"Best of good mornings to you! You're looking rested, Quill. Mistress Mirdley says I'm to take you home or she'll skin me alive and Dery will help her nail my hide to the wall." He gave the Princess a flourishing bow. "I'd say how kind it is of Your Royal Highness to put up with him, but kindness is so much your nature that I'm sure not even this silly snarge could put a dent in your patience. All the same, I'll be taking him off your hands now, for I'm just as sure that kindness and exquisite manners prevent everybody from admitting they're sick to death of him!"

Miriuzca laughed and bade them both a good morning, adding as she walked to the door that a carriage would be waiting for them whenever they were ready. Cade bowed to her as best he could from the bed, and was about to ask Mieka if he'd paid off the hire-hack he arrived in—had he come on foot all the way from Wistly, he wouldn't have been half so neat and tidy—when Mieka inhaled deeply and let the breath out in a little puff of laughter. The door shut behind the Princess, and Cade looked up at a broad grin that showed every tooth in Mieka's head.

"Well done, old thing!"

Cade hadn't a clue what he was talking about. When Mieka sniffed the air again, however, and winked at him, he felt a hot flush suffuse his whole body. The bed didn't smell just of bed. It smelled of sex.

"Lady Megs? Of course! Oh, excellent!"

Looking round for his shirt, which was nowhere to be seen, Cade muttered, "Well, who d'you think it would be? Miriuzca?"

"Never can tell," was the amiable reply. "C'mon, get dressed. Mistress Mirdley is probably brewing up something truly horrible to make you feel better." All at once the humor died on his face. "Quill . . . are you sure you're all right? Your hand *will* be all right, won't it?"

"So everyone says. It doesn't hurt much. Might do soon, though, so whatever Mistress Mirdley is concocting won't be unwelcome, no matter how bad it smells. Find me my trousers, there's a good lad. And don't you dare ever say a word to Megs about this," he warned.

"Me?" Those big, bright, innocent eyes blinked even wider.

"I mean it, Mieka."

"I know. I've a hankering to keep all me most important parts intact, if it's all the same to you. Here's your shirt." He paused, eyeing Cade. "But before I speak of this nevermore, I really do have to say that bite on your neck is *most* impressive."

An instant later he dodged out of the way, laughing as the pillow Cade had thrown at him plopped harmlessly to the floor.

Chapter 1

Overall, it took two years, but Touchstone finally worked their way out of debt.

In the two years following the celebration of King Meredan's twenty-five years on the throne, Touchstone performed more than five hundred times. They performed at private homes and castles; at the Downstreet, the Kiral Kellari, the Keymarker, and the opening nights of three new theaters in Gallantrybanks; at the small theater Princess Miriuzca had ordered built at the Palace for her father-in-law; at Trials; on the First Flight of the Royal Circuit. They performed "Bewilderland" outside during warm summer afternoons and inside during thunderstorms for large audiences of delighted children and parents. They performed "Dragon" and "Silver Mine" and "Hidden Cottage" and "Doorways" and "Caladrius" and all the other plays in their folio for enthusiastic theater patrons four nights out of seven. They performed the length and breadth of Albeyn for Guilds and societies, Lords and merchants, and the only shows for which they were not paid were the two they gave each year at Trials: one to reaffirm their position as First Flight, and one on the last night of Trials. No one, not Black Lightning or the Crystal Sparks or Hawk's Claw, was even considered anymore for the honor of the last-night performance. Touchstone reigned supreme.

The Shadowshapers no longer worked together. They had lasted two summers out on their own. It was rumored that both Vered Goldbraider and Rauel Kevelock were trying to assemble new groups of their own, but the notion that either of them would ever appear at Trials again to win a place on one of the Circuits was laughable. They had their pride—which was what had broken up the Shadowshapers in the first place.

All that Cayden knew about it was that Touchstone had no real rival. He ignored rumors. He had no time for them. He had time only for performing and, very occasionally, writing. When Touchstone wasn't performing, they were traveling. The only real rest they got was at Castle Eyot for seven days each summer. A holiday of a fortnight or longer was something that happened only to other people.

Because the Shadowshapers were no longer available, Touchstone was in constant and lucrative demand, and could command fees for private performances that other groups could only dream about. Two years after King Meredan's celebrations, Touchstone was at last solvent again. There was no need for constant performances, constant travel, constant work.

But they couldn't seem to stop.

That second Wintering, everything fell apart.

It began in late autumn when Crisiant's sisters came to Cayden and told him flat out that if Rafe didn't stop using thorn, his wife would leave him and take their son with her. According to custom, the women who stood with a bride at her wedding were obliged to let her know if her husband was unhappy; similarly, it was the duty of the men who stood with the groom to warn him should his wife become troubled about their marriage. Things rarely came to that point in practice. But in this case, Crisiant's sisters had waited months for Cade to say or do something. He hadn't. They arrived at Redpebble Square one afternoon before a show at the Kiral Kellari and announced their intention to remain until he promised to do more than have a word with Rafe. They wanted him to promise that the thorn would stop.

He didn't bother to argue. He didn't say that the only reason Crisiant and Bram still had a roof over their heads was the scanty profits from the last two years of constant performing, and this had been possible only because of thorn that energized tired bodies and minds for shows and quieted them afterwards so they could get some sleep. He wasn't even terribly shocked that Crisiant, who had set her heart on Rafe when they were mere children, had reached this point of desperation. There were times when he'd been pretty desperate himself. But none of them, not Cade or Rafe or Jeska or Mieka, had been able to stop.

He said none of this. He told Crisiant's sisters that he would do his best, but could make no promises. Rafe was a grown man of twenty-seven and made his own decisions. Cade thanked them for their concern and escorted them to the door.

Then, because Touchstone had a performance in a little over two hours, he went upstairs and got out his thorn-roll.

It might have been Rafe's problems nagging at the back of his mind. Mayhap he'd mistaken one of Brishen Staindrop's special blends for another, concocted just for him because he was so unpredictable in his response to thorn. Possibly he had primed the withies for "The Dragon" to be followed by "Sailor's Sweetheart" so often that he'd grown careless. But something went wrong, and it was Cade's fault.

The performance started well enough. Mieka made his entrance in an immense cloth-of-gold ball gown with frothing purple flounces and acid green gloves. He and Cayden did their usual banter, ending with Mieka stripping off his garish finery to reveal the plain white he usually wore onstage nowadays. But as he selected a withie, there was a worried look in those changeable blue-green-gray-brown eyes that Cade didn't understand.

A minute later, he understood all too well.

There was enough magic in the withies for Mieka to get through "Dragon." There wasn't enough magic specific to that play to make it the triumph it had always been since they first performed it at Trials eight years ago. Watching, horrified and ashamed, Cade wondered witlessly which play he'd had in mind while priming the withies—because it hadn't been "Dragon." The Prince wore Jeska's own clothes because Mieka was working so hard to construct the dragon that he didn't have anything to clothe Jeska with. The cavern looked more like a gray stone castle. There was no female voice describing the battle at all; whatever Cade had put into the withies, magic to do even the captive Princess's dialogue hadn't been included. Jeska coped, as always; Rafe kept a stranglehold on the magic just in case Mieka, frantic to make it through the play, slipped in his own control; Mieka, lunging desperately for the withies, cast just one enraged glance at Cade during the whole performance.

In the tiring room, nobody said anything. Cade collapsed into a chair as if he'd been the one doing all the work. Mieka dumped the spent withies in Cade's lap and went to the drinks table to pour a large quantity of beer down his throat. Jeska paced, using a red silk square to wipe sweat from his face and neck, his golden curls limp. Rafe folded his length into a corner of a sofa and slumped there, exhausted. It wasn't until Cade had roused himself and concentrated on putting the magic needed for "Sweetheart" into the withies that somebody spoke.

Mieka, unable to contain himself any longer: "And here we always thought it would be *me* to fuck everything up!"

"Not quite everything," Jeska offered.

"Near enough as makes no difference! Are those damned things ready yet? All right, then. Just to make sure, it's 'Sailor's Sweetheart' we'll be doing, yeh?" Snatching up a withie, he gripped it in one palm and ran the fingers of his other hand down its length. "Good. I can work with this—and without half-killing meself. You go out first, Cade, and clear all those others from the baskets. Gods only know what's in them. Go on!"

He went.

The performance came off very well. Everyone laughed in all the right places, which was fairly amazing because Cade hadn't been able to find a flicker of humor in himself to prime into the withies. He was reminded of the first time they'd done this piece, years ago now in Gowerion, when Mieka changed everything up and turned a sappy melodrama into a rollicking farce. It had all been Mieka, dancing his delighted way through the playlet, with Jeska adapting and improvising, and Rafe effortlessly managing the flow of magic. Cade, hiding beneath the stairs of the tawdry old inn, had been furious that his new glisker revised the piece without his knowledge or his permission. But the fact that Mieka Windthistle had in the course of that piece become their new glisker was never in doubt.

When tonight's dreadful gigging was over, and they were outside the Kiral Kellari trying to wave down hire-hacks to take them to their various homes, Rafe pushed Cade into the first one that arrived.

"Go home. Sleep. No thorn. I'm canceling whatever we've got on for the next week." When Cade opened his mouth to protest, he snarled, "Do as I say, damn it, or I'll make it a fortnight! And no thorn!"

He waited until he was inside the hack and had given the driver his address, then leaned out the window and asked, "Does that go for all the rest of you as well?"

One thing about being a tregetour: he knew a good exit line. He sat back in the seat, taking home with him the sight of three outraged faces and the sound of three angry voices.

He knew he'd never be able to sleep without thorn. He'd tried. Gods and Angels knew he'd tried, these last two years. He was careful to keep track of what he used and when—that night when his breathing and his heart almost stopped had scared him into at least a modicum of caution—and as he drew columns onto a fresh sheet of paper (date, time, variety of thorn), he purposely did not look at the stack of pages in his desk drawer that recorded the last few months of use. They were no more damning than the marks on his arms.

Snug in a soft linen nightshirt and warm blankets, he closed his eyes and waited for sleep to come. It did not. Sometimes it happened like this: a delay or an outright failure of the thorn to produce the desired effect. He had two choices when this happened. He could use more, or he could endure with gritted teeth. Tempting as another little thorn-prick was, after tonight's near debacle he knew he deserved some discomfort. More discomfort, in truth, than a few hours of restless wakefulness would provide.

His brain nagged and nattered. Guilt over tonight's mistakes warred with self-justification. He deliberately remembered that cold, sick, hunted feeling that came with massive debts and no money to pay them with. He never wanted to feel that way again, that hollow in his guts, the fear. He would still be feeling it, every stomach-churning terrifying icy shard of it, if not for the various thorn that had got Touchstone through these last two years.

They *had* got through. They were safe.

So why was he still using so much thorn? Why were any of them? Even Jeska, who had always resisted and who pricked far less than the rest of them, was still relying on bluethorn every so often for the energy required of certain performances. As for Rafe—well, his wife's sisters were witnesses. Mieka . . . he was occasionally more maniacal, occasionally more somnolent, but at least he'd never had the sort of episode he saved Cayden from: that frightening night when he lost track of what he'd used and nearly died.

Why hadn't he stopped then? He knew the answer very well. It was too easy just to keep on. Not the danger of too much too carelessly used, not the grim scowls of Mistress Mirdley when he declined dinner because he wasn't hungry, not even the scorn in Megs's eyes at the sight of his arms . . .

Fundamental honesty demanded that he admit it: Thorn was also an escape from the confusion she had brought into his life.

There hadn't been just the one night in the Palace. That year's Wintering, when they'd had a week's worth of last-instant well-paid giggings in Lilyleaf, Megueris had shown up to visit Croodle. After Touchstone's performance that night, which both ladies attended, Croodle gave a private party at her inn. Cade had woken the next morning with the memory of Megs on his fingers (his hand had mostly healed by then, and was certainly limber enough for what he and she had got up to that night) but no Megs in his bed. Midmorning, Mieka strolled in from wherever he had spent the night—his wife hadn't had time to make him anything new to wear that would guarantee his fidelity—and once again had only to sniff the air to know who had kept Cade company.

Megs had appeared once more a few weeks later, when her father hired Touchstone to perform at the nearest of his properties to Gallybanks. Only a half-day's drive in the wagon, just an overnight stay at the manor house (where they were as warmly welcomed as the forty other guests)—but when he'd gone up to his room, there she was, calmly unlacing her gown.

There was never a lot of conversation. Talk could be had from almost anyone. What they provided each other was something he couldn't have put into words if he'd tried. Some tregetour.

What he did try was to have an Elsewhen about her. He knew she couldn't possibly be the wife he'd seen years ago, the woman who cared nothing for his work beyond its power to provide for her and their children. Megs wasn't like that. She knew everything about the theater and was coming to know almost as much about fettling as Rafe. She couldn't become the wife in that Elsewhen.

He never saw her. Not since that horrible foreseeing about the North Keep and the explosion that had killed her had she appeared in any Elsewhen at all. Cade had long since figured out that people who didn't show up had made decisions that he had nothing to do with. Whatever he did or didn't do hadn't affected them. He had never seen Mieka, for example, before that night in Gowerion, because it was Mieka's decision alone to follow them there and present himself as their new glisker. He had never seen his little brother, either—something that had not occurred to him until Archduke Cyed Henick asked a mocking question that Cade knew to be a threat. He took this to mean that Derien made his own choices that had little or nothing to do with Cade—but he worried, as with Megs, that perhaps the lack of them in his Elsewhens meant they would not be in his life.

He didn't know if he could bear that. To lose either of them was unthinkable. It implied that whatever they did with their lives, they didn't need him. He wasn't important. He didn't count.

The blockweed combination that Brishen Staindrop had finally hit upon as an effective sleeping aid for him began to stir sluggishly through his mind. About bloody damned time. It was getting on for morning. If he had nothing to do today, he might as well sleep as long as he liked.

Nothing to do . . . *all week*. He couldn't think what to do with himself if he wasn't getting ready for a performance, or onstage, or coming home from a gigging. Write? He had yet to finish—after two solid years—the two plays that told the whole tale of the Treasure. He'd put together new versions of some older plays referred to in *Lost Withies*, and it had been so long since anybody had seen or heard of them that they'd been greeted as originals. This made him squirm inside. He really ought to get back to work on "Treasure." Or mayhap *Window Wall*, which had been languishing unfinished almost as long. That as well was a two-play piece. He saw the structure of each in his mind, there and waiting to be written. . . .

No. He would find something to do that had nothing at all to do with the theater. He needed a rest. A week with nothing to do . . .

He could find out where Megs was these days and go see her. After that night at her father's manor house almost a year ago, she'd never come to him again. Not that he'd noticed, except at odd intervals. He'd been too busy. Was she with Princess Miriuzca at the Palace? Had she spent the autumn at one of her father's many homes? Was she traveling for the fun of it, the way rich people did, and if so, where?

Whom could he ask without sounding like a complete fool?

Easier, more convenient, less stressful to spend some time with Derien. As sleep claimed him at last, he smiled. They might go to the racing meet, or to the Tincted Downs for a day or two. Take a little trip on a pleasure barge, hire a couple of horses and ride out into the countryside. There were a dozen things they could do together that would let Cade get to know him again. The smile deepened, then faded slowly as he slept.

Chapter 2

Being a naturally inquisitive—some would have said prying—sort of person, Mieka could have enlightened Cade as to why Megs had shown at up Lilyleaf that time, and at her father's castle. He knew a lot more about her than Cayden had ever bothered to learn.

He knew, for instance, that the timing of her encounters with Cade was not accidental.

A few months after Touchstone had performed at Lord Mindrising's, they were invited to tea at the North Keep just before leaving for Trials. Mieka arrived early and sought out Lady Megueris where she was supervising the arrangement of flowers on the table set in the middle of the lawn. He casually took her aside, away from the ears of the servants, and asked whether or not she would be attending Trials. She said no.

He looked her straight in the eyes. "In fact, you won't be attending anything anywhere for about—oh, I'd say six months?"

She met his gaze coolly and steadily. "And so?"

"Are you going to tell him?"

"Why?"

"He deserves to know he's going to be a father."

"He could be a father a hundred times over by now," she pointed out, "and he doesn't know about any of *them*." Her green eyes were sharp as broken bottle-glass. Then, hearing the chatter of servants behind them, she laughed an obvious laugh, took his arm, and guided him to a side garden. It was as much privacy as a member of the Court ever knew—except if she had the Princess's personal connivance late at night.

"I think it's disgusting," Megs said as they walked amid flowering trees just coming into bud. "All that bilge about romance and true love and a girl saving herself for marriage—all so a man can boast that he's had a virgin, and he won't be faced with other men who've been with his wife. You men can go out and bed whomever you like, and all anybody does is wink and say, oh, *he's* a bit of a lad!"

Mieka shrugged. "It's different for the upper classes. When there's titles and lots of money floating about, I mean."

"And that's good enough reason to get married?" She snorted. "Any child of mine will inherit the money and the lands, everything but the title. And who cares about a title, anyway?"

"Lots of people." He supposed, but didn't say aloud, that Miriuzca would oblige by persuading King Meredan to grant a Lordship or Ladyship.

"Being a woman who wants to be a Steward is difficult enough. I have this damned 'Lady' in front of my name to wrestle with as well. Why would I want to burden my child the same way?"

"And Quill doesn't have anything to say about it?"

"I've met his mother."

He had to concede the point. Lady Jaspiela was annoying enough about Derien's future. What would she be capable of with a grandson or granddaughter?

"Mieka, if you breathe a word of this—"

He held up a placating hand. "Anything you could think up to do to me wouldn't be half as awful as some of the things Cade has threatened me with."

"Want to bet?" A sudden grin faded rapidly. "If you must know, I'm going to one of my father's houses up north. I won't be at Trials, obviously—I'm planning on a return to Court sometime next spring. This has to be a complete secret, even from Cade. Especially from Cade."

They walked on in silence for a time, towards the river.

At length he pursed his lips and shook his head. "I have to tell him."

"You can't." She gripped his arm with long, strong fingers. Any protest he might have made died on his lips when he looked into her fierce green eyes. "My child, my choices, Mieka."

"Cade's child, and he has no choices at all?" he countered.

"In this instance, no."

And that, Mieka realized all at once, was why Cayden would never know about the child through an Elsewhen. None of the choices were his to make.

Megueris made him promise, and he did, and knew he'd regret it. He was romantic enough to believe that Megs and Cayden would eventually face what had been obvious to Mieka almost from the start: They ought to be together.

Cayden could be romantic, but only if he thought nobody was looking. Mieka had had glimpses of it, how he could be caring, even loving, and gentle and kind. He remembered everybody else's Namingday, though he was deliberately forgetful about his own. Every so often it emerged in his writing—not in a candlelight-and-roses sort of way, but through a defiant belief in happy-ever-always. When he rewrote one of the classics—"The Princess and the Snowdrop," for instance, which he'd worked up about a year ago to appeal to their female audiences—he turned the cloyingly sentimental bits into real poetry, charming and, almost in spite of himself, romantic. He'd deny it, of course, uphill and down dale. That was just Cayden being Cayden.

But Megs wasn't a roses-round-the-porch sort of girl anyhow, Mieka reflected as he escorted her in silence back to the North Keep. What she *did* want wasn't entirely clear to him. She wanted a child, and she wanted to become a Steward. How could she do both? Realistically speaking, she wouldn't get the chance to try. Women in theater audiences was one thing. Women onstage as players, women as part of theater officialdom . . . Mieka felt sorry for her, because her ambition was doomed. Men—obviously—could have careers in anything they chose, and families as well. A woman's place was within that family. For certes, there were exceptions like Blye, but then she didn't have children, did she?

It was all too annoying to think about. The one thing he knew for sure was that she and Cade would work it out eventually. He simply couldn't believe that having chosen Cade to father her child, she'd turn to anyone else for another try if this one wasn't a son to inherit her father's lands and title. But mayhap he was a trifle prejudiced.

When they were nearly at the garden door of the North Keep, he turned suddenly and said, "You'll let me know about the baby?" When Megs shrugged, he added, "I want to know that you're all right. And you'll need somebody to back up whatever tale you end up telling.

Come to think on it, Cade would be the perfect person to include on this—he's a tregetour, he could spin you a great story—"

"I already have one," she snapped.

"I s'pose so," he said musingly. "After all, you can't have seen as many shows as you have without picking up a trick or two about constructing a plot."

She frowned sideways at him, as if trying to make up her mind whether to laugh at him or smack him a good one. Mieka was lucky; she grinned.

But she didn't tell him what her plot was. He was left to wonder for months whether she'd concoct a brief marriage to explain the appearance of a child, or simply brazen it out with not the slightest hint of who the father might be, or . . . or what?

Now, almost a year later, he knew. Not that she'd been the one to tell him. First there'd been an announcement in the *Court Circular* that Lord Sollin Mindrising had, after some twenty-four years of widowerhood, married again, and would be spending the next few months in happy seclusion at his favorite of many far-flung estates with his new wife, the former Lady Tomlyn Cloverbrook. Then had come a brief article in the *Palace News and Views*, which Mieka's wife avidly read, that Lady Megueris Mindrising would not be returning to Gallantrybanks for Wintering, but would most certainly be back at Court in the spring. She had spent the past summer and autumn at several of her father's more remote properties, learning the special features of administering each, for as His Lordship's heir, she would one day own it all. Princess Miriuzca was pleased at the prospect of welcoming her back as a lady-in-waiting, and approved of her diligence regarding her duties to the Mindrising lands and people. Finally—and no one connected these bits of information, one with the next with the next, except Mieka—it was announced that the new Lady Mindrising had given birth to a fine, healthy son. If the timing was a little vague, who would notice?

Five years ago, he might have confronted Megs directly—as gently as possible, of course, because he liked her, but confront her he surely would have done. He'd grown up some since then. Older, wiser . . .

But not brave enough to spend his week of free time at Hilldrop Crescent. After Rafe's edict, he really ought to have jumped in the nearest hire-hack. A whole week with his wife and his daughter . . .

and his mother-in-law. When-oh-when-oh-*when* would the old bitch leave them alone? He knew it was foolish to wish she'd find herself somewhere else to live, preferably at least ten days distant from Hilldrop. He kept hoping.

Mieka stayed at Wistly Hall, telling himself it was for family reasons. This was at least partly true. Sharadel Windthistle, she of the acid disposition and colossal age, had finally died. Her great-grandson, Hadden, had been informed of this fully three months after the event; all the other Windthistle relations, led by Uncle Barsabian, had been busy divvying up and departing with whatever was movable at Clinquant House. Hadden was the rightful heir, but by the time he was informed of the ancient's death, there wasn't much left to inherit. The vast ancestral barn was now his, but pretty much all that remained inside it was thin air.

Whether or not to take sundry Windthistles to the law courts was hotly debated each night around the dinner table. Mieka and Jed and Jez were all for it, declaring that they'd stand the expense of hiring the best advocates in Gallybanks, if only for the pure pleasure of thwarting Uncle Breedbate. Mishia, their mother, was against. She had no desire to waste her family's time and money on recovering the furnishings and garnishings of a house she'd never liked in the first place.

As for Hadden . . . Mieka had the strong feeling that his father was simply glad to be rid of the bothersome old bitch. The only thing that nudged him in the direction of a lawsuit was the prospect of Jezael, as the eldest son (by three minutes or so), eventually inheriting a totally empty house.

On the third night of this ongoing discussion—dinner was the only time the immediate family gathered together—Mishia decreed that until the matter was settled, only ten minutes of the meal would be devoted to arguing back and forth. "It's either that," she told her husband and their assembled offspring, "or I join Blye at the glassworks and you can figure out dinner on your own!" Blye, wise woman, had excused herself from the nightly debate after the first ended in a draw.

Mieka was painfully aware that a few years ago he would have had at his disposal the considerable influence and vast connections of Lord Kearney Fairwalk. When last heard of, His Lordship had taken ship on one of Lord Rolon Piercehand's voyages. That was almost two years ago, and he hadn't been seen since. It was a curious feature of the legal system that those unable to appear in person in a courtroom to defend themselves could be sued but not tried. Because Fairwalk was no longer in Albeyn to answer charges of malfeasance regarding Touchstone's finances, the advocates they'd consulted had advised against bringing suit. There was no point. Neither would it gain anything to accuse any of Fairwalk's subordinates; they would only claim they had been following His Lordship's orders. Touchstone's one satisfaction in the matter was that Fairwalk had exiled himself from his home, and was unlikely ever to return.

Sharadel Windthistle had died most inconveniently. A couple of years ago, Mieka could have called on Fairwalk's influence. Now, even though Touchstone had paid off all debts and was actually beginning to make money for themselves again, their only really important ally was Princess Miriuzca—and she could scarcely be asked to intervene in a private matter of inheritance.

Considering all this, Mieka slumped discontentedly in his chair and barely listened to the now-familiar argument going on around him. Back and forth across the dinner table the suggestions and objections and calculations flew until Mishia, one eye on the clock, finally called a halt. For the next while there was no conversation at all. Mieka glanced down the table at his twin sister, who was applying herself to dismembering half a roast chicken, a sullen frown creasing her forehead as she distributed pieces to Tavier and Jorie, seated either side of her. Feeling his gaze, Jinsie glanced up, scowled more deeply, and mouthed the word *Later*.

Desultory chat began between Jez and Cilka, gradually including most of the rest of the family as well. Mieka had something else to blame on Great-great-granny Tightfist: the destruction of the usual riotous, laughing dinnertime. On any other night he would have taken on his accustomed role of clown, telling wild stories and making everyone forget whatever might be troubling them. He wasn't in the mood right now, no matter how much it was needed. And that made him resent Sharadel Windthistle even more.

After dinner he joined Jinsie on a stroll down the river lawn. They walked silently for a few moments before she kicked at an inoffensive rock.

"We should just sell the damned place and have done with it."

"It's Jez's inheritance."

"Ask him if he wants it. Would you?"

Mieka snorted. "I've better things to do with my time."

"Is that why Touchstone is staying idle for a week?"

At the riverbank, she sat on a weatherworn wooden bench and stared out at the water. The lights from houses and Elf-lit streetlamps danced off the dark river, and Mieka remembered that when they were younger, their mother had told them that these were Fae coming to check up on things, so they'd best be good and go to sleep—*now, Mieka!*

"Oughta get Jed and Jez to mend this thing," he remarked as he sat beside his sister.

"Or have Fa spell it sealed so it doesn't constantly come up splinters."

Behind them, their father's mild voice said, "I realize, my children, that I work with wood all day long, but not with magic."

They made room for him on the bench between them and lingered in silence for a time.

Then Hadden gave a soft sigh. "In fact, I've never been much interested in magic. Oh, I can do it if I please, but it's not necessary to my work. So why bother? Whatever magic I possess seems to sift itself into the lutes and harps of its own accord. I've never analyzed why this is so."

"Like Blye with her glasswork," Mieka ventured.

"So far as I can tell, yes. It's another reason I was so disgusting an object to Great-grandmother. I mean to say, here I am, a Windthistle, one of the oldest Elfen names in Albeyn, and I don't use magic to do anything practical by way of making the family fortune."

Mieka considered this for a few moments. It was true that his father had instilled in all his children the notion that working at a job one hated, no matter how well paid, was no way to be happy. Even if one's personal life was a dream come true, the stress of loathing one's work would be bound to poison everything. For himself, Mieka was grateful that his own calling earned him quite a bit of money (now that Touchstone's debts were paid off). That glisking involved magic made life all the more satisfying.

"Enough to live on," Hadden was saying. "Enough to raise your children. There were times I haven't been very good at it—"

Mieka opened his mouth to protest, but Jinsie was quicker than he.

"None of us would have you any other way than just exactly as you are, Fa."

"We always had enough to eat, and clothes, and the Good Gods know enough places to sleep!" Mieka added, hooking a thumb over his shoulder at the vast disorganized bulk of Wistly Hall.

Hadden smiled and took his children by the hand. "Beholden, my dears. All your mother and I have ever wanted is to see each of you happy. Sometimes that's meant letting you find your own way through things . . . which isn't easy for us or for you." He paused. "It was simpler when you were little. All we had to worry about then was keeping you physically safe—food, clothing, and a place to sleep. And none of that can be done with magic."

There was more to being a parent than this—much more—as Mieka knew full well. He also knew he wasn't as good at being a father as his father was. Well, Hadden had had eight times the practice, after all . . . which Mieka knew was no excuse. Sometimes he worried that he didn't spend enough time with Jindra, especially these last two years— but how could things be different in his profession? How could he provide for his family other than on the Royal Circuit and all the hundreds of giggings that paid the bills?

He could feel, on his father's hand, the ring that had so special a meaning. He'd told Cayden about it years ago. *To hear Mum tell it, one morning Fa just looked at her across breakfast and they both knew neither of them would ever look at anybody else ever again.* His father's ring, plain gold and not just sealed with magic but made with magic, betokened a true bonding, something deeper than love or marriage . . . something, he finally admitted to himself, though he'd known it for quite some time now, that he would not experience with his wife. Deeply as he loved her, for the two of them there did not exist the depthless understanding and commitment his parents shared.

Then again, he argued with himself, Hadden and Mishia had been married ten years before it happened for them. He should just wait a little longer. But tonight he resolved to be much more of a presence in his wife's and daughter's lives.

And all at once he wondered what, if any, magic Cade's father, Zekien, possessed. Whether or not he used it. He couldn't have fathered a son as gifted as Cade without having at least *some* magic in him. He'd never heard anyone talk about it—which wasn't especially strange, considering he knew practically no one who actually knew Cade's father. Considering what he did for Prince Ashgar as First Gentleman of the Bedchamber, Zekien's magic probably consisted of discerning whether the girl chosen for Ashgar's bed on any given night was afflicted with pox.

"So you approve of Rafe's ban on performances this week?"

Jinsie's question startled Mieka from sardonic thought. Evidently they'd gone on talking quietly while he was nattering around in his own mind.

Hadden replied, "You've all been working too hard—not just you boys, but Jinsie and Kazie as well, seeing to the giggings and payment and suchlike."

Everything that Fairwalk used to do, Mieka's sister and Jeska's wife now did for them, with occasional help from Crisiant, Rafe's wife. Mieka knew that Jinsie really took on most of it, for both other ladies had children to care for.

"Now that everyone's been paid," Hadden went on, "Touchstone can afford to relax a little."

"Touchstone can," Jinsie said. "Kazie and I can't. We've managed to mollify the cancelations by promising a gigging at half price—"

Mieka groaned softly.

"—but you realize that Wintering is coming up, and some kind of decision has to be made about where Touchstone will be playing."

"Rafe and I both vote for not playing at all," Mieka said. "A family Wintering—haven't had one in forever." As Jinsie leaned across their father to frown at him in the dimness, he whined, "Oh please! Just this once!"

"Correct me if I'm mistaken," their father drawled, "but wasn't that what you said the first time we found you tottering about in your mother's favorite shoes?"

"I wanted to be tall," Mieka protested.

"That explains the shoes, but not the gown."

"I liked the way the silk sounded. *Swooooosh!*" He laughed. "C'mon, Fa, I was only five years old!"

Jinsie snorted. "And now you're twenty-five, and you've made it all into something of a hallmark, haven't you? That, and the shattered withies. And there's irony for you—the inspiration for getting noticed almost lost Cayden his fingers."

Mieka looked down at his own fingers, remembering how painful it had been for Cade to prime the withies. The bandages interfered, or so he'd said. Mieka had lost count of how many times he'd rewrapped Cade's right hand. The healed wounds had left visible scars, and Mieka suspected that Cayden didn't want them to fade. If they faded, they would be forgotten, and he didn't want to forget.

Chapter 3

When Cade broached the subject, Derien replied with regret that he had too much schoolwork to skip attendance for that week of Touchstone's idleness. When Rafe sent a note round to Redpebble Square decreeing that one week would become two, Cade ripped the page into as many small pieces as he could and threw them fluttering onto the hearth fire.

Fine for Rafe—he had his wife, his son, his parents, their bakery, all manner of things to occupy his time. Equally fine for Jeska and Mieka, with their families. Cade had a brother who left practically at daylight and didn't return until dusk, and a resident Trollwife who showed scant sympathy for Cade's fidgets.

And then there was Lady Jaspiela. No longer arm-in-arm friendly with Princess Iamina or Archduchess Panshilara, she had attempted to insert herself into Princess Miriuzca's little circle, trying to trade on the Princess's closeness to Touchstone. What this maneuvering availed her was almost daily attendance at tea—not with Miriuzca, but with Queen Roshian. Miriuzca, clever and kind, had invited Lady Jaspiela on a day when the Queen was present at lunching. Her Majesty had inquired whether Her Ladyship was of the same Silversun family as that talented young tregetour fellow. That there was no other Silversun family in the whole of Albeyn had evidently escaped her notice. Cade found it sublimely ironic that his mother's entry into the top level of Society had been accomplished not through her husband's position with Prince Ashgar, but through association with the son whose profession she deplored.

If he'd wanted to, he could have joined her at the Palace. He most emphatically did not want to. The Queen was acknowledged (in polite, pitying whispers) to be the most boring woman in Albeyn. Cade was sure that all her ladies were as intellectually radiant as she. Not that this would matter to his mother.

To all intents and purposes, then, Cade was alone in the house. Nothing appealed to him. He didn't want to go to the Archives and do research. He didn't want to go out drinking. He didn't want to sail on the Gally River, or stroll through any of the parks, or visit any of his friends, or even spend a day polishing glass and talking with Blye. Work had been so much the sole focus of his life for so long that without the almost nightly performances, he had no idea what to do with himself.

So he turned to his thorn-roll.

Brishen Staindrop had gifted him with his very own, made of black leather stamped along the edges with small flaring suns in silver paint. They had a color code of their own by now, he and she, and whenever a package arrived from her, it took him only a few minutes to sort everything into its proper place. All the little twists of paper contained thorn prepared for him alone. Cade didn't know precisely what was in them, or what effect such things might have on other people. But he knew how they worked on him, and so did Brishen, and whenever she sent him something new with suggestions about what it might provoke, he was always eager to try it. Lacking anything else he wanted to do, and feeling that he deserved an interesting afternoon, on the third dull day of Touchstone's break he fixed up a new mixture shortly after lunching and lay back on his bed to enjoy. After all, who knew but that he wouldn't get an idea for a new play out of it?

More than three hours later, he surfaced from the thorn sweating and shaking. He had dreamed he was asleep, and in the dream he was asleep and having a dream. It wasn't an Elsewhen inspired and abetted by thorn, it couldn't possibly have been an Elsewhen—but it felt that way. It certainly hurt as much.

He knew he was dreaming.

He remembered sliding between fresh silk sheets that smelled of Mistress Mirdley's herbs, and kissing his wife's shoulder, and settling down for some much-needed sleep. He remembered thinking that the new play was doing very well and its accompanying quarto was selling briskly—the broadsheets were calling it another masterpiece, even though it hadn't turned out anywhere near his original concept. This was a familiar feeling, though not so sharply galling as "Turn Aback" had been. He supposed he was getting used to it, to the dismal truth that no matter how much you wanted it and how hard you worked for it and how grimly you fought for it, not much in life turned out the way you thought it would.

He remembered thinking, and then not thinking, and he didn't remember waking up. So he knew he must still be sleeping. Dreaming. Sitting in a hard wooden chair in a cold and shadowy chamber without doors or windows, he wondered if there was such a word as nightmaring *because* dreaming *was much too pretty a term for what was happening to him now.*

To his left sat a hunch-shouldered figure, thick blond curls hiding the profile. To his right sat a tall, long-limbed man wrapped in his usual watchful silence. Each in his own way seemed beaten, perhaps even broken. He knew that something about him expressed the same defeat. Perhaps his eyes, or the thinness of his lips as he bit them between his teeth to hold back a groan of familiar anguish as he stared at the man sprawled on a black velvet sofa before him.

No, he was not dreaming. Whether it was a word or not, he was nightmaring. *He'd been doing variations on it for years. The subject was always the same—the subject of so many Elsewhens and so many nightmares: a brilliant, funny, clever, mad little Elf. Sometimes Cade would scream warnings that were never heard, or find himself running and running and never getting closer, as if he slogged through invisible knee-deep mud. Sometimes he simply sobbed, helpless with fear and frustration. And sometimes, recognizing with cold anger that here was yet another hopelessness, he turned his back and walked away.*

But always before it had been just him and Mieka. Neither Jeska nor Rafe had ever been there, except as half-felt presences. Rather like the way it was onstage sometimes, the best times: him watching Mieka, Mieka watching him, their communication composed of instinct and intellect and art and pure clean joy. Jeska internalized Cade's words and spoke them as if they'd been his to begin with; Rafe wove his agile magic around the whole to hold it steady; but Mieka was inside the play, living every emotion and image and sensation of it with his heart, his muscles, his brain. He and Cayden would stare at each other for minutes on end, utterly intent on their mutual journey, Mieka dancing behind his glass baskets and Cade completely still at his lectern, always aware of Jeska and Rafe nearby.

Jeska and Rafe were on either side of him now. He had the sudden, sick feeling that this nightmaring was going to be different from the others.

The man sprawled on the wide black sofa was dressed in plain tan trousers and a half-buttoned yellow shirt, ruffled cuffs undone. Unconscious, head lolling, skin ash-pale and clammy, the skin of his arms showed the red dots of healed thorn-marks. There were no new ones that Cayden could see, but that didn't mean anything. There were so many places to find a vein. . . .

"Rather a shocker, innit?"

The voice that spoke behind them was light and soft, the way Mieka's voice had been in his early twenties, before liquor coarsened it. The dark tones of unwilling insight were new. Cade tried to rise from the chair, but could not. Jeska had raised his head. Rafe hadn't moved.

"It's not what it looks like," Mieka went on. "It's not what you're thinking. I think my heart just . . . stopped. Didn't hurt much. I didn't even know what was happening until you lot showed up."

Cade told himself this couldn't be. Mieka hadn't touched thorn in a long time, and his consumption of wine and beer and whiskey and brandy was less than half what it used to be. The change to comparative sobriety had started after they lost Yazz—more than fifteen years ago now. The trauma had sent Mieka to the thorn-roll and the bottle for a solid month thereafter. And then he just . . . stopped.

More or less.

When a tour was too long, or Touchstone had too many Gallybanks performances over too few days, Mieka would turn again to thorn. Every audience must get the show it came for; he was adamant about that, about not disappointing anyone who came to see Touchstone. And sometimes that meant the added energy of thorn. Last year it had taken him over a month to stop again—he'd wryly termed it a "fortyer" after the isolation required of certain ships—but stop he always had done.

Yet here he was, a broken crumple of limbs on black cushions.

"I can't go until you let me," Mieka said behind Cayden. "You've been keeping me here—oh, not against my will, don't ever think that. I don't much want to leave. But this looks like I have to, yeh?"

Jeska was shaking his head. Rafe's long, powerful fingers clenched into fists. Cade couldn't react at all.

"Look at me. Without the thorn, I'm no use to you. Without it, my glisk-

ing is all gone to shit, and I can't do justice to any of you, nor to the work and Cade's words. But with it . . . well, we all know what I'm like."

Jeska's shoulders flinched, and there was the slightest sound from Rafe, something like a whimper. Cade didn't—couldn't—move, or make a sound.

"With thorn or without it, I'm no use to anybody. Not you three, nor Jindra, nor my family, nor myself. It's—"

"Why do you always put yourself last?"

The sound of Rafe's voice, a low, angry rumble, startled Cade so much that he cringed in his chair.

"Anybody and everybody always matters more than you. Worth only whatever laughs you can provide, is that it? The laughs and the glisking, and nobody would keep you around otherwise? You stupid little quat!"

Cade felt his jaw drop a little. He'd never heard Rafe rant like this, not even when he was furious—which happened about once a year. The very air in the windowless chamber seemed to quiver, strange shadows darting round each other behind the black sofa, as if they were as frightened as Cade was.

"You never did figure it out, did you? What you're worth to us, it's more than the work—more than the fact that we weren't anything *until you showed up that night in Gowerion—"*

The scene appeared, hazy and washed of color, in the dimness. Jeska on the deck of a magic-spawned ship . . . Rafe hovering nearby . . . Mieka dancing lightly behind the glisker's bench and the glass baskets . . . the tavern's rough patrons weeping with laughter—then suddenly weeping real tears as the murky "Silver Mine" formed and doomed fathers, sons, brothers bade each other final farewell. But where was Cade? Where had he been that night? Not onstage. He'd never been onstage before Mieka joined them. He'd been hiding, the way he always did, so that no one could see him. Hiding, invisible beneath the stairs, because he didn't want to be seen.

"Yeh, center of everything, ain't he?" Jeska suddenly sneered, and Cade cringed again. "You love it like that, don't you, Mieka? Center of the whole fucking world! Most bloody selfish bastard who ever lived! More thorn, more whiskey, more women—black powder in every pocket to explode whatever takes your fancy, just to see the looks on their faces—"

"That's enough," Rafe warned.

"Not by bloody half, it ain't! He never thought what he was doing to

the rest of us, did he? Never knowing if he was drunk or thornlost or both in a brothel someplace—if the messenger would bring a note that he couldn't be found or was too drunk or thorned to walk—or that he'd pricked his last thorn ever—" Jeska choked with rage. "All those years bein' scared to answer the door—Gods fucking damn you, Mieka!"

"Shut it!" Rafe bellowed.

"No, it's all right," Mieka said gently from behind them. "You both have the right of it. I'm selfish and I'm thoughtless, and I put you through a lot, I know. Too much. Tryin' to make up for it by pranks and jokes . . . playin' the clown because that way I could make you laugh it all off and not kick me halfway to Scatterseed or throw me into the Flood. But in the end, y'see, I don't matter—not like the work matters. It's why I had to keep goin' back to the thorn. Even after Auntie Brishen stopped that part of her business—even though the thorn Alaen and those others died from wasn't hers—I had to find it and use it, or the work would suffer. And I couldn't let that happen."

"Mieka—" Rafe sounded frightened now.

"I try so hard, and sometimes it's all right, but I think maybe I'm not strong enough. I can't do the work like when I was twenty, not without the thorn, and havin' to go back and forth, back and forth—thorn and then no thorn . . ."

A sigh glided through the air behind Cayden. It wafted over his shoulder and became a haze of memory over to his left, forming vague shapes and colors that resolved into Mieka, curled in a narrow bed with sheets tangled all round him, sick and shivering with the lack of thorn he'd used too much of and now must again forswear. Cade didn't recognize the exact circumstances. He knew only too well the feeling of agonized helplessness spiked with anger that Mieka had done this to himself yet again.

As the breath of memory faded, he heard the soft voice behind him say, "I think my heart just got tired out."

"We're here," Rafe muttered. "Damn it to all Hells, Mieka, you have us to help you through."

"No, Rafe. You have me. You're holding on. I need you to let go."

"Fuck you," Jeska said with weary bitterness. "I'm not letting go just because you tell me to."

"I love you, too, y'know," Mieka murmured.

With a brief, keening moan, Jeska bent nearly double in his chair, arms wrapped around himself. Cade wanted to do the same, but he still couldn't *move. He had never known anything could hurt this much, frighten him this much, and yet not kill him.*

Why did he think it wasn't going to kill him?

Rafe rose slowly to his feet, his profile grimly determined. He took the three steps to the sofa where Mieka lay, took one pale hand, held it tight for a moment before placing it at Mieka's side.

"Beholden," Mieka whispered behind Cade.

Rafe nodded once, and turned and walked away.

Jeska almost lurched up from his chair, every muscle tensed for a fight. Then he let out a long breath, shook the hair from his face, and approached Mieka. His hand reached, shied back, then brushed gray-threaded hair back from Mieka's forehead.

"Damn it, Mieka," he whispered feebly.

"It's all right. Beholden."

Cade didn't watch him leave. He refused to stand up from his chair, even though he knew that he could have if he'd tried. He wouldn't do this.

He. Would. Not.

"Cayden."

He shook his head wordlessly.

"C'mon, old love," coaxed the familiar voice that for twenty years had wheedled him into glorious excesses of drink and thorn, mayhem and magic—but now asked for mercy. "Please, Quill."

He couldn't. He wondered if this meant he loved Mieka more than Rafe and Jeska did, loved him too much to let him go. Rafe had been the first to give Mieka what he needed in an act of selfless tenderness that Cade knew himself incapable of matching. And Jeska—the crushing weight of grief and guilt was a thing he could bear. That was love, too. So did all this mean that he loved Mieka less than they did?

He stared at the man collapsed gracelessly on the black velvet. No memories came to claw at him. He saw Mieka as he was—as he knew he must see him. Not the blithe, laughing, clever, mad little Elf, for there was almost nothing left of him. Nothing now but the haggard, worn face that had once been so beautiful; nothing but the healed scars of thorn on his arms.

Cade was the last, the only one left. The only one still holding on.

"Mine you are and mine you'll stay."

"Yes, always—but not like this. I can't live like this."

Cade got to his feet, stumbled a step, then two, fell hard onto bony knees, caught himself on the sofa. His eyes were almost on a level with those closed eyes, so near that he could see every one of the long black lashes weighing the eyelids down.

"You should have let me see," he whispered. "I kept trying to look, but you never let me see."

Still behind him, sounding more remote now, Mieka answered, "I didn't think you'd like the view. I had to keep making you laugh, so you'd forgive all the rest of it. You didn't laugh much, y'know, before I came along."

"And you think that's all you were worth?"

"I had to be what you needed—the best glisker in Albeyn, the one who could always make you laugh—the one who never wanted you to hide your Elsewhens or anything else about you."

"But you never forgave yourself."

Silence.

"I'm right, aren't I? When Yazz died—it wasn't your fault, Mieka!"

Silence.

He knew now. He understood. He saw. "You thought you didn't deserve to be here, not if he was gone. Gods, Mieka, you should have told me! You should have let me see!"

"That's all done with now, Quill. Let go. Please."

Cade bent, resting his brow against the silent, motionless chest. Then he pushed himself to his feet and turned to walk away.

Mieka stood before him, young and strong and beautiful. "Beholden, Quill. I know that was impossible for you. Beholden, for doing it for me."

This wasn't the Mieka of the past. There were lines at the corners of those eyes, threads of silver in his hair as if he'd combed it with moonlight, and knowledge—perhaps even wisdom—that Cade had never seen in that face before. All at once a smile appeared, dazzling and irresistible. The laughter was just as boisterous, but held nothing of the maniacal cackle that meant impending havoc.

"Cayden Silversun, you softhearted fake! All that deep-minded artsy-fartsy wyvern shit you toss around—you're naught but a sentimental old grandmum!"

Yes, Mieka had always seen right through him. Fear pierced him again. "I can't let you go, Elfling."

"It'll be all right. I promise. I'll be waiting for you. For all of you."

He tried to touch Mieka, but the Elf took a small step back, away from him. Ready to leave.

"I'd come with you if I could—and I could, Mieka, it would be so easy—"

"No! You've so much more to write, so much to do that's really and truly important—not like me. I always knew that if the wind blew too hard, I'd be gone. But you—bright as the whole sky, Silversun!" He smiled. "I'm not worried about being forgotten. Not as long as your work exists."

And everything he wrote from now on would have Mieka in it—but how could it ever be performed if Mieka wasn't there onstage to do it? How would anyone ever truly see one of Cayden's plays again, without Mieka behind the glass baskets?

"When Touchstone lost their Elf, they lost their soul."

Where had he heard those words? It didn't matter. With Mieka gone, he would hear those words again and again, and read them, and dream them and nightmare them—

"Every word," he heard himself say very slowly. "You'll be here, in every word."

"Beholden for that, too," Mieka said.

The dimness began to brighten, coalescing into a thin ribbon of silver that broadened to a rippling and glowing pathway. Moonglade.

"Quill?" Mieka whispered. "Break the window. You have to. Just like you have to let me go."

Those eyes. Innocent, wise, mischievous, compassionate—it was the compassion that finally convinced him. This was Mieka as he'd been meant to be, all insecurities and hurts and masks and fears gone, revealing a loving and compassionate man who knew him, understood him, saw him as he was.

But between one blink and the next, Cade was alone. Mieka was gone.

*   *   *

He lay in his bed, the thin sunlight of a winter afternoon impotent to warm his shivering. Something was scratching at the bedchamber door—Rumble, of course, peeved that Cade hadn't let him in. He pushed himself to his feet, pulling the big feather-stitched counterpane around his shoulders in a vain attempt to stop the shaking, and opened the door. Rumble stalked through, lush white tail lashing, and made straight for the soft black armchair. He leaped up, turned, and yowled a demand for Cade to stop being such a fool and sit down and pet him.

When Cade had settled with the cat in his lap, the rhythmic purring provided a background for his thoughts—not soothing, exactly, but calming. He knew, intellectually, that his mind had done what it always did when a dream or nightmare or Elsewhen invaded: took the disparate elements and made a cohesive (but sometimes not quite coherent) story of them. The mind he had trained to organize and remember the Elsewhens always did the same with dreams, thornvisions, nightmares. This time it seemed to him that his brain had been rather kinder to him than usual. It had, after all, presented the entire sequence as if he had been dreaming it. Shorn of all the fantastical elements, though, it was a fair approximation of a possible future.

Two things were conspicuous. First, Yazz had died. Mieka held himself responsible somehow—else why that long debauch of liquor and thorn? Second, Brishen Staindrop had given up Thornlore because too many people had died. *Alaen* had died. Not from her mixtures, but those of other concoctors—Master Bellgloss, perhaps, and the dragon tears that Master Lullfinch supplied to select customers at his brothel. Yes, thorn could be dangerous. Certain kinds of thorn were especially perilous to Elves, Wizards, Gnomes, Goblins, and so on. Evidently quite a few people hadn't been careful, or aware of their own bloodlines. He had the thought that mayhap Black Lightning's little trick of being able to identify each person's background—and to make them ashamed, should it include anything other than Wizard or Elf—could be used at large to warn those who wanted to use thorn just which ones they ought to steer clear of. This wasn't why Black Lightning had worked it out, Cade was certain. Just what they had in mind, he'd no idea.

And it didn't matter right now. Yazz would be dead, and Brishen would stick to distilling whiskey. All Cayden had to do was decide whether this really had been nothing other than a thorn-dream, or if there were elements of an Elsewhen mixed up in it—and if so, how much was a forewarning and how much was his own convoluted imagination.

He heard Derien's rapid footsteps up the stairs, and Mistress Mirdley's call: "Tea right now, or go hungry!" He smoothed Rumble's fur by way of apology, and shifted the cat to his shoulder as he stood up. Well, if nothing else, this nightmare-Elsewhen had shown him how *Window Wall* had to end. And that was something, wasn't it?

Chapter 4

Even though one week's holiday from performing became two, then lengthened into three, Cade didn't much mind. Now that he had the ending for the two plays that made up *Window Wall*, he had plenty to keep him busy.

In the first play, the boy's father, traumatized by magic in the Archduke's War, decided to make an environment for his only child that would keep him safe from all magic. That he had to hire a prodigiously talented Wizard to do it was an irony that escaped him—but not, Cade trusted, the audience. The tale of the man's wounding was the first part of the first play. His experiences in battle of withies that came spinning and shining to ravage the King's Army with magic emphasized that part of the horror was that one never knew which it would be: merely malicious or hideously deadly. Returning home, sick in mind and heart and incapable of fighting anymore, he discovered that his wife and son had fled as refugees. His search for them ended with his making a promise to his dying wife that he would protect their child from the evils of magic.

There were no changes for Jeska to make. He would be only the father as soldier, invalid, and seeker, and then silently cradling his son in his arms as he walked through a war-ravaged countryside, trying to find a place for them to live. Cayden decided to let all this play out with only a backdrop—no emotions gliding through the audience. The scenes and dialogue would be enough. And that meant that the words had to be the best he could find, and the visuals the most evocative he and Mieka could come up with. He knew in his guts that the words were more important, but he would never be so foolish as to tell Mieka that.

As for emotions—the horrors of war and the terrors of Cade's own grandmother's lethal withies, the pain of magical wounds and the desperation of the search, the pathos of the mother's plea and the grim resolve of the father—he trusted to his own words that all these things could be felt by the audience without prompting. Besides, he needed the impact of feeling later on to communicate the sincere determination of the father to shield his son from all magic by locking him away in the room with one huge window.

The Wizard, tall, spindly-limbed, cloaked in dark brown, would pace the stage creating each portion of the boy's prison. This would give Mieka the chance to build the final scene section by section, while the Wizard mused aloud on why anyone should want such a thing, and that mayhap it was a good idea and mayhap it wasn't, but he didn't really much care as long as he was being paid.

At last the boy, five or six years old by now, was brought into the room by his father, who showed him all its marvels: fireplace for cooking, sink for washing, bed for sleeping, books for education, toys for playtime, a lute for music, and a screen to hide the toilet. While rewriting this scene, Cade changed his mind about which of the characters Jeska would inhabit. He'd thought the father, but how much more effective to have Jeska play the son—with the scale of the room upsized to stress the child's helplessness, just the way they'd played about with the Giant at the tournament in the Third Peril at Trials a few years ago. Rather than have the boy brought into the room by his father, Cade would let him wander through it on his own while his father's voice explained everything. Jeska would stay the little boy, bewildered and more than a little scared (Mieka would underscore these feelings with magic) until his father shows him a big wooden rocking-dragon. The play would end with the boy stroking the nose and wide wings of the garishly painted dragon, and contentment would waft gently through the audience . . . threaded with the barest hint of sadness and misgiving.

Cade wouldn't have to give the boy words to detail everything, but only such dialogue as a child would speak. But in the second play, the boy—now sixteen, perhaps seventeen years old—could display the sort of vocabulary one might expect from someone who had learned words only from books and one teacher: his own father. If nobody noticed that subtlety, fine. It was there, and Cayden knew it was there, and that was enough for him.

Staging it would be tricky. Everything depended on the audience's seeing what the boy saw and fidgeting with the lack of sensation. No sounds of the people passing by outside. No smells of flowers or horses or the man pushing the cart of meat pasties. No tastes. (He'd have to figure out how the boy and his father acquired the food they'd cook over the hearth, but . . . well, leave that for some other time, don't get caught up in something that would distract him from the flow of the play.) No feeling of a breeze or sunshine or even the clothes on his back. Cade would have the boy moving around the room, tidying things, shelving books, whatever, while all sorts of things went on outside, beyond the window. The boy would ignore them, having long since exhausted any longing to know what the outside world was like. All the yearning, the frustration that this yearning went unfulfilled, the anger that came from frustration, the weariness of spirit that followed an explosion of anger—he would have gone through all of these a thousand times, and was now simply resigned. He didn't ignore the world beyond the window because it would hurt too much to look. He ignored it because he just didn't care anymore.

What would happen next?

This was where Cayden got stuck. He knew how it would end: the boy using his fists to shatter the glass (*"Break the window, Quill"* echoed in his mind from that horrible dream). But what motivation was there to leave the safety of the unmagical world behind his window wall and risk all the chaos beyond?

Years ago, around the time of "Turn Aback," he would have wrestled with it alone. He would have flogged his brain stuporous and ended by hating the whole piece. He knew better now. He'd take the problem to his partners. They'd be able to see what he couldn't. They'd look at it from their own unique viewpoints and offer suggestions. And he'd listen to those suggestions. He knew their value now and wasn't too proud to admit it.

A memory teased him of the afternoon spent at Seekhaven reworking that piece that the players from the Continent had performed. All three groups involved—Touchstone, the Shadowshapers, and the Crystal Sparks—had functioned quite differently from one another.

Crystal Sparks' tregetour and masquer had done the creative work between them, while their glisker and fettler played cards over in a corner. With the Shadowshapers, it was a mad little dance of constantly changing partners, as Vered and Rauel took turns talking with Chat and Sakary; two of them would meet, then three, then a different pair, then a different three, until all possible combinations had occurred—except the final debate between Vered and Rauel, which would eventually (and with varying degrees of rancor) decide the outcome. Watching these two groups at work had caused in Cayden a profound gratitude for his own glisker, fettler, and masquer. To be sure, the four of them argued—but it was the *four* of them.

Over the years he'd come to rely on that—unknowingly at first, then deliberately and with eager anticipation. All four contributed vitally to each play. What worked for the Shadowshapers or the Sparks wouldn't work at all for Touchstone.

And that, he realized, was one of the great strengths of theater in Albeyn. On the Continent, the scripts were set and the words sacrosanct, leaving no room for anyone to be truly creative. Cade amused himself for a few moments imagining reactions to *Window Wall* in those other countries where magic was seen as suspect at best. The boy battering at the glass with his fists seemed to him symbolic of anyone born there with magic—no, that wasn't it. The window would work the *other* way: those with magic trapped, caged like animals in a traveling menagerie, stared at by a society that considered them dangerous. What if the magically gifted broke the window?

More to the point for his present project, what would happen when the boy broke the window separating him from a world he could see but not live in? And why would he finally choose his freedom to go out into that world, and experience the magic it contained?

Rafe or Jeska or Mieka would have some idea. They could work it out together. A good feeling, that; knowing he had partners as talented and clever as himself. Even better, knowing that he was no longer so blindly prideful, and could freely admit it.

Still, on the ninth evening of Touchstone's self-imposed break, Cade leaned back in his desk chair, rubbed his stubbled face, smiled tiredly at the pages and pages he'd written today of dialogue and performance notes, and chided himself for having avoided this sort of exhaustion for so long. The demands of sheer survival had of course taken precedence over real creativity—or so he'd told himself. For so long now, when he'd done something new, it wasn't really new, only a rehashing of some old play from the copy of *Lost Withies* Mieka had found years ago at the Castle Biding Fair. The plays were new to Touchstone's folio, perhaps, but certainly not original or different. He'd convinced himself that he hadn't the time to indulge. For certain sure, he hadn't the energy.

What he hadn't realized until now was the disservice he'd done to himself, to his partners, and even to the audiences. He'd forgotten how *good* a spate of creativity could feel. (And how hard the work was—its satisfaction in direct correlation to its difficulty. Put simply, the more exhausted he was, the happier.) It shamed him to admit that the desperate necessities of financial survival had become so easy an excuse for not putting in the hard work that left him feeling as limp as a strand of seaweed and as powerful as a crashing wave.

Writing was his outlet and his safeguard as surely as performing was Mieka's. He owed it to himself and to his sanity to create. He owed Mieka and Rafe and Jeska new and original pieces to challenge and fulfill their talents. And he owed the audiences the best work he was capable of, not some warmed-over reworking of a play that had grown gray-bearded fifty years before Grandfather Cadriel the fettler had been born.

And as long as he was admitting things, he might as well admit that the things he had to say could be said by no one but him. Vered Goldbraider and Rauel Kevelock, Mirko Challender, Trenal Longbranch, even Thierin Knottinger—Cade would never be able to write their words (and in one case wouldn't care to try) any more than they could write his. He had something to say. All these pages proved it.

Rafe had been absolutely right to demand a break. They were all sick of each other. This was what they told themselves, and it was true—but didn't openly admit to the overuse of thorn and liquor that frayed tempers and caused mistakes onstage. They'd grown stale, careless, at times complacent and sometimes even bored. And a new play, an *original* play, was just the thing to invigorate Touchstone. Arguing over dialogue, debating stagecraft, proposing effects, rehearsing and rehearsing until they got it right—Cade was smiling as he fell asleep, tired and happy and without the slightest interest in or need for blockweed.

The next morning he sent notes round to the Threadchaser bakery, Jeska's flat, and Wistly Hall, tentatively suggesting that perhaps they might want to gather for a talk about *Window Wall*. Not a rehearsal, he pointed out, just a chat over tea and Mistress Mirdley's seedy cakes and apricot muffins.

Mieka, Rafe, and Jeska all arrived at Redpebble Square within minutes of each other. The bustle of removing cloaks and hats and gloves in the hall got them through any awkwardness of first greetings; Rafe, who had decreed the break in the first place, won everyone's heart when he announced that after fifteen years he'd finally mastered the spell his father used to keep the loaves warm, and proceeded to use it on his partners' shoes.

The fettler was looking less tight about the eyes. Wryly aloof as a rule, thorn had wound him up to a dangerously uncommunicative tenseness. Cade was ashamed of himself that it took this new relaxation to make him notice the difference. They *had* been taking one another for granted, concentrating too much on their own problems, just as they'd done during the time he refused to see the Elsewhens. Of course, the problem this time was a collective one: money. In a way, they hadn't dared talk too much about it amongst themselves. They all knew the mess they were in. Endless reiteration only led to frustration and anger that they took out on each other. Now that they were solvent again, and actually beginning to earn more than the bare minimum for survival, Touchstone had needed a rest from Touchstone.

The fear was still in Cade, though. He wondered if the others were prey to the sick, cold terror that of itself had been enough to send him to the bottle or the thorn-roll, even without the seemingly endless cycle of enforced energy onstage and nervous exhaustion in private. He had the nasty feeling that no matter how much piled up in his bank account from now on, he'd worry about money for the rest of his life.

Seated around a cheering fire, warmed by Rafe's newly learned spell and the lavish tea Mistress Mirdley had laid on for them, it was nearly like old times. *Old*, Cade thought with an inner wince, when it wasn't really that long ago. They'd been so much younger then, and arrogant with it in the way young men were who knew they were good at their chosen calling and hadn't yet known that being good at something didn't always guarantee success.

Back then, they hadn't fully developed the give-and-take of working through a play. As Cade presented his outline of the two *Window Wall* scripts, he was ready and willing to make notes based on their ideas and comments.

And then he got to the sticky part.

"He has to get out. He has to *want* to get out. But what's his motivation? Why does he want to leave that safe little room?"

The three looked at him, and then at one another. He had the sensation that the answer would be so devastatingly obvious that they considered him a total shit-wit for not recognizing it instantly on his own. The looks they turned back onto him were, in varying degrees, amused, pitying, exasperated, and impatient, but mainly disbelieving that he, their esteemed tregetour, could be so vividly stupid.

"All together now?" Rafe asked, and when Jeska and Mieka nodded, continued, "One day he looks out the window and sees—say it with me, lads—"

They obediently chorused, "A *girl*!"

A girl. Of course. Painfully, mortifyingly obvious. Cade wondered if he could use one of his own withies to make himself disappear. Why hadn't he thought of it himself? He knew how plots worked, what motivated characters, why people did what they did and said what they said. The boy suddenly sees outside the window the most beautiful girl in the world, and falls in love with her at sight. Surely Cayden ought to have thought that one up for himself.

Well, it had never happened for him like that, had it? Rafe, gobsmacked by Crisiant while they were still at littleschool; Mieka, stunned, staggered, and stupefied by the first sight of his wife at the Castle Biding Fair; Jeska, stumbling and incoherent upon first seeing Kazie . . . and then there was Cade, and the girls he casually chose for bedding when Touchstone was on the road—but that wasn't love. Not the way his friends loved their wives, with desire ever renewed and a need to be with them whenever possible, with companionship and laughter, arguments and passionate reconciliations, struggling through these last two years somehow together, always together . . . No, he knew nothing of that kind of love. The nearest he had ever come to it was Lady Megueris, and that feeling certainly hadn't happened with his first look at her. It had come only after months and months of getting to know her, being annoyed by her, infuriating her in his turn, and finally, inexplicably, that night of the King's celebrations when he'd hurt his hand and she'd spent the night in bed with him. Was that love? He wasn't sure. Was what he felt the sort of all-powerful, thoroughly overmastering thing that would incite the boy to break through the window at last?

No.

He'd have to leave this part of it to his masquer, fettler, and glisker. They had the experience of it, so he'd trust them to make it come out right in the play. There was usually a happy dearth of explanation from men rendered incoherent and sometimes speechless by falling abruptly and violently in love. So there wouldn't be much by way of dialogue, and he wouldn't have to embarrass himself by writing drivel.

They were already plotting it out. How old was she? What should she look like? Hair, eyes, height, proportions, style of clothing, the expression on her face—something had to set her apart from all the other girls the boy had seen beyond the window wall. Something had to make her so different and so compelling that for love of her, for the need to hear her voice and touch her hair and skin and breathe in her scent and taste her kisses, he would break through the protecting glass and brave the world outside.

Cade was astonished to hear himself interrupt. "Yeh, yeh, that's all very well. But in a way, all he wants is just to *see* her—whether she's really everything he thinks she is, or if the glass has distorted something. He wants to *look* at her without anything getting in the way."

"And that means she's got to see *him* as well!" Mieka exclaimed. "Are we going to show that? Will what she sees make her want him and love him, or will she run away screaming?"

"Well, she'd be nervous," Rafe mused. "Maybe even scared of him. But what happens to her isn't the real point, is it? And it'd be—I dunno, kind of dishonest, to imply that all he has to do is break open the window and go outside for everything to be rainbows and rose gardens."

"I think he waits until she's passed by," Jeska said. "He works himself into a dither, and realizes that he has to see her again but there's a horrible chance that he won't—she might never walk past his window again. And the only way to find her is to break the glass and go out looking in the big scary world."

"And the decision takes him all day and into the night!" Mieka went on, practically jumping up and down in his chair with excitement. "And then—"

"Does he realize that all sorts of people are going to be looking at him now?" Jeska interrupted.

"Looking," Cade stated. "Not *seeing*. That the really important thing—that he finally realizes that even if he never finds her again, he does want to be *seen* by somebody. By at least one person. Seen for who and what he is, as he is."

"—and then," Mieka said loudly, "it's night, and everything dark outside until the moon begins to rise—and on the wet street outside—"

"If it's raining, how can there be a moon?" Rafe scoffed.

"It rained earlier, all right? Think what a nice, gloomy backdrop it'd be for his ditherings and whinings. But when the moon hits the slick of the road—" He clapped his hands together in triumph, beaming all over his face. "Moonglade!"

Rafe scratched at his beard. "And he's so thrilled with the very idea of it that he crashes through the window to get at it? I thought he wanted out because of the girl."

"I want a moonglade, damn it. Cade's been promising me a moonglade for years."

"Maybe," Jeska said, "he imagines her as kind of a spectral figure walking along the silvery path—"

Rafe's groan stopped him. Cade hid a grin.

Jeska glowered and kept going. "Maybe the something unique about her is her blonde hair—silver-blonde, like Jinsie's or Vered's. And when he sees the moonglade, he associates that with—" When Rafe screwed his face up with disdain, he burst out, "All right, then, *you* think of something!"

"Not my job," he drawled. "Leave it to Cade. But I know what we can do at the end, when he shatters the glass." Rising, he came over to where Cayden sat, took a sheet of clean paper, stole the pen, and started to draw. The others gathered round. "Like so—at an angle, the way we do 'Doorways,'" he said. "When he throws the chair, it goes through the window, the glass splinters onto the stage—"

Cade saw where he was going. "—and the chair goes flying out over the audience, scaring the shit out of them!"

"And then it vanishes," Mieka contributed happily, "as a distraction while I change the scene onstage—"

"—to all the sights, sounds, feelings, and smells rushing in through the broken window," Rafe finished, nodding approval.

"I can give a huge yell as the chair vanishes," Jeska offered, "to bring their attention back to me."

"The timing will be tricky," Cade mused. "But I like it. Give me a few days to work it all out and write it up, and then we can meet downstairs here where no one will bother us." He said this last rather feelingly, for a clattering in the kitchen announced Derien's arrival home from school.

"Brilliant," Mieka declared. "We are all of us and each of us collectively and separately absolutely *brilliant*."

Chapter 5

Books piled up around him as he searched through his grandfather's library for something that would help him stage an angled presentation, and how it might affect the bounce of magic. Then, on a soggy gray afternoon, Mistress Mirdley marched into his bedchamber without knocking and snatched a heavy volume right out of his hand.

"Downstairs. Now."

Cade had a moment of sheer panic—Derien? Had something happened to Derien? No, he thought, searching her face as he got to his feet. There was a grimness to her harsh features, a tightness to the lines of her mouth, but no grief. Aware that questions would gain him no answers, he followed her down the stairs to the front hall.

Mieka and Hadden Windthistle were there, brushing rain off the cloaks they had just hung up. The two men turned at the sound of footsteps. Mieka looked subdued. Hadden looked solemn.

"Beholden, Mistress," he said. "Good afternoon, Cayden. Is there perhaps someplace we can sit down?"

Mistress Mirdley pointed to the drawing room door. "Tea," she said, as stingy with her words today as a full-blooded Goblin, and departed for the kitchen.

When they were seated, Hadden glanced at Mieka and then looked Cayden straight in the eyes. "I'm very sorry, Cade. There's been an accident. Your father is dead."

He waited for something more. No, that was all. The father he hadn't seen to speak to in longer than he could remember . . . never more than a vague presence someplace in Gallantrybanks, unless he was traveling with Prince Ashgar . . . to Seekhaven, mostly, for Trials, where Zekien had never so much as acknowledged his own son's presence either onstage or off . . .

Was Cade supposed to cry? Should he express some sort of sorrow? He wasn't that much of a hypocrite. He decided that he was, in fact, rather shocked. Zekien was still quite a young man, by Wizardly standards. Just fifty-one. No age at all.

"Accident?" he asked.

Mieka threw an apprehensive glance at his own father, then said, "It was—the circumstances—oh, Hells, Quill! He took some strange kind of thorn last night and this morning they found him dead in his room at the Palace."

Now Cade was well and truly shocked. Thorn? His father?

"Master Lullfinch," Hadden said quietly, "has a new mixture, it seems. Spiralspin, he calls it. Among the effects are visions and illusions—deliriums, in fact—"

"And a raging cock-rise," Mieka interrupted. "No sense trying to pretty it up, Fa. He obviously took it to—um—renew the fires, as it were."

When one considered what Zekien's position had been in Ashgar's household, it was scant wonder he'd tried such a thing. And considering that Master Lullfinch owned an exclusive brothel called the Finchery, it was even less of a wonderment that he'd cooked up a recipe to stimulate flagging desire. Lullfinch, who had once given Mieka's wife a business card that had led to all sorts of trouble.

"Princess Miriuzca sent to us at Wistly with the news," Hadden went on. "She thought it would be easier for you, coming from friends."

Cade nodded politely. "Does my mother know?"

"Probably. Would you like us to stay until Derien gets home from school?"

"I'll tell him. Beholden for the offer."

Mistress Mirdley came in then with the tea tray. On it, in addition to the pot and cups and saucers and spoons, the milk jug and the sugar bowl, was a small bottle of whiskey. The Trollwife departed and Cade poured out, liberally dosing his own and Mieka's cups, obedient when Hadden shook his head. They drank in silence.

"I'm told that they've packed up all his things from his Palace chambers," Hadden said at last. "I asked the Princess's man to have it all sent here."

"Beholden," Cade repeated.

They sat for a while, listening to the crackling of the fire.

It was Hadden who once more broke the quiet by clearing his throat awkwardly. "I don't like leaving you alone here, Cade, but I have a customer coming by before dinner."

Mieka said at once, "I'll stop awhile, if it's all right with Cade."

It made little difference to him, but he held himself from the dismissive shrug that would have been an insult. He saw Mieka's father out the front door, wrapped in a plain black cloak and wearing a wide-brimmed hat against the rain. Returning to the drawing room, he caught Mieka taking a swig directly from the whiskey bottle.

"Put that down."

Those big, changeable eyes blinked wide. "Huh?"

"Just go easy on the drink, all right?"

The Elf set the bottle carefully on the tea tray, tilted his head to one side, and asked, "You've had another Elsewhen about me, haven't you?"

At least he could answer with the truth—Mieka always knew when he was lying, anyway. He always saw it. "No." And the fact was that he hadn't. "But wasn't one of the reasons Rafe wanted some time off that we should all stop using so much thorn and liquor?"

"You, maybe. You're the one who bollixed the show that night." Then—and it was obvious in his face—he thought better of sniping at someone who'd just lost his father, and said, "Sorry, Quill. Quite the shocker, this."

The words were so much like the ones Mieka had spoken in the dream that Cade had to turn away. He looked into the fire for a time, and all he could see was the yellow of the flames. Yellow, like that shirt Mieka had been wearing—and something to do with a yellow shirt tugged at his memory. It pulled no threads free to be followed back to their source. Perhaps it had been in an Elsewhen that he'd deliberately forgotten. The more fool he.

"I know you weren't close," Mieka went on. "But he was your father."

"No oftener than was convenient." With a shrug, he sat back down in one of his mother's spindly little wooden chairs. *His* chairs now, he supposed, being the eldest son and heir. Dreadful thought. "Beastly weather today, innit?"

"Oh, c'mon, Quill. I'm not sayin' you should crumble down weeping, or wear mourning for a year. You gotta feel *something*, y'know." He made an abortive reach for the whiskey bottle, then settled back in his chair. "Your mother will be home soon, I'd imagine. You'll have to think up something to say to her, at the very least."

"No, I've an idea she'll stay at the Palace as long as possible. Collapse in tears—tastefully, of course, even decoratively if she can manage it—and be fussed over by the Queen's Ladies, that sort of thing. I wouldn't be at all surprised if she manages to spend the night in somebody's bedchamber, unless she can arrange to be driven home in one of the Queen's carriages."

Mieka looked truly shocked. "She's not *that* bad!"

"I've known her a lot longer than you have." He glanced up as someone made emphatic use of the door knocker outside. "That'll be Father's rubbish."

It was. Five footmen wearing Prince Ashgar's livery brought in two large wooden crates and a coffer old enough that Grandfather Cadriel might have used it on the Circuits. Cade directed the men to put everything in the drawing room, and tipped them a couple of coins on their way out. Touchstone was solvent again, and he had to start behaving like it.

The first crate, its nails pried up with a fire iron, contained just what Cade had predicted: rubbish. Clothes, mainly, plus a large collection of unmatched buttons; broken boot laces; empty ink bottles; a rusty flint-rasp; one of those glass neck-cloth rings, Mieka's idea that had been briefly popular and made Blye such a tidy profit, finely worked but chipped at one corner; shirts that needed mending and stockings that needed darning; and a whole slew of slippers, shoes, and boots in various stages of wear and disrepair.

"Why'd they bother to pack all this lot?" Cade muttered as he reached a layer of smallclothes and embroidered nightshirts thrown in at the bottom, unfolded and rather forlorn.

"Well, if it's the Court, whoever packed it must've gone through and pinched whatever was actually worth anything," Mieka said reasonably. "Did he have any personal servants?"

"No idea. If so, I imagine they'll be round here sooner or later, angling for a job or a means of support while they look for other work." His lip curled when he found, at the very bottom of the crate of useless things, a little wooden box, delicately carved and inlaid with iridescent shell fragments, that held three glass thorns and a tiny pewter bowl for mixing. Thorn—his own father!

"Next?" he asked, and Mieka obliged him by opening the second crate. More clothing—everything from stockings of all colors to a heavy woolen cloak, black and trimmed with matching fur at the hem and hood. This last he shook free of the crate. "No holes that I can see, and the fur's probably worth a goodly bit. I'm surprised it's here, considering—" He broke off as something fell from the undone folds of the cloak. "What in all Hells—?"

Two things: two framed drawings done in pencil.

"Good Gods," he murmured. "Mieka, look at these."

They were not imagings done with magic, but simply pencil sketches done by some unprofessional but mildly talented artist. The drawings were labeled at the bottom. CAYDEN. DERIEN.

Mieka laughed with delight. "Quill! You were adorable!"

Embarrassed, he protested, "I couldn't have been more than a year old. All babies are adorable at a year old."

But he couldn't take his gaze from the infant whose features were his. There was no mistaking that nose, even in a face barely a year old. He could understand his father's having kept the portrait of Derien—a beautiful baby, he was growing into a beautiful young man—but *him*? Cade had often doubted that his father remembered his existence more than once or twice a year.

"I wish—" he began incautiously, then stopped.

"What? Tell me, Quill."

After a moment's struggle, he gave in to those thoughtful, compassionate eyes. "I just wish I could go back and tell this boy that it'll be all right. That he'll be all right. That there will be friends and work he'll love. And even with all the problems and even the Elsewhens, his life really will be all right."

Mieka was quiet for so long that Cade felt his face begin to burn with renewed embarrassment. At last the Elf spoke.

"There's a drawing of Jed and Jez and Jinsie and me—Fa couldn't afford to hire an imager or anything, and he wanted to give Mum something special for Wintering one year—this was before Cilka and Petrinka were born, and way before Tavier and Jorie. Anyway, he had this musician friend who had a friend who was an artist, and the four of us made such a picture—two redheads, and Jinsie and me being opposites in coloring—that the man did the work for free. I don't remember sitting for it—"

"I can't even imagine you sitting still that long!"

"I probably didn't! But the thing of it is, Mum keeps it in their bedchamber, with drawings of the others, and I was in there about a month ago for something or other, and . . ."

"And?" Cade prompted.

"I looked at it, and I thought . . . Quill, don't laugh at me."

"I won't. Just tell me."

"I wanted to ask that little boy if he minded much, growing up to be me."

"Why would I laugh at that?"

"Well, it's kind of funny, when you think about it. You thinking what you did just now, and me thinking the exact opposite, in a way."

"We had opposite sorts of childhoods."

"Me with this huge family, you all alone until Dery was born."

"You the *really* adorable little boy who made everyone laugh," Cade said, more slowly now, "and me something of a freak."

"Stop that! That isn't what I meant. You were unhappy. I wasn't."

"I don't think I was *un*happy, exactly," he mused. "I always knew what my mother thought of me. My father wasn't around much. But my grandfather was wonderful. I just figured that this was the way things were supposed to be, that it all was normal. Children are very accepting. They don't know any different."

"But what did you think when you saw this just now? You wanted to reassure him that things will turn out all right. I wanted to ask the little boy I was if he thinks I totally fucked up."

"Why would he think that?" Cade asked.

Looking uncomfortable, Mieka opened his mouth to reply. At that precise moment Derien came clattering in from the kitchen, fourteen years old, as tall as Mieka now, all legs and arms and big brown eyes and a rowdy tangle of curly hair. The noise came from the satchel slung over one shoulder, full of books and pencils and what sounded like a dozen of the small, hard wooden balls used in various games. He let the bag drop and went immediately to Cade, and flung his arms around him.

"They let me out of school early. Is it true about Father? What happened to him? I heard the Palace footman say something to the teacher about thorn."

Cade exchanged glances with Mieka, who shrugged. Was Dery old enough to understand the sordid circumstances of Zekien's death? It would be common knowledge all over Gallybanks before tables were set for dinner tonight.

"It's better that you hear it from me," Cayden said, pulling away, taking the boy's shoulders in his own thin hands, and looking straight into those wide, trusting brown eyes. "You know what position he held at Court?"

"Of course. Ashgar's pimp."

Cade winced. Mieka let out a little snort of surprise.

Derien made a disgusted face. "Do I look as if I'm still five years old? What happened, Cade? How did he die? In bed with some girl, trying her out for the Prince?"

"Not exactly. More to do with—with getting too old to do that anymore, I think." He was just as glad that he wouldn't have to find the exact words to explain. "Lullfinch has some new kind of thorn."

"Oh, it's not new," Derien said. "We learned all about thorn in class. Consecreations and Consequences, taught by a Good Brother who's about a thousand years old. Thorn isn't approved by High *or* Low Chapel, y'know."

"When did that happen?"

"First I've heard of it," Mieka said at the same time.

"It's Princess Iamina and the Archduchess." He drew away from Cade and fell into a chair, sprawling long legs and still somehow looking graceful, as Cade had never been. "They're taking an interest in the King's College. It's said they'll focus on Shollop and Stiddolfe this summer. A whole new university discipline, the study of sacred writings to turn out highly educated Good Brothers—but not Good Sisters, the usual Chapel schooling is education enough for women." He made an impatient gesture. "But who cares about that, anyway? How's Mother? Does she know? Will she be home soon? And what's all this stuff?"

"The Palace sent it over from Father's rooms. I'm not sure when Mother will be home." Cade saw Derien's face change, a frown and a bitten upper lip alerting him. "What?" he demanded.

Dery slid from his chair to the floor, scooted across the rug to the coffer that was still unopened. "What's in here?"

"Haven't gone through it yet."

He knelt beside his brother to examine the coffer—heavy oak with the outline of a dragon carved into the lid, bound in brass that had long since lost its shine, with worn leather straps easily unbuckled and a lock for which they had no key. Mieka, more practical, took up the fire iron and wedged it between the lock and the coffer, and yanked. Derien was looking more fretful with each passing moment.

Cade hefted the heavy lid open and began removing items—good clothing this time, made of fine silks and whisper-soft woolens, with a plentitude of intricate embroidery and silver buttons. For a moment Derien's face cleared as he fingered a longvest decorated with gold thread, but then he bit both lips between his teeth and started flinging garments out of the coffer as fast as he could.

"Have a care, mate!" Mieka protested, snatching up a particularly elegant jacket, dark blue brocade, the collar and cuffs stiff with silver embroidery. "I guess his best clothes didn't get pinched after all, Cade." He held the jacket up to himself and extended his arm, measuring the sleeve. "Take some cutting down to fit—what is it with you Silversuns and your arms and legs that go on forever? Can I have this one?"

"Take whatever you like," Cayden said, irritated at the interruption. Dery was hunting for something and not finding it. He didn't distract the boy—not when that look was on his face. Did he himself look like this when on the trail of a plotline? Or an Elsewhen?

And then it struck him: Derien's magic. Gold. Something in that coffer was gold.

He thought it might be the opaque green glass box—something Blye's father had made long ago, by the hallmark on the bottom, but not magically sealed as a keepsake box, like the one Blye had made for Cayden to give to Princess Miriuzca. This one contained jewelry. Cuff links and shirt studs, brooches and stickpins, all made of gold and silver and precious stones, and worth a tidy sum.

Dery was still jumpy, still frowning.

At the very bottom was an old tea canister, square and slightly rusted. Cade took it from his brother's hand, impatient to see what was in it. Dery didn't give it a second glance, even though the coffer was now entirely empty. Cade wrenched off the lid and saw what was inside: business cards. Dozens of them. He picked one at random and although it was not from the Finchery, he knew it must be another whorehouse by the feminine names written on the back and the two, three, or four stars drawn beside them. So this was how Zekien had kept track of Prince Ashgar's bedmates.

Cade put the canister aside. Mieka was still sampling clothes. Dery sat back on his heels, scowling at the empty coffer. All at once he gave a wordless exclamation.

"What?" Cade asked again.

"It's bigger on the outside than it is on the inside—see the difference in depth? There's another three inches or so at the bottom. Help me get it open."

"Wait a moment. It might be magical." He touched the sides of the coffer, the open lid, the inside and bottom, where another dragon with outspread wings had been burned into the wood. "Did anybody ever say what sort of magic Father had? Mother never mentioned it."

"He must've had something, mustn't he? I mean, if *we* do, and Grandfather Cadriel did, then—"

"Magic or not," Mieka said, "me mum says she never met any magic that iron couldn't conquer. Remember that slip I threw at the Fae, Quill?" He slammed the business end of the fire iron straight down into the coffer, as if stabbing to the heart of a real dragon.

Dery cried out in protest, Cade in alarm. They really didn't have any idea whether or not their father had possessed any magic, or how it might manifest itself, or if the coffer had been bespelled by him or someone else.

Evidently not. No flashes, no smoke; no surge of noxious smells; no sudden feeling of panic or anything else. No magic here.

Except Derien's magic, which had sensed what was hidden in the false bottom of the coffer. Cayden felt his jaw sag open a little. Gold. Packed tightly in row after row after row, with a shred of gold velvet in between each coin to prevent the telltale ring of metal. A small fortune in gold royals.

"Where did he get it?" Mieka's voice was hushed in the presence of so much wealth.

"Isn't it obvious?" Derien asked. "Proceeds from all the brothels. Bribes to get their girls into Father's bed, and then Ashgar's." He sat back again, disgusted. "There's years of it here."

"Can't be," Mieka argued. "All these clothes must've cost—and that box of jewelry, none of it was cheap—"

"Look at the velvet," Cade said. "Gold. Like the bags Lullfinch gives out with Dragon Tears in them. He cut up a few of them so the coins wouldn't chink against each other." He slid a neat little circle of velvet from between two of the coins. "See that? The bit of black ink stamped into the material? If that's not part of a bird's wing—" He let the coins fall back into the compartment. "Dery's right. It has to be bribes. But what was he saving it all for?"

"Why didn't he offer some of it to Touchstone last year or the year before?" Derien asked. "Or at least to pay for my schooling? Or—" Viciously now, sounding twice his age. "Mother's liquor bills?"

Cade began tallying the rows. "Lord and Lady, look at all this."

"Six hundred," Mieka said. "Thirty rows of twenty each."

"That's enough for—for—" What it would buy rendered him incoherent for a moment.

Again he met Mieka's gaze, and saw rueful understanding there. The Elf picked up one of the splintered slats of the false bottom and turned it to show Cade and Derien the dragon's tail curled across it, sooty black against pale oakwood.

"My little brother Tavier will be pleased," he drawled. "It would appear that dragons really *do* guard treasure."

Chapter 6

Sick to his toenails—that was how Mieka felt when he saw those rows of lovely, glittering gold coins. All Touchstone's hard work; all their fear; all their bone-weariness and frantic travel from one gigging to the next and scrimping and everything else they'd gone through in the last two years—and here was the solution to their troubles lying silent and shining in a shabby old box. If Zekien Silversun hadn't already been dead, Mieka would have hunted him down and killed him.

The iron poker had come down on three of the coins, slightly bending the soft metal, and he waited until Cade and Dery were looking at each other before palming them. Instantly ashamed of himself, he cleared his throat and held out his hand to Cade.

"Damaged but still legal, I think."

"They're all yours. I mean it. Take what you want. I'm not touching any of it—except to pay for Dery's school for the next two years."

The boy glowered at his brother. "And how d'you think *I* feel about using his—his immoral earnings—"

"I don't care how you feel about it," Cade replied roughly. "It's yours because you found it, and Mieka's because he opened it." Reaching behind him, he snagged the fur-trimmed cloak. "Here, Mieka, you might as well take this, too. Your wife can size it down to fit you, I'm sure. And if there's anything here of the clothes you think your father or Tavier might want—none of it would fit Jed or Jez in the shoulders."

"Cayden!" Dery's brown eyes were flashing every bit as furiously as Cade's gray ones. Mieka knew that the Silversun family was about to have it out with itself. So, bundling up the cloak in his arms, he rose to his feet.

"If there's about to be yelling, I'll get myself gone. Just please do consider, Cayden, that you can't prove how these coins came to belong to your father, so why assume the worst? Maybe they were his share of a business venture. Who knows? The point is that what once was his is now both of yours, and though I'm not sure about inheritance laws and I've no idea if your father made out an actual will, although I rather think he didn't because all of this was delivered to you practically the moment he died without the courts being involved— although he might have done, but that doesn't matter. What I want you to do is think what would happen if *your mother* had got hold of all that money." Having run out of breath, he smiled his sweetest and bent down to take a single coin. "My fee for singular brilliance in opening the bloody box. Beholden for the clothes."

He left them sitting on the rug, gaping at him.

Paying for a hire-hack with a gold royal was a stupid notion; no driver would have that much change to return to him. So he folded up the fur-trimmed cloak and blue brocade jacket as best he could, hunched into his coat, and walked home.

Wistly Hall in the rain was a dismal sight. He had to admit it. Even though the leaky roof had long since been repaired and the cracked windows replaced (a glasscrafting sister-in-law was a definite advantage), the crumbling stonework shored up and the dripping gutters patched, the place still looked forlorn. He couldn't decide whether or not the latest alteration—wooden window frames repainted the purple of blooming thistles—looked bravely jaunty against stolid gray rock or simply silly.

Mieka couldn't help but imagine how it had been in its prime. The center of Elfen society in Gallantrybanks, with Ministers of the Crown and all the important people in Albeyn and even the occasional Royal Personage attending meetings and receptions every night of the week. Light, magical and otherwise, blazing from every window; music spilling onto the river lawn; pretty women in bright gowns flirting with good-looking men and every race and magical heritage represented without fear or favor. And then had come the Archduke's War, and Elfenkind had almost unanimously declined to participate on either side . . . and Great-great-granny Sharadel Tightfist had handed over Wistly to Hadden because the law compelled her to, but kept all the money for herself. Mieka was no writ-rat to understand how she had legally done it. And, in truth, he had no ambitions to restore his home to all its former glories. It was enough for him that the roof kept the rain out and the upper floors were in no danger of falling down (like the turret that had once been his lair, and now lay at the bottom of the Gally River). It was enough for his parents as well, and for all his immediate family, that their home was warm and snug again, and filled with friends—and, of course, the dozens of leechlike relations who inhabited the warren of upstairs rooms. There had been talk of sending all of these to Clinquant House, now that Hadden owned it as well. Mieka hoped his father would sell it and have that be an end to it. He doubted this would happen, for at the Clink was the family urn garth, where the ashes of generation upon generation of Windthistles waited out eternity in tidy rows of buried pottery or glass, with little stone markers to indicate who they had been.

Mieka wondered as he heaved the front door shut behind him where Zekien Silversun's ashes would end up. And whether or not, in time, Cayden's would be buried there, too, just as Mieka's would join all the rest of the Windthistles at the family urn garth, below a carved marker set into the grass.

He shivered and ran up the stairs. He could have said that his feet were chilly inside his boots, but the truth was that imagining himself as naught but soft gray ash inside a glazed pot made him feel just about as sick as had the sight of all that money—laid out in similar rows, he thought suddenly, and just as dead. Unless Cade and Derien overcame their ridiculous scruples and spent it . . . that was what money was for, wasn't it? Wistly Hall was proof enough of that, he told himself firmly as he entered the bedchamber kept for him on the third floor. The money he and Jed and Jez had made meant there was not a chink in the walls where the wind could get through or a creak in the floorboards beneath faded carpets. And there was a firepocket in each corner of his room to keep the place nice and warm.

"Mieka! Where have you been, darling?"

His wife stepped out from behind the open door of the standing wardrobe, where she'd been hanging up gowns and skirts. The three large chests nearby told him she intended a lengthy stay. The gown she held was one he didn't recognize, made of palest pink silk and decorated with gold lace flounces accented with thin brown velvet ribbons, and this told him she intended to go to some lavish social event. He hadn't the slightest hope that he wouldn't be going with her.

She didn't wait for him to tell her where he'd been. "Mieka darling, I've such wonderful news! The night before Wintering, we're going to Great Welkin! For a *ball*! I can't believe the Archduchess sent us an invitation—but I suppose you're so famous that having you at one of her parties is *quite* the triumph!"

He smiled. How innocent she was. Whatever reason Lady Panshilara, the Archduke's wife, had for issuing the invitation, it had nothing to do with his fame. "Why not Wintering Night itself?" he asked, crossing the room to take her in his arms.

"I think the Queen is giving some tedious dinner. Pity the Archduke won't be there—he's at New Halt, I think, something to do with trade or the merchant fleet—but we're going to Great Welkin and I'm going to dance and dance and *dance*!"

Laughing, he obliged her by twirling her around the room. They ended by falling breathlessly onto the bed.

"But only with me," he warned her, fingers busily seeking out buttons and laces and hooks.

"Don't be so silly! You'll have to dance with the other ladies—Mieka, you can't pass up this chance! Jinsie and Kazie aren't invited to this sort of thing, so they can't make the contacts that you can, with all those people there—"

"Do I *have* to?" He turned his attention to the pins and clips holding up her hair.

"Yes. And while you dance with the ladies, I have to dance with their husbands, for the same reason." With a laugh that drove him wild, she lay back in the bronze and gold glory of her hair and smiled up at him. "And *that* means you can't spend half your time in the refreshments room, no matter how expensive the wines are!"

It was gently said, teasingly said, but there was a warning behind it that he knew he deserved. He made an unhappy face because he was expected to, then said, "All the way from Hilldrop and you're not even a little bit ill?" Usually the long drive left her queasy and exhausted.

"I'm too excited to feel the journey." She twined her arms around his neck. "And I've been missing you so much. . . ."

When he could think again—much later, naked, and grateful when she pulled the blankets up around him, for the bespellment of the fire-pockets had waned—his first thought was a hope that the night before Wintering would be clear and cloudless, so that she could arrive at Great Welkin not in a hire-hack but in her very own little carriage. He'd meant it as a Wintering present, knowing how the drive unsettled her, reasoning that a light, fast rig would cut at least an hour off the journey (though not if she insisted on bringing all these clothes with her every time).

He'd seen the rig yesterday at the wainwright's, almost exactly as he'd envisioned it. Light and fast on its two huge wheels, wondrously sprung for comfort, it sat two comfortably or three at a pinch—just roomy enough for him and her and their daughter, which her mother wouldn't much like. The driver's bench was behind and above, in the design of some of the newer hire-hacks. The wooden body was painted Windthistle purple, with black leather upholstery and brass lamps at front and rear and on either side of the driver's high bench. The one thing it lacked was the retractable cowl, which was still being worked on at the tanner's, after which the wainwright would fit it to the steel frame and make sure it would fold easily and efficiently, without tearing or coming loose.

A good thing, he told himself as he watched his wife get dressed for dinner, that he'd claimed that gold coin as a reward for opening the hidden compartment of that coffer. He'd scrimped on everything for months, cutting back on drinking and even thorn (except when he really, really needed it for a performance), saving up to pay off the wainwright. Now it wouldn't be a problem.

All at once he felt guilty for being so wrapped up in his own life when Cade and Derien had just lost their father. Should he have stayed at Redpebble? No; he'd only lose his temper as they continued arguing over which of them ought to abandon his high-mindedness in refusing to spend Zekien Silversun's brothel bribes. Such scruples were ludicrous, as far as Mieka was concerned. If they thought the money was tainted, then why not remove the taint by using it for something worthwhile?

Ginnel House, for instance. He felt guilty again, knowing that his own contributions over the last two years hadn't been so generous as before. He ought to have sent some of what he'd spent on the new rig. Making a mental note to have Jinsie give Ginnel House half his share

for Touchstone's next gigging, he opened his mouth to tell his wife
about what had happened that afternoon—and shut it again, knowing
he could never explain about the hidden gold royals without revealing Derien's odd magical quirk. He'd revealed one Silversun's magical
secret to her (though he'd been drunk at the time). He wasn't about
to make the same mistake twice.

As his wife, half-dressed again for dinner, searched one of the chests
for something-or-other, she said, "I don't know if the others were invited to Great Welkin—do you have any idea, darling?"

"Couldn't say. But Cade's father just died, so he won't be going much
of anywhere until after the burn-and-urn."

"His father!" She swung round, petticoats making a swift, rustling
sound that he instinctively filed away for use onstage. It was a glisker's
annoying habit to notice such things—sounds, sunsets, the taste and
texture of cherries as opposed to apples or peaches or plums—he
couldn't help it, and sometimes he missed a word or two while his brain
was scurrying to add some reference or other to his arsenal. It happened thus now. She was in the middle of a sentence. "—in mourning
for someone so close to Prince Ashgar, but surely that won't extend to
the Archduchess, will it?"

He shrugged by way of answer, and pulled the blankets up to his
chin.

"Well, if Cade's not there, Lady Megueris won't be, either. And it's
not as if she owns a suitable gown, wouldn't you say?"

He ignored the unkindness and concentrated on the implications
of her first remark. "Why wouldn't she be there?" Did everyone know
about Cade and Megs? Did they suspect any of the things that Mieka
actually knew?

She shrugged in her turn, and shook out a pair of trousers he didn't
recognize—new, made of orange velvet. He suspected they were meant
for the Archduchess's party. Damned if he'd wear the Henick colors
of gray and orange—

"I don't know if she was even invited. But she does have a soft spot
for Cayden—or used to. After she left Court this year, everyone was
wondering whether or not he'd asked and she'd refused, or more likely
that *she'd* asked and *he'd* refused. She's just the type to push herself
forward and not wait for him to notice her, the way a girl with proper
manners would."

She eyed him sidelong, obviously waiting for what he knew he should say: *The way you hung back in the booth that day at the Castle Biding Fair—as if any man within a hundred paces couldn't see you shining from that dark corner you tried to hide in, silly girl!*

He didn't say it.

She waited a few moments longer, then went back to shaking out and folding clothes. "But I s'pose she's so rich that she can behave exactly as she pleases. It's much more convenient for her now, being able to go to the theater openly—how I wish I'd been there that night, Mieka!"

He chuckled as she threw a smile at him over her shoulder. "That *was* a night. But you never would have got through it, and we both know it. Too modest to wear men's clothes like Lady Megs and the Princess, and too nervous about getting caught to arrive in a gown! Did I ever tell you what Fa asked on the way there? He wanted to know if Megs was rich enough to buy off the constables—and I told him she's rich enough to buy the whole jail."

"I daresay all her money means she really can do most anything," she replied. "Except get through a dance without stepping on someone's feet!"

He realized then—half-wit as he was around her both before and after bedsport—that it was a *ball* at Great Welkin that they'd be attending, and at a ball there would be dancing, and the dancing would take place—

—in the ballroom.

That horrid ballroom with the hideous paintings on the walls. Goblins and Giants, Pikseys and Sprites, Gnomes and Harpies and he didn't want to remember what-all else, depicted in scenes from the most vilifying and unfounded legends ever concocted to shame and belittle and cause fear and revulsion and—

He couldn't do it. He couldn't go into that room again. Especially because Cade wouldn't be there to calm him down. But how could he tell her that? How could he deprive her of something she wanted so much?

He'd escort her to the doorway and make up some excuse, like needing the garderobe, and wander around the house and gardens for an hour or two, and then collect her and come home. She'd be so excited at being there that she wouldn't even notice.

He didn't want to think about what else he might find at Great Welkin. Paintings? Sculpture? Tapestries dedicated to the most awful slurs against any magic that wasn't Wizardly or Elfen?

But why those two, particularly? Black Lightning's horrid play clearly indicated that all other magical folk were inferior. Filthy. Evil, the way folk on the Continent thought all magic was evil. Was it simple self-protection on Black fucking Lightning's part, because Wizard and Elf dominated in anyone working in theater?

He'd have to pose the question to Cayden. It would give him something else to think about besides his father's upcoming burning and all that gold.

Oh, what Mieka could have done with even a tenth of it . . . Cade and Dery were stiff-necked fools. He loved them both for it, of course; they wouldn't be who they were otherwise. But . . . all that *gold* . . .

"Show me what I'm wearing on Wintering Eve," he said to his wife. "And would you have time to do some stitching on a cloak, and mayhap a jacket? Cayden just gave them to me, and they need a bit of taking in and taking up. And," he finished, glad that he'd be able to please her in the matter of the new rig if nothing else, "tomorrow morning put on your warmest gown. I've something I want to show you."

Chapter 7

At lunching on the day before Wintering—the same night that Mieka and his wife would be attending the Archduchess's party at Great Welkin ("Gods help me," he'd groaned)—Cade received and accepted a last-moment invitation to dine with Vered and Bexan Goldbraider. The alternative was to sit across the table from his mother and listen to her yet again on the subject of her husband's burning. The ceremony had taken place two days ago. Prince Ashgar himself had been in attendance with all his household, and spoken kindly to Cade and Dery. (Widows were never addressed at such times, for they were assumed to be much too distraught even for words of comfort.) Everything proper had been done. But that morning, Lady Jaspiela had learned who her friends were. The Queen's Ladies, while willing to admit her into their private circle, could not publicly be seen accepting a woman whose husband had done for the Prince what everyone knew but nobody acknowledged out loud that Zekien Silversun had done. Naturally, Lady Jaspiela said nothing about this. Her comments centered around the absence of her sisters and their families. Useless for Cade and Dery to point out that it was a very long way to Gallantrybanks from the craggy moor where their aunts lived. She felt that they ought to have attended, citing numerous examples of her bounty to them over the years that ought to have ensured a little effort on their part. She had spoken of it that night at dinner, and the next night at dinner, and when Cade learned that Dery had chosen to have tonight's meal on a tray in his room, he felt no guilt at all in accepting Vered's invitation.

When Vered divorced his first wife, she took with her their house, more than half their money, and their sons. This was unusual (and scandalous; sales of broadsheets featuring the story had surged during the half a year it took to settle the matter), but the lady's interests had been seen to by the justiciar who became her second husband. Thus were the atypical terms of the settlement—so advantageous to the divorced wife—explained. The simpler truth was that Vered wanted to be free to marry Bexan Quickstride sooner rather than later. As it happened, the first Mistress Goldbraider missed out on the wealth earned by the Shadowshapers after they abandoned the Royal Circuit and went out on their own. The justiciar kept her in silks and silver; nowadays Vered could have kept her in diamonds.

Vered and Bexan lived in a small mansion outside Gallantrybanks, in a gracious neighborhood just off the road that led to Great Welkin. Cayden left town early enough to avoid any traffic heading for the Archduchess's revelries. It was a fine, starry night, if chilly, especially here near the river. Vered's house was named Wavertree, presumably for the weirdly spiral shape of the oak out front, rumored to have been warped by magic during the Archduke's War. Cade personally doubted this. No battles had ever been fought so close to Gallantrybanks, though he supposed it was possible that someone had attempted to get into the house and defensive magic had rebounded onto the poor oak tree. More likely it had been the effort, two or three generations earlier, to sculpt the tree trunk the way Cilka and Petrinka Windthistle now sculpted hedges.

Wavertree crouched on the north bank of the Gally River in an acre of pretty parkland. The house comprised six bedrooms, an appropriate number of baths, two drawing rooms, one large study for Vered and a second for Bexan, and a long dining room that could hold thirty. At either end of this was a painting—one a portrait in plain oils of Vered and Bexan, and the other of the magical sort. This was of a sumptuous empty stage. Bexan had shown it to Cade after she and Vered moved into the house; properly bespelled, it filled with a scene from Vered's play about the Balaur Tsepesh, where all the various magical races contributed gifts to the chosen Knights in spheres of multicolored fire.

It was in this room that Bexan, Vered, and Cayden sat at one end of the vast polished table, having dined on plain fish, plain bread, plain vegetables from the hothouse, and no wine. Not only was Vered notoriously unable to carry his liquor, but Bexan was at last pregnant, and sticking to the simplest possible diet. Cade assumed that like every-one with a good dollop of Piksey blood, she was carrying twins. She looked big enough to be carrying two sets of twins, and possibly three.

Conversation during the meal was general and amusing. Bexan turned out to have a rather bawdy sense of humor that sent Vered into gales of laughter. Cayden joined in, even when he felt himself blush-ing a bit. He'd heard racier stories, and even told some himself, but to hear them from the lips of a pregnant woman was slightly disconcert-ing. More so was her insistence, when the talk turned (naturally enough for a pair of tregetours) to the impulses and actions of creating, that writers (and painters, sculptors, musicians, and all others who could be considered practitioners of a creative art), while working to exter-nalize their own internal selves, had a duty to the public to make the product "uneasy," as she put it.

"The value is in the effect," she stated. "Something pretty is worth-less if pretty is all it ever is. Ideally, a work must evoke a sense of uneasiness, so that people think about what they've seen and experi-enced, and change that which is wrong in themselves."

"Who defines *wrong*?" Cade asked—unwisely, he was aware, but curious as to what she would say.

To his surprise, she smiled. It was Vered who replied: "Never be-fore has she fallen into that trap, and she won't do it now—not even for you!"

"All that I mean," Bexan went on after giving her husband a sidelong wink, "is that something sweet and lovely that only makes people feel good is useless in the end, and a betrayal of the gifts given by the Gods."

A direct swipe at Rauel, Cade gathered. "And laughter?" he asked, thinking of Mieka. "Is there room for that? It seems to me that there's a usefulness in making people laugh." Unless that was all you ever did, and it came to define you, and you thought that it was all you were worth—no, he had to stop brooding about that damned nightmare.

"Laughter to forget troubles, to distract from pain—yes, that is a worthy goal. Because such a play *does* something, you see." She leaned forwards, her face pale and intent. "We pull things from our own per-sonalities, you see, and put them on display. We're forced to do so by the creative urge—to rid ourselves of thoughts or feelings that weigh so heavily upon us that we have no choice but to externalize them. Such things are rarely pretty—but they can be beautiful."

Cade nodded slowly. "Beauty being quite accidental, in this case. And rare, I should think. So much of what's inside everyone is downright ugly."

"But the expression of it," Vered broke in, "can be beautiful. Simply its expression, in words and pictures—getting it out, that's a worth-while thing for the creator—"

"—and when an audience sees what he's done with this not-very-pretty something inside him," Bexan said quickly, "that he has made from it a play that makes them think and respond—"

"—and apply it to themselves, to improve their own lives—"

"—interior or exterior—"

"—then even a thing that started out ugly becomes beautiful because it has *value*," Vered concluded triumphantly, raising his water glass to his wife. A glance told him it was empty; he grimaced sheepishly, poured from the pitcher, and toasted Bexan. She covered her face with her fingers and giggled—an oddly girlish sound to be coming from this earnest, self-possessed woman.

At this point, Mieka would have said something mischievous about being dizzy from swiveling his head back and forth to follow the conversation, worse than a battledore match. This occurred to Cayden, but he didn't say it. He recognized that this subject was something they had often discussed between them, refining ideas. Further, he saw several other things: that they were glad of an audience, an audience who moreover understood exactly what it was a tregetour did; that Bexan was only the second woman he'd ever met who could speak of such things with real knowledge, leave alone authority; and that Vered was superlatively happy with this woman who understood him and his work. Cade wanted the same thing for himself and knew he was unlikely to find it except with the only other woman he'd ever met who *knew* theater—and he had no idea when or if he'd ever see Megs again.

Vered was summing things up for Cade's benefit. Cade hoped he wasn't expected to argue any of the points, or even to think about them just now. He'd succeeded in depressing himself anew with wondering about Megs. It would take more to distract him than Vered's announcing that the worth of any work had to be judged by the actions it provoked, and if these weren't good, then the work had no value at all. Cade nodded; Vered looked slightly disappointed; Bexan gestured to the servants to clear the table.

"Shall we relax in my drawing room?" she asked the men, and led the way.

But for the carpets, her drawing room was entirely black. Walls, curtains, furniture, upholstery, everything from the fireplace bricks to the candlebranches hanging from the ceiling, all of it was black, except for the rugs, which were white with black patterns. These were no two alike, and competed with the shadows thrown by candles and firelight until one was uncertain which was which. The idea, Cade guessed, was that one *felt* that there were shadows, rather than actually saw them individually. Which was as nice and neat a representation of Vered's former partners as anything he could have come up with even if he'd thought it out with both hands for a fortnight.

Bexan indicated a comfortably deep chair, black velvet on black walnut with black tapestry pillows. Cayden sank into it, extending his legs towards the fire. The dancing red and gold and orange flames were a relief to look at; so was the swirl of blue and gold in the blown glass of the brandy snifter Vered handed him.

"Just for you, Cade," he said with a grimace, and went to sit in a chair next to his wife's. Cade noted how effectively the room emphasized Vered's hair and Bexan's skin, leaching from it the faint blue Piksey tint. Her pallid face seemed to float in an aura of black; his white-blond hair formed an Angel's halo around his dark face. Cade amused himself by speculating on the effectiveness of such a set onstage: all one color but for whatever one wanted the audience to notice—or, no, what the audience should notice *instead* of what was really important in the room . . . it had interesting possibilities for teasing the audience's expectations—

—much like the play Vered had staged on his own last winter, with a hired glisker, masquer, and fettler. Cade remembered this just in time to keep his mouth shut regarding notions of mucking about with perceptions. The play had not been a raging success. Intended as a present for his sons, to lure their mother into bringing them to the theater so Vered could see them, it had featured a boy searching for a girl he'd glimpsed only once. The lovelorn, perquesting youth drifted through various fantastical scenes, traveling in a hire-hack plastered all over, including the wheels and harness, with broadsheets whose black-and-white headlines screamed the breakup of the Shadow-shapers. Eventually the young man caught sight of the girl down by a river. Gigantic flowers of yellow and green, transparent and shining, grew beside the arch of a stone bridge, and as the hack came to the middle of the span, the rest of the scene vanished. The youth hovered above rushing pink water—supported not even by the bridge—calling frantically for his love as stars twinkled like a scattering of diamonds in the clear blue sky.

This stars-in-daylight scene was as far as the audience had allowed the play to get. No glisker could have evoked emotions powerful enough, and no fettler could have spread them compellingly enough through the theater, to keep people in their seats, not when their perceptions were being jumbled like that. They walked out severally and then in groups, muttering that Goldbraider had lost his touch and mayhap his mind. Vered had pretended not to care that much. His children hadn't been in the audience anyway.

But the tale of the great Vered Goldbraider's humiliation had wildfired through Gallantrybanks and the length and breadth of Albeyn. Cade's own mortification with "Turn Aback" was nothing to it. He was very glad he'd remembered Vered's play in time not to mention anything that could be remotely connected to it.

Vered settled into his chair, a thing of cast iron painted black and cushioned with velvet pillows, adopting a lord-of-the-manor pose and a grin.

"Finished it," he said.

Cade knew instantly what he was talking about. "Finally? Well done!"

"After so many years of writing and research—and then rewriting after the research turned up something new—curse you for that, Cayden Silversun!—I have the thing the way I want it."

Cade raised his glass. "Magnificent, I trust."

"Of course," Bexan purred. "Only now he must find someone to perform it with."

He had the sudden, hideous thought that perhaps, after the catastrophe of hiring a glisker, fettler, and masquer, Vered wanted Touchstone to present the play—or to borrow the rest of Touchstone while Cade stood around backstage, unheeded and useless.

But that wasn't what Vered had in mind at all. Looking anywhere but at his wife, he said, "Been thinking about that. A lot. And it occurred to me that mayhap we left money on the table, as it were. The Shadowshapers, I mean."

"It isn't the money," Cade said. He knew this man. More to the point, he knew how much the Shadowshapers had made during the time they'd been out on their own, turning their backs on the Royal Circuit. "You've more than enough. It's the work, Vered. The *work*."

"Well . . ."

"Nobody could do it the way you four could." It was only what Vered wanted to hear. It also had the virtue of being true.

Vered's gaze drifted from side table to window to door: a blackness as lacking in answers as whiteness would be. No shades of gray here—Cade found it intriguing that Vered's black eyes sought the flickering fire in the hearth. "That's a thing, yeh."

Bexan murmured, "We've looked for gliskers and fettlers. None were good enough."

He was *very* glad he hadn't mentioned that wreck of a play. "They can take direction," he guessed, "but have no ideas of their own." When Bexan's eyebrows arched almost to her hairline, he added swiftly, "—that they can use in service to the work. Your work, I mean." He regarded first one and then the other of them, then thought about that painting of an empty stage. There had been arguments between the two of them, he felt certain. So now they were discussing it with him, with an eye to . . . what?

"Would you like me to approach Chat and the others?" he asked softly.

Vered nodded, palpably relieved that Cade had got the idea. "You can be subtle. You can sound them out, sideways-like. You can—"

"It would be Vered's play, without question," Bexan interrupted. "They would have to understand that from the outset."

Each group worked differently, of course, according to talents and personalities, but every group's members analyzed and contributed to each piece. Everyone had a say. Everyone in the best theater groups, anyway. Greater than the sum of the individuals—part of something worth being part of—

"I'll see what I can do," Cade said.

Vered nodded gratefully, Bexan graciously enough but with less enthusiasm. It was clear to Cade that however reluctantly they had reached this decision, they both knew that Vered's work required the best performers they knew.

"Mayhap you'd care to hear her latest?" Vered asked Cayden, who understood at once that this was his peace offering to his wife for gulping down enough pride to ask for help.

Just how Cade would go about helping, he had no idea. Imaginary conversations played out in his head, and always ended badly. He sat in that remorselessly black chair, listening to Bexan read her own work, and wondered how much of Vered's *balaurin* play had been influenced by his wife. Her words were good, but as a play, this piece being recited for him now would be impractical to perform. That was the difference, he mused, between professionals and amateurs, no matter how talented. Whatever Bexan might have contributed to her husband's play, it was Vered who knew what worked onstage.

Amateurs, he further reflected, were always absolutely convinced that the way they'd written the thing was the way it absolutely must be performed. No changes. No compromises. The mark of the professional was the ability to see difficulties and make changes to solve them—and to listen when the professionals one worked with pointed out problems. One could not get so caught up in one's own brilliant visions that flaws were never admitted and altering even one word was like a dagger to the guts. "Turn Aback" had taught him that lesson; Vered had learned it with the play about the girl and the boy and the diamond sky—

And all at once he heard Bexan's voice screaming. An Elsewhen, not the here and now. Blood on her hands—screaming, screaming—

Chapter 8

Nothing good would come of this night, Mieka was sure. He hadn't wanted to go to Great Welkin. Now he was here, and he wanted to be someplace else. Anyplace else. But his wife had been so delighted by the invitation that he couldn't deny her. This would be her first foray into real Society, the kind that was always capitalized in the broadsheets, with all the famous names printed in bold type. Were the name Windthistle to appear thus, she and her mother would be in ecstasies.

He'd had a weak moment yesterday night, mentioning that it would be a long drive there, a long evening, and a long drive back, with another long night to follow as the Windthistles and all their friends celebrated Wintering. He ought to have known better. He ought to have kept his mouth shut.

That her pleas had included a lot of "Mum says" and "Mum told me" merely made him shrug. Her mother was not a happy topic of conversation. Back when they'd first found out that Touchstone wasn't just broke but also deeply in debt, Mistress Caitiffer had raged at him for so thoughtlessly endangering her daughter and granddaughter. *"Everything we've worked for, everything we have—all at risk because of your stupidity! And if you're thinking to sell this house to help pay the debts, think again, boy!"* Further, it was her opinion that his share of the proceeds ought to be bigger than Cayden's, for he had a family to support and Cade did not. *"His parents are still alive to support his little brother, aren't they?"* And she didn't see why they all had to contribute to paying off what she saw as individual debt. *"Reckon up whose bills are whose! Why should my daughter suffer because Threadchaser bought his mother new furniture for the parlor? Pay your own debts, not theirs!"*

Mieka wondered if it was a symptom of growing up that he hadn't pointed out the obvious: that if divvied up strictly by who had bought what—and never mind the mess Kearney Fairwalk had made with ordering things in their name for his own properties—Mieka's share would more than likely have been the biggest of all. His wife spent whatever he gave her and then some. This amount had to be greatly reduced while Touchstone was struggling, and Mieka had heard about it. Vehemently.

No, her mother was not a preferred subject for discussion. But last night Mieka had hidden his annoyance at his wife's constant references to her mother's advice, and to end it had taken her onto his knee, listening with a smile as she told him how she'd decided on the color and cut of her new gown. Not that anyone who would be there had seen any of her old ones, but they *were* old, or at least not *new*, and there was something about wearing new clothes that gave additional confidence. He understood that right enough, recalling that first Trials, that first performance at the Kiral Kellari. There was an extra and often vital bit of self-assurance that came with knowing there wasn't a single loose stitch or remnant of a stain to betray poverty—and knowing, too, how good he looked. So she had made herself a new gown. And he had a new jacket and trousers to match his favorite of the wondrous embroidered waistcoats she had made for him over the years. As they dressed that evening in their room at Wistly Hall, she chattered about who would be there and what they might say to her and she to them, ending with, "And Mum says that Lady Jaspiela has had a falling-out with the Archduchess and won't be there! Imagine it, Mieka, *we're* going to a party where Lady Jaspiela Silversun isn't invited!"

This was a life she dreamed about: wealth, fame, elegance, admiring mention in the most fashionable broadsheets, glances directed at her wherever she went that paid tribute not only to her beauty but to her social standing as well. Mieka didn't comprehend her ambitions himself; perhaps it was because Windthistle was one of the oldest of Elfen names, and perhaps it was because he'd met plenty of the nobility and been bored silly by them—not to mention having been swizzed to near-bankruptcy by one of their highborn number.

Still, he loved his wife, and seeing her in her new pale pink silk gown with gold lace trim, her bright hair swirling into a high pile of braids and curls set off by thin brown velvet ribbons, he was exhilarated at the prospect of showing her off. The stiffened collar rose up around her jaw and behind her head like an opened pink calla lily, framing that exquisite face in a much more elegant manner than the newly fashionable starched ruffs ever could. But for all the modesty of long sleeves (necessary in this weather), she was exposed from throat nearly to nipples, with the pink pearl he'd given her resting just above the deep cleft of her breasts. She was the most beautiful thing he or anyone else had ever seen, and she was *his*.

And any man who sought to change that would repent of it at the point of Mieka's blade.

It had turned out that he was rather good with sharpened steel of varying length and lethalness. Not surprising about the knives; the dexterity required for plying one withie after another onstage served him well when it came to daggers. With a sword, though, he hadn't expected to be this good this soon. Neither had his instructor, who supplemented his income at the King's College by giving private lessons.

"Not built for it in reach," Master Flickerblade had told him. "Needs Wizard blood for that. Height, long bones. But you Elves—rarely do I see such as your kind for speed, and that will do you fine, just fine. And you've a sharp eye and you keep your wits about you. Theater training, I expect."

His instructor was descended, like Jeska Bowbender and many others, from a foreign soldier who had fought for the King in the Archduke's War and stayed on in Albeyn. Unlike Jeska, he showed no signs of magical inheritance. Human to his toenails he was, and so accomplished with any sort of steel that Mieka understood why the Archduke had lost. Send Flickerblade up against any dozen other men, no matter how armed and armored, and within the space of a dozen breaths a dozen corpses would litter the landscape.

The lessons had come about because of Mieka's determination never to be caught again in any situation where he couldn't defend himself with more than magic—at which, lacking a withie, he was admittedly not very good. He hadn't anticipated enjoying himself. As he was naturally indolent except when onstage, the hard exercise required ought to have made him cancel the lessons on the first afternoon. Yet from the beginning he thought of it as a dance, just as his glisking technique was a dance, and what he wielded could be just as dangerous. He also found that if he kept up with his practice, he could drink as much as he pleased without consequence to his waistline. So, all in all, the decision to hire Master Flickerblade was a grand success. He'd never had to use his developing skills yet in earnest, but they were there if he needed them.

And, truthfully, it was most satisfying to be good—really good—at something besides glisking.

Tonight, even though he was headed for Great Welkin, the very place where he'd vowed to learn swordsmanship after an unpleasant encounter in that horrible ballroom, he'd left his long blades at home. At his back, in a special sheath disguised by careful tailoring, was a six-inch knife, steel with a thistle and leaves inlaid along the blade, hilt tipped with an amethyst; a short plain knife was in each of his tall boots. Rafe teased him about this new fixation for armament—all very well for *him*, over six feet tall and more solidly built than most people with Wizardly bloodlines—but Mieka shrugged off the mockery. If they ever got into the kind of trouble they'd encountered on the Continent, with a gang of toughs chasing them for no other reason than that they were magical folk, Rafe would be singing quite the different song.

The sheath at his back had the additional advantage of making him sit up straight. His mother had nagged him since boyhood about good posture, and his glisking master had insisted on it; they would be proud of his straight spine and squared shoulders as he settled beside his wife in the new rig.

Yazz was driving. Robel was at Hilldrop with the children, and Giants didn't make much of a fuss over Wintering anyway. Mieka was grateful for Yazz's offer to drive them tonight, for not only was Mieka useless at the reins but he disliked horses on principle, and the horse between the shafts tonight was one of Romuald Needler's huge white breed. Chat, who owned several of them, had obliged Mieka by lending him the filly for the evening, with the caution that she was young, fast and feisty.

It was said that over the years since the Archduke had come into his majority, Great Welkin had been transformed from a starkly utilitarian fortress (suitable for the constant observation, if not the imprisonment, of the only offspring of the most infamous traitor in five hundred years) to a pleasant, even gracious home. Archduchess Panshilara was credited with much of the transformation. To Mieka, comparing it to the place he'd visited two years or so ago, it still looked like a big, ugly box with a squat protrusion on top for lifting the lid. The trees had grown some, and the last quarter-mile to the gates was lined with big-bellied urns flaunting flowering plants, lit by strategically placed torches. All the flowers were red, and all the urns were dark blue. The effect was pretty enough, Mieka supposed. His wife gasped her raptures. He wondered how long it would take him to talk her out of buying something similar for Hilldrop Crescent, where such things would look preposterous.

He wasn't surprised to see scores of people crowding around the gates. Long as the walk was from the main road, there were coins to be begged and even purses to be snatched if the perpetrators were fast and lucky and managed to evade the notice of the guards.

Had the Archduke been in attendance tonight, Mieka would not have gone no matter how desperately his wife pleaded with him. As it was, the mere thought of being in that ballroom again with its horrible paintings gave him the wambles, his stomach churning around his dinner and making him wish for a tall, cold beer.

Carriages and lesser conveyances (no hire-hacks—those invited to these festivities owned or borrowed private vehicles) drove through the gates, leaving the crowd behind, and waited in turn to decant their occupants. Mieka gazed idly around the courtyard, wishing he could escape with the drivers and grooms for some convivial drinking and storytelling. Instead, a footman in the Henick orange-and-gray livery opened the door of the rig, bowed, extended an assisting hand, and gestured to the steps where the great doors had been thrown open. Light and music and voices poured from the entry hall. As Mieka escorted his wife inside, vases crammed with whole meadowsful of flowers every imaginable color of red and blue—scarlet, sapphire, crimson, azure, blood, turquoise, cherry, peacock, apple—assaulted his nose with so many different scents that he was terribly afraid he was about to have a fit of the sneezes.

The Archduchess Panshilara stood at the top of the stairs, receiving her guests. Princess Iamina was at her side. Both wore simple gray gowns, but Panshilara's was of figured silk and embroidered everywhere with silver, and the necklet of silver filigree and huge moonstones around her throat matched the gems twisted in her dark, high-piled hair. Iamina no longer wore her famous yellow flower jewel; tonight, her only decoration was a silver coronet indicating her rank. The cloth of her dress was wool—a very fine-spun wool, to be sure, but wool just the same. Mieka bethought him of the story Cade had told about a Wintering more than twenty years ago, where the young Princess had been among a party who stripped naked a Woodwose (played by a convicted murderer) and then devoured him. Surely it was Mieka's imagination, or Cade's evocative storytelling, that even tonight the Princess's lips seemed very, very red.

From somewhere along the gallery, a choral group commenced a loud, complicated song while the reception line moved slowly upwards. Mieka nodded and smiled as his wife excitedly whispered the identities of various people ahead of and behind them: Lords with their Ladies, Lords with their mistresses, Ladies with their lovers, colossally rich merchants with their wives. She seemed to recognize almost everyone at Great Welkin that night, with gossip about many of them that he pretended to find fascinating. He needed no help from her to identify the tall, lean, dark young man just arriving through the main doors, a blonde girl of perhaps sixteen (and perhaps not) on his arm. Thierin Knottinger, dressed to the teeth in black satin accented with blood-red lapels and cuffs and a high, upturned collar picked out in black spangles, saw Mieka at the same time Mieka saw him. The slight stretching of lips and minimal baring of teeth they exchanged bore no resemblance to smiles.

As they neared the top of the grand staircase with its gleaming brass handrail, Mieka saw that after introductions everyone headed for the ballroom. Having not the least desire to set foot in it again, he had prepared an excuse for his wife—that he had theater business to discuss with several people she didn't know and would be bored by, and would see her a bit later on in the evening. He anticipated pouting objections, and to them planned to say that she had suggested it herself, hadn't she? She wanted Touchstone to keep on earning lots of money, didn't she? Enough to afford the flat in Gallybanks she'd been hankering after these five years and more? And to move ever higher in social circles? *And* to send Jindra to the best schools? And so on and so forth until she finally gave in and went to dance and left him alone.

This, at any rate, was his plan.

"Master and Mistress Windthistle, Your Royal Highness, Your Grace."

Mieka bowed. His wife curtsied. Princess Iamina stared at something in the distance. The Archduchess smiled.

"So pleased you could tonight accept our invitation and come, remembering how long it was ago when Touchstone were performing at dear Princess Miriuzca's home, and charming also," she said.

How the Archduke managed to communicate with this woman was beyond Mieka's understanding. Mayhap with simple, direct commands: *Sit. Roll over. Shut the fuck up.*

"We are so very much beholden to Your Grace," breathed his wife, with a second bending of the knees. Silk scrooped on silk, a soft seductive rustle as the rose overdress shifted atop the silver-trimmed white petticoats scalloped below it.

An unrepentant bit of Elfen blood sparked in Mieka. He smiled at Princess Iamina. "And glad I am to see you at last, Your Royal Highness, in the full and flattering light of all these torches and candles! It seems that every time I've had the good fortune to be nearby, it's been very dark, or very dusty. Which remembers me, did my family ever express our gratitude for the use of your carriage that awful day at the Gallery?" He let his smile widen as Iamina's color changed. She had been partly responsible for the exploding withie that had injured so many, including his brother Jezael, and his smile let her know that he knew it.

Her head jerked downwards in a spasmodic little nod, her eyes brimming with helpless hate.

Mieka turned his attention to the Archduchess and made of his face a mournful mask. "And I'm grateful, my own self, for the chance at last to give Your Grace my personal condolences on the untimely death of the Tregrefin Ilesko. A special friend of yours, I know."

One thing to be said for Iamina: *she* knew when she was being needled. Panshilara was too stupid to get the point, as it were. Somberly, the Archduchess said, "Yes, so very sad, and him so young and the promise of his life, regarding which we all hoped for so much, a tragic ending and for his family as well."

Mieka wondered if he should try again—some reference to her husband, perhaps. The Archduke had owned the vessel that had been wrecked on its way to Vathis, with the Tregrefin on board. Everyone had survived but the little weasel and two of his entourage, plus a Good Brother sent as a gesture of friendship between the High and

Low Chapels of Albeyn and whatever it was they called their religion in the land whose name he had never been able to pronounce. Cayden had seen it in an Elsewhen while recovering from the wounds on his right hand, and remarked that losing a whole ship was an expensive way to be rid of one little quat.

No, he decided, looking into Panshilara's eyes, as big and dark and intellectually astute as a cow's. She'd never understand what he was really saying, and whereas Iamina would, he'd stuck her enough for one evening. Besides, thinking about Jez's leg and Cayden's hand made his fingers itch for the blade at his back. This would never do, not in this company and with so many witnesses.

So he bowed again and coaxed his wife from their presence. Or tried to.

"Such a pretty pearl," Iamina crooned sweetly, nodding at the necklace. A phrase of gratitude from his wife ought to have come next, but as a Princess of the Blood, Iamina could flout social rules as she pleased. She went on, "But only the one? No earrings? Pity." And with that she turned to the next guests in the presentation line.

Mieka felt his wife's trembling joy become shivers of mortification. Slipping an arm around her waist, he coaxed her along the gallery balustrade, looking down on the hall so she could compose herself without anyone noticing.

After a few moments, he whispered in her ear. "There's only one like it in all the world," he told her. "Just like you."

She gave him a grateful smile. He guided her across the broad gallery to a window overlooking the torchlit grounds below. The trees had grown a bit since the last time he was here. So had the hedges. No matter the greenery and gardens meant to soften its aspects, Great Welkin was still a stone island in a marshy sea, girt with stout walls, all approaches glaringly exposed.

Nothing down below was lit with any sort of magical light. Torches only. There might have been some dramatic effects produced by some Wizardfire here and there, but the Archduchess had a reputation for piety. This meant horrified avoidance of everyone and everything magical.

Mieka began to wonder why he and Thierin Knottinger were here. A footman came by with a tray of glasses brimming with bubbling wine. Mieka took one for his wife and one for himself, drained his instantly down his throat, and took another. It was going to be a long evening.

Behind him he heard some woman speak in the almost-murmur that meant she wanted to be overheard but that no one with manners could admit to having eavesdropped. "The rest of Touchstone isn't here, I see."

A companion replied in the same sort of voice, "Oh, my *dear*! Didn't you know? One of them is the son of a *baker*—and the other married some little flirt-gill with skin like the darkest of Dark Elves! *Foreign*, you know."

Mieka consciously relaxed his fingers around the crystal in his hand. If he didn't, he'd shatter it and end up with scars like Cade's. And speaking of whom—

"The Islands, I'd heard. Absolute barbarians. As for Silversun . . . well, his father just died, didn't he?"

Refined giggles ensued. As the two women moved on, the second finished up with, "The Windthistles are *ancient* Elfen stock, but the wife is nothing, daughter of a *dressmaker*, which accounts for her clothes, which one must admit are quite nice."

"Shocking, how these old families have fallen. A theater player! My father would have drowned him at birth!"

Mieka turned. Overpainted, overbred, overdressed, and over-matched. He smiled his sweetest smile once again. "It's a shame," he purred, "that your father was evidently absent when *you* came into the world. Then again, mayhap he couldn't be sure he actually *was* your father."

Taking his wife's arm, he drew her over to another window. She had pretended not to hear any of it. He rather admired her self-control.

"It's so lovely," she murmured.

He watched her dreaming, perfect face. Nothing in this world was as lovely as she. "Shall we take a walk, later on?"

Eyeing him sidelong, flirting with thick lashes, she told him, "Only if I don't have to hold you up. You will be careful with the drink to-night, won't you? And dance with me before you start sampling the whiskey?"

He knew he deserved it, and hid a flinch. "I shall stay as sober as a Good Brother on contemplative retreat," he promised, and to prove it set his glass on a windowsill. It wasn't quite time yet to present his case for staying out of the ballroom. He was about to point out the spectacle of an elderly lady dressed in an excess of the current fashion that would have challenged even a fresh-faced eighteen-year-old when a familiar voice spoke behind him.

"Mieka, old son, we all know you much too well to believe *that*!"

Chapter 9

Deeply shocked, Cayden jolted himself out of the Elsewhen. Bexan was too busy reading aloud, and Vered was too busy admiring her and her words, for either of them to notice.

Only two sounds in the black room: Bexan's voice and the faint crackle of the fire. No screaming. Cautiously, he opened his mind to the Elsewhen, trying to observe rather than to lose himself in it. Night; Elf-light streetlamp shining on the blood covering Bexan's slender white hands; her voice, screaming and screaming as she knelt outside someone's doorway; Minster chimes very close by—Cade struggled to keep himself both in the black drawing room and in the Elf-lit darkness—eight, nine—

A different scream and different bells pierced a different night.

{ Her face—that exquisite, innocent face—distorting to a mask of terror. The whip Yazz never, ever used on horses cracking high over the heads of rough-shaven men and straggle-haired women, to warn but not to hurt. The white filly, dancing nervously between the shafts of the absurd purple-blue rig, flinching at the sound. Yazz tightening his grip on the reins as he flick-snapped the long leather whip again, lower this time. }

In another place, another time, Bexan was still screaming with agony and fear and, curiously, a note of disbelief, as if such a thing couldn't possibly be happening to her. Cade had no time for that. Where the girl was, Mieka must also be. He pushed aside the vision of Bexan and the Elf-lit darkness, and sought the torchlit night where Mieka must be.

{ The crowd surged forward. This was not the usual ragabash of lifters and loafers, cutpurses and beggars, all looking as if they'd been scraped out of drains, that clustered about a great house on a festive night, hoping for

easy pickings or at least an easy grab at flung charity coin. This was a purposeful mob with angry eyes and resentful faces and plenty of torches held
high. How had they got within the main gates of Great Welkin?

How had Mieka and his wife managed to get through this seething throng
to their carriage?

Mieka pushed her down, trying to shield her, tucking the big fur-trimmed
cloak around her as if it held some sort of extra protection. Someone leaped
up to the driver's bench, and then someone else, and suddenly a dozen or
more swarmed up, tearing at Yazz, who roared his outrage as they dragged
him down to the cobbles. Another man wearing a bright yellow vest over a
ragged white shirt climbed into the rig, teeth bared in a snarl, powerful fingers tangling viciously in Mieka's shaggy black hair. They wrestled, scrab-
bling for the loose and flapping reins. Mieka snatched at the heavy silver
hoop in the man's earlobe, ripping it from his flesh. He bellowed in pain and
rage. The girl shrieked as the horse reared and the man clapped his open
palm into Mieka's shoulder, trying to hang on as Mieka fought to heave him
bodily out of the carriage onto the cobbles. The Elf reached one hand behind
his back, fumbling for his knife. Swaying suddenly, grasping for the coachman's bench in a vain try for balance, the knife dropped from his hand.
Slowly he toppled onto the seat and rolled onto the floor.

The man kicked Mieka and grabbed for the girl. "Witch! Witch!" he
yelled, and all at once she reared up, both frightened and furious, with such
rage and hatred in her gorgeous eyes as Cade would never have dreamed he
would see.

Long, sharp, pink-varnished nails sought the man's eyes. "Fuck off!" she
screeched, and with blood running down his cheeks now as well as his neck,
he lurched as the rig jolted back and forth, the horse flinching and starting.
The girl took advantage of his precarious footing and pushed him out of
the rig.

"Mieka!"

But he lolled, senseless, without a fist-mark on him. She sobbed and shuddered, pulling the fur-trimmed cloak around her, and snatched up the reins
in her slender bare hands.

All the while Minster chimes were ringing, and ringing, and ringing—}

The muffled ringing of fine crystal against the wooden arm of his
chair startled him out of the Elsewhen. Bexan and Vered were staring,
puzzled and worried. He managed a smile as he bent to pick the glass

from the carpet, grateful that it was empty and hadn't shattered. When he straightened up and met their gazes, he had his story ready.

"Sorry—a combination of excellent brandy and the most evocative voice I've ever heard. Bexan, my apologies. Vered, you are simply a snarge for marrying a woman who could turn the attention of a king from his own crowning. I was busy imagining the scenes of your play, and—" He finished with a self-deprecating shrug.

In point of fact, Bexan's voice was high-pitched and nasal; a less generous man would have called it shrill. Cade hadn't the vaguest notion what she had been reading—doubtless more of the same impossible-to-stage declamations. But Vered's appreciation and approval were so complete, and Bexan's willingness to believe his estimation of her work so powerful, that they accepted his excuse without realizing for an instant how ridiculous it was.

"And now," he said, setting the glass aside and rising to his feet, "I really ought to go home. I know it's a bit early for you and me, Vered, but I'm guessing it's a bit late for them!" He gestured to Bexan, who put a hand on her belly and giggled that incongruous giggle again.

"How did you know there's more than one?"

"Piksey, my dear. Piksey."

Had Bexan still been pregnant in that Elsewhen? He thought not. Kneeling, she hadn't been clumsy or cautious in her movements. Whatever danger threatened, it was months in the future. No need to worry about it now.

"And because you can bid farewell to sleep for the next year, I'd best leave you to get some rest while you still can." Aware that he was babbling, he got himself out of there as quickly as he could. As he donned his coat and a thick woolen scarf, and waited for the hire-hack summoned by Vered's footman, he counted up the ringing bells in that other Elsewhen. The one about Mieka and his wife and Yazz. That meant reliving it, but he was able to keep himself aloof enough from the quick, intense terror of it to number the sounding of the Minster chimes.

Nine. At least nine, for they might have gone on after Mieka's strange collapse onto the seat of the carriage. Perhaps ten, even eleven—but he couldn't take that chance. He climbed into the hack, waving farewell to Vered and Bexan, who stood within the warmth of their front doorway, and for just a moment he wondered why she had been screaming so desperately, so disbelievingly. Some other time, he told himself firmly, and to the driver said, "Great Welkin, as quick as you can!"

The man knew whose house this was, and the identity of his passenger. He urged his horse to a fast trot. The hack was almost beyond the main part of Gallantrybanks when the hour struck all up and down the river, an urgent clamor that nearly split Cayden's skull as he tried to single out just one bell for counting. Five . . . six . . . times twenty, thirty, all mingling together . . . seven . . . so many different notes, from high sweet chimes that slid across the water like a moonglade to the stern knell of a gigantic bronze bell bawling out eight . . . He thought it was eight. It had to be eight. Why hadn't he found a clock at Vered's and made certain of the time? Panic and the need to hide it had made him careless. He had to think. He had to reconstruct that Elsewhen again and see what he could change so that Yazz didn't go down under the churning mob and the hooves of that huge white horse—so that Mieka wasn't slammed to the floor of the carriage—

{ She yanked the cloak more closely around her and reached for the tag ends of the reins that twined about her shoulders like snakes. She sat up, bracing her feet on her husband's back, and pulled on the thick leather with all her might. The carriage rocked violently, then jerked backwards. The horse reared between the shafts, oversetting the girl's precarious balance, and Mieka rolled bonelessly on the floor like a log pitching in the tide. }

Cade tried to grab on to the image. It dissolved into a new Elsewhen, as if the first hadn't been warning enough and this subsequent vision had come to urge him to action—though he had no idea what action he'd have to take once he arrived at Great Welkin—couldn't this damned hack go any faster?

{ Cade looked at the wyvern-hide thorn-roll on the bedside table, emptied of all but a scant few twists of paper; at the bottles littering the floor and the counterpane, emptied of brandy, whiskey, wine. The quantity and properties of what Mieka had consumed would stagger anyone but him. In point of fact, he really ought to be dead right now. Cayden was sure Mieka thought so himself—that *he* ought to be dead, not Yazz.

Cade sat on the bed, regarding the face on the pillows. Asleep or merely unconscious, puffy with drink, flushed with thorn, eyelids bruised with weeping, it was a travesty of the beautiful Elfen face Cade had first seen years ago in Gowerion, with those bright changeable eyes and that sweetly wicked grin. He'd known somehow that night, without any Elsewhens to tell him, that his life had just changed forever with Mieka's arrival in it. And in spite of everything, Cade wouldn't have had it any other way.

Somehow he had to bring Mieka back. Considering the amount of liquor and thorn that must still be in him, Cade had little hope that anything he said would be understood, and forget about actually being believed. Hadden and Mishia's desperation had led them to appeal to their son's best friend for help. But he hadn't the first damned clue.

Threaten Mieka, and he'd walk away. Plead with him, and be bitterly mocked. Reason calmly, and he'd listen with every evidence of attention, then burst out with a scathing observation about Cade's own lack of judgment on any number of occasions. Accuse, and be accused right back. The only way Cade had ever been able to reach him was to arrange things so that he saw the truth for himself.

And just what the truth was here, he didn't know. He hadn't made it to Great Welkin in time.

Mieka shifted in bed, moaning low in his throat. His fists clenched, then opened as if reaching for something, then went lax, upturned on the counterpane. Cade stared at those fine-boned hands. They were clever hands, wielding the withies so confidently, twirling the glass twigs between flashing fingers. The wrists were encircled by heavy silver bracelets signifying his marriage, the palms pale and uncalloused.

"Cayden?" Mishia called softly from the doorway.

"He's asleep." Cade stood, taking the thorn-roll from the table, gathering up empty bottles so he didn't have to look at Mieka's mother and tell her he didn't know what to do for her son. "Might as well bin some of this."

"No," said Hadden Windthistle. "Leave them. He has to know when he wakes what he's been doing to himself."

Cade didn't think Hadden was right—when had Mieka ever concerned himself with how much or what he used?—but had no better suggestion. Together they collected all the bottles and lined them up on the table like Royal Guards on parade. They had to remove everything else—vials of scent, candlestick, flint-rasp, small canisters of lotion, pots of salve—to make room for all the bottles.

When they were done, Cade looked once again at Mieka. Strands of lank, greasy black hair stuck to his cheeks as he twisted in the bed, legs kicking feebly as he dreamed, hands clenching and unclenching in spasms and then once more slackening on the bright coverlet, open-palmed. Cade felt his own hand tense around the container of salve he still held. It was the same ointment used on his hand after a withie exploded on the night of King Meredan's celebration. He remembered how blessedly numbing it had been to the cuts and welts—}

Cayden came back to himself slumped across the seat of the hirehack, seething with anger. What a thoroughly useless Elsewhen—how dare something that told him nothing take up so much of his time! He *knew* that everything depended on how quickly he arrived at Great Welkin. What was he supposed to do, leap up onto the bench and seize the reins and whip the horse to speed himself?

"Faster, damn it!" he shouted to the hack driver. "Get me there in time!"

The man didn't ask *In time for what?* The answer, Cade knew, was *In time to save Yazz's life and keep Mieka from destroying himself.*

Chapter 10

Sullen and out of temper, Mieka fixed his gaze on the torchlit gardens. Mayhap if he was very lucky and very obvious in ignoring him, Thierin would betake his scrawny self off to the ballroom or, for preference, an untended garderobe with a broken seat that with any luck he would fall through and end up in the shit where he belonged.

"Allow me to introduce myself, Mistress Windthistle. Thierin Knottinger, of Black Lightning."

What Mieka would not have given right now for a pocketful of black powder. Plenty of candles around for a quick light . . . .

"Delighted, I'm sure," she replied. "And your charming friend?"

Mieka shifted his spine against the sheathed knife and regretted more than ever his promise to be good tonight.

"Oh, I'm sure she's delighted, too. Go get a drink, my dear, there's a good girl."

Mieka gave it up and turned to face Black Lightning's tregetour. The nameless and apparently voiceless girl departed. Thierin, handsome and pretentious in black and blood-red velvet, was making no attempt to disguise his assessment of Mieka's wife. His dark eyes roamed at will from her face to her bosom, down to her waist, back up again, and settled on the pink pearl just above her cleavage.

"I've heard that Mieka's lady was beautiful beyond his deserving. May I say that I can't think of any man, living or dead, who could possibly deserve you?"

She blushed. "You tregetours! All alike, with your easy eloquence!"

"A dagger to the heart, lady!" He clutched at his chest, grinning.

"Only grant me the favor of a dance, and I swear I will think up something original—"

"That'd be a bit of a strain," Mieka observed. It was beginning to look as if he'd have to go into that horrid ballroom after all, to protect his property.

"—inspired by clasping you in my arms," Thierin finished smoothly.

Three things happened almost in the same instant. Knottinger reached with both hands for her waist. Mieka growled and reached for the knife sheathed at his back. And someone in the hallway below cried out, and screams moved rapidly up the steps as if the sound were being passed like a leg of mutton from throat to frightened throat, echoed bizarrely by a series of shrill ascending yelps.

Gowns ripped and shoes clattered as people flung themselves out of the way of something unseen. Thierin took a step back, laughing at Mieka's knife. A moment later his grin was gone and he kicked at the sinuous russet shape that, with a flourish of a furry white-tipped tail, scurried to a safe haven beneath pink skirts and white petticoats.

That Gods-be-damned fox! Mieka fumbled to replace the knife, seeing shock and then horror on his wife's face. The miserable animal must have slunk into the carriage, hiding beneath the seat. Escaping, following its mistress's scent, it now whimpered from its hiding place beneath her dress.

"What a sweet shelter it's found for itself," drawled Thierin. "Tell me, Windthistle, did you train it thus to keep her netherlips warm when you're not at home?" He leaned forward slightly, eyes shining like a cat's by night, and murmured, "I'll wager they're surely as plump and ripe as the lips everyone can see."

She gasped and turned white. Mieka discovered that relative sobriety (just a nip of whiskey before the drive here) did not make for quick decisions. Indeed, it brought about an effective paralysis. The knife was still in his hand and he wanted keenly to use it, but another part of his brain told him that it wouldn't be quite the thing to gut one of the Archduchess's guests.

Fully aware of Mieka's dilemma, Knottinger leaned in close. "Send for me anytime, lady—I'll do much more than keep you warm!"

Mieka grabbed Thierin's collar and pressed the knife against his throat. The amethyst in the hilt winked and glittered. "D'you like breathing? D'you want to keep on doing it?"

As Knottinger froze, Mieka smiled sweetly at him. This was more like it. A thin little slice with the blade, and a line of blood would be even better. Nobody would see it against that ridiculous red collar—

"Gentlemen! Please!" A senior flunky, chain of office dangling round his shoulders, hurried up, flapping his hands. "We cannot have this, we really cannot!"

"No?" Of all the things Thierin might have done—collapsed to the floor, lunged backwards, lashed out at Mieka with both fists, kicked, spat, screamed—he chose perhaps the most ill-advised course. He punched Mieka in the gut, then bent down, grabbed a handful of skirt and petticoats, and snatched up the fox by the scruff of its neck. It growled and snapped at him, wriggling as he held it aloft.

"Good Gods!" he cried with a masquer's pitch and volume that riveted anyone who wasn't yet staring. Dangling the terrified animal high, he exclaimed, "What in the name of the Lord and the Lady is this? Is it—? Could it possibly be—?" He turned so that everyone could see what he held. "Is this *the creature of a Witch*?"

The fox freed itself with a terrified convulsion and scratched Mieka's jaw on its way to the floor. It streaked away, screams and guttural snarls following in its wake as people fled in all directions, chaos rippling from the balcony down the stairs to the front hall.

The three of them were alone by the window, as isolated as if they had suddenly been discovered to be escapees from a fortyered ship known to be carrying plague. Mieka, having caught his breath with a couple of whoops, seized Thierin by the shirtfront. The tregetour's dark eyes were weirdly fixed on Mieka's jaw, but flared with fear as Mieka inserted the blade tip into his left nostril.

"You enjoy *opening* things, don't you?" he whispered, mocking Black Lightning's most famous play. "Let's start here, shall we?"

Thierin jerked away. The knife didn't slit his nose, only nicked him. Yelling, he clapped a hand to his face and stumbled back. His blonde came skittering to him and as they stumbled away, a path was instantly made for them towards the end of the gallery.

Mieka wiped his jaw, rubbing away the blood from the scrape of the fox's claw. He turned to his wife, whose beautiful eyes were full of angry tears. Still, she refused to weep in front of all these people, and Mieka admired her for it. All her extravagant Society dreams had just crashed into rubble, but pride kept her upright and set-faced.

He took her arm, gently coaxing her across the expanse of tiled floor towards the stairs. Down below, a sudden shriek near the front doors indicated the departure of the fox into the night.

A few moments later, someone in the crowd began a low, sibilant chant: *"Silver needles, golden stitches / These be weapons used by Witches—"* It spread across the great hall and up the stairs to the ballroom doors, never more than a few voices at a time but all of them tense with menace.

Grimly, Mieka urged his wife towards the stairs. Princess Iamina was directly in their line of sight now, aristocratic brows signaling outrage. Archduchess Panshilara stood beside her, fingers twisting nervously, gaze darting about as if seeking someone to explain what was going on.

"Astonishing," Iamina said coldly, carryingly, "the sort who feel themselves welcome at Great Welkin."

Mieka felt his wife's body readying for a submissive curtsy. He gripped her elbow tighter as a warning not to try it. The low, hissing chant went on all around them, like the background of stream-rush and dragonfly-whirr conjured for one of the scenes in "Doorways." If only he had a withie to hand right now—he'd magick up a monster to rival those hideous paintings in the ballroom, and the crowd would scatter like sea-spray against a rocky island.

Panshilara had turned pale beneath her makeup; it had obviously not occurred that Iamina would blame *her.* "I don't—I can't—yes, of course, and apologies are—"

Mieka gave them both his most adorable smile, feeling it stretch his lips across his teeth. Top of the stairs now . . . one step down, two . . . keep walking, hold on to her and to his knife, three steps . . .

Panshilara turned a look of bewildered appeal on the Princess. "I'm not understanding—I mean, *this* wasn't supposed to happen—"

"And would not have," came the icy reply, "had you not insisted on having *these* people here tonight."

Mieka turned, twirling the knife between his fingers as deftly as if it were a glass withie, steel and silver and gemstone twinkling. He let his smile fade slowly as he said, "Talking of suitable company— Archduchess, dear old sugar-lump, I'm afraid we won't be accepting any more invites until you rethink your guest list." Then he grinned. "Cheery-bye, old dears!"

They descended the staircase, crossed the entry hall, and went out the front door. The fox had cleared the way for them in its frenzied bid for escape; people shrank into chaotic clusters all over the courtyard, leaving a meandering path of cobbles all the way to the gates. Hoping the damned animal had bolted for good and not found its way back under the rig's seat, Mieka beckoned a footman over and charmingly requested that his vehicle be brought round. Only then did he return the knife to its sheath.

And only then did he realize that his wife was trembling. Not with mortification this time, but with fury.

He chose to interpret it as fear. "It's all right now," he soothed, stroking her shoulder. "We're quit of them."

Someone nearby said, "She's certainly beautiful enough to be a Witch—aren't they supposed to be the loveliest women of all?"

"Who knows but what it's a spell spun over all of us, to make us *think* she's beautiful?"

"Mieka, how *could* you?" she breathed, barely audible.

"How could I what?"

"Say that—to the Archduchess—and the Princess st-standing there—and everyone w-watching—"

"They're only a bunch of toffs," he said with a shrug. "Who cares?"

She made no reply. But he knew what her answer would be. She cared. Her mother cared. As if the fox and Thierin hadn't ruined every hope they'd ever had—

The footman came running. "Sorry, m'lord," the boy panted, "can't get your carriage any closer than over there—too many people still arriving, m'lord, a hundred apologies."

It annoyed him to be addressed as if he were a nobleman. "I'm naught but *Master* Windthistle, lad, and we can walk fifty paces on our own feet." Wishing he'd brought a few coins so he could tip the boy, he stood as tall as he could and squinted. Yes, there was the big white filly, and Yazz standing at her head. Torchlight gleamed from the purple rig and the brass and glass of the lamps. He took his wife's hand firmly in his own and started through the incoming crowd, thinking that they'd all be kicking themselves for not arriving sooner to witness the incident that would be the subject of conversation for the next fortnight.

Let 'em talk, he thought. His wife and her mother could care all they liked. He gave not the tiniest shit, and proved it by elbowing and prodding his way as rough as he pleased through the crush of silk gowns and velvet jackets and rainbows of jewels glittering by torchlight.

Silver needles, golden sewings,
Witches bind with Witchly knowings—

They'd taken up the chant outside. He pulled his wife closer to his side. "Yazz!" he shouted.

Silver needles, golden fabrics,
These be Witches' wicked magics—

"—never know what spinnings and threadings a Witch will do to good honest folk—"
"Yazz!"
"—evil in so pleasing a shape that everyone's fooled—"
As he pushed deeper into the mob, Mieka realized that these people didn't smell like persons invited to a ball at Great Welkin. The accents they used weren't highborn. Their clothing was plain and in some cases actually dirty. Where had these people come from? How had they got through the gates?
"Yazz!" he bellowed.
The voice that answered—called his name—made him wonder if Elsewhens weren't contagious. Forget all these roughs and toughs—what in all Hells was *Cayden* doing here?

Chapter 11

The scene at Great Welkin was almost the scene of the Elsewhen, only now Cayden was constrained within the crowd, aware of a vital and menacing change: the chant of an old children's rhyme.

Silver needles, golden stitches,
These be weapons used by Witches.

In littleschool, it was a taunt to any girl just that bit *too* different. Himself, he'd heard all the ones about Trolls. He'd managed to forget those on purpose, but this came clear into his mind even after twenty years. The shrill of childish voices that really didn't know what they were saying was now a deep, snarling threat from people who knew exactly what they meant. Why? How?

He knew. Someone had accused Mieka's wife of what Cade himself knew to be true: She *was* a Caitiff, a Witch.

Silver needles, golden sewings,
Witches bind with Witchly knowings.

He bellowed Mieka's name once more, and saw by the quick turn of the Elf's head that he had heard. Their gazes met. Mieka wasn't yet frightened. The girl was; Cade was certain of it. As for himself—he couldn't afford to be scared. He had to get to the rig, he had to protect them all somehow. If he didn't, Yazz was going to die.

There weren't quite so many people as in the Elsewhen. That would change swiftly, he knew. People were still arriving. The rowdies from beyond the gates were reaching the courtyard. Yazz hadn't yet climbed onto the coachman's bench, wasn't snapping the whip over their heads. Shouldering through the crowd, Cade's height allowed him to see the distinctive yellow vest—that damned color again—and heavy silver earring of the man who would soon accost Mieka in the carriage. Cade struggled towards him, thinking that mayhap if he grabbed him and wrestled him down somehow, none of what he had seen would happen.

Ridiculous, of course. The man was as tall as he and half again Cade's heft. And Cade would never get to him in time. There was nothing he could do—

Warp and weft, shuttle and loom,
Witches' fingers weaving doom.

All at once he was eleven years old and listening as a group of younger girls at littleschool chanted verses they didn't even understand at another girl—he didn't know who, only that it must be someone who looked or spoke or dressed differently from the rest of them. He cowered behind a corner as the bullies surrounded the girl they tormented. He'd known similar chants himself, ones having to do with Trolls, over and over until one day he'd had enough and wished so hard that his tormentors would be silent that one of them had begun to choke. Immature and clumsy as his magic was at that age, it had *worked.*

Not a minute after that, he learned that foolish, impulsive children who tried to use their magic against others were punished. Painfully. Publicly. Once taught, it was a lesson never forgot.

Witches weave evil!
Witches weave evil!

That was new. The difference dissolved the remembered scene of childhood, but the shame lingered. He'd done nothing for that girl. When he'd tried to do something for himself, he'd been disciplined. But tonight the threat was real. He could justify magic against these people. Yazz's life was worth more than the singeing of a few ruffians. The chant grew louder, no longer a rhyme but a single word: *Witch— witch—witch—*

In the same instant he bethought himself of magic, he knew it would be a mistake. Magic would turn an already ugly crowd into a lethal mass of fear and fury. More people than Yazz would die.

Mieka and his wife had reached the rig. He had taken off the fur-trimmed cloak and wrapped it protectively around her. Yazz, still holding the white filly's head, called out to Cayden and waved at him to stay back. *Not bleedin' likely*, he told himself, keeping one eye on Mieka and the other on the yellow vest.

The horse reared. The bridle must have slipped from Yazz's fingers. The carriage rocked, unbalancing Mieka. Cade surged forwards— almost there, almost there—

Another upward lunge, hooves clawing the air this time, like a *vodabeist* or its landbound cousins ridden by the Fae—as if the white filly remembered some remote era when she, too, had brandished claws to shred flesh from bones. Yellow Vest was beside the rig now, reaching for Mieka, who had tumbled to the floor. But Cayden was there, too, on the other side, trying to climb into the carriage as the girl screamed and the Minster chimes pealed the hour.

He couldn't see Yazz. The rig jolted back and forth. Yellow Vest was bleeding from his ear now; Mieka had torn the silver hoop from his flesh. But instead of grasping Mieka's arm, this time he slapped his open hand against the Elf's thigh just as the girl seized the flapping reins and Mieka went for the sheathed knife at his back. Cade hauled himself over the side of the rig. It pitched backwards as the girl hauled on the reins. Yellow Vest fell to the cobbles. Mieka swayed, wilted to the floor. Losing his handhold, Cade tumbled onto hard stone cobbles. As the huge wheel turned beside his outstretched fingers, inches from crushing his hand, he scrabbled out of the way—and heard Yazz howl with astonished pain. The rig jolted back and then forwards. This time the wheels kept turning, and there was a space where the carriage had been, quickly filled by chanting people—and three, and then five, and then a dozen guards in orange-and-gray livery.

Somebody trod heavily on Cade's shoulder, and he cried out.

Then a guard was tugging him to his feet. "You all right, Master Silversun? Not hurt?"

For the first time in his life, Cade was grateful for an unmistakable nose. "Yeh." He rubbed his shoulder. "Yeh," he repeated. "What about Yazz?"

"Yazz?"

"The Giant—the coachman—where—?"

And then the crowd was cleared off by guards wielding cudgels, and he saw the massive body lying inert on the cobbles. Just beyond was Mieka's new carriage, under the control now of two guards who together held the horse's head. Cade supposed he ought to see to Mieka and his wife. He didn't. He stumbled over to where Yazz lay.

Alive. The great chest rose and fell, the right hand clenched and unclenched, the eyes fluttered open. Cade knelt beside him. He heard one of the guards snarl for people to get back, and another yell for a physicker.

"Yazz. It's me. Don't move. Everyone's all right."

"Miek?"

"Fine." Out cold for reasons Cade didn't understand, but fine. "She's not hurt, either. Just you. What happened?"

"Wheel, I think. Hooves." He tried to shift his left shoulder. Only then did Cayden see, by uncertain torchlight, the gash in his upper arm and the sickening white of bone. Yazz snorted and tried to sit up.

"No. There'll be a physicker here in a moment, and then—" And then take him inside Great Welkin? Not bleedin' likely. "We'll get one of the Archduke's carriages and go home. Mistress Mirdley will see you to rights in no time." Or so he hoped. The arm and shoulder didn't seem to fit together the way they ought. Yazz was looking down at his left hand as if he'd tried to move the fingers and couldn't. "Is Robel at Hilldrop? I'll find someone to send her a message—"

"No. Tomorrow."

Cade nodded. Stupid of him; what would Yazz's wife think, being rousted out of bed in the middle of the night with no real word on his condition? Best to wait, and send for her early tomorrow morning.

The young guard who had recognized him approached and extended an open flask. "The physicker thought you might be needing a bit of this, sir."

"Kindhearted man. Beholden." He took a swig, and then another. Good whiskey, it was, a slow sweet fire sliding down to his stomach. "Find me a carriage, won't you? There's . . . a . . . good lad. . . ."

He ought to have known better, he really ought. In these circumstances, at the Archduke's own house—excellent whiskey, and effective thorn. Crumpling against the guard's chest, he wondered vaguely if this was the limit or if he was capable of being even more stupid than this.

*   *   *

The thorn was effective, so far as it went: rendering him unconscious and physically pliable. But as usual, his odd inheritances meant it didn't work on him quite the way it would work on anyone else, and by the time the guard had draped him across the leather seat of a closed, darkened carriage, he was fully awake.

And immediately in the middle of an Elsewhen.

{ ". . . dreadfully homesick, after all this time here," said the Archduke, a sympathetic sigh leaving his lips. A footman came by with a tray of drinks, and he chose one for himself and one for Princess Iamina. "Poor darling. Of course, I can deny her nothing, but if Your Royal Highness has need of her here . . ."

"Do you know," said Iamina, "she asked about a fortnight ago if I'd care to join her." She sipped wine from frail, long-stemmed crystal that spat rainbows in candlelight.

"Did she, now?" He smiled deeply. "I'm sure your company would be more than welcome. You are such close friends. And my wife's country is very beautiful. A summer there would be most enjoyable for you both, I'm sure."

"She mentioned also," said the Princess, looking him in the eyes, "that you have forgiven her for what happened at Great Welkin the night before Wintering."

"There was nothing to forgive!" he protested. "How could she have known that Windthistle and his wife would cause such an uproar?"

"That's what I told her. And how were any of us to know that the girl is a Witch?"

"Oh, I don't know that it's true. I think I heard that someone was trying to vex Windthistle by saying such, and who knows better than Your Royal Highness about the malicious rivalries between young men for the attentions and favors of a pretty woman?"

"True. True. Still, someone ought to warn Lord Ripplewater's son about that girl." She smoothed her plain black skirts—wool nearly as thin and soft as silk. "I hope your children will be all right without their mother for a summer."

"They will miss her, of course. But Princess Miriuzca has kindly offered to let them spend the summer at the North Keep, with Prince Roshlin and Princess Levenie."

"Your plans are further along than I'd thought."

"I'm afraid I have no idea what Your Highness means."

"Of *course* you don't." Rising, she looked down on him with a sour, cynical smile. "I must consult my brother the King about a Royal ship for the journey."

"My own fleet—" he began.

"I wouldn't hear of it. If *I* am to go, it will be a Royal visit, and ought to be in one of my brother's own ships. Good day to you."

He watched her go, pale eyes narrowing, then laughed silently to himself and drained the glass of wine. }

Cayden, all alone in someone's carriage—he didn't recognize the sigil, a six-petaled rose, painted in gold on the interior of the door—righted himself on the seat and rubbed at his sore shoulder. Quite the revealing little vision. He'd seen it, which meant he could do something to change it if he chose.

He did not choose. Why should he? Whatever the Archduke had in mind for his wife—and, evidently, Princess Iamina—it was none of Cade's business. So Cyed Henick was planning to send those two awful women into exile for a summer. How lovely it would be for him if Panshilara decided to stay at home for a year, or two, or three, in a religious and magical climate that suited her much more than Albeyn. It would suit Iamina as well. They'd make a long, long visit to the Archduchess's ludicrously unpronounceable country while the two children wheedled their way into the lives and affections of the little Prince and Princess. Cade considered that he really ought to be ashamed of himself, attributing despicable adult motives to small children—but could anyone doubt what the Archduke had in mind? Iamina certainly didn't—and it had been a mistake, he'd seen that in Henick's face, to reveal what she thought.

Let him plot and plan all he likes, Cade told himself. *Definitely not my problem.*

Curling up on cushioned leather, he closed his eyes and prepared to sleep the rest of the way to Wistly Hall. Or Redpebble Square. Or wherever. He decided to do his best to forget all about that Elsewhen. All the same, he thought as he worked his sore shoulder around to a comfortable position, it would be interesting to know why Iamina had mentioned the son of Lord Dappleweather . . . Riddlefeather . . . no, that wasn't right . . . Quibble-something . . . Nibblewater . . .

Eh, fuck it. None of it really mattered compared to what he'd just done. Yazz was injured but alive, and Mieka wouldn't spin down in a spiral of thorn and alcohol—and that triggered the memory of Hadden telling him what had killed Zekien—Spiralspin, wasn't that what it was called, thorn to cure the droops—which all the Gods knew would never be Mieka's problem—he nearly said that out loud, which worried him a little, and then he heard himself giggle as inanely as Bexan, and knew it was the remnants of the thorn in the whiskey.

Forcing himself upright again, he struggled with the catch of the window and shivered in the rush of clean, cold winter air. A clear head, he must have a clear head before reaching Wistly Hall so he could explain to Hadden and Mishia what had happened—and to Mistress Mirdley, and why hadn't he thought to send a messenger to Redpebble so she'd be waiting for Yazz?

Cayden huddled into his coat, breathing deeply of the icy night. How stupid of Mieka to drive in that open rig. No wonder the girl had been wearing that fur-trimmed cloak.

The carriage stopped. Cade stuck his head out the window.

Not Wistly. Not Redpebble Square. Not even a town. The outskirts of Gallybanks, the last substantial building on the road to Great Welkin. The place was squat and brown-brick, and on either side of the iron-barred oaken door were Elf-light lamps that lit the sign:

HIS MAJESTY'S CONSTABULARY

Cade tumbled out of the carriage, unsteady on his feet. He took a few more lungfuls of air, a mistake that made him light-headed. Bracing a hand against the carriage, he peered around. Mieka's carriage was already there, and empty, the white filly unhitched and led away for a cooldown and stabling. He heard another carriage roll past on the road.

"Here, coachman—" Cade saw the man turn and look down from his bench, strong arms pulling and locking the brake. The click seemed absurdly loud, and Cade held himself from a wince. Damned thorn. "Where's that carriage going to? Any idea?"

"Back to Gallybanks—Wistly Hall, with the Giant in it."

There was something he ought to be remembering, something about Yazz showing up in the middle of the night at Wistly—Oh. Of course. He dug in his pockets, grateful to find some coins.

"Here," he said, tossing them up to the coachman. "You know Red-pebble Square? Drive to Number Eight and pound on the door for all you're worth. There's a Trollwife named Mistress Mirdley. Tell her to go to Wistly Hall quick as she can—in fact, you take her there, right?"

"I'm due back to Great Welkin, taking Lord Ripplewater and his party home."

Ripplewater. That had been the name. "Nobody will be leaving there until dawn. You'll have time to go back." Seeing the frown of reluctance, Cade added, "And a gold royal at Redpebble if you take the Trollwife to Wistly Hall."

"Easy enough to promise. And what about my horses, eh?"

"Two gold royals. Ask for Master Derien Silversun—I'm his brother, Cayden—he's got the money, don't worry about—"

"Silversun of Touchstone?" But he was less interested in theater than in his own profession, for he said immediately, "Then that bloody enor-mous white horse is one of Master Needler's? Lord and Lady save us." He pocketed the coins. "Two gold royals, and if Lord Ripplewater hears of it and complains—"

"You can blame me, and I'll settle with him. Hurry!"

"They won't be driving fast, not with the Giant hurt the way he is."

"Just go, all right?"

He waited to see the man drive off, wanting nothing so much as another drink to steady himself. Clear head, he repeated again as he stepped up to the constabulary door. He had to keep a clear head. Because whoever had ordered Mieka taken to the nearest establishment of the King's Writ did not have the Elf's best interests at heart.

Chapter 12

Regretting that he had ever been born, Mieka woke on a hard wooden bench, positive that a contingent of prisoners from Culch Minster quarry were digging their picks into his skull. For some reason they were paying special attention to the tip of his left ear. He opened his eyes, tried to sit up, groaned, and decided that horizontal was much the better option right now.

Hesitantly, he touched his ear. The little pink pearl stud he'd bought to replace the topaz given to Ginnel House was gone, ripped right out of his ear, leaving a painful slice that stung like all Hells. His fingers came away red with clotting blood. If it didn't heal up well, he would look as if one ear had been very badly kagged. And what sort of selfish, shallow, disgusting rotter was he, to think about his looks when Yazz was dead?

The Giant had to be dead. Otherwise he'd be here to guard Mieka and his wife—whose soft sobbing he could hear from the hallway outside this room.

Bench, table, two chairs, barred window. Brown-brick walls. A tarnished brass three-armed candlebranch hanging from the ceiling, reeking of tallow. Mieka forced himself to sit up. He hadn't the strength to stand; he could barely remain upright. He hadn't had that much to drink, so perhaps it was the pain in his head and his ear that was making his stomach roil. All at once he knew he was going to be very, very sick.

And he was, all over himself. The beautiful brocade jacket that his wife had so swiftly and cleverly downsized for him, his trousers, his boots—he couldn't even find the energy to bend over and direct the vomit onto the floor.

A young constable about Mieka's own age opened the door and peered in. "Sir? Are you all right?"

Any number of sharp retorts occurred to him. It also occurred to him that for some reason he was in a constabulary. That reason was obvious: He'd killed Yazz. Run over him with the rig, the horse's hooves had got him, mayhap both—or the mob in the courtyard had managed to overpower a part-Giant and—

He felt sick again, but there was nothing left in his stomach.

The young man came forward and helped him to stand. "Washroom down the hall, sir. I've some spare clothes in me locker—they won't fit, but . . ."

Mieka nodded gratefully. Anything was better than the stained and stinking clothes he wore now.

The constable joined him in the washroom. Mieka stripped off down to his smallclothes—nothing could soak through suede trousers, but they would need a good cleaning before they were wearable again—and was handed a cloth. He ran some water in the sink and scrubbed himself down.

"I seen almost every play you ever done," the young man said suddenly from his post by the door. "Since I were seventeen, anyroad, and earning. Touchstone's me favorite and no mistake. No one else even comes close."

"Beholden," Mieka managed. He examined his ear in the looking glass. Not so bad as he'd feared. It would heal with only a tiny scar. All at once he understood Cayden's attitude towards the scars on his hand. He didn't want this one to vanish, either. He wanted the reminder of what he'd done. "Did you mention clothes?"

"I'll send someone for them." He opened the door and called out, "Here, boy! My shelf in the alcove, the gear there—look sharp!"

Only then did Mieka realize that the constable was under orders not to leave him alone for an instant. Him. The murderer.

"Do I need a brief?" Mieka asked abruptly.

For the first time the man looked uncomfortable. "I wouldn't be knowing nothing about that, sir."

In other words—*yes.*

He needed a lawyer. He had killed Yazz. He didn't remember a thing about it. He was familiar enough with memory loss; there had been times, Gods help him, when he'd courted it quite deliberately. But tonight he'd pricked no thorn, he'd had only a small whiskey and a glass and a half of wine—this wasn't possible. He ought to remember. Unless he'd been knocked on the head. Yet aside from the pain in his ear and a generalized headache that was now receding a bit, there were no wounds on his skull. He ran his fingers through his hair to make sure. No lumps, bumps, bruises, or blood.

He'd killed Yazz and he remembered nothing.

The constable's clothes arrived. Mieka's were taken away. The shirt and trousers were much too long, but he could roll up cuffs and sleeves and use his own unblemished neck-cloth as a belt. Ridiculous it would look, wispy violet silk fringed in black at either end, especially against rough wool and unbleached linen. For once in his life he didn't much care about his appearance. He was too busy being grateful for thick woolen socks. The floor was cold and his boots were disgusting. He was in the shirt and about to haul on the pants when the constable cleared his throat.

"A moment, sir, if it pleases you. What's that mark on your leg?"

"Mark?"

"A sort of welt, like. I'm to take notes on any injuries. It were a rough crowd at Great Welkin, I heard one of the drivers say. And if you was hurt anyplace besides your ear in the fighting . . ."

Mieka understood. A bash on the head could be responsible for more things than a blank memory. Temporarily insane, not responsible for what he was doing.

No. There were no excuses.

"We don't get many legal gentlemen here on the edges of Gally-banks," the young man went on, "being as most of our work as constables is drunks and accidents from bad lighting on wagons and such. But I seen enough to know that everything should oughta be took note of, and not just for the records, if you see what I mean. That mark, now. I'd like to have a nearer look."

Mieka sat on the bench so that the constable could have a squint at the mark on his right thigh. It did look like a welt from the sting of a bee or wasp. Mieka wanted to vomit again when he recognized what it really was.

A thorn-mark. Not the sort visible over veins in his arms, there was a slight swelling centered around the tiny pinprick. It was something powerful that worked very quickly—but had it knocked him out completely or merely stolen his memory?

"No! Take your hands off me! I want to see my husband!"

Mieka looked up at the constable, whose sympathies he was now counting on. Rising to his feet, he hitched up the trousers and reached for his neck-cloth to tie them into place. "Let me see her. Please. Just for a moment or two. Just to calm her down."

After a grimace of hesitation, he said, "Only with me in here, and the door wide open."

The next thing Mieka knew, she was in his arms. She was at that stage of weeping when there are no tears left, only dry convulsive sobs. He held her close, rocking her, murmuring, trying to soothe. The compassionate young constable let the time lengthen, and finally she stopped shaking.

"Mieka—oh, Mieka—they're saying you did it!"

"I wouldn't say nothing more, me lady," the constable warned. "There's folk listening as will remember anything you talk of."

Mieka nodded his gratitude. She took no heed.

"I was so sc-scared—and afterwards, when you w-wouldn't wake up—and that man barely able to control the horse driving here—"

He'd wondered about that, someplace in the back of his mind. Yazz was the only one strong enough to handle that big breed of Rommy Needler's, and Yazz was dead.

"It's all right now. Hush."

"And now they say it was you!" She choked. "And they'll keep you here, and send me away, and I can't bear to be parted from you, Mieka, not now, not when everything is so horrible!"

The constable nodded confirmation of all of it.

"Don't worry," Mieka told her—foolishly, he knew. "It'll all come right. Just—just go home, they'll find somebody to take you home, and when you're there, get word to Robel—"

"Don't leave me, don't let them take me away—"

"Mieka! Is he in there? Please let me talk to him—"

"Cade!" he called out. She shivered in his arms and he held her tighter, turning his head to see Cade in the doorway. "He can take you home. Will you, Cade? This is no place for her."

"Yes, of course. Are you all right? Never mind, stupid question." It was in Cayden's cloud-gray eyes that he knew how moronic he sounded, but with the constable standing by, there would be no chance to speak openly.

He knew he should say something about finding a lawyer, and had the dismal and shaming thought that the retainer would gobble up his share of Touchstone's performance fees for months to come—and that was assuming the authorities would let him out to go onstage, an assumption that was sublimely shit-witted. Touchstone was dead, too.

"Mieka—oh, Mieka, please—don't let them take me—"

"Go on out to the carriage—is there something for you to drive home in?" he asked Cade.

"They've sent for a hire-hack. It should be here in a little while. We're a ways from—I mean, there's not much out here, this far from—" He stopped himself with an annoyed gesture.

"Yeh, I know. Take her home."

"Here, me lady," said the constable, "you just come along with this boy here, he'll get you all settled." The lad who had brought clothes for Mieka snapped to attention, looking abashed when his superior frowned. "What's this, then? Didn't nobody see to her getting a cuppa, or even to wash her hands and face? Are we common brutes, to treat a lady like this? You find her some hot tea—*hot*, mind!—and a bowl of warm water and a clean cloth to wash with, and be quick about it!"

Mieka gently extracted himself from her frantic grasp. "They'll see to your comfort, darlin', and then Cayden will see you home. It'll be all right."

She trembled and looked up at him, her face framed in the elegant pink lily-collar and thick black fur. Smudges on her cheeks, consisting of makeup and dirt and tears, her lower lip swollen where she'd bitten at it in her terror—his heart contracted painfully in his chest. She needed him, and he would not be there. They'd keep him here for days, perhaps weeks, unless the lawyer could get bail, and after that would come a trial, and he'd be sent to prison for murder—surely they wouldn't hang him, not when everything had happened in such chaos, not when he couldn't remember—

"Go with the boy now," he murmured, and kissed her lips very lightly. "Try not to worry."

She sniffled, and nodded, and slipped out of the cloak. "You're shivering. They'll let you have this back, won't they? I needed it on the way here, but a hire-hack won't be so c-cold—"

"Hush now. Of course. I can't think why they wouldn't let me have it back. Have some tea and wash your face. Go on, now."

She touched her cheek, then his, then looked at her hands and flinched. "Yes, Mieka. I'll do that now."

She left him standing there, holding the cloak. Cade stepped out of her way, then moved a pace or two into the room. The constable remained precisely where he'd been all this time.

"I won't ask what happened," Cade said roughly. "I don't need to." He paused, which gave Mieka time to grasp that he meant an Elsewhen. "It's obvious enough, after all. I just want you to think about two things, and have answers ready for the lawyer."

Bless Cade; he knew without Mieka's having to ask. "What things?"

"Why do you think you were invited to Great Welkin tonight? No, don't talk about it now, just think it over. And the other—if there's anything that was said or done that seems strange to you, looking back on it—"

"But that's just it! I don't remember!"

"Don't tell me about it right now," Cade warned.

"There was Knottinger and his girlfriend, and then the fox—"

"The fox?" Cade echoed, startled.

"She brought it with her from Hilldrop. Tonight it must've sneaked into the carriage, under the seat or something. It followed her up the stairs, and—" His temper ignited all over again. "That cullion, that slimy fucking cocksplat Knottinger—"

"Never mind him. Not right now. Just *think*, Mieka. Go over it all in your mind and sort it, as if it were a new playscript to go through."

Would he ever do that again? Gather with Touchstone over tea, the way they had not even a fortnight ago, discussing and arguing and proposing ideas, working through each aspect of a new play—had that been the last time he would ever do that?

Suddenly feeling the cold once more, he hunched into the cloak and sat back down on the bench. "Yeh. All right."

"Good."

His life hadn't been meant to turn out like this. He'd been meant

to be onstage, magicking his way through play after brilliant play of
Cayden Silversun's until he was too old to keep a grip on the withies.
It wasn't supposed to be like this—

And had Yazz been meant to die under massive sharp hooves? That
wasn't supposed to—

"Quill!" he exclaimed. "She said that! It wasn't supposed to happen!"

"She? Who said what?"

"The Archduchess! No, I have to tell you, it doesn't matter who
hears it. This is important. When everything went all crazy, she said,
'This wasn't supposed to happen,' but the way she said it was, '*This*
wasn't supposed to happen,' as if—"

"As if something different *had* been supposed to happen?" Cade's
long fingers clenched, tightening the skin across the backs of his palms,
throwing the white scars into sharper relief. "Which brings us back to
the question of why you were invited in the first place. She's no advo-
cate of magic, and she hates theater. So why?"

"Something's been gnawing at me, sir," the constable interrupted.
"How did all those people get inside the gates? From what's being said,
they weren't the sort to have invites, even less than what you just
said about him and his good lady—begging your pardon, sir," he
finished with an apologetic glance at Mieka, "for you're famous and
she's prettier than anyone as ever lived, and an ornament anyplace she
goes."

Cade shrugged. "Whenever there's a big party at some nobleman's
house, there are always people around, begging or stealing or just there
to see the spectacle of jewels and gowns. That's why you constables
are always told well in advance of a dinner or ball at a rich man's home."

"But Great Welkin's not easy walking from Gallybanks. Why'd they
come? How'd they get there?"

"What you're saying," Mieka ventured, "is that not only did somebody let them in at the gates, but somebody *wanted* them there to be
let in at the gates to do just what they did—which was why my wife
and I were invited."

"Somebody recruited them?" Cade asked incredulously. "Got them
there and let them in just so they could do damage to you?"

The constable said in a quiet voice, "'*This* wasn't supposed to happen.' If that's what she said, then something else *was*. And it's my thought that the chanting was no accident—again, sir, I'm sorry, but it has to be said."

"Yes," Cade replied. "It has to be said."

"But why would I be that important?" Mieka protested. "Who would go to all that trouble—and *expense*, hiring all those people—who'd do that for *me*?" He beat his fists helplessly on his knees. "Gods, Quill—who'd want to kill Yazz?"

Cade stared at him. "Yazz? Mieka, he's not dead. He's hurt, but he's alive. Didn't anybody tell you?" This with an angry glance at the constable.

"I thought he knew, sir. Honest to the Lord and Lady and Angels, I thought he knew."

"It's—it's all right." His voice sounded strange to him, high and thin. "He's not dead. It's all that matters." He looked up at Cade. "I'm really tired, Quill. Can you take her home? I guess I'll see you tomorrow or something. I'm just—Is there anyplace I can lie down, besides this damned hard bench?"

Chapter 13

A blanket borrowed from the constabulary was no fit drapery for a fine lady. For one thing, it smelled faintly of stale beer. Cade settled it over the girl's knees anyway, reasoning that keeping her warm was more important than genteel delicacy. Gentlemanly, he had given her his jacket—but kept his overcoat. He had no intention of freezing for her sake.

For the first few miles, there was a dull silence within the hire-hack. This late at night there was no noise on the road but for the clatter of the horse's hooves. That would change as they neared Gallantrybanks, where sheep and goats and cattle would be driven to market and wagons of winter produce would be rolling in. Parties would be breaking up, taverns would be closing, theaters would be letting out. There would be more light, with Elf-lit lamps on every corner and usually in the middle of the block. Cade wondered when the fear of darkness captured inside those lamps by Wizards after the Archduke's War would ever fade. Or if.

At length, Cayden roused himself. "I'm sorry you had to go through all this," he said, meaning it. He still remembered that little girl at school . . . and the child he had once been.

"They won't keep Mieka more than one night, will they?"

"I don't know."

"But he didn't do anything! All those people attacked us!"

He shouldn't have opened his mouth and allowed words to come out. It meant she'd be talking now, too. "Strange thing, that," he said.

"I expect an apology from the Archduchess tomorrow afternoon."

She shivered, tugged the blanket up to her chin, and scooted a little closer to him.

He didn't take the hint.

"I hope they give poor Mieka something decent to eat for breakfast tomorrow. And somewhere better to sleep than that cold hard bench! And what will happen to our carriage, and Chattim's horse?"

"At the constabulary. They were taking care of the horse when I arrived. They'll probably stable the carriage and drive Mieka home in it tomorrow." He had no idea whether they would or not. He was trying to find something definitive to say so she'd shut up.

"But they won't let Mieka drive, will they? He's just simply hopeless. Like tonight, when he grabbed the reins."

Cade fixed his gaze out the tiny window, where the lamps were spaced closer together now. He didn't dare look at her. He knew as well as she did that Mieka hadn't touched the reins.

"I hope poor Yazz isn't too badly hurt," she went on. "Robel will be so worried, and with two children to take care of as well as her husband, she won't have much time or energy to help us around Hilldrop."

"No doubt. You should probably close your eyes and try to rest a little."

"I'm quite wide awake. But you're kind to be concerned." She paused. "Especially since you've never liked me very much, have you? Not since the first time you ever saw me, at Rafe and Crisiant's wedding."

He could think of nothing to say. Nothing. Where was his tregetour's glibness now that he needed it?

"Mieka spoke constantly about you, and I knew of course which one you were the instant I walked into the Chapel. The look on your face . . . why? Why don't you like me? Why have you never accepted me?"

"I don't dislike you." That was true enough.

"That's no answer. That's not even polite. My mother says that if nothing else, we can always count on you to have beautiful highborn manners. I do wish Mieka would learn from your example. And correct his speech more often. And—"

"And *that* is why I don't fall at your feet with adoration," he suddenly snapped. "You wanted to change him from the moment you met him. You don't want him to be what he is or who he is. You want him to be what *you* want him to be. How is that love?"

He thought perhaps that had done it; he thought she'd be so outraged that she'd preserve an affronted silence the rest of the way to
Wistly Hall. No such luck.

Still, what she did say wasn't predictable. It wasn't *How dare you!*
or *What do you know about love or marriage?*—either of which would
have been perfectly justified.

What she said was, "I want him to be what I need him to be."

Cade decided he really didn't want to know what that was. So he
asked a more interesting question. "Why?"

She turned her head and stared at him with those magnificent iris-
blue eyes. "Because I deserve to be happy!"

"Do you?"

"Yes! Happy and loved and rich and respected—"

He asked again, "Why? I mean, why you, more than anyone else?"

"Because I'm beautiful."

She believed it. She truly believed it. He remembered what Bexan
had said only hours ago at dinner: that a pretty thing was useless if
pretty was all it ever was. Witch or not, he could imagine nothing more
useless than this girl sitting beside him.

Well, useless except for one thing. She had produced Jindra, and
Cade loved Jindra as if she were his own. He could just imagine Blye's
face if he ever said in her hearing that a woman, any woman, was worth
only her ability to bear a child. Blye, who was still childless and likely
to remain so. Blye, who had taught him from childhood that a girl
could do anything a boy could do except piss standing up.

Nevertheless, he couldn't see much use for this particular woman
beyond Jindra's birth. He couldn't help thinking it, even though he
knew that if he ever said it, Blye—and Megs and Jinsie and Vrennerie
and even Princess Miriuzca—would have his balls on a silver plate.
He shook his head and smiled.

"Don't you dare laugh at me!"

"I'm not laughing. There's nothing funny about it, really. Actually,
I feel sorry for you."

"Sorry? For me?"

Indeed. She *was* beautiful. The most beautiful thing Mieka had ever
seen. Cade regarded that exquisite face, the sweet childlike mouth,
the wealth of gold-bronze hair. Her face was pallid with weariness, her

mouth defensively tight, her curls drooping and looped braids fraying. He saw her plainly now in the growing light of dawn, saw the sudden fear in her eyes, and knew what she was about to say. He let her say it.

"Why do you feel sorry for me?" she demanded. "What have you seen? What is it that you know?"

Softly: "Someday, my dear, you will grow old."

Her face betrayed her for an instant—but only for an instant. He was who he was, after all, and she knew it. A glint in her eyes, a twitch of her lower lip, the slightest flinch in the muscles around her eyes . . .

And then she laughed at him.

It was a terror that would not really touch her until the morning she looked in a mirror and saw the first line, the first hint of sagging, the first white hair. She who could never pass a mirror without seducing it would one morning find the mirror had become her enemy.

"Never," she scoffed, secure in the magnificence of her youth and beauty.

Cayden shrugged. She'd find out someday. "Would you tell me something, just for the sake of my own curiosity?"

"What would you like to know?" She was confident again, a little smile on her lips.

"The business cards. One from Finicking and one from the Finchery. Please don't bother to deny that there were two of them."

For a moment she looked as if she were considering doing just that. Then she lifted one shoulder in an indifferent little shrug. "My mother gave me the Finchery card. I was to pretend I'd found it in Mieka's things."

"Ah. Of course." He could have written the scene himself, if he'd had a taste for melodrama: her anger and hurt and accusations; Mieka's denials, increasingly frantic because he had never been faithful to her while Touchstone was on the road. Whatever she asked for, he would have given, just to stop her from crying.

"But you did something else with it," he said.

"When the man at the races gave me his card, I decided to switch them while Mieka was busy with his thorn." She hitched her shoulder again, angrily this time. "He wasn't supposed to be angry at *me*!"

Cade could well imagine how shocked and frightened she must have been. But not so shocked that she hadn't realized that when Mieka hit her, it was something she could use for the rest of their lives. Even now she made the gesture: dainty fingers touching her cheek. It would have been easy enough to switch the cards once more, after Mieka had realized what he'd done.

He regarded her thoughtfully in the dimness. She wasn't a wicked person. She was guilty of nothing worse than stupidity and ambition. It was her mother who was behind it all—her mother, who must have been livid when the girl's heart was set on Mieka instead of some wealthy lordling.

"Beholden for clearing that up," he said. "I'd wondered."

"I'm so pleased." She curled herself into the farthest corner of the hack, drawing the blanket around her, and proceeded to ignore him. *At last, silence,* he thought, and returned his gaze to the drowsing streets of Gallantrybanks.

She surprised him again when they reached Wistly Hall. Tavier, evidently set to be on the lookout for them, ran down the front steps to open the hack's door. Every bit as susceptible as his brother, he worshipped the girl with his eyes as she descended unsteadily. He held out both hands to her. She waited until Cade had alighted before swaying, crying out in a soft whimper, and at last collapsed backwards into his arms.

"Pay the coachman," Cade told Tavier. Rather than swing her up to carry her inside, he set her down on her own two feet. He knew what she was doing. Beauty was one thing; helpless, vulnerable beauty was so much more. When she realized that he wasn't going to do what she expected, she walked a few artfully unsteady steps. Inside, Cade heard Jinsie's voice from the balcony and looked up.

"What's wrong? Is she hurt?"

"Just tired. Still a bit in shock." He knew that had to be true; now that she knew herself physically safe, she could give way to what had been an appalling experience. He had the grace to be vaguely ashamed of himself for treating her as he had.

Jinsie ran swiftly down the stairs. She took charge of her sister-in-law, helping her up to her room, throwing a glance back over her shoulder at Cade as she said, "Yazz is in the drawing room. Good thinking, Cade, to send for Mistress Mirdley."

Of course it would have been impossible to carry the Giant upstairs to one of the bedchambers, even assuming Yazz would allow the indignity of being carried. Cade trudged wearily to the door of the drawing room, hearing as he neared a consultation between the Giant and the Trollwife, with Mishia Windthistle's softer voice occasionally contributing. He didn't listen to the words. The calm tones were enough. Yazz would recover. And Mieka wouldn't be charged with murder.

What he *would* be charged with, however, was an open question. Anything from disturbing the King's Peace to assault—not on Yazz, who would never press charges, but what if someone in the crowd had been injured or even killed? Cade wondered if the thorn dissolved in that whiskey was still slowing his brains down. He should have thought of all this before, and never left Mieka all alone at the constabulary.

And now he had to tell Mishia and Hadden that their son was more or less in custody, and he'd need a good lawyer—not some snollygoster with every crooked trick of the law at his fingertips, but someone clever and just this side of ruthless.

He was so weary, he could hardly think. He found a chair just outside the drawing room door and sank into it, and it might have been moments or hours before he felt a gentle hand shake his shoulder.

"Cayden?"

He hadn't expected Derien to be here—but of course he would be, roused out of bed in the middle of the night by someone who demanded two gold royals from the stash in Zekien's coffer, and the attendance of Mistress Mirdley at Wistly Hall with all her medical supplies. Cade examined his little brother's face. He looked older, and not just because of lack of sleep. Something about the eyes, something more mature in them, something strained about the muscles around them . . .

"Yazz is doing much better," Dery said. "Come talk to Mistress Mirdley."

A corner of the drawing room had been set up for Yazz's comfort. A large mattress had been brought in (Cade suspected that someone among the Windthistles had perfected the hovering spell that Mieka never seemed to get quite right) and supplied with pillows and blankets. The Giant lay in this makeshift bed, his left arm immobilized in a sling tied close to his chest, looking mutinous. Judging by the frown directed at Mistress Mirdley, they had just concluded a discussion about his getting up and going home, and Yazz had lost.

Approaching with a smile on his face, Cade warned, "You'll not persuade her to let you up for at least another day, so don't even bother to try." That Yazz was alive was the truest relief he had ever known. "I've never won any kind of argument with her in the more than twenty-six years I've been alive."

"Longer than that," the Trollwife retorted. "Made signs of coming into the world early, you did, until I bade you stay where you were for another fortnight. And that was the very last time I had no dispute from you in the meantime."

Mishia rolled her eyes. Derien and Yazz laughed—one clear high note, one gravelly low. Perfect sounds. Just simply perfect.

"I'll let you rest," Cade went on. "I just wanted to see for myself that you'll be all right."

Mistress Mirdley cast him an odd look. He let an eyebrow arch slightly, and her expression changed to one of understanding.

Deaf to Yazz's protests that he didn't need to rest, the two brothers and the Trollwife went out into the hall, leaving Mishia to deal with the grumpy patient.

"You saw this, didn't you?" Derien challenged. "You knew."

"Not here, bantling. Wait until we get home." Turning to Mistress Mirdley, he said, "Mieka's wife could probably use something to help her sleep."

She gave him as fierce a frown as he'd ever seen from her, and stalked off towards the front door. Too late, he remembered that one of her nephews had been done to death by a Caitiff. She would move not one inch to help any of that breeding. He recognized this attitude as being the same kind of narrow-minded prejudice as was painted on the walls of Great Welkin's ballroom. But somehow he couldn't blame her.

He draped an arm across Derien's shoulders and followed the Trollwife. Wistly Hall was beginning to wake up—he wondered how the rest of the family would react to the Giant in the drawing room—and Cade wanted to be gone before people began descending the stairs to breakfast.

He had barely set his hand to the front door when it opened inward to reveal a white-bearded man wearing the black tailcoat of the legal profession. His ears had been skillfully kagged. Evidently his teeth had been hopeless to change while still in his jaw, for Cade could hear the faint watery click of dentures when he said, "You're not Hadden Windthistle."

"No, I'm not." Full points for incisive logic. If this was the writ-rat Hadden was counting on to get his son out of nick . . .

"I'm sure he's just coming," Derien said. Full points, Cade thought again, for paying attention during lectures on social niceties. He'd make a diplomat of himself, Derien would, if only to voyage to those lands he fell in love with on his maps. "Will you come in, sir, and wait inside?"

"Oy, Burningcrag? Is that you?"

Cade turned to find Mieka's father hurrying down the stairs, knotting his neck-cloth into an approximation of tidiness. It was dark purple; his shirt was pale green; his longvest was an indeterminate blue; and his socks, visible between the hems of black trousers and the laces of a very old pair of leather shoes, were bright red. Mieka had definitely not inherited his elegant sense of dress from this man.

"Cayden! I'm glad you're here. Can you stay a moment longer and tell us what Mieka's like to be up against?"

He sent Derien (protesting) home with Mistress Mirdley in the hack Master Burningcrag had arrived in. Then he joined a family conclave in the dining room. Mishia was already there, and Jez and Jinsie, and when Hadden arrived with Cade and the lawyer, the doors were firmly shut.

"She didn't say much," Jinsie began at once. "Too jumpy to answer any questions. So I put her to bed. Maybe later on today, she'll have something to tell us, but not now."

"Yazz doesn't know exactly what happened," said Mishia. "He'd turned to confront the mob when the horse reared, the carriage lurched, and hooves came down hard on his shoulder and arm. He fell, and the carriage ran over him. Twice," she finished with a wince.

"You could see the marks of the wheel on his shirt," Hadden said. "We didn't want to upset him any more than he already was, so we told him Mieka would be back soon and to let Mistress Mirdley work."

"Mieka." Jezael was shaking his head as he spoke his brother's name. "He's for it this time, I think. Yazz won't press charges, but the Archduchess surely will. Does anybody know if other people were hurt? Cade?"

"No idea. Somebody slipped some thorn into a flask of whiskey, and I came to in a carriage just outside the constabulary. But here's the thing. The constable noticed a welt on Mieka's leg. Thorn."

"Somebody—" Jez began, but Jinsie interrupted curtly.

"He's known to use it. Proves nothing, Cade."

"Nobody who uses would jab himself in the thigh like that." He almost said, *In the first Elsewhen, it was his shoulder—but both times the man in the yellow vest did it. If he's not in the Archduchess's pay, I'll swallow a withie.* But not everyone here knew about the Elsewhens. Only Jinsie.

Master Burningcrag said, "Disturbing the King's Peace is what *all* those people should be charged with. But they'll have vanished by now. Your son is the most likely target, Windthistle. The young lady is right. A thorn-mark proves nothing."

Cade folded his hands together atop the table. "Mieka mentioned something before I left with his wife. The Archduchess said, 'This wasn't supposed to happen.' In just such a way: *This*. Which tells me that *something* was supposed to happen, but not the *way* it did happen."

"Can't prove a thing that never occurred, either," Master Burningcrag pointed out. "Well, if there were no serious injuries or fatalities, the charge won't be anything but mischief or whatever the current weasel-word is for causing a ruckus. I shouldn't think anything more would happen than a fine and a month or two in jail. Not prison," he hastened to say when Mishia caught her breath. "That's reserved for felons. I'll do my best to keep him out, or at least limit the sentence. But that's assuming the official report doesn't include any injuries more serious than your friend's. Are you quite certain he won't—"

"Yazz?" Cade snorted. "Never."

"Moreover," Jez added, "he'll say the whole bloody mess was his fault, not Mieka's, and try to take all the blame himself. Not that Mieka will let him."

"If that's all, then," said Master Burningcrag, "I'll return to my office. My clerk will inform the constabulary that I'm representing him, then wait for the official notification of Mieka's arrest."

"And after that?" Jinsie asked.

"I'll go bail him out and bring him here. Can't do anything until the proper paperwork arrives, you see." He rose and swept the table with his gaze, then cleared his throat awkwardly. "I'll send to you later with—that is to say, I won't know what will be necessary, as it were—"

"I'll take care of the money," Cade said. Derien wouldn't have approved the bluntness, so thoroughly indelicate, but he had no time for polite back-and-forth. "No arguments," he said quickly as all the Windthistles opened their mouths to protest. "He can pay me back out of our next giggings. If that's all for now, I should get home."

"And get some sleep," Mishia advised, practical and motherly. Then she shivered and rubbed her hands over her face. "A son of mine," she murmured to no one in particular, "arrested and tried and jailed . . ."

Hadden paused to clasp her shoulders gently before accompanying the lawyer to the front door.

Jinsie held Cade back with a hand on his arm and drew him aside in the hall. "It's good of you, offering to stand my idiot brother's bail."

"And Master Burningcrag's fees," he insisted, thinking that at least all those gold coins could be put to good use.

"Oh, there won't be any. He's a Windthistle a couple of generations back—I'm sure you noticed the ears—and one of the few who never came freeloading at Wistly. But his sister did, and then left with Uncle Barsabian after the famous afternoon Jed and Blye got married. So he owes us both for giving his sister a roof over her head all those years *and* for the insult she offered when she left." Her smile was uncannily like her twin brother's, though her dark face with its frame of silky pale hair was the opposite of Mieka's coloring. "We never saw it as an insult, of course. One less gaping, greedy mouth to feed!"

One of the younger gaping, greedy mouths had run to the corner and fetched two hire-hacks. The lawyer got into one. Cade climbed into the other, told the man his address, and sank back, closing his eyes. He could prove Mieka's innocence—well, not prove it, exactly, but at least turn people in the right direction, the direction of the man in the yellow vest, who was certain to have a connection to the Archduchess. If Cade revealed what he'd seen in the Elsewhens—evidence of something that hadn't happened, but it wasn't as if he'd be testifying on his oath before a justiciar—he could direct the investigation.

Who was he kidding? There would be no investigation. Mieka's carriage, Mieka's driver, Mieka's fault. And what even two days, leave alone two months, in jail would do to the Elf was something Cade couldn't begin to contemplate.

He went home to Redpebble and slept. Sometime after noon, Derien came upstairs to wake him, bringing notes from Jeska and Rafe.

Both expressed fury and the unyielding determination that Mieka would not be tossed in jail for something that wasn't his fault. Oh, and they assumed that the usual Wintering celebration at Wistly was canceled. Let them know if Cade or Mieka needed anything, from money to a couple of pairs of fists.

"You wrote to tell them?" Cade asked Dery.

"Just after we got home this morning. Mistress Mirdley says to come downstairs and eat something before you turn into a walking skeleton."

"Mm." He scanned Jeska's note again. Wintering. Jindra's Naming-day. A fine revel it would be for the child tonight, with her father probably still in the constabulary jail. The Windthistles might not want to throw their annual party for family and friends, but Cade knew they'd see to it that their only grandchild wasn't disappointed on her sixth Namingday. Cade decided to join them. He had questions to ask of Jindra's mother.

Jindra's mother was unavailable. She had taken to her bed and would see no one but her mother. Mistress Caitiffer had arrived from Hilldrop Crescent with Jindra that morning, and on finding her daughter prostrate and her son-in-law absent, had pushed the child into her other grandmother's willing arms and vanished upstairs. Cade, arriving just after tea, learned all this from Jinsie, who finished by saying, "And it's not a word nor a whimper we've heard from either of them since. Now. Sit down and tell me what you saw my brother do last night."

Lowering himself into a chair—sturdy of construction but threadbare of cushion, and thus relegated to the little room Jinsie used as an office—Cade spread his hands in a gesture of helplessness. "It was pretty much what actually happened. I don't know how much I changed, except for one thing. What I saw before . . . Yazz didn't make it."

River-blue eyes narrowed fiercely. "He *died*? That's what was going to happen?"

"Yeh."

"Did you know about the fox? What little she told me last night didn't make much sense—especially the pet fox. I can't find the wretched thing, and I've looked all over Wistly Hall." Jinsie scowled when Cade maintained a blank silence. She reached over and shook his arm. "What? Tell me!"

"I don't really remember it."

"Try."

"It's a long time ago. I was driving Fairwalk's carriage, and Mieka was up on the coachman's bench with me . . . it was night, and I saw a fox in the road, and the next thing I knew, the horses had bolted and I could barely pull them to a stop." He looked down at his palms, crossed with faint scars from the exploding withie, where once the skin had been smooth. "It was something about the fox on a leash at some party. She didn't take it with her last night on a leash, did she?"

"Of course not. But it might have stowed away in the rig and followed them into Great Welkin." She laughed suddenly. "Oh, what I'd give to have seen the uproar! All those fine frustling ladies scattering every which way!"

"And *that* must be what the Archduchess meant!" he exclaimed. "When she said that *this* wasn't supposed to—she did have something else planned, but if the fox was there and messed up those plans, and whatever she'd arranged with the man in the yellow vest didn't happen the way she thought it would—"

"Yellow vest?"

"He seemed to be the ringleader. I'm guessing so, anyways. I did see him, and very clearly. Mieka ripped the earring out of his ear."

"Did he return the favor?"

"Yeh. If Mieka gets bail today, take him some salve or something so it doesn't get infected."

She might have nodded or spoken. He didn't know. He was too busy chasing down images in his mind. The fox in the night-dark road, abruptly illuminated by the carriage-lamps . . . the fragment of an Elsewhen that he'd deliberately forgotten . . . hauling on the reins . . . the memory of what had happened next, inerasable: Mieka taking the blame with Fairwalk's coachman . . . salve on the reddened marks of leather streaking his palms . . . and another Elsewhen, seen just last night, standing in Mieka's bedchamber after Yazz's death, and the little pot of salve on the table—and in the coach that night long ago, when the reins had marked his palms with welts and blisters . . .

"Cade? Cayden!"

He glanced at the desk chair where Jinsie had been sitting. She was no longer there, but standing at the office door.

"Are you back? Because Mieka is."

"I didn't go anywhere." He pushed himself to his feet. "I have to see him. Right now. Before he even goes upstairs to his wife. Right now, Jinsie!"

Chapter 14

Neither the amount of his bail nor who had paid it interested Mieka at all. The night he'd spent on that hard wooden bench, with only his cloak for a bed and a constable posted just inside the open door, had been cold, sleepless, hungry, and miserable. That they didn't consider him dangerous enough to lock up in a cell was a very good thing; that they didn't trust him not to sneak out unless somebody was watching him at all times annoyed him. By the time Master Burningcrag showed up (Mieka dimly recalled the old man's sister, a whiny hag who used her long, sharp nails to pinch any Windthistle child who got within reach), Mieka was feeling sumptuously sorry for himself. At least he'd got his own clothes back—the jacket and shirt still bloodstained, to be sure, but nothing stank of vomit anymore. The kindly young constable had long since gone home, so Mieka simply walked out of the constabulary when Burningcrag said he could, without a word to anyone. He was in no mood for pleasantries, not even to relay his gratitude to whoever had cleaned his clothes.

He made the lawyer stop the hack at the first food-cart he saw. Once he'd washed down a chicken pasty with a bottle of beer—the driver obliged with a corkscrew—he felt much better. This feeling died as Burningcrag began harassing him about what exactly had happened last night in the courtyard of Great Welkin. Mieka lost count of the times he'd said, "I don't know! I can't remember! Somebody smacked me with some kind of thorn!"

At length Master Burningcrag observed, "Loss of memory can, in some instances, be a useful defense. Not in this case. You really must try to recall."

Fortunately, they arrived at Wistly before Mieka could lose his temper.

Cade was waiting for him in Jinsie's little office, into which she hauled him before he could do more than assure their mother that he was all right and ask after Yazz. Sight of his tregetour's bleak gray eyes sent Mieka's spirits plummeting again.

"Sit down and shut up until I've finished."

"Tell me about Yazz first."

Cade's expression softened. "He'll be all right. Mistress Mirdley isn't sure if he'll regain full use of his left arm. But he's alive."

"It was my fault, Quill."

"I said *listen*."

Mieka sat down, shut up, and folded his hands in his lap.

Cade seemed to be having some trouble knowing how to begin. Finally he said, "It wasn't your fault. You were unconscious. The man wearing the yellow vest—the one who tore the earring out of your ear—he slapped your leg with a glass thorn. A few moments later, you were out cold."

"How do you—?"

"Let me finish. Yeh, I saw it—in a different version, where Yazz was trampled and he died."

Mieka felt his stomach lurch.

"But it wasn't your fault, either time. You were right about what the Archduchess said. She had something planned, but not what happened. Whether you and your wife left too soon, or whether I got there in time to change things just enough, I don't know. I think it was probably that fox. She couldn't have allowed for that. The important thing is that when Yazz was injured, you were rolling about the floor of the rig and didn't know a thing."

"But—"

"Look at your hands."

"What about them?"

"Are there any marks on your palms or fingers? If you'd been holding the reins, trying to control that huge horse, there'd be welts and bruises all over your hands."

He stared at his palms. Not a mark on them. Some bruising and split skin on his knuckles—he remembered fighting the man wearing the yellow vest—but nothing on his palms.

"They said it was me, didn't they?" Mieka whispered. "That I was the one who couldn't rein in the horse, and that's when Yazz got hurt, and—"

"It wasn't you."

"I thought it was just that I couldn't remember. They said it was me. Why did they lie, Quill?"

A telltale hesitation. "They spoke the truth as they knew it."

"Who told them?" He sat forward in the chair. "Somebody from Great Welkin? One of the drivers, or one of the crowd in the courtyard? Somebody who belongs to the Archduchess, for certes! Who saw it? Who told them it was me?"

Cade said nothing.

There was no one else. No one. But that couldn't be true. Desperate now, Mieka demanded, "What did *you* see? In the Elsewhen *and* for real? Who was holding the reins?"

Cade stared down at his own hands. At length he said, "Do me one favor, Mieka. When you go upstairs . . . look at her hands."

The rage was swift and total and like nothing he had ever felt before. Because Cayden was right, and Mieka knew it. "You've never liked her! Never!"

"No," Cade replied, looking up, grim-faced. "I don't like her. Or her mother. D'you know why? Because I saw them planning how they were going to win you, as if you were a medal for First Flight on the Royal. Oh, don't look so shocked! What if I'd told you back then? What if I'd said, 'Mieka, she wants to own you, and she's going to use magic to do it?' What if I'd told you what Mistress Mirdley told me later on? What the crowd was chanting last night—it's true. You know it's true. She's a Caitiff, a Witch. She used thread-magic on you, from the first neck-cloth she sewed for you back before you were married. I saw her making it. You never would have believed me. You're in love with her. You never could see anything but her. But I've seen what she'll end up doing to you, one way or another, and what you'll do to her."

This scared Mieka more than he would ever admit. Cayden stood there, implacable, his eyes cold. How could he be so cold, when the fury and the hate were burning Mieka up from the inside?

"It's actually quite simple, when you get to the bottom of it. Do you trust her or me? Do you believe the lies she's told you, she and her mother, or do you believe that I'm telling you the truth? Don't answer now, Mieka. Just go upstairs and look at her hands."

For long moments neither man broke the gaze that was almost a physical linkage between them. Mieka became aware that he wasn't breathing, and sucked in breath through his teeth.

"I betrayed you to her," he whispered. "You said so. I told her what you are. But you betrayed me, too. You never told me. You knew all these things, and you never told me."

"I couldn't."

"You didn't warn me!"

"You never would have believed me. Not then. Probably not now, either." He went to the door, opened it. "Look at her hands," he repeated, and walked out.

Mieka sat there, shaking with rage, staring at his own unmarked palms. As his heartbeats settled down, he pushed himself to his feet. There seemed to be more stairs than usual on the way to the bedchamber he shared with his wife when at Wistly; he was out of breath and his heart was rampaging again by the time he reached their door.

Her mother emerged, saw him, and anger tightened her features. "Don't upset her. She's not well."

"I won't stay long," he said. Just long enough to look at her hands. Feeling a traitor, he crept into the room. He put off the moment with a detour to the wardrobe, where he shucked off last night's clothes. He wanted something clean. Old clothes, soft and comfortably worn against his skin. Examining the discarded jacket, he decided that even if it and the shirt could be salvaged, he never wanted to see them again. As he yanked the belt from his trousers, he heard the spine-sheath drop to the floor and only then realized that the constables hadn't returned his knives. This nettled him; they were excellent blades, perfectly balanced, set at the hilts with an amethyst each and engraved with thistles. No use asking for them back. Knives of such quality would be long gone by now.

At last, dressed in soothingly worn pants and an old green woolen shirt, he could delay the moment no longer. He turned to the bed.

She was as beautiful as always, as beautiful as an Angel with her soft childlike mouth and her bright hair in two long braids like a little girl's. He approached quietly, but something woke her and she looked up at him, her eyes red with weeping.

"What is it, sweeting?" he whispered, sitting beside her. "Are you hurt? Should I call your mother back in?"

"N-no," she stammered. "Oh, Mieka, I'm so sorry!"

"Why?" he asked, keeping his face and voice very gentle. "What could you have to be sorry for?"

"I lost the baby!" she sobbed, and threw herself into his arms. "I didn't t-tell you before, because I wanted to be sure—I was going to tell you tonight at Wintering—but I was so frightened, it was all so horrible—I felt so cold and weak all the way home—and then—and when Mother came this m-morning she knew, and she helped me, and I'll be all right and there can be other babies—but not this one, Mieka, I'm so sorry!"

She was lying. He heard it in her voice. Even thick with tears, the words broken and rushed, he knew it as surely as he knew by the expression in Cayden's eyes when he was lying. And he'd heard this tone in her voice so many times. So many lies, over the years. Trifling lies that didn't really matter, so he ignored them; significant lies, such as the Finchery card. And now this.

His own wife had lied to him for years. And he'd let her get away with it. Why should she assume she wouldn't succeed this time? She always had before.

"Hush. It's all right. Hush now."

Cade was right: Mieka loved her. She was his.

Did he love her *because* she was his?

"Mieka, say you forgive me for losing the baby—"

What he would give not to be thinking these things. To have everything back the way it was. To not know that she was a Witch who had been using magic on him since the day they met.

"Please, darling, say that you don't blame me—"

All the signs of magic had been there, too, as obvious as the note in her voice when she lied. What had he touched in that booth at the Castle Biding Fair, what had his fingers brushed against of skirts and shawls and neck-cloths that had gone straight to his heart? He thought about the first gift she'd given him, that first time she'd come to Gallybanks. At the feel of it on his fingers as he tied it, he could think only of her. All the things she'd sent him while Touchstone was on a Circuit—easy enough to explain his increased longing for her as the result of her sweet thoughtfulness in sending him presents she made with her own hands. And the sporadic weeks of celibacy? Could those be explained, too?

He drew away and took both her hands in his. "Of course I don't blame you. You were scared and I didn't keep you safe." Holding her gaze with his own, he brought her hands to his lips and kissed each palm. Each bruised, reddened, welted palm. There was a vague taste of medicinal salve. But he didn't look at her hands. "Poor darling," he murmured, still looking directly into her eyes. "Poor sweet girl."

Her face changed, so subtly that if he hadn't been watching for it, he wouldn't have seen. She had won. She thought she had won.

"You must be so tired," he said, letting her go, standing up, grateful that his knees were holding him. What he wanted to do was fall into a mindless heap, or shout and scream and break things—or find a barrel of Auntie Brishen's whiskey and dive into it and never come up for air. What would that solve? Nothing. Stupid idea. He stroked straying strands of hair from her face and said, "I'll leave you to get some rest."

"Don't tell anyone—" She clutched for his hand. "Mieka, please don't tell anyone what happened. Don't say anything about the baby."

A private matter; he understood. Yet the renewed panic in her eyes signaled something else. Oh. Of course. A miscarriage was a messy business. Someone, most probably his sharp-eyed twin sister, would have noted that no bloodied sheets had come downstairs today.

Amazing, this ability to set aside his feelings and look at things rationally; to find causes and reasons rather than simply explode; to suss out the whys and the hows, instead of running straight for a bottle or his thorn-roll. Cayden was a bad influence.

Or mayhap Mieka was just too deeply in shock to feel much of anything at all. Even the fury was gone.

"Nobody needs to know. You sleep now, sweeting."

Master Burningcrag was waiting downstairs in the dining room. Mieka's parents were with him, but none of his siblings. He closed the door and sat in his accustomed place. He was glad of his wool shirt, for no fire had been lit in the room. But his hands were cold, and he folded them together atop the table.

"You'll have to appear in a court of law," said Master Burningcrag. "There are witnesses who saw someone wearing a fur-trimmed cloak yanking back on the carriage reins. If that's their only identification, and no one actually saw your face, then we may be able to shake their certainty."

Aware that his parents were watching him intently, Mieka allowed nothing of what he was thinking to show on his face.

What he was thinking was that the witnesses were telling the truth.

And that he hadn't been the one wearing the cloak.

And that if *he* told the truth, and let them look at her hands, she wouldn't last more than five minutes in a courtroom before collapsing in tears. Genuine tears born of genuine terror, not the quick manipulative weeping she'd used on him for so long.

At least she'd spared him the fingers brushing her cheek where once he'd struck her across the face. At least he hadn't had to see that again.

"But surely," Hadden was saying, "the fact that he was trying to calm the horse—there were so many people about besides Yazz who could have been injured or even killed—Mieka was trying to get the horse under control—"

Cade had seen Yazz die. No, that wasn't quite what he'd said. Yazz had died; Cade hadn't seen it for himself, had he? None of that mattered as evidence, anyway. One could hardly go into a court of law and say, *Well, it's this way, Your Worship. My friend here has visions.*

Cade had seen the man with the yellow vest, too. Mieka remembered him, remembered ripping the silver hoop from his ear and scoring his jaw with his knuckles. That must have been right before the thorn went into his thigh and the man tore off Mieka's own pearl earring. He'd spent a long time looking for just exactly the same shade of pink as the pearl necklace he'd given her.

"Negligence," said Master Burningcrag. "That's the best we can hope for. A deliberate disturbance of the King's Peace—"

"Mieka didn't start it!" Mishia objected.

"No, I didn't," Mieka told her. "Actually that damned fox was what set everything off." He explained what had happened, leaving out Knottinger's insults, and how Mieka had threatened him with his knife, and everything about the fox being a Witch's familiar. Thierin had been following the Archduchess's orders, Mieka was certain of it. But he had strayed from the arranged script when the fox appeared. "This *wasn't supposed to happen*—"

"I suppose the poor thing ran off into the grounds at Great Welkin,"

Hadden mused. "But am I right in believing that this has nothing to do with it?"

"Very much you are right," said Burningcrag.

No, Mieka couldn't blame her for being afraid.

What he blamed her for was lying.

"What do the witnesses say, again?" he asked. "And who are these witnesses, anyhow?"

Burningcrag consulted his notes. "There are four. Sir Nouel Elkbottom's coachman, Lady Quarryhold's maid—"

"What was she there for?" Mishia looked bewildered.

"Evidently Her Ladyship was wearing a gown that required the services of her maid to put right after the drive from Gallantrybanks."

And all these women who couldn't even dress themselves were the ones his wife wanted as her intimate friends.

"Who else?" Hadden asked.

"A vendor of mocahs and hot teas, who was doing a brisk business amongst the coachmen and other servants on that cold night. And a footman in the employ of the Archduke." He paused. "You'll have perceived, I'm sure, that all these people are simple working folk. With a jury of similar backgrounds, their word as to what they saw will be the more readily believed."

"Meaning," Hadden said, "that Windthistle is an old Elfen name, Mieka is famous, and it would be their chance to stick it to the upper classes?"

"I merely point out the facts," said Master Burningcrag.

Mieka gestured impatiently. "How close were they? What else did they see? Was the teaman wearing a yellow vest? Did he have a torn earlobe?"

"I'm not sure what you mean by asking—"

"The man who did this—" He waved a hand at his own ear. "—was returning the favor. It was a thick silver hoop, and I pulled it right off him. Hells, it might still be on the floor of the rig!"

"I am uninformed as to the apparel of the witnesses. Though I would imagine the coachman and the footman were both in livery."

"I'd bet damned near anything it's the same man."

"I'll have my clerks ask around." Burningcrag didn't sound all that enthused.

"If someone can recall what he was wearing," Mishia said, "then there's someone else who could be responsible for what happened, and that would cast doubt on those who said it was Mieka. Mayhap he was the one holding the reins!" Then she shook her head. "But so many people saying that whoever held the reins was wearing a furred cloak . . ."

"What was it Cayden said?" Hadden looked at his wife, frowning. "Something about the Archduchess. Something she said."

Mieka knew what it was. He'd told Cayden, and now he told his father. "Once the fox got loose and we were leaving, she said that *this* wasn't supposed to happen. Like she'd intended one thing, but this happened instead."

Mishia asked, "Mieka, did you smell anything on the man in the yellow vest?"

"Like cinnamon tea or spiced mocah?" He shook his head. "Sorry, Mum."

"That would be too easy, wouldn't it," she sighed.

Burningcrag readied pen and paper. "Again, I'll set my clerks to asking. What we must do right now, however, is record the whole of what happened that night as *you* experienced it." He cocked an expectant eyebrow at Mieka.

"Mum," he said, wanting just a little more time to get his story straight—not what he would tell, but how much of it would be believed, "could we maybe get some tea? This sounds like thirsty work."

Chapter 15

Giving him no chance to refuse, Jinsie had told Cayden to stay until her parents had finished talking with Master Burningcrag. He found his way to the river lawn and stood on the terrace, shivering in the icy wind off the river. Tonight everyone else in Albeyn would celebrate Wintering. Staying at Wistly for Jindra's sake competed with a deep need to go back to Redpebble Square, to get out of the way of all this trouble for a day or two. *Coward.*

"So you're still here."

He turned to find Mistress Caitiffer a few paces away, wrapped in a gorgeous woolen cloak woven, no doubt, by her own hand in patterns of white birds flying on a blue background.

"Why him?" he asked all at once. "Why Mieka Windthistle?"

The woman shrugged. "Why not?" Then, as if the casual lie were poison on her tongue, she went on fiercely, "Stupid girl! She could have had anybody! *Anybody!* Any man she fancied—but she fancied that foul-mouthed, useless little Elf! She had to choose *him*! All ready I was, and her fifteen and ripe as a peach—"

"Ready? For what?"

"A man worthy of her." She calmed again, explaining as if to a none-too-bright child. "Any man with two eyes could have been hers, up to and including the Prince himself. Ready? She was to take my place, where I ought to have been all along. Years I spent sewing frustles for rich women's backs, waiting for my girl to get her full beauty, waiting for the right time—"

"And that year, at Castle Biding, you were ready."

"Never pay attention to anything that doesn't directly concern you, do you, boy? Never considered how many lords come to that fair, swanning about with their bags of coin, looking to cheat honest folk—but I was ready for to be cheating *them*. Gowns and bodices for sisters and mothers, wives and mistresses—but woven to bring them to my girl, none other."

He pondered for a moment. "Frimham . . . ladies go there for seaside pampering. All that was needed was to send her out walking in the best part of town, and—"

"And looking more of a lady born than any of the noblest blood. And why shouldn't she? Isn't her blood both noble and old? Better than yours, Silversun! Back to the First Escaping we trace our line, and farther back even than that. And when those women saw men watch her because of her beauty and her gowns and her shawls, they came to me for the same."

"But the ladies weren't enough," he said. "They came to your shop, but they didn't bring their menfolk, did they?"

"Oh, and it's a right bright lad, isn't it? At Castle Biding, I was ready. Waiting for the right lord to come by. And then she saw that bedamned placard! He seemed all the prettier, didn't he, imaged next to that ugly face of yours. She went out at night and stole one of the fool things, and cried when I burned it in our cook fire the next morning."

"That wasn't very smart," he remarked mildly. "A girl that young . . . they tend to be stubborn."

"Found that out with her mother, didn't I? I ought to have learned then."

Cade felt the stones beneath him shift a little—or maybe it was the muscles of his legs automatically keeping his balance. "Her mother?"

"Didn't you ever do the sums?" she jeered. "Her fifteen, and me past sixty and looking it, what with all I've had to do in my life to survive! I made sure my girls didn't overuse their magics—I taught them our craftings, but made them save themselves for the man they chose. And who did they choose?"

"Her mother fixed on an Elf as well?"

"Aye. But she bore the child alone, with only me to help her through it, and send to her lover to tell him. He came, I'll give him that. He came to have a look at the child. And when he saw that her ears were round and small and perfect, he turned his back and left."

"More Elf than the First Elf," Cade murmured, thinking of Mieka's description of Uncle Barsabian and Granny Tightfist.

"He was that prideful," she agreed. "And my daughter died of it. She set her face to the wall and died."

"Did you ever find him again?"

"I had better things to do. I had my granddaughter to raise."

"But you failed there, too. She wanted Mieka."

"He had an old name, at least. Not the heir, but the prospect of money. If only he could be turned from prancing about the theater—" She clutched the cloak more tightly around her. "I tried, at the Threadchaser wedding, to show her and warn her. But him she'd have and none other. Every rich and titled lordship at Castle Biding came by our booth for a look at her, and that spring at Frimham there were dozens more. Ah, what she could have been, if only she'd never seen his face!"

Well, Cade thought cynically, at least they'd fallen in love on equal terms. Wasn't Mieka always saying that she was the most beautiful thing he'd ever seen?

More important was something else she'd said. *"Not the heir"*—were Jed and Jez in danger? Jez had been injured in the accident that was no accident while building Lord Piercehand's Gallery—but that had been nothing to do with Mistress Caitiffer, Cade reminded himself, nothing at all. Still . . . was this woman's magic the reason Blye remained childless? He wanted to run home and beat down the door at Criddow Close and tell Blye to throw out every stitch of clothing she and Jed owned, and their sheets and counterpanes and towels and dishrags, every thread of upholstery and all the carpets and anything that had been woven, no matter how old it was. A Caitiff's spell lasted only for the turning of the moon, but Jed and Blye were here at Wistly all the time. How simple to switch off a shirt or a neck-cloth, how easy to tuck something into their satchel on the occasions when they stayed all night.

As calmly as he could, he said, "So you resigned yourself to the inevitable, and helped her."

"You were there for most of it," she said bluntly. "You know what it took. I kept telling her that if she wanted a faithful husband, he was the wrong one. All those months traipsing round Albeyn, and on the Continent—and that interfering bitch of a sister, hiding her letters to him and his to her! Without that meddling slut, there would have been a proper wedding, and no sniggering chaverish about how quick the baby came!"

The baby. Jindra. What would her life become, if this appalling woman continued to be part of it?

"And last night?" he asked as something occurred to him. "Was the invitation your doing? You still make clothes for the Archduchess, don't you?"

"That was naught of mine. She's a silly cow who must have overheard her husband say as he was always saying—that to ruin you, he had only to ruin Mieka." She laughed when he reacted with a flinch. "Neither of them saw that he's got his ruin in his own blood. Drink, thorn, any woman he sets eyes on—destroying himself comes natural. He can't help himself, and there's no help as can be given him. Not even yours, Silversun. Not even yours!"

All too true, unless Mieka saw for himself. As Cade hoped he would see for himself the girl's hands. And that reminded him, and he smiled. "Well, Mistress, you'll be packing up your things soon enough, and you and she can go live at Hilldrop—or back to the Durkah Isle where you came from."

She smiled back. "Are you so certain of that?"

"You know, I really am. But before you go, just for curiosity's sake— my Trollwife would like to know—how did you leave in the first place? And why did you take the name Caitiffer?"

"My own mother was the greatest of her generation. She wove for me a cloak so powerful that it lasted the whole of the journey here and twenty-five days of the fortyer."

"I suppose it could be done. But what did they think, when the person they'd let on board simply vanished?"

She laughed low in her throat. "What makes you think anyone ever saw me at all?"

Invisibility? Preposterous. Nobody could—

Nobody in Albeyn could. She was a Caitiff, a Witch.

"It was the provisions they began to wonder about. As for the name . . ." She shrugged her shoulders. "If you thought about it, you could work it out. It's only our women who inherit the magic. It's not unknown for our men to leave the Isle. It's permitted, now and then, so long as the name is used as a reminder. And as a woman takes her husband's name—" She broke off, and looked at him as would a teacher expecting a passably bright student to take up the lesson.

Cade saw no reason not to oblige her. "You passed yourself off as the completely ordinary wife of a Caitiff male who had lived in Albeyn, a whole long line of them as far as anybody could guess. There'd be no prohibition about a Caitiff man living here, because only your women have magic. I see. Very elegant." He inclined his head slightly, grateful for the information. "I suggest that you make arrangements to return to Hilldrop Crescent. Mayhap they'll let you stay here tonight, but tomorrow you and she will be gone."

"Is that how it seems to you? And what of Jindra, in this little fantasy of yours?"

"She stays," he said curtly. "Jindra stays."

She laughed again. "There's laws, boy. And magic. I have both on my side."

"How do you reckon that? Men always retain custody of the children in a divorce—" But Vered hadn't, he remembered suddenly. "And anyways, I doubt Lord Ripplewater's son would agree to raising another man's child."

This stunned her, though she made an admirably quick recovery. "Seen it, have you? Then you ought to know that he has influence. What justiciar will say him nay? Especially when the husband she wants to be rid of is serving a term in jail! Oh yes, great tregetour, that's one point where the law is on a woman's side!"

"Does she really want to be rid of Mieka? I wonder."

"She'll do as she's told."

He smiled, because he knew it would irk her. It did.

"Oh, and have you seen that future, too?" she sneered.

"What I've *seen* is the welts on her hands where she was holding the reins."

"That's proof of exactly nothing."

"I didn't mean legal proof. I meant that it can be proved to Mieka. He'll know what she did. He'll never forgive her for it."

"Whether he forgives or doesn't forgive makes no difference to me. He'll be a guest of His Majesty for time enough to secure the divorce." She chuckled. "How long d'you think he'll last inside a prison—pretty little thing that he is!"

Cade laughed aloud, and again she twitched with surprise. "What makes you think that Mieka will ever even see the inside of a court-room?"

"That disgusting brute he's so fond of is hurt, crippled for life, most like. Mieka will be held responsible by the law."

"Don't count on it." Cade wasn't laughing anymore. "*He's* the one who'll hold himself responsible. And that's something *I* won't forgive. Make no mistake, woman. I know a few things that I'm sure you'd rather remained unknown in certain quarters."

"You don't know a damned thing!"

"Don't I? You know what I am. What I can see."

She stared up at him, eyes narrowed. "And you'll offer it to the Archduke in exchange for the Elf."

"I don't have to offer him anything. What will happen . . . well, I've seen it, you know," he said, lowering his voice to a scheming little whisper. "Just as I saw you write a letter to the Archduke telling him what I am. 'Something to His Grace's advantage,' that's the way you phrased it. Purple wax to seal it. I saw it all."

"And couldn't prevent it! No more than you could prevent that vulgar little Elf from spilling the whole tale one night, or prevent my girl from telling it all to me!" Then, as if the question had been feeding on her insides all this time: "Why didn't you kill him? You know what he did, who he told—what I did with the knowledge—"

"Kill the finest glisker in the Kingdom? Oh, I don't think so. He does have his uses."

Mieka was the means by which the Archduke had sought to break Cayden. Cold common sense dictated keeping him close, a target to divert the Archduke from Cayden himself. Yet no one with a scrap of sense would abandon the Elf who had triggered Touchstone's success. They'd been going nowhere fast, before that night in Gowerion.

Compassion for the Elf required sacking him for his own safety. Yet to exile Mieka from the art and artistry of the theater would be to sign the warrant for his slow, agonizing death.

Cade contemplated the fierce and angry eyes of this woman he despised. "One more question," he said. "Just one. Your ambitions for her—it can't be just money and position. What do you want?"

Turning her gaze to the rain-drenched lawn and the river, she seemed to be thinking it all over. At length she said, very quietly, "You know the story, so you'll understand when I tell you that we refused to share our gifts when the Knights were made. For this, we were condemned to serve them. Shunned by all other races, from Wizards to magicless Humans—after a time, they forgot why and hated us out of habit."

Nothing she might have said staggered him the way this did. A connection between Caitiffs and the Balaur Tsepesh?

"Those Knights who survived were outcasts as well," she went on. "They needed servitors to hide them when necessary, to take care of their needs."

"Need for what?" he whispered.

"What do you think?" she snapped, all the pensive depth gone from her voice. "We were hunted down and sold as slaves. And those brave Knights? What did they do to help us, we who had hidden *them* and fed *them* and helped *them* escape for centuries? Nothing!"

He could guess what feeding them required. As for the rest—

"Money and social position would allow you to take your vengeance?" he ventured, feeling his way through it. "But if your grudge is against the Knights, what's the sense in punishing Albeyn?"

"Work it out for yourself," she said. "It's cold. I'm going in."

"Not until you tell me—"

"Cayden!" Jinsie called from the dining room window. "Can you spare us a minute?"

The old woman was halfway to the door. He stared after her, mind reeling, until he remembered something Drevan Wordturner had said—or had it been Vered Goldbraider, regarding his play? It didn't matter. The vital thing was that Henick was a *balaurin* name. The Archduke descended from a family that had given at least one son to the Knights.

"Cade?"

"Yeh," he said automatically. "Be there in a tick."

Chapter 16

Even considering the urgency of his need, Cade was well aware that it was no use sending a message all the way to New Halt, where the Archduke had gone for Wintering. He waited until Tobalt Fluter gave him the nod that Henick was back in Gallantrybanks, in his chambers at the Palace, and then he wrote a letter. He delivered it personally, making his way with stubborn persistence through multiple layers of Court functionaries, trading shamelessly on his late father's name.

It required several hours of kicking his heels in reception chambers, hallways, and private waiting rooms, not to mention following flunkies up and down stairs, to get to the Archduke. Finally admitted to Henick's presence, Cade bent his head in as minimal a token of respect as he could get away with, and handed over the letter.

"For Your Grace's immediate attention," he said.

"Ah. I thought I might be hearing from you, Master Silversun. Permit me to offer my condolences on the death of your father. How is your mother?" He paused, watery blue eyes watchful in a face unhealthily pale. "And your little brother?" he added at last—echo of the veiled threat he'd made years ago.

Cade forced himself not to react. "As well as can be expected. And now I ought to leave, and not take up any more of Your Grace's time."

He had to get out of there. He couldn't stand being in the same room with that man. Returning to Redpebble Square, he sat in his room to wait for the Archduke's reply.

He knew what it must be. He'd written only four words: *Look to your obligations.* That should be sufficient reminder to Cyed Henick that he owed Cayden, and Cayden now intended to collect.

Wintering had been a strange, anxious holiday, with everyone adamantly avoiding any talk about Mieka's problems or his wife's indis-
position. They made Jindra's Namingday celebrations as much fun
as they could. Cade had the feeling that at six years old, the child understood that the grown-ups were worrying about something, and
suspected their at times artificial laughter. He didn't like what it
said about Jindra that she didn't ask questions. Soon enough, he
told himself, soon enough she'd be separated from her mother and
grandmother—*great*-grandmother, he reminded himself—and could
grow up unstifled in the happy confusion of Wistly Hall.

He hadn't reckoned with Mieka's thoroughly unexpected streak of
self-sacrifice.

Just before Cade took Dery home on Wintering Night, Mieka pulled
him aside and said, "I did like you told me, Quill. I looked at her hands.
But it doesn't matter, don't you see? I'm to blame. And that's what I'll
tell Master Burningcrag tomorrow."

"Mieka!"

"It was me they were after. I can't let her go through all of it—court,
and lawyers, the broadsheets—I *can't*. And if you say a single word
contrariwise, I'm gone as your glisker." When Cade only gaped down at
him, he shrugged and said, "She's my wife."

After all this, all the lies and the manipulation, he still loved her.
Cade searched the changeable eyes, seeing the well-known stubbornness. He saw also honor and gallantry and self-sacrifice—useless
things, things she didn't deserve.

"You are without question the stupidest man I have ever known."

Mieka only shrugged and walked away.

Now, five days later, with the witnesses formally identified, located,
and informed by magistrate's writ that they would be summoned to
court in Gallybanks within the fortnight, Cade sat waiting for the
Archduke's reply to his letter. Yazz was on the mend, Robel had arrived with their two children, and Touchstone hadn't performed in
more than a month. Jinsie warned Cade that while the populace could
stand another week or two of deprivation, Touchstone's bank accounts
couldn't.

In the dismal winter months, theater was one of the few diversions
available, provided, of course, that one could get through the snow
and the wet. Every group in Gallybanks and its surrounding area—

even the barely professional ones who hadn't yet been invited to Trials—performed every night to large audiences and made pots of money doing it. People were beginning to ask what had happened to Touchstone.

When news of the disturbance at Great Welkin hit the broadsheets, people no longer wondered. They talked of it constantly (scandal being another major winter entertainment), and the few times Rafe and Jeska ventured outside their own front doors, they were stared at. Accustomed to it for much more agreeable reasons, they stopped leaving their own homes unless absolutely necessary.

While he waited for the Archduke's response, not leaving the house except to visit Blye at the glassworks, Cade carefully composed another letter. This one was to Vered Goldbraider, and covered eight pages. He told the story that Mistress Caitiffer had told him, fitting it into what he already knew about the Balaur Tsepesh and garnished with gleanings from his grandfather Cadriel's library. It wasn't just this research that took him so long; it was also deciding on the best way to tell the tale without giving away the name of the person who had supplied him with this astonishing source material.

Cade was aware that Vered might already know some of it or all of it, and incorporated it into his plays. If this was new to him, he'd do one of two things: rewrite, or ignore it. Cade felt sure he would do the former, because it was a poor tregetour indeed who ignored such dramatic possibilities.

By that fifth morning after his visit to Court, there was a rime of stubble on Cade's cheeks, chin, and upper lip. He hadn't bathed or changed clothes in days, shucking off only his trousers and shoes before crawling into bed at night. Derien brought him food at irregular intervals, and usually stayed to eat with him. Of Lady Jaspiela there was no sign. Presumably she was at Court. Cade didn't much care one way or the other.

He experienced no Elsewhens during this time. He was nightly tempted to use the thorn that Auntie Brishen had devised to trigger those odd visions that were part dream and part Elsewhen. Yet he couldn't stop thinking about the one where Mieka had pleaded with them to let him go. His heart had just . . . stopped. Did anyone who used that much thorn—or used it at all—live to a ripe old age? Look at what had happened to Cade's father.

That fifth morning, Derien came running up the staircase and burst into Cade's bedchamber, waving a copy of *The Nayword*.

"It's done, it's all over," he panted. "They've all recanted!"

"They—?"

"The witnesses! All of them—well, except for the one who drowned in the Gally."

And that, Cade thought as he took the broadsheet and began to read the article, was why the other three had recanted. Oh, there had undoubtedly been scenes: the footman, told by his mistress the Archduchess one thing and ordered by his master the Archduke to say another; the coachman and the lady's maid, informed by their horrified employers that merely appearing in a court of law, even though they were only witnesses and not charged with any crime, was a scandal that could not be forgiven, and they had best think thrice about their jobs. The fourth witness's death, however . . . that would have shut their mouths completely about what had really happened that night.

He read the details of the recantations: "Very dark . . . bad lighting from the torches . . . hundreds of people milling about . . . happened so fast . . . couldn't be sure enough to swear to it . . ." The interesting mention of a wound in the drowned man's ear, as if an earring had been torn from his flesh. Yellow Vest, Cade thought.

> His wife told the official inquiry agents that he had indeed been injured at Great Welkin, and that Mieka Windthistle had not only hit him in the jaw but also ripped a silver hoop from his ear. The Constabulary, deducing from this that he had been in the carriage with the Windthistles, have postulated in the light of this new evidence that Master Tanglemure's were the hands holding the carriage reins.

"So Mieka's safe," Derien said, a tinge of a question in his voice.

"Of course he is. It's all sorted now. I thought it would be." Leaning back in the soft black armchair, he tossed the broadsheet to his brother. "I wonder when they'll refund the bail money."

"Is that all you can say?"

"What do you want to hear?"

"I dunno—it just seems—" He kicked at a leg of Cade's desk. "After everything going all crazy, it feels—"

"Like a bit of a letdown?" Cade asked, amused. "Like a play that sets up something frightfully dramatic, a confrontation that will change everything completely and for all time, and then . . . *Phut!* Nothing!"

"Well . . . yeh."

"I agree, it's lousy theater, but life usually is."

"At least we got to do something good with some of Father's money."

"Y'know, I'm coming round to Mieka's way of thinking about that," he admitted. "What if we give it all to Ginnel House?"

"I think that would be *excellent*. That nice Mistress Cavenester will be so pleased."

"All right, then, it's agreed."

"But save a bit," Derien said with a sudden grin, "for the next time Mieka gets into trouble and you have to bail him out of nick!"

Alone once again, Cade leaned his head back, staring at the ceiling beams and the cracked plaster between them. So much for Master Tanglemure, his tea-and-mocah cart, and his yellow vest. Cade supposed he'd never know exactly how the Archduchess had contacted him in the first place, or what she had agreed to pay him, or even what his mission had really been. That it had all been Panshilara's idea he had no doubt. The Elsewhen showing him Princess Iamina and the Archduke had been indication enough that he was angry with his wife. Sending the ladies to the Continent was effectively sending them into exile for a whole summer—always assuming they survived the voyage, as Miriuzca's brother Ilesko had not. The Archduke had two children now: a boy to marry Princess Levenie, a girl to marry Prince Roshlin. He had no more need of Panshilara.

Cade reasoned that any decent man ought to be appalled by such thoughts and surmisings. True, he had spent years thinking for other people, putting himself in the places of all manner of folk so that he could write their dialogue and portray them as faithfully as close observation and extrapolating imagination could do. Still . . . that he could so easily perceive what Cyed Henick would probably do, up to and including murder, ought to have alarmed him. But he was too busy being disgusted.

The trading of favors—his service to the Archduke in the matter of Ilesko's plan to blow up the North Keep, the Archduke's paying off the debt by getting Mieka out of trouble—made him sick. There was no justice and the law was a mockery. One woman's treachery had led to a man's death, and all of it would be covered up and smoothed over because the Archduke owed Cayden a favor.

Starting with Kearny Fairwalk, Cade had taken full advantage of the advantages that knowing powerful men could bring. He'd paid for it, quite literally. But balancing out favor for favor didn't make it right. There was nothing honest or honorable about it. He despised the powerful and himself and the whole corrupt system. But he'd used that system when it suited him. It seemed to him that in the end, all any man could do was conduct his own private affairs with as much integrity and honor as possible, and be as honest in his own life as he could. The greater life, that of society, was hopeless of remedy. Years and years ago, Sagemaster Emmot had spoken eloquently for the advantages of order. How had his little speeches gone? Every man in his proper place, doing his proper job. The great turning wheel with a million spokes, each one secure in its socket—glued in, with no risk of rattling free . . .

"But what about people who have talent? What I mean is, my friend Rafe is the son of a baker, but he's also going to be a really wonderful fettler—he's got the magic for it and more. Should he become a baker like his father just because that's where he was born?"

"I can't see that this could overset the proper order of society."

"Well . . . no. But lots of people are born into one kind of life and want something else. Something better or different. If they're taught not to want anything different—I mean, if they ask, should they be told it's impossible?"

Though Cade had forgotten what Emmot had replied, he had concluded that *order* meant that answers need never be provided, because no one would know enough even to frame the questions.

Tregetours—the truly gifted ones, like Vered—wanted people to ask questions and demand answers. Tregrefin Ilesko and his friends were right about one thing: Theater of the type performed in Albeyn could be dangerous. Looking back, it puzzled Cayden that Master Emmot had encouraged him in his ambitions.

Rousing himself at last, he went to his desk and took out three sheets of paper. On each, he wrote the same words, then signed his name.

Rehearsal here tonight at seven.

The fourth and fifth sheets were for Jinsie Windthistle and Kazie Bowbender, telling them that Touchstone needed to work. It didn't matter where or for how much. They needed to get back out there before the public again.

He folded these notes, addressed them, and set them aside. Then he dug his letter to Vered from a drawer and read it through one last time.

Caitiffs had refused to contribute when the other magical races had bestowed certain gifts on the Knights. For this, they were condemned to serve the Knights who survived after the invaders were expelled. The Caitiffs hid them when necessary, provided them with food, helped them in any way they could, until they were themselves expelled from the Continent. (What the Knights had done after their servants were sold into slavery, Cade couldn't begin to guess.) Sequestered for centuries on the Durkah Isle, the Caitiffs—one of them, anyways—now wanted a path back to power, or at the very least to live in Albeyn instead of on their frozen island. Not that Cade told Vered this; it had nothing to do with the origins of the Knights, which were the subject of Vered's plays, and Cade would have had a tricky time explaining how he knew.

As he folded and sealed the letter, he mused on the implications of that servitude to the Knights. Freed from their island ostracism, would they try to honor the old agreement and set about finding the Knights who still survived? It would make a good story, he supposed. But he doubted very much that the Caitiffs would choose to return to the old ways. Unless, of course, any amongst those Knights had become powerful—

The Knights, or their descendants.

No. Were this true, Mistress Caitiffer would still be working for the Archduchess—

But hadn't she been the one to tell the Archduke about Cade's Elsewhens? A thing not just to his advantage, but to hers as well. Had she played on the old relationship? Did he know anything about it at all? Had any tales been told in the Henick family for generations, conveyed in hushed secretive voices, about the sacrifice made by their ancestor in becoming one of the Knights who would vanquish the invaders?

It was all much too tangled for him to unthread the knots. Frankly, the whole concept scared him. Witches who worked in textiles, allied with what logic dictated the term Vampires—it was too awful to contemplate. They would count on that, wouldn't they? Two mostly legendary peoples, experts at hiding what they were . . . could the Knights even be accurately described as *people*? Few had even the slightest, vaguest knowledge of Caitiffs and the Knights. Even Cade, Wizard and tregetour and arrogant enough to consider himself a scholar, had never heard any of what Mistress Mirdley had told him whilst she was un-working any possible spells from that counterpane. He glanced over at it, scrunched at the foot of his bed, years old now and harmless. The Knights were even more obscure. No one would take Vered's plays seriously. No one would believe.

Except Caitiffs. And the Knights' descendants.

Drevan Wordturner had had the right of it. Vered shouldn't be writing what he had now finished. It was much too dangerous. Cade looked at the sealed and addressed letter. Would a few more pieces of that centuries-old puzzle help or hurt?

Before he could change his mind, he tore the letter into shreds.

Chapter 17

Being a good, kind, thoughtful husband, Mieka didn't sleep in his wife's room. His mother made up a bed for him in one of the empty chambers. Jindra chose to stay in her aunt Jinsie's room. All of this was for the best, because every night since Wintering, Mieka had nightmares. Actually, the same nightmare. Always the same.

Enormous carriage wheels, tall as Yazz himself—even taller—red-rimmed, shining torchlit blood dripping from every spoke as the wheels turned slowly, slowly . . . He shouted for it to stop, but the rig kept moving, wheels and axles and springs screeching, grating, grinding. He leaped and grabbed the spokes and the wheel turned with him on it, over and over, and Yazz wailed with pain. . . . He fell off, through miles and miles of air to the courtyard, sobbed with grief as the carriage moved away, exposing the great broken body on the cobblestones. Blood frothed from Yazz's lips in a last gurgling breath. Blood streamed towards Mieka, filling the little gulches where the stones met. Blood puddled at his feet, rising inexorably to his ankles, a pool of thick wet blood that caught on fire, gold-red fire that should have been reddish-brown because that was the color of Giants' fire in Vered's play wasn't it but this was gold-red and licked up his legs like a starving beast and he was going to die, he wanted to die because he didn't deserve to live, he'd killed Yazz and it didn't matter that he hadn't been holding the reins and his hands weren't marked with welts and blisters, it was his fault, his fault, he hadn't been able to stop the wheel and he pulled in a breath that was gold-red fire that burned his throat and he screamed Cayden's name—

Always the same. He would wake in a bone-chilling sweat, shivering, nearly convulsing with lack of thorn and alcohol. It would be so easy to stop the dreams and the shaking terror with a little of this or a trifle of that. But he deserved to suffer. All of it had been his fault. He was the one who had drunkenly blabbed to his wife about Cade's Elsewhens. And from that, all this had come.

By the time Cade called for a rehearsal at Redpebble Square, Mieka had been cold sober for more than a week. He felt like all Hells were competing for precedence in his brain and body, and the only person he made the effort not to snarl at was his daughter. That nobody ever snarled back—warned, he surmised, by his mother—didn't help. When the note from Cayden arrived, he was more than glad to get out of Wistly, where his parents and siblings either replied gently to his spiteful moods (with a look of sympathy in their eyes that drove him wild), or simply walked off while he was still snapping at them. Refreshing, he thought as he walked over to Redpebble, to be with those who would answer insult for insult and sneer for sneer.

He hadn't counted on feeling so *good* after the even minimal rehearsal use of the withies. He'd missed performing. He hadn't realized how much he missed it until he sat in Cade's drawing room, glass twigs in his hands, and wished fiercely for an audience to play to.

Jeska had brought with him the news that his wife and Jinsie had got Touchstone a gigging at the Keymarker the next night. This put Mieka in such a cheerful frame of mind—onstage again *at last*—that he didn't even miss the usual tot of brandy in his tea. It was only when he realized that nobody else had indulged either that he became grouchy. Someone at Wistly had tattled on him. Cade, Rafe, and Jeska were abstaining to show their support. What was one little sip, for fuck's sake? One little sip, one little pinprick on his arm where all the marks of thorn use had smoothed over . . .

Mieka had always been adept at smoothing over whatever he was feeling by playing the clown. So, in rehearsal, when it came time to magick up the peerless vision of a girl who caused the boy behind the window wall to fall headlong in love, instead of a vagueness (all that was needed in rehearsal) featuring Kazie's dark creamy skin, Crisiant's height and grace, his own wife's lips and eyes, and Cade's contribution of shimmering golden hair, he used the withie to conjure up a version of Cyed Henick. Stooped, wheezing, scarlet-faced, squelchy of body and pallid of eye, Mieka put him in the gown he'd seen the

Archduchess wearing that night at Great Welkin, and gave him a big flashing necklace besides, the carkanet of shining gold and silver plaques they'd devised for "Treasure." Rafe and Jeska whooped with laughter. Cade growled. But there was a spark of laughter in those gray eyes, and for Mieka, that was enough.

Throughout the evening, nobody talked about what had happened at Great Welkin and what had happened since. They all knew that the man who'd ripped Mieka's ear (also healing nicely) was dead; they also knew who had ordered it. It was ended, and over, and not worth discussing.

Perhaps they should have. Mieka couldn't be the only one who recognized that now things were even between Touchstone and the Archduke. Nobody owed anybody any favors. He wondered how Cade felt about that, but didn't ask. Was losing that advantage worth keeping Mieka out of jail? The answer had to be yes. Still, he couldn't help wondering if there might be an even greater cockup in the future, when the Archduke's influence might be needed for something more important.

Then again, it was a weird sort of relief to know that they wouldn't have to endure Henick's fat slimy fingers twiddling about in their lives. In the next instant, he knew how vain that hope was. The Archduke would *always* be there, sometimes more prominently and sometimes less, but always there.

The rehearsal ran very late, so he took a hire-hack to Wistly. It was nice to be able to afford such things again. He was so pleased by the quality of the work tonight, and so happy to be feeling so much better, that he told the hack driver to stop a few streets away from Wistly Hall, and got out, and went into a tavern for a celebratory drink.

He was on his third whiskey when the Minster chimes rang out all over the city. He downed the rest of his drink, bowed genially to the three gentlemen from the neighborhood who did their drinking at the tavern rather than in the elegant confines of their mansions in the vicinity of Waterknot Street, and walked home whistling under his breath. And instead of seeking the little cubbyhole his mother had prepared for him, where he'd had nightmares every time he slept, he went to his wife's room.

She was in bed. Her bronze-gold hair was loose, freshly washed, gleaming in soft curls that framed her face. She wore a nightdress of purple silk and frothing black lace. The bed was made with clean, fragrant white linens and embroidered pillows. She was sound asleep.

He spoke her name, very softly. She did not respond. He watched her breasts rise and fall with her breathing and said her name again. Still no answer, nary a twitch nor a twinge.

But he *wanted* her. She was his wife, she belonged to him, and he *wanted* her. Striding over to the bed, he touched her smooth shoulder, then shook it. Nothing.

"Wake up!" he exclaimed. "What's wrong with you?"

He picked up one of her hands, avoiding the sight of the still-reddened welts, and stretched out her arm. No thorn-marks. And she wasn't one to drink herself into a stupor.

"Open your eyes, damn it!"

"She won't. Not even for you."

He spun on one heel, swaying a little. Her mother stepped from a shadow, arms folded, watching him with unconcealed hostility.

"I gave her something to make her sleep. She's been crying her eyes out every night, grieving for the baby. Not that you, her own husband, could be bothered to come to her and comfort her! No, you spend your nights anywhere but with your wife!"

Mieka echoed stupidly, "The baby." And didn't trust himself to say anything more. He hadn't had enough whiskey to make him numb, nor yet to make him reckless. The baby that had never existed. The lie she had told, right to his face. The lie she had told the constables, which had got him a night in jail that could have turned into years. The lies she and her mother had been telling for years.

It wasn't precisely a lie that her mother had given her something to make her sleep. The nightdress and the sheets and the cushion-slips were new. He knew, now that he accepted what she and her mother truly were, that had he crawled into bed beside her, he would have been asleep, too, as soon as he closed his eyes. He wanted that, even more than he wanted her. But he couldn't bear the thought of waking beside her, and looking into her face, and listening to more lies.

So he nodded, and went past the old woman into the hallway, and found the room he'd been sleeping so badly in, and right where he'd hidden it behind the chest of drawers with the stove-in back was his thorn-roll.

It wasn't really cheating on his resolve to give up drink and thorn.

After all, it was just to get some sleep. He needed sleep, if he was to perform tomorrow night. It wasn't as if he'd be going onstage drunk or thorned.

He arrived early and clearheaded at the Keymarker, laughing in delight at the placard in the window:

The Keymarker proudly announces
the return of the legendary

TOUCHSTONE!

Once backstage, a peek through a parting in the curtains showed him that the place was already packed, an hour before they were due to go on. Everybody would make bags of money tonight. His partners made fun of him for showing up so early. In his top-loftiest accent, he informed them that he was a Legend—it said that very thing on the placard outside. Early, late, it was all the same to him, for a Legend didn't bother with trifles like time.

"You can't be a Legend," Rafe told him. "You're too short. So's Jeska. I'm too young and too pretty to be a Legend. And as for Cade . . ." He pretended to scrutinize the tregetour. "He can be a Legend if he likes. In fact, it rather suits him."

Cade favored him with a crisp little bow. "Beholden to you. As your resident Legend, I decree that it's bloody well time we got onstage. Move it!"

The break from performing had done Touchstone a lot of good. "Hidden Cottage" was funnier than ever; "Silver Mine" more intense and moving. Cade had chosen the old standards rather than attempt any or all of *Window Wall*, reasoning that they needed to stretch any kinks out before getting ambitious. Mieka, Rafe, and Jeska agreed with him. Though they knew these plays backwards, forwards, and sideways, the sheer joy of being back onstage and the special alertness for flaws made them perform as if they'd never done either play before. The audience responded with wild applause, and broke convention (for, even though drinks were served, this was more theater than tavern) by pelting the stage with coins. Jeska, laughing, gathered up the trimmings and flung them high in the air over the crowd. Mieka tossed a withie even higher over his own head, and shattered the glass into a million glittering shards.

Tobalt Fluter was present, and Mieka knew that tomorrow *The Nayword* would be singing Touchstone's praises yet again. Backstage, he virtuously declined a mug of beer, stuck around for about a half-hour of congratulations, then took a hire-hack home to Wistly. He was very tired, for his performance had not been assisted by thorn tonight—but how good it was to put everything into the withies, and have it all come back to him in applause! The clean, fresh, positive energy made him truly happy. Touchstone was still the best in Albeyn.

She was awake tonight, breathtaking by candlelight in the sweet tumble of soft sheets and her long bright hair. Purple silk and black lace were again on display. She pushed herself up onto the pillows, smiling, a tiny sleeve slipping down one shoulder.

Mieka was cold sober and she was unimaginably beautiful and he didn't feel even a spark of desire. This was unbelievable. He ought to have been shocked out of his wits. What was the difference between last night and tonight?

She saw it, of course. The lace shifted across her breasts, exposing lush curves. "Mieka, darling," she whispered.

He sat down in a chair to take off his boots. The difference was that his wits were precisely what he was *in*. No thorn, no liquor, just himself.

"Was it a good show tonight?"

"Mm-hmm." Stockings next. He reminded himself to replace all three of his knives, the ones for his boots and the one that went into the sheath at his back. And he ought to send a note to Master Flickerblade, and set up a training session.

"I can always tell when you've had a good time," she went on. "Those eyes of yours always turn more green, with a hint of blue in them."

He unbuttoned his shirt. Now that Lord Kearney Fairwalk was no longer dictating Touchstone's wardrobe, all four of them wore what they pleased, what they were most comfortable in. Mieka had taken to dressing in plain black or tan trousers and white-on-white embroidered shirts. Just a hint of flash, no distraction. His jackets expressed his more flamboyant impulses: multi-colored brocades, figured silks, crushed velvets, decorated with gold or silver braid. He didn't wear them onstage. They interfered with his work.

"Do you want me to pour you a drink, darling?"

What he wanted was for her to shut up. For if she did, he would hear no more lies.

"Mieka . . ."

Shirtless, he sat back in the armchair and looked at her. "Why did you do it? I mean, I know you must've been scared. I was, too. But why did you tell them I was the one holding the reins?"

"What? I never—"

"Don't lie to me," he said wearily.

"I'm not lying! I didn't tell anybody anything! They took you away and I was all alone in that horrid place—nobody even spoke to me! How could I tell them anything when they didn't even speak to me?"

He lifted a hand in a dismissive gesture, let it drop to his thigh. "The baby, then. Was that your mother's idea?"

"What do you mean?"

"There was no baby. I know it as well as you do. Were you scared of what I might do when I found out that you'd lied about who was holding the reins? Did you tell that lie about a baby to—Gods, I don't know, to make sure I didn't yell at you? All you had to do was tell me the truth. I would've taken the blame anyway. I would have protected you. Why couldn't you believe I'd protect you? Why couldn't you tell me the truth?"

"There *was* a baby—I was waiting to tell you, I was waiting to be sure—"

"Don't lie to me! Don't you fucking dare lie to me!"

Shrinking into the pillows, she put a hand up to her cheek.

That gesture. *Again.* How many times had she used it in the past few years? The anger was suddenly a living, writhing thing in his guts, compounded of betrayal and hopelessness and the mockery that was his life with her. Springing to his feet, he tore at the buttons of his trousers. He saw the want kindle in her eyes, her stunning iris-blue eyes, and it sickened him and he suddenly wanted her right back—which made him even angrier.

Naked, he stood next to the bed, glaring down at her. Never had he made love to her with anything other than the most exquisite tenderness. He didn't recognize himself in the man who yanked the sheets off her body, who took the lacy front of her nightdress in both hands and ripped the flimsy thing in half.

Certainly he was no longer the boy wandering the Castle Biding Fair, falling over his own feet when he first caught sight of her, hopelessly tangling his fingers in fine-webbed woolen shawls, stammering and blushing as she retreated shyly into the shadows.

Nor was he the boy who had written callow, passionate love letters until finally, *finally*, he'd been allowed to spend a wondrous night in her bed.

No, he was not that stupid, lust-struck boy, insensible to the magic swirling around him whenever he touched her, blind to her mother's secret smiles.

He wasn't that boy anymore. But he didn't know who he had become, either. He knew nothing right now except that he felt furious and betrayed and he wanted her and he hated himself for it.

"What are you waiting for?" she taunted. "You know you want me. You always want me!"

He didn't know who she was, either. Had he ever?

She laughed and held out her arms to him, spread her thighs for him. Her gaze roamed his body, her breath coming faster, her swift heartbeats visible in the pulsing of her throat. Lust in a woman's eyes was nothing new. It was the possessiveness, the glitter that meant "I own you," that had always excited him, even though he knew it wasn't true.

Cade was possessive, he thought suddenly. *"My glisker you are, and mine you'll stay"*—what Mieka was, what he could do onstage, belonged, in a way, to Cade and Touchstone.

Therein lay the difference. The work owned Mieka. The magic and the work had laid claim to him long ago. She claimed ownership of— of what? An upper-class accent, a flat in Gallybanks, clothes and jewels and social position—how much happier she would have been if those things had come to her in the form of a man with some pompous title. A man who came home every night at a reasonable hour, who escorted her to grand parties, who followed the Court from Gallantrybanks to Seekhaven and back and otherwise never went more than ten miles from the city, not even in imagination, because imagination had died years ago, dead along with youth and ambition and magic.

It wasn't her, he told himself. It was her mother. His accent, his grammar, his clothes; the luxurious flat in Gallybanks instead of the cottage in the piddling little village of Hilldrop; why did rehearsals take up so much of his time, why was he gone so long on the Royal Circuit every year and gone all over Albeyn during the winter and spring; he could work with his brothers, they'd be pleased to hire him, and what about the Princess, she liked him so much, he could ask her for a position at the Palace or the Keeps, and he could preserve his interest in theater by giving lessons to aspiring young gliskers—

As he looked into his wife's eyes, he saw another pair of eyes and they were the same. It didn't matter whose ideas she had spoken. The fact remained that she was the one who had spoken them, and that meant that she belonged to her mother. Not to him. The most beautiful thing he'd ever seen. His? No. She was her mother's creature. She had never really been his.

"Mieka—I know it's too soon, but—I do want another baby—please, darling, let's make believe that the other baby never happened, and that tonight I'm ready—oh, Mieka, I want to give you a son—"

"You don't want to *give* me anything." He heard his own voice, thin and cold, and knew it must be his own voice because he felt the movements of his lips and tongue, the breath leaving his throat. But he didn't recognize this brittle, bitter tone, any more than he recognized this man who was suddenly, horribly unable to make love to her. A man to whom the touch of her fingers would be as the flaying of flensing knives. "All you ever do is take. But you're gettin' nothin' from me, not ever again."

She didn't believe him. How could she believe him, when he had never refused her bed? She tossed the hair from her face and reached one hand down between her thighs. A whimper, and then a soft moan. He stayed where he was: watching, listening, unmoved.

"Mieka—!"

She was crying now and he didn't care. He picked up his trousers, his shirt, put them back on.

"What are you doing?" An instant later, suddenly furious: "Go on, then! Get out! Just you *try* to leave me!" Then she laughed at the sheer absurdity of the notion. "Where would you go?"

"Anywhere."

"There's nowhere and no one would have you! Come on, Mieka— think of someplace you could go that would—" With a gasp, sitting bolt upright in bed: "To *him*?"

He'd always known she didn't like Cade. He hadn't known before tonight how much she hated him. "Get yourself gone by tomorrow afternoon, and your mum with you."

"You *can't* leave me! I know things—about *him* and—and all of Touchstone—I could tell the Princess—"

He shrugged. "Just as you please. I'll see you're taken care of, but only if you don't make a fuss. And that means Jindra stays with me."

"You'll never take my child away from me!"

"Pull up a chair, make yourself comfortable, and watch me."

"You *can't!*"

"Fight me, and it'll be back to workin' for a livin', and you've had all these years of doin' as you like." He deliberately coarsened his accent, mocking her. "Back to Frimham with you, me girl, paradin' about all frustled up in your mum's makin's—"

It was an odd thing: even weeping with frustration and shaking with rage, she was exquisite. He wondered why he didn't fall onto the bed and take her right here and now. Who *was* this man who didn't want her anymore?

"You think you're the only man as wants me?" she taunted. "You think there aren't dozens of them—hundreds!—who'd do anything I ask?"

She was counting on the piercing jealousy she had worked on to such powerful effect for so many years. Mayhap she was right to do so; he did feel a stinging like acid. But only for a moment.

"Yeh, I don't doubt there's hundreds who'd walk through a mile of Wizardfire or stare down a real live dragon, just in the hopes of a smile. I oughta know. I was one of 'em. You go and do whatever it is you want. Jindra stays."

"No!"

Anger began to nip at him again. But not jealousy. How odd. He'd spent years bristling with possessive wrath whenever any other man so much as looked at her. It really was singularly strange to feel . . . nothing.

Except that he did feel something. He'd not allow his little girl to be trained up as a Witch.

"I know things about you, too," he said grimly. "What if I was to mention that what they chanted that night at Great Welkin is true?"

"No it's not!" A breath later she gave the game away with a panicked cry. "You wouldn't fucking dare! If you whisper a word of it, you condemn Jindra, too! Witch-blood runs in the female line—if I am, so is she!"

"And that's why she's staying here. I'll have no more of your mum's teachings to poison her. No more 'silver needles and golden stitches.'" He tucked his shirt into his trousers, and the heavy silver bracelet caught on a belt loop. Too bulky for his wrist, weighing down his hand when he worked—on purpose, he knew that now. Replacement marriage-gift for the originals, thin and slithery, which she'd got him because he hadn't wanted a necklace or a ring. Bracelets could be tucked away, hidden, invisible beneath shirt cuffs. A chain would have glinted around his neck, and a ring would have shone from his hand. He'd hidden her away, just the same as the bracelets, pushing her out of his mind while he roamed Albeyn and bedded whomever he fancied and behaved like a lust-struck sixteen-year-old newly liberated from an all-boys school. Whatever had gone wrong between him and her, he was willing to take his share of the blame. He'd admit to his full portion of lies, his shameful part in this farce of a marriage, with its heavy, shiny symbols weighing down his hands.

He'd kept forgetting to have his mother or Blye or someone seal the silver bracelets with magic. He could take them off now without pain. He undid each clasp in turn, glancing at the inscription on one small, flat silver disk: his name, hers, the date of their wedding. It turned out that there *was* pain, but only a little. Tossing the bracelets onto the bed, he told her, "Here—I'm guessing you might be short on coin, so take these. Might be worth a bit, enough to get you back to Hilldrop, anyways."

As he sat down to pull on his boots, she snatched up one bracelet and threw it at him. It glanced off his shoulder. He arched a brow at her and returned his attention to his boots.

"Mieka! It's the middle of the night! He'll slam the door in your face!"

"Maybe so." It was a possibility. Not a strong one, but it was possible that Cade wouldn't believe him, wouldn't listen to anything he had to say. It was possible that he could explain himself until next Wintering and Cade wouldn't believe him. But that was all right. He could be patient. The Lord and the Lady and all the Angels and Old Gods knew Cade had been amazingly patient with him.

Stamping his feet into the boots, he stood up and grabbed his jacket.

It occurred to him that this would be the last time he'd ever see her alone—certainly the last time he'd look on her naked body in a bed. He tried to remember a time when this would have broken his heart.

"Tomorrow afternoon," he repeated. "You'll hear from Master Burningcrag within the fortnight. You can have the house—"

"Go back to that squalid little village? When I could crook my finger and have—"

"—have a silk-lined bedchamber in a mansion here in Gallybanks? Have fun deciding which of 'em it's to be. And be sure to let me know. I'll need the address, so I can send the divorce papers."

Chapter 18

Oh, Gods. What have I done?

It was very late, long past curfew. There were one or two hire-hacks available in the streets. Mieka chose to walk to Redpebble Square.

What have I done?

He knew what he *wanted* to do: get drunk. Return to Wistly, find his thorn-roll, and—

Oh, yeh, that would mend everything, wouldn't it?

Better he should throw it into the fire. He remembered that Jeska had done the same thing years ago, and how furious he'd been, foolishly taking a swing at the masquer. He'd ended up flat on the floor, laid out by an expert, efficient fist.

Actually, unconscious sounded like a good thing to be right now.

Surely he could not have just said and done what sharp clear memory told him was true. For the sake of a few lies—which hadn't even caused that much trouble, when it came down to it—he was about to divorce his wife. The woman he adored. The most beautiful . . .

What have I done?

He tripped off the curb and into the cobbled street and cursed floridly. For a few minutes it felt as if he'd twisted his foot right off his ankle. Back on the pavement, he limped past a block of flats, the music of lutes and singing voices floating down from the upper floors. He recognized one of Briuly Blackpath's songs and walked faster. Elf-light lamps were plentiful in this stylish section of Gallybanks. He left it behind, venturing into neighborhoods darker and shabbier, his ankle throbbing. He forced himself to be alert for pickers and lifters and plain unvarnished thugs. No knives in his boots, no blade tucked against his back—what had he been thinking, to go out unarmed?

He avoided Chaffer Stroll, for some of the whores there knew him. Not because he had patronized them—he'd never paid for bedsport in his life—but from the Touchstone placards posted all along Beekbacks Lane. In fact, on almost every street his own face smirked at him. Jinsie and Kazie had evidently ordered up new designs: TOUCHSTONE written down the right-hand side, and individual imagings of himself or Cade or Rafe or Jeska, four times life-size. He frowned at his own face, not liking it that each member of Touchstone was set apart from the others on these new placards. Part of something worth being part of . . .

What have I done?

Rounding a corner into a better neighborhood, he encountered Cayden's face, stark black lines on bleak white posterboard; severe, unsmiling, cold—not his Quill at all. Yet it was that face and those eyes that gave him his answer. What had he done? He'd grown up.

He couldn't say that he liked it much.

No wonder he hadn't recognized himself.

Sober. Unmoved by beauty that had hitherto rendered him helpless and quivering with desire. No longer willing to gloss over what he knew to be lies, just for the sake of keeping a woman who had never truly been his. Aware now, without lying to himself, of what she was—and filled with a new and unyielding resolve that his daughter would never be like her.

Was it a feature of sobriety to see things as they really were? And, worse, to know that there was no haven to be found in all the things that had made the world more bearable?

He kicked at a mounting block, snorting through his nose at the sharp stubbing of his toe and the renewed pain in his ankle. Childish, foolish—he wasn't a little boy anymore. He wasn't even a grown man playing (rather desperately sometimes) at being a little boy. Elf-lights, luminous with fear, glinted off hanging signs and shop windows, and he paused to study his own dim reflection. A child and a fool and the best glisker in the Kingdom because of those things—or mayhap in spite of them.

He wasn't deep, like Cayden. He didn't like poking around his own

insides, picking himself apart just to see how everything worked. He
didn't spend his time studying other people to figure out their moti-
vations, their emotions. It was enough for him to observe how those
emotions were expressed, and use those impressions in his work, evoke
them in an audience through his skill and his magic and his withies.

He'd felt so happy tonight after the performance. So *alive*. Onstage
was where he belonged. Being a part of Touchstone was his truest identity, the thing he had chosen for himself, the only thing that could crush
him if he got it wrong. He'd come scarily close at times, too drunk or
thorned to give the audience everything they'd come for. Never again,
he promised himself. He would never betray his partners or himself
onstage again.

Offstage . . . he was a husband, a father, a son, a brother, a friend.
He'd done badly at all those much too often. But he'd do better. He
swore he would do better.

Again it struck him as being uniquely odd, that the sober confrontation with his wife had nudged him without his even knowing
it towards the truth. And the truth was that he could have one of
two things: the work and the people he loved, or the reckless delights
of being thornlost or drunk or both. He could be a better man for his
daughter and parents and siblings and Touchstone, for Blye and Chat
and all his other friends . . . or remain a foolish child.

He had reached Redpebble Square without realizing it. The bricks
and bushes of the central garden were lumpy snow-shapes, the paths
between them cleared by a weathering witch. He thought the word
and flinched away from it.

Gods, why couldn't he have left well enough alone?

There was a tavern a few blocks away. He'd been there with Quill.
He could go there tonight. He had coin for a few drinks. He could go
back to being—

There wasn't any going back, and he knew it. Just like the morning
at Ginnel House, there was no going back to ignorance.

But what use was he to anyone, if not as a clown? That, too, was
something he'd chosen for himself. What if the drink and the thorn
were what made him funny? What if without them he was a *bore*?

He had no Elsewhens, but he did have an active imagination. He
could never have succeeded in his profession otherwise. He saw himself sober, upright, earnest, conscientious . . . never. He couldn't be

that way if he wanted to, and the Lord and Lady knew he wanted to
about as much as he wanted to go back to Wistly and his wife. To go
back to being stupidly, adoringly blind.

If he did what he'd just promised himself he would do, it had to be
for himself. He couldn't shove it all onto other people, because even
people one loved—mayhap *especially* the people one loved—could disappoint. In a moment of anger or a perceived betrayal, he could blame
them if he took a few drinks too many or sought out Master Bellgloss
for a quick infusion of thorn.

He saw that with vicious clarity. Damn Cayden, anyway. It was all
his fault, taking him to Ginnel House and making him *see*. That had
been the start of it. He understood that now. If not for that one rainy
morning, Mieka would be in his own bed at Wistly Hall right now,
making delirious love to the incomparably beautiful woman who belonged to him.

The woman who had lied to him again and again. The Witch who
did and thought and spoke as her mother bade her. Who had never
betrayed him with her body but had betrayed him with her words—
was he right in thinking that the latter was somehow worse than the
former? She had loved him; she probably still did. But she had never
really been his.

He limped slowly across the brick square between ugly lumps of
snow-shrouded shrubs. He fixed his gaze on the door of Number Eight,
and knew that here was his reason for not going back. Whatever else he
was, whatever his own actions had made of him, he'd been born with
a glisker's magic. It defined him. The work was the truest expression of
himself. Proof? It made him happy. Not liquor nor thorn nor bedding
his wife had ever made him as happy as being part of Touchstone.
Without it . . .

He tried to imagine Cayden without pen and ink, Cayden without
all those words. He didn't have to imagine Cayden without the Elsewhens; he knew exactly what that looked like, felt like. Cade hadn't
been truly himself without them, any more than Mieka could be truly
himself without the work.

If he did this, if he swore off thorn and limited his drinks to one
after a performance, it had to be for himself. Nobody else. Just him.
The alternative was a long, sluggish deterioration into someone he was
certain sure that Cade had seen more than once in his Elsewhens.

"Mieka?"

Cade's voice. Cade, standing in the open doorway of Number Eight, blinking with sleepy surprise. Mieka felt the prickle of his knuckles that meant he'd knocked them hard and repeatedly on the door.

"Can I stay here tonight?"

"Sure."

Mieka stepped into the entryway, shrugging out of his cloak—the fur-trimmed cloak that was so easily identifiable to the "witnesses" of events at Great Welkin. He didn't remember grabbing it on his way out of Wistly. Handing it to Cade, who hung it next to his own and Derien's coats, he said, "No, I don't want to talk about it. Not tonight. Maybe not ever."

"All right," Cade said warily.

Relenting just a little, Mieka smiled a rueful smile. "I had trouble enough finding words to explain it to myself. Don't make me do it all over again, Quill, not tonight!"

"And maybe not ever." Cade nodded, still bewildered but willing to wait for understanding. He pulled his dressing gown closer around him. "C'mon, it's cold."

Ah, but that was where Cade was wrong. Cold *outside*, yes; here, inside, climbing the stairs, Mieka was warm. Safe. Cade would help him if he needed it. He wasn't fool enough to think that he'd never need anyone's help. The habits of years would take time to overcome. Still . . .

"No more long breaks like this, all right? We have to work, Quill. We all get a little crazy when we don't work."

"Just not like the last two years. Not anyplace and everyplace that'll hire us."

"Right. But takin' weeks and weeks off from the stage . . . that'll come eventually, when we're too old and feeble to hold the withies, so why rush it?" He flung a glance over his shoulder as he reached a landing. "How old did you say you were in that Elsewhen?"

"Forty-five."

"And losin' your hair."

"Don't remind me!"

But the grin belied the groan, and Mieka knew that he'd enjoy being reminded for the next nineteen years.

Jindra would be all grown up by then. Hells, she would probably have made him a grandfather. And it was another odd thing on this night of oddities that this new man he had become didn't shy back from the thought of growing older, and actually found himself rather looking forward to it.

*   *   *

If it was work that Mieka wanted, Jinsie and Kazie delivered it and then some.

With the Shadowshapers no longer performing together, Touchstone was the most besought theater group in Albeyn. Though the lucrative season of Wintering was over, boredom was always a factor everywhere but Gallantrybanks, and requests came in from all over the Kingdom. They accepted those that required only two nights' travel, but refused (politely) everything else. For one thing, Mieka had his divorce proceedings to consider. For another, Cade was in the process of selling Number Eight, Redpebble Square.

It belonged to him now, according to his father's will. Lady Jaspiela was livid about it, but there was nothing she could do. Cade told her she could have half the sale price to establish herself in congenial lodgings wherever she pleased, but he'd be using the other half to buy a place on the river. Derien would be living with him. End of discussion.

Finding this new home had been the result of one of Mieka's long walks through the city. Sometimes Cade or Dery accompanied him; sometimes he was alone. Since childhood he'd explored nearly every part of the city from the Plume eastwards along the river, and his profession had taken him to most of the other sections in hire-hacks. On the days when he felt good, he deliberately chose routes that would take him past as many taverns as possible, and smugly congratulated himself on not entering any of them. When he was feeling the grinding, aching need for a drink, he stayed near the river, trudging through districts of grand mansions or wharfs and warehouses and manufactories.

One night, when he was especially thirsty, and his tongue remembered the taste of whiskey, and his blood sliced through his veins like shattered withies with the lack of it, he decided he deserved the torture of a walk down Curglaff Road, where sailors and dockhands could find an open tavern at any time of the day or night and constables never, ever enforced curfew. The street name had its origins in a warning, for the buildings and the pavement outside them fetched right up to the steepest part of the riverbank. With no barrier to keep the unwary (or the very drunk) on dry land, a curglaff's "sudden shock of icy water" was a very real danger. Mieka walked down one side of the street, forcing himself to look in at the windows of each and every tavern, then turned at the end and walked up the other side, his hands almost shaking. Then a brace of ludicrously drunken men burst out a door, lurched into the street, and were vehemently sick all over themselves and each other. Mieka stood awhile and watched them stumble upright, go down on their knees, yark again, and finally stagger to their feet, laughing like candidates for permanent residence at the Shelter, where Cade's insane uncle had spent the last forty years of his life.

They were filthy, sloppy, contemptible, and disgusting. And either one of them could have been him.

He hurried back to Redpebble Square, needing to feel the warm safety of just being in the same house with Cade.

It was a fine, cloudless day, though very cold, when Cade came along on one of Mieka's walks. He wanted a break from polishing the final version of *Window Wall*. They crossed Gallybanks, heading south to the river, then turned west to stroll along the meandering path of the water. Nothing so spectacular as the Plume featured here, just a broad expanse of clear, rippling water winding its way to the sea. Few bridges, few businesses, no manufactories at all—it was much quieter, and in places almost rural.

Mieka tramped along with his cloak pulled tight around him and his gaze on his boots, grimly denying that he had any desire for a drink before sundown. He allowed himself one beer with dinner and one small whiskey after a performance; he'd convinced himself that so little could do him no harm, and it did diminish the cravings. He could've used a drink—to be honest, quite a few drinks—after receiving news this morning that his wife and mother-in-law were still at Wistly Hall. Mieka refused to return home while they were still there; they refused to leave without Jindra; Mishia and Hadden refused to allow Jindra to leave. Master Burningcrag had drawn up various documents necessary to divorce proceedings, and as generous as the terms were, they had been rejected.

In any divorce, the wife was assumed to be at fault. The husband might be a dedicated bedswerver, a famous drunk, a pock-armed thorn-thrall, a giddy spendthrift, and a downright flaming bastard (all present and accounted for in Mieka's case), but responsibility for the success of the marriage was always a woman's. If she wanted out, she got nothing. If he wanted out, he had to pay back her dowry. But that was all. Thus it was rarely to a woman's financial advantage to free herself from a rotten marriage.

Unless, of course, she had a wealthy lordling waiting to become her second husband. In the last week or so, Mieka had heard the name Ripplewater mentioned. He pitied the man profoundly.

Master Burningcrag, with stiff though mostly silent disapproval, had drafted a settlement that gave Mieka's wife Hilldrop Crescent to live in for her lifetime—but the deed was changed to make Jindra the legal owner. A set amount would be paid quarterly for housekeeping and other expenses, which would stop the instant she became Lady Ripplewater. Mieka, in accordance with tradition and the law, kept full custody of Jindra.

His wife knew that their daughter was her best asset. To be sure, he had no real fault to find with her as a mother. It was *her* mother that worried him. (In point of fact, her grandmother—and his amazement when Cade casually mentioned it had lasted several days.) Mieka had said and meant that he wouldn't allow Jindra to grow up under the old woman's influence. If he had to pay to keep his little girl safe, then he'd pay.

However, moral outrage was no substitute for the sustaining comforts of ale, whiskey, or thorn.

Mieka plodded along the path, wondering how far he'd have to walk today to wear himself out for a few hours' decent sleep tonight. Touchstone was free for the evening, and those nights were always both the best and the worst. He loved giving a show, but the tiredness that came after a gigging was always matched by the exhilaration of the work itself and the applause that half-deafened Touchstone whenever they performed. He'd talked this over with Cade several times, and they'd concluded that various kinds of thorn could either evoke that sensation or dampen it down, depending on one's needs of the moment. How they would learn to cope was still problematic. But Mieka was touched and humbled that Cayden had decided to support him by swearing off thorn, too. Almost five weeks now; Mieka told himself it was getting easier, and mayhap it was, because he didn't have to tell himself that quite so often.

All at once he realized that Cayden was no longer beside him. Turning, he saw his tregetour rooted to the narrow pavement skirting the slope to the river, staring at the opposite bank.

It wasn't an Elsewhen. He knew what those looked like on Cade's face. He also knew what recognition of part of an Elsewhen becoming reality—a scene, a conversation—looked like. Retracing his steps, he squinted to see whatever was clutching Cade's attention so hard.

Brick steps led up from the narrow dirt track beside the riverbank to a terrace that fronted a very peculiar building. It had a hole through the middle. The tall three-story house, constructed of warm dark-gold stone accented by silvery-gray window casements, was split in the middle by an archway wide and tall enough to drive a coach through. Studying the place, it seemed to Mieka that it might have been a gatehouse of sorts, with stabling for horses and carriages, and the grooms and coachman living on the floors above. Or maybe *all* the outdoor servants, he thought, counting windows. But such a building ought to have been on the grounds of some huge estate. There was no such mansion visible; hedge fences and stone walls marked the boundaries of the property to each side and around back, and beyond were other houses, modest in size and embellishments—though some ambitious soul had provided his somewhat squat two-story dwelling with a ridiculous row of columns across the front facing the river.

Mieka returned his attention to the odd building, wondering firstly why anyone would put a gatehouse on the river, approached by stone stairs up the bank, when it ought to have been at the road, and secondly whether there was a kitchen and suchlike so it could be turned into a real house—for a kitchen hearth was no safe thing to have anywhere near the wooden stalls and straw bedding of a stable. Unless, of course, one knew a Wizard or, more likely, a Goblin with a seriously brawny spell that restrained fire to hearths and torches and candles where it belonged.

"Quill?"

At last he got a response. Cade looked down at him, gray eyes bewildered. Yeh, this was an evocation of an Elsewhen, all right. Mieka thought for a moment, then laughed.

"Forty-five?"

The confusion increased for a moment before Cade's face cleared and he laughed, too. "Exactly! I only saw it at night, but this has to be it. There couldn't be another place like this, could there?"

"Looks like a gatehouse stables or something." He tilted his head slightly to one side. The shape of the thing was like the letter U, only upside-down and bottom-heavy. Top-heavy. Whatever.

"It'd probably cost a bleedin' fortune to make it livable," Cade mused.

"Lucky, then, that you've credit with Windthistle Brothers, that renowned and accomplished firm of builders, who, for reasons that utterly elude me, like you so much that they'll give you a discount. C'mon, let's go have a closer look."

They'd passed a bridge about a half-mile back. Returning, they crossed to a tidy little street of shops, and chose the shoemaker at random to ask about the neighborhood and that strange building.

The door opened with a brisk ring of a bell. Mieka looked up instinctively at the sound—but there was no bell for the door to hit. Magic. He grinned to himself. Nobody around here was likely to look askance at a Wizard tregetour, at least not for being a Wizard. The disreputable profession of traveling player might be another matter. But if Cade spent generously at the local shops, they'd all get to liking him right quick.

Cade had already made his ask of the shoemaker—who was Wizard-tall, Troll-faced, and looked at least two hundred years old. From the array of wares on his display shelves and the tools at his workbench, he was not just the maker of shoes but also the snobscat who repaired them.

"Hopeless pile of rock, ain't it?" he said to Cayden. "Sir Blasien Linstock, as whose grandsire had the firings of all the King's cannon under his eye—this was during the war, mind, and I doubt me Sir Blasien could light a candle with both hands and a book to guide him, he's that thick, the poor looby, and everyone's always said that whichever land his grandsire came over to Albeyn from must be swimming in stupid. Anyways, with the knighthood the grandsire got that nice bit of land on the river to build himself a home. He'd barely married before he was buried—the custom of his homeland, and savages they must be as well, to put a man in a box and put the box in the ground!

But his wife had a son three months after he died, and spent all her years in that big house up the road, the one with the roofline that heads off in twenty different directions and a hundred different angles, which makes it a puzzle to thatch, and I know this for why? My daughter married the thatcher."

Cade cast a quick, laughing glance at Mieka, who knew exactly what he was thinking: *This old crambazzle talks more than* you *do!*

"But now we come to Sir Blasien, the grandson, who bethought him that it was high time the house got built, and by this time had to sell off half the land to do it with, for *his* mother was naught but a lovely little lozel who spent everything she could get her hands on and then some."

"Beg pardon?" Cade asked, unwisely, marking himself as a lackwit in the shoemaker's scornful eyes. Mieka hid a smirk by pretending interest in a pair of heeled suede boots. *Lozel* was another of Uncle Barsabian's preposterous words. This man looked to be of the same generation, and maybe even older.

"Wasn't I just saying that she couldn't hold on to a coin if it was glued to her hand? All Sir Blasien could get built was the gatehouse, according to a plan his grandsire sketched up. Tribute to the old man, all that." He shook his head. "There *was* talk at one time of a road, a proper road, with pavement and all, along the river, and that's why the cobbles were laid to the gatehouse and through the middle, for they were supposed to connect with the road. The steps down to the river were meant to receive guests, even Royalty, coming along by boat. But that never happened, neither."

"I see," said Cayden. "Has anyone ever lived there?"

"Rats, mice, birds, and the cats what dine off 'em. All empty on the inside, and for why? Sir Blasien invested his last penny in some voyage of Lord Piercehand's ships to some distant place or other, and lost it all. Been trying to sell the gatehouse ever since."

Mieka nodded sagely. Cade ought to be able to get the place cheap. But as for what might have to be done to it to make it habitable . . .

Ah, but hadn't Cade seen it in that Elsewhen? What if possession of that strange house was a requirement for that Elsewhen to happen? Or might it happen anyway, wherever Cade—and evidently Mieka himself—lived?

And then he had it. It wasn't just Cade's house, it was *his* house, too! How perfect it would be: half of it his, half of it Cade's, with a shared drawing room and dining room and whatever—and most of all, a shared kitchen where Mistress Mirdley could reign supreme. . . .

He heard Cade express gratitude to the shoemaker for the information, and followed him back outside. When the door had shut behind them with a sharp ring of its magical bell, he peered up into Cade's face.

"Well?"

The gray eyes were staring down the road, where the top of the house was visible through the trees. "Can't afford it."

"*You* might not, but *we* can." Laughing at the shock he'd just administered, he danced a few steps into the middle of the street, then whirled round. "Just think of the discount my brothers will give *me*! Now, what shall we call it?"

"Call what?"

"You're the tregetour. Think something up!"

"Mieka, I don't even know if I want to buy the place or not!"

"Did you or did you not see us there? I mean, *here*? And look—it's a nice little village—not quite enough people to be a real village within the meaning of the Royal Census, I expect, but it's got what's needful, greengrocer and butcher and baker and everything in between, and they don't mind magic, and it's an easy drive from Gallybanks and right on the river and Jed and Jez will have a fine old time frustling it all up for us—"

He stopped talking only because Cade reached out a hand and clapped it over his mouth. He grinned and pretended to bite the heel of Cade's thumb.

"I'll think about it," Cade said firmly. "C'mon, it's getting late and we ought to get home for dinner."

Stepping back, Mieka waved extravagantly in the general direction of the house. "We *are* home, Quill!"

Chapter 19

Ready and willing as Cade had been to give Mieka a room for the night—or as many nights as he wished—Cade had been too sleepy that first night to feel much besides bewilderment. Six weeks later, he was still bewildered, and nowhere near growing used to it.

No Elsewhen could have warned him. The choices had been Mieka's to make. Cade had thought that Yazz's survival and getting the girl out of the way—and, totally unexpected, finding the house—would negate all those futures of drunkenness and thorn-thrall and death too young. He cherished this notion until one morning about a month after Mieka moved into a spare bedroom at Redpebble Square, when an Elsewhen disabused him of his hopes.

{ Tobalt sat at his desk, sorting old issues of *The Nayword*. All the issues dealing primarily with the Shadowshapers went to his left; everything that was mostly about Touchstone was placed to his right. He paused in his methodical sorting when an issue appeared with a front page bordered in black. The imaging was of Vered Goldbraider. This he set aside. Searching for something in the unclassified stack, he finally pulled out a similar issue. The black border was the same, but the imaging was of Mieka Windthistle. Tobalt contemplated each in turn, then placed his palms, fingers spread wide, to cover each face.

"Fa? Are you done yet?"

He snatched his hands back as his daughter peeked around his half-open door. He waved her in.

"Funny," he remarked. "Just about the same number of years for both groups, and almost the same number of column inches."

"Did you include the ones about the Shadowshapers after Vered Gold-braider?"

He gestured to a plain wooden chair in the corner. Stacked on it were more issues of *The Nayword;* another pile was on the floor beside it. "There. And those about Touchstone after Mieka Windthistle."

"Fa!" she chided. "You're being like Rauel or Cade—only *they* pretend that what they lost doesn't matter as much as the way they dealt with losing it. A life is a whole and entire thing, not bits and snatches and only what you want to remember—or things that you want others to remember about you." She pointed to a framed imaging on the far wall. "Is that how Touch-stone would want to be remembered? Or would they want that one over there?"

The first was of Cade and Rafe and Jeska, dressed to the teeth, beside a tall young man who looked a great deal like Princess Miriuzca. Around their shoulders were ornamental chains from which depended oval medals. The second was an old placard of Touchstone, one of the first imagings Lord Fair-walk had ever commissioned of the four of them. Tobalt contemplated each, his eyes clouding with memories.

"For Rauel and Sakary and Chat, I suppose it simply hurts too much to think about it. What they were, what they might have become . . ." He looked at his daughter, gaze sharpening. "But Cayden . . . He despised Mieka for his weaknesses. The one he really despised was himself, for his lack of compassion. What he did to himself afterwards showed that clear as Blye Wind-thistle's finest glass goblets."

"Well, Fa, you can understand that, can't you? Trying to rein in Mieka Windthistle would wear out anybody's patience."

"Maybe. Maybe not. Once Mieka was gone, he went about trying to do him one better. Dragon tears—daring Mieka's ghost, I think. He knew by then—how did Jeska put it, in that interview he persuaded me not to print?"

"That Cade had thrown Mieka away with both hands."

"Yeh. So how could he have compassion for his own failures when he'd had none for Mieka? I remember how he used to look at Mieka—disgusted at what he'd willingly done to himself, horrified at what he'd unknowingly done to himself. As if it made him physically sick to see him. Well, that was true of everyone who knew him, of course. Nobody could look at him, not even those who loved him, and not wince. Dear Gods, he'd been so beautiful. . . . And after Mieka's death, Cade set about doing the same things."

"Punishing himself," she remarked. "As much as he could, without actually dying."

"Y'know, I've spent years trying not to see Mieka as a tragedy—not in the way Vered was a tragedy, of course. I've tried to see it as merciful, that death took him before age and illness could, that he didn't wither slowly but burned out instead, like a snuffed candle flame." He paused. "No. More like he burned up from the inside."

"Fa," said his daughter, pointing now to the stacks on his desk, "do you think Mieka would want to be remembered for being there—" Once more she indicated the imaging of Cade, Rafe, and Jeska with the Prince. "—or for *not* being there?"

"You know," he said slowly, "I'm not sure which would scare him more."}

That made no sense to Cade. Mieka wasn't scared of anything. Well, mayhap one or two things. But not of the dark, like almost all Elves. Certainly not the kinds of things Cade feared—making a fool of himself in public, presenting a play that everyone loathed, losing Mieka . . .

He was in his room, seated at his desk, when the Elsewhen came. His gaze focused once more on the rows of figures before him: calculations as to how much he could afford to pay for that peculiar house he had found. It was his; he knew it was his. He'd seen it in Elsewhens— the best Elsewhens, his forty-fifth Namingday. Recently he had become obsessed with finding a way to pay for that house and everything that would be necessary to make it livable. If he could only establish himself and Mieka there (with Derien and Mistress Mirdley and Jindra), then everything would turn out all right.

And now this new Elsewhen—but had it shown him that it wasn't as simple as buying a house (or not buying a yellow shirt, memory gibed at him), or did it mean that until he held the deed in his hand, losing Mieka was still possible?

He chose to believe the latter. And if even that choice was one that affected the Elsewhen . . . well, he had second-guessed and outguessed himself so many times that he really couldn't bring himself to care. There were only so many things a mind could deal with at once. Doing a thing, not doing a thing—he had to take responsibility for the outcome either way. Wasn't that what adults did?

Cayden had suggested that Blye and Jed take over Number Eight, using the downstairs as a reception and office space for Windthistle Brothers and the upstairs as living quarters. Jez was bespoken to a girl who was just finishing up her apprenticeship in weaving (one of the few trades that officially admitted women to its Guild), and once they were married could live at Redpebble Square as well. Rikka Ash-bottle, whose Goblin teeth had been straightened and filed to Human perfection, was married now, and could live above the glassworks and handle the sales room while Blye worked at the kiln. Lady Jaspiela would have enough to buy a flat someplace fashionable. She wasn't happy about it, but his mother's happiness was at the bottom of Cade's list of things to worry about. Jed and Jez could repay Cade in kind, by working on the new house.

"Got it all arranged as neatly as one of your plays, have you?" Blye had remarked.

"Yeh," he'd countered, grinning, "and it's a shame and a pity that I can't write the rest of life the same way! But you'll do it, won't you? I mean, just because it's perfect doesn't mean you have to buck at the traces like a contrary filly."

"Are you calling my wife a horse?" Jed had demanded, then spoiled the effect by laughing. He ducked as Blye threw a pillow at him. "Peace, woman! All right, yes, it sounds as close to perfect as anything will ever get in this life. We'll talk it over with Jez and Eirenn, but I can't see that they'd have any objections."

All Cade needed now was enough to buy the house. He didn't want the distraction of puzzling out what Tobalt had meant in that Else-when. Scared of being remembered for being there, for being the best glisker in Albeyn? Or for *not* being there—for being dead?

Now Cade understood better the other Elsewhen, the one wherein he and Hadden had arranged bottles on a table like the King's Guard on parade while Mieka lay in a drunken daze. Mieka hadn't cared about living or dying. He'd held himself responsible for murdering Yazz. Well, Yazz was alive, and would recover—though it would be years, if ever, before he would have the use of his left arm again.

Remembered for being dead. Cade didn't like that idea much him-self. Remembered for being alive? For the glisking, for his skills as a player . . . or for his pranks and jokes and hilarious outrageous stunts onstage and off?

The work mattered to Mieka now more than it ever had, because he finally understood that it was the truest expression of who he was. It defined him, provided him with release for his impulses and emotions, left him both exhausted and elated. What Mieka felt about performing, Cade felt about writing. And he began to see that Mieka would indeed be afraid of being remembered for the faults and follies that had ended up killing him, rather than for the brilliance of his magic.

However, living with Mieka at Redpebble Square was much the same as living with him in the wagon on the Royal Circuit. Mistress Mirdley had fixed up a bedchamber for him right next to Derien's—the boy was ecstatic at having, as he put it, *two* brothers—but somehow Mieka seemed to spend most of his time in Cade's room. To someone who required solitude and plenty of it, the presence of someone who required company and plenty of it became rather wearying.

It took one sentence, a fortnight after Mieka moved in, to silence Cade on the subject. He'd asked if Mieka could possibly find it in his heart to go bother Mistress Mirdley or Derien or Blye or indeed anyone within a five-mile radius for the rest of the afternoon, because it really would be nice to get some work done.

Mieka, with equal measures of shame and defiance that convinced Cade as nothing else could, replied, "I'm sorry, Quill, but you're the only one that when I look at you, it reminds me why I threw my thornroll into the fire."

There wasn't much Cade could say to that. So he didn't. But it made him wonder if he wanted to spend the rest of his life watching Mieka's every move.

Not that the Elf had suddenly turned Angel. Cade was unsurprised when, the night his wife agreed to Mieka's terms for divorce, he vanished after Touchstone's performance at the Kiral Kellari and only showed up again a little after noon two days later. Where he'd been was something Cade never discovered; what he'd been doing was all too apparent.

As Mistress Mirdley mixed a cure for a hangover, she remarked, "I hope at least that it was expensive liquor, and worth all this."

"It was," muttered the Elf. "Almost."

Cade noted that even though he'd spent the time at the bottom of successive bottles of whiskey, he'd chosen nights when Touchstone didn't have a gigging. Maybe Mieka really had grown up.

Now that his soon-to-be-former wife and her mother (grandmother) had decamped from Wistly Hall, Cade expected that Mieka would move back home. He didn't. Mishia was happy to continue caring for

Jindra while the winter and spring wore on. With Trials coming up soon, Cade finally asked why Mieka was still living at Redpebble Square.

"Not that you're not welcome," he added hastily. "You can stay as long as you like. I was just wondering."

Mieka was quiet for a moment, ruminating. "You want the nasty old truth? I'm scared to face Jindra. I don't know what to say. Look at it, Quill—how do I tell her that I sent her mum away, and that her mum went willingly once I agreed to pay her enough money? And I just *know* she's going to think it was her fault somehow, because that's what Vered's boys think. You said it yourself, last year when he did that play for them, and they didn't come, and he told you their mother said some pretty awful things—"

"All the more reason you should go home and talk to her."

"I'm scared to."

Cade opened his mouth to urge him again, then shut it. Although he'd purposely forgotten quite a few Elsewhens, bits and pieces of them lingered (probably because he'd wanted them to; he didn't care to analyze that too deeply). Scenes like imagings, just flashes—and a couple of them had to do with Jindra, and were the source of his determination not to see her grow up spiteful and embittered. With the purchase and renovation of that house, a home for him and Dery and Mieka and Jindra and Mistress Mirdley, he considered that he was keeping his promise, however unexpected the means would be. He hoped so, anyway.

Blye had been right about him. He wasn't an ordinary sort of person who could live a normal life. She was right as well that he didn't want to be ordinary. But he felt that now, with this new home, he was constructing a life that would be normal for *him*—and to all Hells with what anybody else thought of it. After all, Blye's household wasn't going to be ordinary: husbands *and* wives working at their chosen professions. Would so-called normal, ordinary people look askance? Who cared? Blye certainly didn't.

Planning which rooms would belong to whom, envisioning the life they'd lead there, he decided that *normal* was a word used by boring people to disapprove of those who weren't just as boring. *Normal*, to Cayden, had come to mean whatever made a person happier, more productive, more at ease with himself and the world, and caused no bother to anyone else. Picturing the way he and Mieka and Derien and Jindra and Mistress Mirdley would live at the new house, he knew that it would become normal for them, and that was all that really counted. As for people who found it strange, people who disapproved . . . fuck 'em.

The planned renovation would be done while Touchstone was away on the Royal Circuit. Jed and Jez would make sure the place was structurally sound, create walls to divide off rooms, install the most modern plumbing available, and oversee the placement of paving between the river stairs and the two front doors (one into Cade's half of the house, one into Mieka's). Mishia and Mistress Mirdley would make sure it was actually livable, with things like beds and tables, chairs and sofas, standing wardrobes and cabinets and sideboards, plus all the necessary sheets and towels and curtains. Dery would supervise the book room—Cade considered his collection too limited to be termed a *library*—and pick out which of the furnishings from Redpebble Square would look best and be most useful. They would also raid Wistly, with Mishia's help. Derien had already confided a plan to Cade that involved framing selected placards from Touchstone's career, and a display of their Trials medals inside the boxes Blye had made.

It was just as well that his personal life was getting itself nicely organized, because his professional life was about to become a chaos he could never have foreseen in the most detailed—or brutal—Elsewhen.

First, there was the secret reunion of the Shadowshapers.

Then the news that Lord Kearney Fairwalk had returned to Gallantrybanks.

The day after, he learned that Princess Iamina and Archduchess Panshilara would be leaving in the summer for a journey to the latter's homeland.

And the day after that, Derien came home and announced that a competition would be held at the King's College to select three students—those intending a career in diplomacy or in government service—to accompany the Princess and the Archduchess, and he intended to enter.

Chapter 20

It ought to have been impossible to keep the secret about the Shadowshapers. Yet day after day, Cade was astonished to find that almost nobody knew that they were rehearsing in the undercroft at Number Eight, Redpebble Square. Judging by the half-smiles Cade intercepted from time to time, Tobalt Fluter might have guessed, but Cade surmised that he was too excited by the prospect of a reunion to say a word to anyone who might blurt out the news and ruin everything. The most he revealed in *The Nayword* was that "those who know are anticipating this year's Trials with more eagerness than at any time since the spectacular first performance by Touchstone."

Romuald Needler had long since sold the Shadowshapers' wagon to Black Lightning. It had been repainted white with jagged black lightning bolts. At the time of the sale, Vered had got together with Chat and Sakary, who insisted that Rauel be included even though he and Vered were scarcely speaking to each other by then, to leave Black Lightning a little home-cozying present: a spellcasting in the firepockets that emitted a faint odor of manure whenever the things were lit. Anything stronger would have been discovered and dealt with immediately; by being subtle, they guaranteed at least a week and possibly longer of frenzied speculation—and open windows in autumn cold.

Cade had used that fondly remembered trick to remind them—after arranging an "accidental" meeting between Vered and Rauel at Redpebble Square—that it hadn't been all acrimony and spite amongst them. The event hadn't been all that difficult to organize. Rauel was invited for tea. Just as he settled into a chair by the fire, Cade heard the front door open. For once in his life, Mieka was right on time.

Instantly Cade began a plaintive moan about please could *somebody* teach Mieka a little subtlety in his pranks, like the firepockets left for Black Lightning? Rauel was laughing when Vered walked in. Cade repeated his grievance, and Mieka chimed in with protests that elegant as restraint might be, it could never be half so funny as, say, a fistful of black powder.

Vered had looked Rauel in the eyes and said, "Aren't you glad this mad little Elf showed up to torment Cade and not us?"

From then on it was easy. Well, relatively easy. Once Chat and Sakary were brought in on things, Cade offered the use of Number Eight's undercroft for rehearsals. There being two entrances to the house, Redpebble Square and Criddow Close, they could lark about with the timing and the combinations of their arrivals as they pleased. And there were so many people coming in and out these days that no one would notice four more men in the mix, what with Lady Jaspiela moving to her new flat, and some of the furniture Cade wanted for the new house going into storage, and Jed and Blye and Jez and Eirenn planning their move.

Thus nobody—except Tobalt—outside their immediate circle knew that the Shadowshapers were together again. A few of the workmen might have guessed, but if they were familiar enough with theater to know these faces, they were, like Tobalt, eager to see this group reunited. Of course, what went on downstairs in the undercroft was known only to the Shadowshapers themselves. Not a wisp of stray magic escaped to hint at anything. Cade admired their control, but rather wished he could have a bit of a preview.

With Redpebble Square in fairly constant uproar, his own working time was nonexistent. Touchstone was performing at least three days a week. They took overnight trips in their wagon to giggings outside Gallybanks, using those huge white horses of Needler's and the Shadowshapers' former driver, Rist. He had not been part of the bargain with Black Lightning—in fact, he flatly refused to work for them. Cade presumed they'd found somebody with enough muscle to control the beasts. Yazz assured them that until he was well, he was perfectly content that his good friend Rist should be on the coachman's bench. But Yazz did summon him out to Hilldrop Crescent, where he was recovering under Robel's stern wifely eye, to read poor Rist a long lecture on taking care of Touchstone both in the wagon and out of it.

Cade wondered sometimes—not that he really cared—about the atmosphere at Mieka's old home. The girl and her mother—*grandmother*, he still had to correct himself—lived in the cottage. Yazz and Robel and their children occupied the converted barn. Did the inhabitants of the two dwellings have anything to do with each other at all? Did they even speak? Did Yazz—or, more to the point, Robel—know that right next door was the person truly responsible for Yazz's injury? No news reached Gallybanks of mayhem or maiming, so he assumed Robel had no idea of the truth.

He stopped wondering and started worrying when, about a month before Trials, it was announced in the *Court Circular* that Lord Ripplewater's son had married Master Mieka Windthistle's former wife. Cade had seen in an Elsewhen what Yazz's death would have done to the Elf. Surely the same or worse was possible now that he'd irrevocably lost the woman he'd adored. So Cade held his breath for a day, and then two, and then three, and all of a sudden a week had gone by with no outburst from Mieka. No wild binges of drink or thorn; no frenzied raging; no dire vows of vengeance; no suspicious sharpness to the emotions emanating from the withies at performances. If he wept or raged into his pillows by night, Cade didn't hear it and those eyes didn't betray him in the morning. He watched carefully for signs of anything, anything at all, knowing it was futile to try concealing his watchfulness. But Mieka didn't even snarl at him to for fuck's sake stop staring at him as if he were a stewpot on the boil. It would seem he'd taken out all his anger and misery months ago. By now he was either purged of the emotions or simply numb.

This was unprecedented. Mieka had never been shy about expressing himself. Silence and reticence from him were unnerving.

Cayden hadn't really seen before how radically their lives were changing. He'd seen his new house and Mieka's divorce as inevitabilities more certain than any Elsewhen. Cade was free of his father, his mother, the house he'd lived in all his life. Mieka was free—or so Cade hoped—of helpless passion for a woman who'd betrayed him and lied to him for years. Where both of them might journey from this place was not an inevitability. And Mieka, in choosing to abandon his habitual methods of escape, had done what Cade had never really thought he would. He'd grown up.

Cade was appalled with himself for having even a moment's worry that a Mieka who was no longer a child would also no longer be the glisker Touchstone needed. There was proof enough to the contrary three nights a week. He was as brilliant as ever. Mayhap now he would become even better. Who could say?

Chances were good that there would be no hideous decline into an early death, that no one would ever say that when Touchstone lost their Elf, they lost their soul. He'd seen it so many times . . . and so many of the alternatives were things seen once and never again. And sometimes on their evenings off, when they sat with Mistress Mirdley in the kitchen at Redpebble Square, drinking hot tea and just talking, Cade saw Mieka laughing and told himself that this was how it would be in the new house, too. *Mine you are and mine you stay.*

So the Shadowshapers worked at Cade's house, and Cade couldn't get any work done at all, and one dreary afternoon Dery came home from the King's College fairly bursting with news. He couldn't even wait to shuck off heavy layers of wool and hang it all up, but raced into the drawing room where Cade was waiting for him and their tea, shedding scarf and coat and gloves as he talked.

Lord Kearney Fairwalk was back in Gallybanks. His own elegant residence in town had long since been let to someone else, so he was staying in a flat, two pitifully small rooms in an inferior part of town, all he could afford.

"But here's a puzzler for you, Cade," Dery said as Mistress Mirdley brought their tea to the drawing room. "My way home goes past his old place, where the Scrapebolts live now, and there's something different about the house."

"Different how?" Cade nodded his gratitude to the Trollwife and bit into a mocah-walnut crispie.

Mieka came downstairs just then and pounced on the plate of crispies, muffins, and cakes. Dery waited until he'd seated himself on the floor by the fire and Mistress Mirdley had returned to the kitchen before he spoke.

"It's the cellar." Sitting back in his chair, his dancing eyes belied his elaborately casual pose. Cade caught a glimpse of the diplomat Derien wanted to be—glad that for now, he was still a little brother, alight with excitement.

"Well?" he prompted, because he knew the boy wanted prompting. "What's in the cellar?"

"Something he brought back with him. It wasn't there yesterday, but it is today. Probably sneaked it in overnight. Or maybe out in the open, because it's still his cellar, after all, and he can store things there if he chooses."

"What did he bring back?"

Derien smiled.

"Out with it!" Mieka demanded.

But Cayden already knew. He set his cup down carefully on a side table. "Tell me you're joking."

The boy shook his head. "The house is on my map, and—"

"What map?"

All traces of the self-possessed future ambassador were gone. Dery wriggled a bit in his chair, then burst out, "It's of Gallybanks—most of the houses, anyway, the ones where rich people live. I started it a couple of years ago, after what happened at Piercehand's Gallery. I don't have to check it to know that there's a lot more gold in that cellar today than there was yesterday. A *lot*."

"Dery . . . about this map . . ."

"I was curious! I wanted to find out if I could tell quantity and all that—"

"Why didn't you say anything to me about—"

"It was just an experiment—once the Gallery was finished and everything, and I knew for sure how much gold was in the glass cases on the second floor, I could figure out what it felt like—how different amounts of gold felt, I mean—so I drew a map of a few neighborhoods, and—"

"Hells with the map!" Mieka exclaimed. "How much gold does the cellar feel like?"

"A *lot*. It feels all heavy and cold. Maybe ten times the coins in Father's coffer."

There was a brief, respectful silence.

"What's he going to do with it, though?" Mieka mused. "Dole it out bit by bit to his creditors? Such as *us*?"

"Yeh, that's likely," Dery scoffed.

"Living in a piddly little flat," Cade said slowly, "it's perfectly clear that he wants to hide the gold, not spend it. He doesn't want anybody to know it exists."

"What good is it if he can't spend it?" Mieka reached for another cake. "Can you tell what it is, exactly? Coins or lumps out of the ground, or what?"

Dery shook his head. "I don't know. But whatever it is, he'd have to trade it for real money, wouldn't he? Coin of the realm, and all that."

"The Goldsmiths Guild?" Cade guessed. "Where do they get their gold?"

He glanced over to the door. Blye came in from the kitchen, carrying a fresh pot of tea in one hand and a mug in the other. Her cheeks were flushed with the cold—or perhaps her own kiln fire—and her pale hair was dampened by the rain.

"Well, aren't we the cheery little group." She joined Mieka on the hearthrug and waited for somebody to speak. When no one did—unprecedented for this company—she stretched her lips in a purposely bright-and-shiny smile. "Frightful weather we're having, isn't it? Did you ever know such a chilly spring?"

Derien hid laughter behind a cough. Mieka assumed a face to match Blye's and looked expectantly at Cade. Cade, who had been trying to work out a way of asking if she knew anything about the Goldsmiths Guild without asking outright, wordlessly passed over the plate of muffins.

"If you want me to leave, just say so," Blye advised. "I started with the weather. It's your turn. Court gossip, theater gossip, it doesn't much matter to me so long as I can have a slice of cake before Mieka guttles it all."

With injured dignity, the Elf replied, "I have *never* done anything so vulgar as *guttle*. And as long as you're here, make yourself useful. Where do the people who make jewelry get their gold from?"

No hiding Dery's laughter this time. Cade stifled a sigh. So much for subtlety.

"Interesting conversational opening," Blye observed. "Much better than the weather. The jewelers buy their gold in ingots of various sizes from the central stores of the Guild."

"Ingots?"

"Sometimes my father would do up glass ingots for sale to other crafters—if they'd run out of a particular additive or something and needed the glass quick. The Guild would come round and register the ingots, and make sure they were stamped with a number. The Goldsmiths and Silversmiths do it the same way with their own raw material."

"Why?" Mieka asked.

Derien answered, "Because it's like diamonds. We had it in class—well, most of those boys have the family diamonds to worry about after they inherit. Anyways, if you flood the market with too many, the price goes down. So the Gemcrafters Guild regulates what shiny rocks the goldsmiths and jewelers can have on hand to make into goods for sale."

"Then what would somebody do with—" Mieka began, but a stern look from Cade shut his mouth.

Blye's gaze went slowly from one to the other of them. "Don't mind me," she advised. "Pretend I'm not here. It's not as if you can trust me or anything."

Casting a defiant glance at Cade, Dery said, "Lord Fairwalk's home and he's got a secret stash of gold in the cellar of his old house. What we want to know is, how can he get rid of it?"

She blinked once or twice, set her mug down, scowled, then spoke. "Even if he finds somebody who'll buy it, he won't get full value if it's an underhand deal."

"The financial condition he's in," Cade said, "I can't imagine he'd worry much about that. But somebody would guess, wouldn't they, if a few goldsmiths started making more stuff than they've officially got gold for?"

Dery asked, "Could he sell it to the Royal Mint? Whatever else he is, he's still a nobleman. He might have connections."

"Didn't get him anyplace decent to live, did it?" Mieka countered. "You said it before—why live in some rat-hole if he's got all that gold? No, this is a secret stash. Who's he friends with that's powerful?"

Blye narrowed her eyes and looked straight at Cade. "Who's powerful enough to do something with that much gold?"

They all knew the answer to that one. But as to exactly what the Archduke might do with it . . . that was another puzzlement entirely.

A knocking sounded at the front door, and Cade cursed under his breath. "That'll be Chat and Vered. They'll all be here while we're at the Keymarker tonight." Realizing what he'd let slip, he shut his mouth with an audible click of his teeth.

Blye said mildly, "Quite the social gathering place these days, is Number Eight. Should I hide behind a chair?"

Another knock, more insistent. Mieka snorted a laugh. "For pity's sake, somebody go let the poor sods in!"

More tea, more muffins and cakes, more apprehensive significant glances, and some genuinely inane attempts at conversation while Blye sat there looking innocent and Mieka sat beside her looking delighted. Rauel entered by the kitchen door, saying as he came in, "Sakary's about ten minutes behind me, with the bag of withies," then saw that there was a person present who was not officially in the know, and winced.

Cade gave up and laughed.

Later, once the Shadowshapers were downstairs rehearsing and Blye had gone home, Derien found Cade upstairs and said, "I might be able to tell how much gold there is—get a better idea, I mean—when I go past the house tomorrow. Better still, if I could sneak into the cellar—"

"Absolutely not!"

"I could get in there, easy. One of my friends at school has a little brother who's friends with one of the Scrapebolt boys—"

"Do I have to tell Mistress Mirdley on you?"

Derien sighed. "You will, anyways. I should never have said anything."

"Save the slippery stuff for when you're an ambassador telling lies to a foreign king. I'm your brother."

"Yeh, and you used to be more fun." Dery grinned. "How about this? If you won't tell Mistress Mirdley about it, then I won't tell Mieka!"

Cade groaned. That was all he lacked: his brother and his glisker in quod for breaking and entering. "No. To *all* of it!"

A day or two later, Cade was wishing he hadn't been quite so stern about forbidding Derien's expedition to Fairwalk's cellar. This time the boy came home with the news that a competition would be held at the King's College for three students to act as pages on the Continental trip planned by Princess Iamina and Archduchess Panshilara.

Derien wanted to enter the competition.

Of course he did.

"How many times do I have to say no?" Cade snarled after half an hour. "How many different ways must I say it before you get it through your skull—"

"I've only heard a dozen," Derien retorted. "Pretty paltry for a tregetour!"

"You're not entering! That's it! Final!"

"How many times do *I* have to say that when I win, people will remember it for years, and when I get old enough for an important posting, I'll be streets ahead of everyone else?"

They were arguing in the kitchen. Mistress Mirdley had wisely found something to do in her stillroom; Mieka was nowhere about. Cade glared into his brother's furious brown eyes and decided he would never, ever have children. He had enough yelling, beholden all the same, in his professional life. He didn't need it at home as well.

"Are you scared I'll win, and you won't be the only Silversun with a name to his name?"

Cade gasped. "No! Dery, how could you think—"

"Not like Father, but people thinking *good* things when they hear—"

"Apologize at once!"

They both jumped when Blye roared the command from the back door. She came in, fists clenched and breathing fire.

"What's the matter with you two?" she demanded. "Mieka said you were at it hammer and tongs and I should come at once, but I couldn't believe that the two of you would be that stupid! Now, say you're sorry, both of you. Go on! Say it!"

"Sorry," Derien mumbled.

"I don't have anything to be sorry for!" Cade exclaimed, still hurt that his own brother could think so little of him.

Blye took a threatening step towards him—which should have been ridiculous, as he was more than a foot taller than she was, but he retained plentiful memories regarding boxed ears and bruised ribs. So he set his jaw tight and stubborn, and glowered down at her.

She glowered right back.

Mieka poked his head around the kitchen door, then—evidently deciding that Blye was protection enough—came in. "C'mon, Quill. You owe him a *sorry* and you know it. This is his future you're stomping on with those great huge feet of yours. Let him enter the contest."

Derien turned on him. "I don't need his permission to do anything!"

"As long as you're in this house," Cade began.

"Silence!"

This time the command came from Mistress Mirdley.

She could do more with a single word than anybody Cade had ever met. He knew he was going to apologize, and rather than draw out the mortification, he started for the door, flinging, "All right! Sorry!" over his shoulder.

Mieka caught up with him halfway up the stairs. "He'll enter the competition will you or won't you. But when he wins—and we both know he will—it isn't as if he'll actually *go*."

"And why do you think he has sense enough not to get within a mile of that ship to Vathis?" he snapped. "We'll be at Seekhaven, or out on the Royal, I won't be able to stop him."

They had reached the fourth floor, where Mieka's room was. "Mistress Mirdley will."

He had to admit that the Elf had a point. Cade followed him into the bedchamber, where Mieka's only personal possessions were his clothes and one of the candleflats Blye had made for him on his eighteenth Namingday. Jinsie still had one, and the third had crashed into the Gally River when the turret housing Mieka's childhood aerie parted company with the rest of Wistly Hall.

"I need to be certain," Cade said with considerably less heat. "I saw something—did I tell you? The Archduke is sending his wife and Iamina to the Continent to get rid of them. And the look on his face . . . Besides, he said something to me, that time at Great Welkin. He asked if I'd ever seen my brother in the Elsewhens."

Mieka visibly paled. Then his chin jutted out and he said, "He was only trying to scare you. He couldn't possibly know anything, not the way you do."

"He *did* scare me."

"It was a threat, yeh, but it was also a mistake. He should never have shown that he knows you love your brother, and that he's the easiest way to get at you."

But Dery isn't the only *way to hurt me.*

"You're on your guard now," Mieka went on. "You know to protect him. But, Quill, the Archduke will *expect* Dery to enter the contest— if he's kept up with the boy at all, through the governors of the College, maybe, he knows there's a lot of ambition there. Hells, he might've suggested the competition himself! If Dery doesn't compete, he'll know you're watching for mischief—but if he does compete, he'll think you're not worried. Like I said, asking you about Dery in the Elsewhens was a mistake. And anyways," he finished, bouncing down onto his bed, "all *that* means is that you don't have any choices or decisions to make that would affect Dery's future."

"And I'm supposed to find that comforting?" He knew Mieka had destroyed his thorn-roll, and to ask him to procure from Auntie Brishen what Cade wanted would be a cruelty. Even to mention thorn would be heartless. He'd have to write the letter himself, requesting whatever it was he'd used a few years ago that had brought on an Elsewhen, rather than wait for their erratic occurrence.

"What're we playing tonight?" Mieka asked suddenly. "By which I mean, of course, isn't it time for you to prime the withies?"

On the nights when Touchstone had a gigging, Cade didn't worry about Mieka and drink or thorn. It had been very hard for him at first, and Cade knew perfectly well why: after the paradoxically exhilarating exhaustion of a performance, after all that applause, it was difficult to regain one's equilibrium. Onstage there was magic, constant magic, jubilant magic. A too-abrupt return to life offstage often felt like being pushed off a castle parapet. Nothing like liquor or thorn to cushion the fall . . . nothing, except having someone there to catch you.

Mieka's wife had been unable to do that for him, even if she'd understood why it was necessary—and Cade had no reason to think she'd ever understood. So: whiskey and brandy and thorn. Mieka allowed himself one after-performance beer these days, and Cade should have been worried sick that it wouldn't be enough. But he'd been right about how essential performance was to Mieka. Through the magic, his emotions were used, expressed, calmed. What Cayden gave him in the withies, he turned to the service of the play. This rid him of tension, and that was where the exhaustion came in. The exhilaration was in the knowing that *this* was what he was made for, *this* was what he was meant to do, using the brilliance of his own magic to create.

The danger for Mieka had always been the prospect of being trapped in a perpetual performance. As the days and weeks moved on, that seemed less and less of a threat. He was learning—slowly, to be sure, but learning—that not every moment of every day should be a riot of outrageous pranks and constant laughter. A thing Cade had noticed about him long ago was that he fidgeted only when bored or anxious.

At all other times—except onstage—he was physically rather muted, sitting or standing without restlessness as he paid close attention to everything around him. Cade had always suspected that behind that quietness of body, his brain was working intensely so that he could at an instant's impulse play the clown that everyone expected him to be. Yet as incredible as it was for someone as impatient as Mieka, who except for when he was performing always wanted to do tomorrow yesterday, his body at least knew how to be still. It seemed that somehow his mind and emotions were learning that lesson.

Cade didn't worry anymore on the nights Touchstone performed. It was the other times that were a danger, when Mieka didn't have a gigging to look forward to during the day and to give his all to at night. Days when he went out walking and brooded about his wrecked marriage, his daughter, his promise to himself that he would never again touch thorn and would strictly limit his drinking. Nights when he simply couldn't sleep, and sometimes went out walking, and showed up at breakfast the next morning looking a step away from death.

Jindra and Kazie, after a private discussion with Cade, knew to arrange as many giggings as they could without overly wearying either Touchstone or the public. A tricky balance, it was; he appreciated their appreciation of the rigors of performing and the danger of oversating their audiences. It was Cade's job to produce enough material to make every gigging special. This ought to have crushed him, but he found it oddly invigorating after two long years of writing only at odd intervals without the sustained and satisfying effort that made him lose all track of time and place. Now that their money worries had eased, the writing part of his job was glorious. There was no scratching of his pen; the ink flowed smoothly, soundlessly across page after page, leaving words in its wake. Leaving upon the paper pieces of his mind, and perhaps even of his soul.

And when he thought about those years of bone-weariness and scraping for even the price of dinner—because the horses had to be fed first, after all—and that his father could have put an end to it by disgorging even half of what had been in that coffer . . . it made him more determined than ever to procure from Brishen Staindrop the special concoction that, as far as he could tell, actually stimulated the Elsewhens. He wanted to know what Lord Kearney Fairwalk, author of those two miserable years, intended to do with all that gold.

Chapter 21

Sometimes, Mieka was fully aware, he could be a complete idiot. Over the last few years, he'd had his faults presented to him on a succession of silver platters, usually by Cade. Moronic as he could be sometimes, though, he wasn't stupid. And he had his pride. He wasn't doing so well as Cade surmised and he spent a lot of energy hiding it.

He didn't reveal that some nights he sought physical weariness of a kind that didn't involve walking at all—except upstairs in a tavern. He went to these places for the willing girls who were keen for a tumble. It would have been easier to direct his footsteps to Chaffer Stroll or any of the dozens of flatback houses where the girls were clean and the clients were of the upper classes, but he had never paid for it in his life and wasn't about to start now. Besides, he enjoyed flirtation, the game of words and glances and smiles and teasing fingers necessary to woo the nonprofessional. He liked it when they succumbed to his looks, his wit, and his charm. And he was very, very careful, which they always appreciated. He kept his stockpile of lamb-gut sheaths as hidden from Cade and Mistress Mirdley as he had, when very young, kept his thorn-roll hidden from his mother.

It was never the same as making love to his wife. But it sufficed, in a way, and if one had to be in thrall to something, it might as well be to bedsport with pretty girls.

He thought about thorn constantly and not at all. It was always there in his mind someplace, but he never allowed himself to remember its pleasures. He knew Rafe was in much the same predicament—Crisiant had laid down the law and Rafe abided by it—but he didn't seem to be struggling the way Mieka was. Perhaps he was less susceptible; perhaps he was stronger; perhaps the simplicity of the choice he faced—his family or thorn—made it simpler for him. Mieka didn't know and didn't ask. So determined was he to forget everything about thorn that it never occurred to him that Cade would seek a special blend from Auntie Brishen and use it in an attempt to answer certain tormenting questions.

One night about a week before Touchstone was due to leave for Trials, Mieka returned from a brief but delightful visit to a young lady (whose parents were, appropriately enough, spending the evening at the theater) and wandered into Cade's bedchamber, just to say he was home. His tregetour sprawled in the big soft black chair, slack-jawed and wide-eyed and oblivious. He knew instantly what Cade had done. It didn't take the glass thorn, the discarded twist of paper, and the little cup of water on the bedside table to tell him.

Mieka was furious. And scared. There was nothing he could do but wait it out. So he sat on the bed cross-legged with a pillow in his lap, hands folded, and watched the pale, staring eyes. Rumble, having returned from his own nightly ramble, sauntered through the half-open door and joined Mieka in his vigil. Did the cat look at Cade's eyes and see what Mieka saw? Or, rather, what he didn't see: there was no light. There were two gray holes in Cade's face and no gleam of sense or intelligence in them at all.

Eventually Rumble uncurled and jumped down, winding himself around Cade's shins. A few moments later, with a twitching of fingers and a grimace writhing briefly across his face, Cade was back. He looked at Mieka, and then at the cat, and chose the latter for official notice. Bending down, he scratched ears and chin, saying with an almost desperate casualness, "Good hunting tonight?"

"I could ask the same of you," Mieka said. "What, exactly, were you hunting down? Derien or the gold?" When surprise flashed in his eyes, Mieka snorted. "Yeh, Quill, I really do know you that well."

"Both, in a way. And something else that doesn't make any sense."

"Tell me." It wasn't a question. It hadn't been for a long time.

Leaning back in the chair, with Rumble on his knees, fingers stroking idly through fluffy white fur, Cade waited a moment and then began. "I saw a letter he was writing—the Archduke. I don't know the recipient—this was the third or fourth page. Something about everything being ready for his wife's trip to the Continent, and how peaceful it would be at Great Welkin with her gone. Joking that the King would be in his debt for getting Iamina out of his way. But the way he wrote it, Mieka—it's as if he doesn't expect either of them to return."

"Well, Panshilara's served her purpose, right? A daughter to marry Roshlin, a son to marry Levenie. And it ain't like he's madly in love with her. Who'd even notice if she and Iamina stayed on the Continent for the rest of their lives? What else did you see?"

"He wrote that Fairwalk's gold was at the workshop in New Halt, and he'd seen the designs and looked forward to the samples. A couple of weeks, he thinks, before they arrive for his approval."

"Samples of what?"

"How should I know? He complained about how much he's having to pay Fairwalk for the gold and his silence, and he's aware that whoever he's writing to will say it's worth it."

Mieka thought that over. "Why doesn't he just have Fairwalk killed?"

"Maybe Kearney was smart enough to write down everything about the deal, with the threat that if he dies of anything other than fully demonstrable natural causes, the letter will be sent to the King. It's what I'd do."

Mieka chewed the inside of his lip for a moment. "The gold is going to a workshop. Not to make a dinner service for forty, I'll wager, or a hundred goblets, or a couple of thousand wedding necklets."

"There was something about an exchange rate, too. Five for three to start, then down to five for four as a warning to those who didn't act fast enough." He sat up straighter, dislodging the cat, who slithered down from his knees to the floor and stalked off. Cade ignored the animal, scowling as he tried to remember. "It's coins, Mieka, it has to be coins. He wrote about melting down the old to keep up with demand for the new, and prices would be unsteady for a bit but that didn't matter, things would settle soon enough, when—no, *after*! 'After the people become accustomed to my profile'!"

Mieka hugged the pillow to his chest, trying not to shiver. "His profile . . . on gold coins . . . made at the New Halt workshop . . ." Meeting Cade's gaze, he said quietly, "You know what this means, Quill. For the first time we can be absolutely certain that he's going to make a try for the throne."

"But we still don't know *how* he plans to do it." Cade wrapped his arms around himself, as if he struggled against the same chill that had come over Mieka. "And I don't know what to do about any of it."

"What else did you see?"

"I didn't see it, exactly. It was kind of like another Elsewhen was trying to crowd out this one. That's happened before." Mieka wanted to ask *When?*, but Cade went on quickly, "Just a voice, low and harsh. And darkness. A man's voice. 'It's not the drinking that makes them what they are, it's what they are that makes the drinking necessary. So you see how wrong you were.'" He looked surprised, as if recalling something he hadn't noticed at the time. "And there was another voice. I could barely hear it. He was saying, 'Do it, do it.' Then someone screamed." He sat forward, arms still wreathing his chest. "I don't know what that means. Any ideas?"

"He could be talking about liquor, couldn't he?" Mieka asked uncertainly. "Enough whiskey or thorn, and they become necessary. Nobody knows that better than me." He saw the compassion in Cade's eyes, and the pride that Mieka had been fighting this grim battle and (mostly) winning. "But I've never heard of anybody who *has* to drink in order to survive, and that's what *necessary* sounds like, doesn't it?"

"I should've followed it," Cade fretted. "I should've ditched what I was seeing about the Archduke, and gone after this other one."

"The gold is more important," Mieka stated. "And—listen, Quill, I've just thought of something. Mightn't it be inside your head anyways? When you've seen an Elsewhen, you store it away so you can look at it again later, I know that. But what if even if you didn't really *see* all of it, couldn't it be there all the same?"

Pursing his lips, then biting on the lower one, at length he shook his head. "I think it's like something that happens in life, like meeting somebody or taking a walk. It has to happen before I can remember it."

Disappointed that it hadn't been the brilliant insight he'd hoped, Mieka was about to ask what Cade thought could be done about Fairwalk's gold when Derien stalked through the door, followed closely by Rumble.

"Are we speaking to each other today?" he asked Cade, who accepted the cat onto his lap again and eyed his brother warily.

Mieka repressed the impulse to roll his eyes. Sometimes the two of them forgot that they were supposed to be furious with each other, and things were as they'd always been. Then one or the other would remember. Mieka had just about had enough of it.

"Even if we aren't, there's something you want to tell me," Cade said.

"Yeh. Well, actually, Mieka." The boy faced him. "One of my friends at school heard something the other day. It's about that fox."

"Fox? Oh. Yeh." Along with thoughts about drinking and thorn, he diligently avoided thoughts about his former wife. "What about it?"

"His mother's maid is cousin to one of the gardeners at Great Welkin, and she heard from him that the fox got caught in a trap—it couldn't get out of the grounds because of the walls. Lived on mice, I suppose. Anyway, after a couple of months of thinking they could catch it using the dogs, the Archduchess finally said to kennel the dogs and set traps. If it was running around free, she said, it might attack one of the children. Well, it got caught in one of the traps. They found—" He looked sick, but finished steadily, "It had gnawed its own foot off to escape, but of course it couldn't run, and bled to death."

Mieka shivered for real this time. "Poor little thing."

"Better than being torn to pieces by the dogs," Cade said. "Think about it. Cornered and ripped to shreds, or doing what it could and setting itself free."

Mieka almost made a protest, but Derien was nodding. "I happen to agree with you. Better to go out free and fighting than overpowered and helpless."

Mieka looked from one to the other of them. Did they honestly believe that? For himself, in an equivalent situation, he'd prefer to be surrounded and talk or magick his way out of it, rather than have the escape kill him. Well, at least Cayden and Derien were in sympathy with each other again. Mieka said, "Mayhap you can help us with something, Dery. What should we do about the Archduke's gold?"

The boy frowned. "Don't you mean Lord Fairwalk's gold?"

Mieka cast an apprehensive glance at Cade, as if the slip had been an accident and he was sorry. It hadn't been an accident, and he wasn't sorry.

Cade made short work of telling it. Elsewhen; Archduke; coins with his profile minted in New Halt from Fairwalk's gold; entirely evident now that he intended to make himself King.

"We can't demand that Fairwalk give it to us, to compensate," he concluded. "We can't use ingots or whatever any more than he can."

"And if you do let on that you know about the gold," Dery said, "that would bring the Archduke down on us like a wyvern on a flock of sheep."

Mieka asked, "Could we tell Miriuzca?"

"How much does she understand about finance?" Cade countered.

Mieka snorted. "She doesn't have to understand anything about finance. All she has to understand is that the Archduke intends to make himself King. She'll understand that much, right enough."

"If she knew," Derien said slowly, "wouldn't she do something? Let it slip somehow, say or do something the Archduke finds threatening—"

"—and then she'll be more of a target to him than she was to her own brother," Cade finished, grim-faced.

Dery had decided to sit down, choosing the desk chair, turning it to face his brother. "Doesn't it work that you become King and *then* get the coins minted? When Meredan came to the throne, the coins were struck and exchanged for the old ones at the banks, and went into general circulation that way. Slowly. As the merchants came to deposit at the banks, they were given the new coins in place of the old, and those got melted down to be restruck as Meredan's coins."

"If the Archduke grabs the throne and has the coins all ready to be distributed—"

"Quill, didn't you say he'd trade five for three? That'd make him real popular, real fast!"

"Five for three?" Derien's brown eyes widened. "That would muck up prices for months!"

"Ah, what a thing it is," Mieka sighed, "to have an actual education!"

"If you'd bothered to pay attention in school, you might've learned something we could put to the purpose now," Cade retorted. "Miriuzca must have *somebody* near to her who can 'discover' that gold and confiscate it or something."

"No good. Same result as if she confronted the Archduke openly. It would put her in terrible danger, her and Roshlin."

"Not the Prince," Derien said without doubt. "He's supposed to marry the Archduke's daughter, and the Princess is supposed to marry his son. Oh, don't look at me that way, Cayden, everybody's known that forever! Even if nobody ever talks about it openly."

"Granted," Cade said, "but isn't it also true that the thinking is he'd wait until Prince Roshlin and little what's-her-name were old enough, and *then* take the throne? That would give everybody a lot more time."

"To do what, exactly?" Mieka asked. It was the obvious question, and obviously not welcomed. He answered it—sort of—himself. "We need somebody a whole lot smarter than any of us who can figure the whole thing out."

"We can't tell anybody, Mieka!" Derien was shaking his head emphatically. "Nobody can know about Cade's Elsewhens, and how could we explain what we know otherwise?"

"Blye already knows about the gold," Cade mused. "Maybe she'll have an idea what to do about that, anyways. As for the rest of it—you're right, Dery, it can't go any further than the three of us."

Mieka decided that the evening—by the sudden chiming of the Minster bells, it was fully midnight—could come to a close on this happy note of agreement between the brothers. It was long past Derien's bedtime, and Cade's face was ghastly pale. Elsewhen and thorn; bad combination. "Maybe tomorrow one of us will've had a scathingly brilliant idea. For now, I'm for sleep, or I'll never be able to stagger to the glass baskets tomorrow night."

Good nights were said, and Derien departed to his own bedchamber. Mieka lingered to make sure Cade got into his nightshirt and between the covers.

"And no blockweed, neither!" Mieka warned.

"Don't have any. All I asked Brishen for was this." He stretched head to foot, long bones cracking. "Mieka . . . you know that I can't really trust anything I see when it's thorn that provokes the Elsewhens. It could be just my brain plotting out things like when I'm writing a play."

"Tell me this, then. Do you trust your own mind? Your instincts?"

A shrug. "Mostly."

"Does anything else make any sense about this gold? Any other way of turning it into an asset for Fairwalk, I mean, instead of just a lot of shiny metal in boxes?"

"Not that I can think of."

"All right, then. Go to bed, Quill. Get some sleep."

He was at the door before Cade spoke again. "Mieka . . . I still haven't seen Derien."

And that was one of the things he had most wanted to know about. "An Elsewhen might come to you all on its own, y'know."

"You have more faith than I do."

Over his shoulder, Mieka smiled and said, "You only just noticed?"

*　　*　　*

On the first part of the drive to Seekhaven for Trials, Touchstone was privileged to host two distinguished guests. The coach that would carry the pair the rest of the way, with appropriate stops for food and sleep, tagged along behind Touchstone's wagon, ready at any moment to receive its passengers, as any Royal conveyance must do.

The coach had been borrowed from Princess Miriuzca. The guests were Lady Vrennerie Eastkeeping and Lady Megueris Mindrising. And the reason they'd caught up to Touchstone and demanded to ride along for a while was that they had a tale to tell.

The gentlemen made the ladies welcome with a tour of the wagon's comforts and marvels—which Vrennerie had already seen—then brought out chairs, wine, oatcakes, and sharp cheese. Jeska elected to sit in his strung hammock, while Rafe and Cade, being tallest and long-leggedest, took the other two chairs and Mieka perched on the sink shelf. All four prepared to listen to the ladies as they took turns telling their story.

"I'll start at the start, or where it started for Megs and me," began Vrennerie. "Blye sent her a note, and she showed it to me, and I showed it to our Lady, who read it through several times before burning it."

Mieka nodded wholehearted approval. Miriuzca was no fool.

"She had me write back to Blye," Megs continued, "with a single question: How much gold was there in this cellar?"

"And she asked me," Cade said, unable to contain himself, "and it took *hours* to figure it out!"

Mieka knew what this had involved: trying to calculate how much it would take to make a five-to-three exchange for every coin now held by the banks. They'd taken a gold royal down to Mistress Mirdley's stillroom and weighed it on the scale she used for mixing potions, come up with an approximate answer, and went to tell Blye their estimate. But as to why the weight of the gold was important, none of them had been able to say.

"When we received Blye's answer, we told the Princess, and she thought for a while more," Megs went on. She glanced at Vrennerie, whose eyes sparkled over the rim of her wineglass. "We talked for a long time, almost all night. And the next day, wouldn't you know it, we just happened to run across Lord Fairwalk along Narbacy Street!"

"Such luck to find him," Rafe drawled.

"Wasn't it?" Vrennerie grinned. "And considering that we're telling this to the best players in the Kingdom, we'll do the next bit in the form of a play. Megs, you be Fairwalk, and I'll be you and me."

Megs instantly ruffled up her hair to mimic Fairwalk's untidy fringe and assumed a smile that was a marvel of fawning snobbery. For her part, Vrennerie made her eyes wide and guileless, all trace of mocking humor gone. Mieka stifled a snigger.

"A private performance!" Jeska exclaimed. "Play on, good ladies, play on!"

Cade hushed him with a gesture that turned into a graceful invitation to proceed.

"Your Lordship!" Vrennerie simpered. "Oh, how fortunate to find you here! We were just speaking of you!"

"Were you?" Megs seemed to be struggling between wariness and delight. "I am undeservedly honored, don't you see, but I can't really imagine what anything to do with me might—well, as I say, greatly honored, I'm sure."

"Now, don't be so modest! We all heard of your exploits across the Ocean Sea! How many thrilling adventures you must have had! But the Princess is terribly hurt that you haven't come to see her and tell her all about it in person." Now Vrennerie changed her voice a little, giving it Megs's northland inflections. "As busy as he's been, Lady Vrennerie, you can't really expect him to fritter away an afternoon like that! Besides, my Lord, we've discovered your secret!"

Megs frowned. "Do I really sound like that?"

"Don't break character!" Jeska cried.

"Simply not done!" Cade seconded. "If this were my play and you were my masquers, I'd sack you both!"

"Well," Rafe said kindly, "you have to make allowances for amateurs."

"Oh, shut it," Mieka complained. "I want to hear the rest!"

Megs graciously nodded her gratitude to him. Then she looked at Vrennerie. "What did I say next?"

"Your Lordship has been waiting to call on Her Royal Highness, haven't you? Waiting until the gift is ready?"

"G-g-g-gift?" Megs ran her fingers through the hair spilling across her forehead, disordering it into tangled feesks. "Your Ladyships have me at a disadvantage—I—I don't—"

"Oh, come now!" Vrennerie said, back in her own voice. "We heard it from one of the mistresses of the wardrobe, who had it from her cousin's husband's sister's niece—" Again she switched voices; Mieka reflected that the stage really had lost two accomplished performers when they'd been born female. As Megs, she said, "No, no, it was her husband's cousin's *brother's* niece! And she's walking out of an evening with the grandson of the chief cook of the Goldsmiths Guildhall, who says everybody's in a positive tizzy over the lavishness of the gift!"

Megs didn't repeat the stuttering; Mieka admired her instincts. "Your Ladyships mustn't demean yourselves by listening to idle gossip from servants, beneath your notice, don't you see—"

Vrennerie pulled a mournful face. "Then it's not true? We haven't ruined the surprise? It's only that we just can't hold back our gratitude and amazement at so wonderful a gift for the Princess!" She paused, but didn't change voices as she exclaimed, "A bathtub! A solid gold bathtub! It's simply *too* good of you!"

Megs became incoherent.

"Oh, it must be true—do tell us that it's true! She'd be so disappointed!"

Megs flapped her hands and tugged her forelock.

As Megs again, Vrennerie purred, "But do you know, she also said that as wonderful as such a thing would be, she wanted us to tell you that it's really the thought that counts most, and she'd be perfectly happy with, for instance, a little golden cup for each of her children, so that they'll always remember your goodness and generosity." Another quick shift to her own voice. "And as for the rest of the gold—Lord and Lady save us, there must be an awful lot of it, to make a bathtub!"

"Not so very much," Megs mumbled.

"She says she'd be so pleased if you'd make it the very first contribution to her new sanatorium. She's very concerned that there are so few facilities for the sick, and many people unable to afford a physicker, and if you present the gold to the Goldsmiths Guild, they can give you the value of it and you can give *that* as the start for building the sanatorium! Isn't that a wonderful idea?"

Megs seemed to make a mighty effort. "Wh-whatever Her Royal

Highness wishes is of course m-my command. Honored to obey, don't you see!"

By now Touchstone was having a collective seizure from laughing so much. Vrennerie and Megueris rose from their chairs, steadying themselves against the gentle rocking of the wagon, and bowed their appreciation of this tribute to their performance. Jeska slid gracefully out of the hammock and onto his knees, hands clasped before him.

"Considering well and truly what I have just seen with my very own eyes," he intoned, "I pray most sincerely to the gracious Lord, the gentle Lady, every single one of the Angels, and all the Old Gods that women are *never* allowed onto a stage!"

"Was that a dare?" Megs asked.

"Sounded like it," Vrennerie replied.

"Hmm. Well, give me a year or two—"

"And a conversation with Princess Miriuzca," Mieka interrupted slyly. "I'm sure she'll help."

"Oh, Gods," Rafe moaned. "Lads, we're done for!"

"I do hope so," Megs said sweetly.

Mieka hopped off the shelf and refilled everyone's glasses. Toasts were drunk, and at length Vrennerie said with regret that they'd best be getting back into their own coach, or the driver and footman would be telling salacious tales.

"My husband won't believe a word of it," she said with mock chagrin. "But Megs can't afford any slights to her reputation that a certain attractive young lord might be hearing."

Mieka glanced sidelong at Cade to see if this had struck home. No such luck. In fact, he joined with Jeska in trying to tease the name out of Vrennerie. They had no luck, either, and soon enough they'd called up to Rist on the coachman's bench for a halt and were escorting the ladies to their own coach.

Managing to slow Megs down enough for a brief whisper in her ear, he said, "I hear your father married again, and has a son."

"Yes, isn't it wonderful?" She turned and looked him straight in the eyes.

This really *was* a dare.

"It's why I've been away from Court for so long. A first baby at thirty-six can be dangerous, and I couldn't bear to leave Lady Tomlyn or my father until everything was quite all right."

"They must be very happy," Mieka said, signaling that she needn't do any more persuading. He would keep her secret. "What did they name the boy?"

"Guerys," she replied, smiling her pleasure at his interest—or mayhap her relief. "It was sweet of her to name him after me, wasn't it?"

If he'd expected some subtle tribute to Cayden, he didn't show it. "So now your father has a male heir, and you can do as you like—well, even more as you like, I mean! You can become a Steward."

"I mean to," she told him.

"Megs!" Vrennerie called. "Hurry up! We have to reach the first stopping before nightfall!"

Mieka had one more quiet question as he walked with her to the coach. "Will we be seeing your father and his wife and son in Gallantry-banks?"

"Of course! Just as soon as Guerys is old enough to travel."

He understood this to mean that the boy had inherited nothing readily recognizable from Cayden—not the gray eyes, nor the wide mouth, nor the distinctive nose. Pity. As for the other things he might have got from his father . . . well, they'd all have to wait and see.

As he handed her onto the coach's bottom step, she murmured, "You've never asked 'Why him?'"

Startled, he looked up to find her frowning down at him. For an intelligent girl, she asked some very silly questions. "Why *not* him?"

Megs settled in the coach beside Vrennerie. Mieka shut the half-door and made sure the latch was secure.

"Beholden to you, Mieka," said Megs.

"Yes," he replied softly. "You are."

Chapter 22

"The Shadowstone," announced Rist, and there they were, greeted with pride and pleasure by Mistress Luta. Upstairs they discovered signs—not slips of paper, but etched brass plates—on the chamber doors that read VERED GOLDBRAIDER, JESCHENAR BOWBENDER, CHAT-TIM CZILLAG, and so forth. After bidding farewell to Rist for the next fortnight, Touchstone settled in. Cayden, who had not inhabited a room with his name on the door since leaving Sagemaster Emmot's Academy, was alone in it for less than an hour before Mieka came in with all his gear.

"Makes me feel a right fool, it does," he announced, dumping his belongings on the second bed. "Sleeping someplace with me name on the door, as if they're worried I'll get so drunk, I won't remember where the bed is!"

Cade knew instantly that *drunk* was the key word here. Mieka needed to be near him. At Redpebble Square, a corridor away was good enough. Here, with a well-stocked bar only one flight downstairs . . .

"A nice tribute, though," Cade said. "D'you think anybody really thinks that by sleeping in the same bed where Rauel slept, some of his talent will transfer to them—like fleas?"

Mieka laughed and walked over to the window, where the trees were rustling in a gentle wind. "It was nice, seeing Vren and Megs again. And I'm thinking that some of *our* talents as players must've rubbed off on them. A solid gold bathtub, forsooth!"

Cade stretched out on his bed. He'd long since grown used to the wagon hammock, but there was nothing like the luxury of a good, wide-armed sprawl. "Shame I can't work that one up into a nice little ten-minute farce."

"One day. One day. Only, the thing of it is, Quill . . ." He turned, and his voice deepened to seriousness. "None of it is a farce. It's real. We know bits and pieces, but we don't know enough. Are you sure that what you heard from the other Elsewhen didn't have anything to do with it?"

"I'm sure." It had, in fact, been a part of the Elsewhen he'd rejected on the night before Wintering. In that one, Bexan had been scream-ing; Elf-light shone on her blood-covered hands; Minster chimes struck the hour close by. Was this second Elsewhen even related to the first? Instinct told him it was. Yet this time he'd not heard Bexan, and it had been so dark, he'd seen nothing and heard only one man's rough voice talk about drinking, and the other man say *"Do it."* No chimes, no screaming. Something had changed because of something he'd done. Or not done. He would never know. The scene might return, and it might not. But he had no regrets about not following it. Had he done so at Vered's house, Yazz would be dead and Mieka would be in prison waiting to be executed for murder. In the second instance, the Archduke's plans for Lord Fairwalk's gold would be progressing apace and the whole of Albeyn would be at risk. Which it still was, he re-minded himself, solid gold bathtub or not.

He couldn't help but smile and shake his head at the thought of it. "If anybody had ever told me that Vren and Megs were capable of what we saw on the road here—Mieka, we are a terrible influence on those ladies."

"Princess Iamina and the fanatic crowd were right all along," the Elf agreed. "Theater is dangerous."

"Subversive. A threat to the good order of society."

"Don't forget salacious—but only if you do it right!"

The Crystal Sparks and Hawk's Claw joined them at the Shadow-stone Inn for dinner in the back garden. To the surprise of everyone except Touchstone, Chattim Czillag and Sakary Grainer strolled in the gate after the table had been cleared.

Trenal Longbranch widened his eyes. "What're you doing here?"

"Missing the old days?" asked Mirko Challender.

"Bored out of our skulls," Chat responded, and called for another

round of ale. "Gallybanks with nary a player in it for a fortnight and
more—nobody to talk to or drink with or heckle from the cheap seats."

The excuse, though plausible, wasn't the real reason for the presence
of half the Shadowshapers. Touchstone knew it; the others didn't.
Cade had absolutely forbidden any sly glances, mysterious smiles,
meaningfully arched brows, or any other silent hints that they knew
something nobody else did. As for talking about it—the secret was no
ordinary secret, and much too scrumptious to be shared.

Before their withdrawal from the Circuits, the Shadowshapers had
accomplished something for which all the other established groups
were abjectly grateful. For them, there was no more draw for the Thirteen. The younger and less experienced players were still assigned a
Peril for the competition, but those with a few Royal or Ducal Circuits behind them could do whatever piece they wished. This year
Cade intended for Touchstone to perform *Window Wall*. Both plays
were finished. Teasing the audiences with the first play would bring
them in droves later on to see the whole of it. On their third day at
Seekhaven, they did a run-through in the rehearsal hall, then proceeded to relax and enjoy themselves as they'd never been able to do
in the days when the Shadowshapers were still in competition.

These days there was actually a Duke for whom the Ducal Circuit
was named. Prince Roshlin, five years old, had been created Duke of
Overbourne. ("Ovenburn?" Mieka had asked, bewildered. "No, *Overbourne*," Cade had replied. "It means a 'bridge.' *Bourne* is a Northern
word for a 'stream.' So if something is *over* a *bourne*, it's a bridge." "Why
couldn't they just say so, then?" "It's a very old—" "It's a stupid word,
a stupid name, a stupid title, and I bet when the little mite grows up,
he'll think it's stupid, too." "Think if he'd been the son of somebody
named Prickwell. He'd be stuck with it." "You made that up." "Did
not. I went to school with—" "Even if that's true, it's not stupid, Quill.
It's just tragic.") The dukedom had been in abeyance since Meredan's
great-uncle died childless about sixty years ago, and, with its accompanying revenues, had been granted to Roshlin now that he had a small
household of his own. Miriuzca was bringing him to Seekhaven this
year—not to attend any performances, for he was much too young
even for "Bewilderland," but to meet the three groups who won places
on the Ducal Circuit.

Lederris Daggering of the Crystal Sparks, thin and jittery and with a look about him of too much thorn, asked after Vered and his family. He addressed the question to everybody in general, for it was anybody's guess which of the former Shadowshapers were actually speaking to each other again. The members of Touchstone, of course, didn't have to guess.

Sakary answered, smiling slightly. "The twins are thriving. So are the other twins."

"Bexan is so little!" Mieka said. "How did she ever manage to carry *four* babies?"

"Pikseys are born even smaller than Elves," Jeska commented. "I agree, though, it's an amazement that they all lived and that she survived labor. That Wizardly heritage of Vered's could've meant tragedy."

Or, Cade reflected, a complete incompatibility of bloodlines that made conceiving a child impossible. Blye and Jed had given up hoping. Jez's new wife, Eirenn Wooltangle, had declared that Number Eight, Redpebble Square, was plenty big enough for a dozen or more children. If not sons and daughters, then there would be nephews and nieces.

"To Bexan," Chat said, raising his glass. "Hearty and heartful, that's the kind of woman to marry!"

"To Bexan," Cade seconded. "And to the nurses who have to keep track of four infants at once!"

"I think they hired one for each," Sakary said. "Which doubled their household staff and probably tripled the housekeeping budget. Good thing Wavertree is a big place. They're gonna need it!"

Mieka went out walking that night and didn't return until dawn. Cade suspected that he'd found congenial female company for at least part of the time, but didn't ask. All that mattered was that he was no longer using thorn, and the drunken revelries of the past were just that: in the past.

Touchstone treated the fortnight of Trials as more or less of a holiday. Everybody knew they'd be First Flight on the Royal again. Talented and celebrated as the Crystal Sparks, Hawk's Claw, and Black Lightning were, none of them quite measured up. Touchstone had indeed become the standard by which all others were tested. Occasionally Cayden fretted that they might begin to take things too much for granted. The adoring applause that ended their every performance argued otherwise. He started to wonder, though, if it mightn't be time for them to do what the Shadowshapers had done, and strike out on their own. He'd abandoned the idea for the two long years of paying off their debts; even though the Crown took a goodly share of the profits, Touchstone had needed the guaranteed income of the Royal Circuit. Maybe next year . . .

As he lolled in the sunny garden or strolled the street beside the river, Cade knew he'd needed the relaxation. Worry about Mieka was fading; Rafe had stayed true to his word to Crisiant, and had become as abstemious as Mieka; Jeska was calmly ecstatic in his marriage and fatherhood; Cade had the satisfaction of writing again. Touchstone was everything Cade had ever hoped it would become, and more.

As for heading out on their own, forsaking the Royal Circuit . . . he had no concerns that what had happened to the Shadowshapers would happen to them. Touchstone had never had that problem of two competing tregetours. And the thought of being paid what they were really worth, rather than what the Master of the King's Revelries could bargain, was tempting. Never worrying about money again . . . never enduring another sleepless night of wondering where Dery's school fees would come from . . . never steeling himself for a visit to the bank to find out how much money he didn't have. Tempting? Absolutely seductive.

He managed to resist the seduction of another thorn-stimulated Elsewhen. He still didn't know how the Archduke meant to seize the throne. He'd never yet seen Derien. And there were those two fragments to tantalize him. The more he thought about them, the more nervous they made him. To whom was the gravel-voiced man talking in the darkness? What did the other man mean by *"Do it"*? Why had Bexan been screaming?

By the tenth day at Seekhaven, Hawk's Claw had entertained the ladies at the Pavilion with a rowdy comedy that Trenal Longbranch had been working on for a couple of years now; the competition had been held, with Touchstone winning First Flight yet again, and the invitation had come to perform on the last night of Trials. Prince Roshlin, Duke of Overbourne, had met the three groups assigned to the Ducal Circuit, distinguishing himself by marching right up to each cluster of tall young men and saying in a high, clear voice, "I'm very pleased to meet you," just as his mother had taught him. She had *not* taught him to peer up at the Kindlesmiths' red-haired glisker and ask, "Can you show me how to do magic?" The young man cast a panicky glance at Princess Miriuzca, then recovered himself and replied, "I'd be glad to, Your Grace, but I haven't my glass withies at the moment. Perhaps another time?"

One or two of the courtiers gasped at this presumption. But the Princess smiled; all was well. Still, the incident got several people to wondering whether the scant dollops of Wizardly and Elfen and mayhap other sorts of magical blood in the Albeyni Royal line might just work their way to the surface, and endow the young Prince with abilities that would not please his pious great-aunt Iamina.

Touchstone was favored with their usual lunching in the Castle grounds, attended by Princess Miriuzca; Lady Vrennerie; her husband, Lord Kelinn Eastkeeping; and Lady Megueris. Cade was both grateful and irritated when Mieka maneuvered him to a seat at the table next to Megs. That he no longer interested her as a bed companion was obvious by the fact that she treated him exactly as she treated everyone else. Hells, she flirted more with Jeska than with Cade. This was irritating, too. Some part of him was grateful, though, for it appeared this was the end of his own nervous anticipation whenever he was around her. He had enough to fret about these days without worrying whether or not Megs would show up at the Shadowstone Inn one night and slip into his bed. And he knew that Mieka and Rafe and Jeska—Hells, any man worth the naming as a man—would be disgusted with him.

Vered and Rauel arrived (separately) and took up residence in the rooms named for them at the Shadowstone. Vered sneaked in at dawn one morning, but Rauel made an entrance, sauntering into the tap room at dinnertime with a bag of withies slung over his shoulder. Blye's new sister-in-law had woven several lengths of wool in Windthistle purple and Cindercliff gray, accented with thin threads of silver and gold. From these she had made drawstring bags for Blye's favorite customers: Touchstone, Hawk's Claw, and the Crystal Sparks—and now the Shadowshapers. Sakary and Chat were dining with friends on the other side of town, so they missed this silent public declaration of the Shadowshapers' intentions. Tobalt Fluter, leaning back with his chair propped against the wall while he sipped an after-dinner brandy, choked on the liquor as the chair righted itself with a soft thud. Vered laughed at him. Rafe pounded him on the back. Rauel gave them all his innocent, boyish smile.

"Just like that fool glisker of ours to leave the most important bits at home," he told Vered.

"Then it's true?" Tobalt managed in a half-strangled voice.

"Many, many things are true, my son," Vered intoned, examining the play of lamplight through the single glass of beer he'd been nursing all evening. "What exactly did you have in mind?"

The next day, during Touchstone's turn in the rehearsal hall, they were joined by the Shadowshapers. At Vered's request, they stayed to watch and comment upon a couple of scenes from *Blood Plight*—a play on words, for the latter meant both a "promise" and a "predicament." The young Steward-in-training who presided over the hall during Trials this year was goggle-eyed when the Shadowshapers showed up. He was enjoined to absolute secrecy.

"To be honest," said Sakary, scrubbing long fingers through his dark red hair, "me mates here promised I can try out a bespelling that me old granny taught me years ago. So it makes no nevermind to me if you shout it from the rooftops. I've always wanted to turn somebody into a two-headed lizard who can't agree with himself on which way to go." He paused. "Of course, if you don't know where you're going, you can't get lost."

"My lame hop-frog is better than your old lizard any day of the week," scoffed Vered.

"Shut it," Mieka chided. "You're scaring the lad." He smiled kindly at the young man, who seemed half-certain he couldn't possibly be turned into a lizard or a frog, and half-certain that if anybody could do it, the Shadowshapers could. "Just you stand right outside that door in the front hall, and make sure nobody gets in. Right? Right!"

The first play of *Blood Plight* was done and dusted. The second had been seen by no one other than the Shadowshapers themselves down in the undercroft of Redpebble Square. Cade thought he might have a few ideas about what Vered would do, but had kept them to himself. He and Mieka and Rafe and Jeska sat on the floor in the middle of the hall to watch, listen, and marvel.

To set themselves up for the concluding play, the Shadowshapers

ran through a brief scene from the first. There was no scenery, no costuming, no magic at all as Rauel, the Wizard, confronted his old friend
who would choose to become one of the *balaurin*.

"That which troubles you, my old friend, also troubles me. How
long have we known each other? How well do I know you, and you
me?" Rauel's voice was suddenly deeper, more resonant, as he met
Vered's gaze. "We are known, one to the other, after all these years. So
tell me, my old friend. Share your thoughts and your fears—share your
soul with me."

Vered replied, with a slight tremor in his voice, "With you and no
one else."

This was real, Cade realized with a wrenching of the heart, more
moved by this exchange than by anything he'd ever witnessed on a
stage. He always held himself aloof from the magic, observing rather
than experiencing. There was no magic here; Chat's hands were empty;
there was only the honest emotion of the words and the men speaking them. His mind began to analyze the possibilities, so clearly and
poignantly demonstrated to him, of a theater with no magic at all—
until he recognized that he was backing off again, uncomfortable and
even a little resentful that Rauel and Vered had made him feel so
much. He forced himself to pay attention, to open himself a little to
what was being done onstage, because he owed it to his friends who had
asked for his opinions. But an idea nagged at him that perhaps magic
in theater was not so much a tool as a crutch. Did it interfere with or
even prevent moments such as these, moments that were real and
true? Did it compel rather than evoke emotion in an audience? Did it
hide the inadequacies of a player or the players behind the flash-dazzle
of—of black lightning splitting the cold white air?

That group from the Continent—considered the best, presumably—
they wouldn't be in business if they didn't satisfy *something* within their
audiences. They adamantly condemned magic. Nothing to work with
but wood and paint, cheap cloth and shoddy props—and words. Yes,
it could be done just with words. Cayden had just had that proved to
him. He'd not give up Mieka's skills of scenery and costuming, scents
and textures, tastes and sounds. What Mieka did was art. But so could
the words be. In Jeska's handling, with Cade's own special gifts . . .

What if all the maneuvering of emotion by the withies were left
out? How many plays could stand on their own?

And, the question with the most sting to it, the only question that meant anything: *Are my words good enough?*

When his gaze refocused onto the rehearsal stage, Chat had clothed Rauel in a flowing blue robe over brown leather trousers and a white shirt. Vered was in chain mail, sword at his side. Cade settled down to concentrate on the scene being played out before him.

Because it was Vered's work, it was talky, with ideas piling up one onto another. Because Rauel had worked on it, too, there was physical movement, emotion, and a breathtakingly difficult sequence where the Wizard conjured up the aftermath of a battle, hazed with smoke and reeking of blood. The horror wasn't in the slaughter. It was in the manner of the killing. The scores of bodies. The corresponding number of heads nearby.

"It's the only sure and certain way," Vered said wearily. "The silver and the garlic, all they can ever do is repel and repulse *balaurin*. I know, because I've experimented on myself."

Rauel flinched. "You're not like them!"

"Am I not? Do you see those pathetic dead things stacked like cordwood, their heads like a mound of rocks to be smashed down to gravel? I did that! I alone! And even to accomplish only those deaths, we lost more than two hundred of our own!"

The Wizard waved a hand, banishing the conjured scene. "Let me be clear on this. You're saying that you cannot do it alone. That others must become like you—"

"Like *them*."

"Like *you*," the Wizard repeated forcefully. "You're no more one of *them* than I am!"

The Warrior sighed deeply. Slowly, softly, he began to walk the width of the stage towards the Wizard, talking all the while, his voice as gentle as his footsteps. "Does it burn inside your body, the smell of blood? Does it howl through your veins? Does it claw at you with the hunger? Does it shroud your eyes with crimson in those sweet, sweet instants after a kill, when it knows it will soon feed? Until you can say, *Yes it does*, to all of these things—"

He paused, within arm's reach now of the Wizard, then took a single, small step. The Wizard took a quick, involuntary step back, instantly ashamed.

"You see?" asked the Warrior. "You're wondering if the hunger has been sated recently enough. Can I see the vein pulsing in your neck and hear the beating of your heart without wanting *your* blood?"

"No!" the Wizard cried. "You are the same man! The same face, the same eyes—the same honor—the same heart!"

"Give me your hand."

The Wizard hesitated only a moment—but it was enough to bring a bitter smile to the Warrior's face. The Wizard's hand was guided to the Warrior's chest, pressed there for long seconds. The Wizard leaped back, horrified.

"Do you understand now?" asked the Warrior. "Oh, it's still there. Silent and still. Tell me, my old friend, what is a heart without a beat? When this is all over, and their armies are defeated and the heads have rotted to skulls enough to build a warning wall lest they think again to conquer us, you will do for me what I cannot do for myself. And the rest of me will be as dead as my heart."

The scene faded into shadows. Cade felt himself shaking. He hadn't known that about the *balaurin*. A heart, but no heartbeat . . .

Mieka was trembling, too, curled beside him, arms wrapped tightly round his knees. Cade wanted to touch him, comfort him, reassure himself that—well, he wasn't sure what kind of reassurance he needed, but it involved feeling Mieka warm and alive beside him.

Then the stage seemed to flare with light, capturing his gaze and his mind. He only had time to think how masterful the Shadowshapers were—and how much he resented their ease in manipulating him—before a scene emerged from their signature shadows.

The Wizard, all in white and garlanded with the crown of fragrant green leaves that betokened victory, stood in the sunlight in the mouth of a small, rough-hewn passage that became, behind and to the left, a torchlit cavern. A woman knelt before him, so gray of clothes and hair that she might have been a heap of fallen rock.

"And do you so plight yourself and your descendants?" he demanded. "To dedicate your life and their lives to this task?"

"I do so plight and swear," she answered, head still bowed in submission.

"For all that you have no choice but to do so." His voice thinned with contempt. "No one else will tolerate you."

"And *you* have no one but us," she retorted.

"Just the same . . ." He cupped in his hands tiny orbs of glowing color that merged into a single sphere that pulsed a deep blood red. "A binding, to keep you to your word—a mark upon your flesh—"

"Oy! What's this goin' on in here?"

The shout from the suddenly open doorway made everyone flinch. Chat was too good a glisker to lose control of his magic, and Sakary was too good a fettler to lose control of Chat's admirably controlled magic, and thus no one experienced a second shock that could come of a sudden break. Even though the magic extended only so far as the middle of the hall where Touchstone sat, and was being used on those who were themselves possessed of magic and theater players besides, any too-abrupt ending was dangerous.

After the threads of magic had gently disentangled him, Cade jumped to his feet and strode angrily to the door. "Who the fuck d'you think you are?" he demanded, furious not just for himself—he'd been caught up in the play—but more especially for the Shadowshapers. How dared this man interrupt? How dared he intrude?

"And who the fuck are *you*, to be that rude?" He was about forty, dressed in a regrettable excess of fashion, with slightly bleary brown eyes and a reek of alcohol about him. "High and mighty, are you?" he went on, sneering. "Think the whole world is your own just for the asking?"

"This is a private rehearsal!"

"So get the fuck out!" Rafe was suddenly beside him, grabbing one of the man's arms. Cade took the other one. They lifted him right off his feet and started for the door.

"Oy! You can't do this to me!"

"We've already done it, snarge." After a brief glance at Cade, he helped fling the man into the vestibule.

Just then the Steward-in-training who had charge of the rehearsal hall came running up, babbling apologies interspersed with "checking on time allotments" and "said he'd stay outside" and "rehearsal schedule missing from the front door" and "ran to get another one, but when I came back—"

"Just get him gone," Rafe growled.

"You've not heard the last of this!" blustered the ejected intruder.

Cade advised him to do something socially unacceptable with the nearest diseased goat, and slammed the door shut.

All traces of magic were gone now. Vered, Rauel, Chat, and Sakary stood center stage, as if preparing to take their bows. Cade, Rafe, Mieka, and Jeska stood in the middle of the hall, facing them, and it seemed for many long seconds that nobody could think of anything to say.

All at once Vered laughed out loud. "I'd like to say beholden to you on behalf of the group and ourselves, and I hope we passed the audition!"

Chapter 23

Heart beating as hard as if this were the very first time he'd ever been on any stage, Cayden slid between the curtains and waited for all eyes to focus on him.

"Your Majesty, Your Royal Highnesses, my Lords, Ladies, and Gentlemen," he said, "it is Touchstone's very great privilege to cede the honor of this performance on the final night of Trials to another group of players." Jeska had told him to wait out any reaction. There was none. The whole audience sat there stunned. So Cade said, very simply, "The Shadowshapers."

He scanned the faces as he spoke. Startlement, delight, amazement—and on a very few faces, suspicion. He made note of these. They were all together in the eighth row, and they belonged to Black Lightning and two young men who worked for them. Mainly there was shock. And there were more shocks to come.

Cade joined his partners in the wings as the Shadowshapers took the stage. Chat and Sakary were eager, quick to assume their places. Vered looked defiant; Rauel's smile kept coming and going like sunlight on a cloudy day. It was the first time they'd been in front of an audience in at least three years.

"That's it, lads," he heard Mieka whisper at his side. "No worries. Get out there and give it to 'em so great that even people who *look* like them will weep."

The familiar shadows swirled through Fliting Hall. Cade wasn't sure if it was better to be out there in the rows of seats, experiencing the whole of the plays, or here, watching and appreciating the artistry. Whichever, it would be a grand tale to tell in his old age: that he had seen the reunion show given by the inimitable Shadowshapers. Hells, he'd been instrumental in making it happen. Definitely a tale for the chroniclers.

The first play he had, of course, witnessed when it had first been performed. He'd seen much of the second in the rehearsal hall two days ago. Now, as the story of the invasion, the desperate gifting of special magic to a select group of Knights, and the voluntary transformation of the Warrior into a *balaurin*—for the battles could not be won otherwise—part of his mind was busily documenting the performance. The techniques of voice and gesture, the small details of setting and costume, sound and sensation, that made everything *real*. Where he stood, there was the gentlest backwash of magic, so he felt wisps of emotion as well. As the Wizard stood waiting for the outcome of the final battle, Cade felt again the sting of tears. He knew what was coming.

There was a slow fading of magic as gray and white shadows once again spun lazily through the hall. A brief respite for the audience—and for the players. Cade saw Princess Miriuzca, seated between Lady Vrennerie and Lady Megueris, take a long, steadying breath. He wondered suddenly if she had ever seen Black Lightning perform their awful little play where every member of the audience who had any sort of Goblin or Troll blood, or anything but Wizard or Elf forebears, felt dirty and ashamed. If she had seen it, and felt that shame, had she understood why?

He lost the train of thought as the Wizard and the Warrior argued back and forth, ending in a stalemate. Well, that was Vered and Rauel, wasn't it? Two stubborn, forceful, outrageously talented personalities, clashing over and over until they'd torn the Shadowshapers apart. It must have been very easy to write . . . or very, *very* hard. . . .

The Wizard argued that the *balaurin* Knights could live apart from those they had saved, and indeed must go on living lest the invaders return and their special, terrible skills be needed once again. He would see to their protection—and to the protection of the world of men from the Knights. The Warrior, unconvinced, forced the Wizard to repeat his promise: that once the danger was definitely over, the Wizard would kill him with his own sword.

The scene changed to the cavern. Cayden watched more carefully now, for this was the part of the play he hadn't seen. He could feel

Mieka at his left, trembling with tension, and Rafe to his right, still as stone, hardly even breathing.

There was something new in the background: a long, wide, rough-hewn stone plinth. The gray woman knelt and accepted the charge the Wizard placed upon her: to protect the Knights of the Balaur Tsepesh, to serve their needs, to see them safe in their exile from the society of men. In addition to the sphere of blood-red magic that hovered at her nape before melting into her bent spine, the Wizard proclaimed that he had set a secret mark upon her flesh that would appear on all her kind, so that they might identify themselves one to the other.

The Warrior entered, and the old woman faded into the shadows between torches. Beneath chain mail was a gray tunic, and wrapped around him was a gray velvet cloak. The Wizard explained his plan—or tried to.

"No."

"But it's perfect, I've thought everything through—"

"No." The Warrior unsheathed his sword and extended it, hilt-first. "You promised. You swore to me."

"I cannot—do not ask that of me!"

"You must."

"No!"

The Warrior cast the sword aside, clanging and sparking off stone. "You promised," he said softly, taking one step, then two, then three, towards the Wizard. "You and the other councilors, in your wisdom you thought to fight evil with magic. This I acknowledge was noble. It was brave. But it didn't work, did it? Evil cannot be overcome by goodness, even if magic fights on good's side. Evil can be met and over-matched only by its like. Thus I and the others took upon ourselves the same evil."

The Wizard was in agony. "How can you and they be evil, if you fought on the side of good? I will never believe that of you—I will never believe that!"

"Mayhap I ought to show you precisely what we have become."

Moving faster than seemed possible, he grabbed the Wizard's arm and stripped the sleeve back. His voice was low, soft, seductive.

"Blood. Thick, rich, sweet, pulsing blood. Within the bone cage of your ribs beats your heart, and at your throat, and here, at your wrist. Faster now, stronger, as the fear grows. Did you know that the fear is almost as nourishing as the blood?" He lifted the hand towards his lips, his gaze never leaving the Wizard's horrified face. And then, with a rasping cry, he lurched back and let go, falling to his knees.

"Trust me, do you?" he shouted hoarsely. "Nothing changed between us? Were that true, there would be no silver at your wrist—"

"My wife's gift to me upon our marriage! I always wear it, you *know* I always wear it! It's nothing to do with you!" The Wizard extended a hand, let it fall to his side, the sleeve covering the glinting silver bracelet. "It is you who cannot trust," he said sadly.

"No one," the Warrior agreed. "Not you, not myself. I beg of you. Show me that you do indeed trust me—by doing what you swore you would do. For I am such things as should not be left alive and free."

Slowly, with tears streaming down his face, the Wizard picked up the sword. He lifted it high and swung it wide and lopped off the Warrior's head.

Every single person in Fliting Hall screamed. Even Cade. Standing out of range of the more powerful magic, always holding himself aloof, going through even Touchstone's performances essentially untouched even when it was his own magic in the withies—Cade cried out with all the rest.

The torches flared, flickered, died into shadow. Then the gray woman appeared, carrying a candle, with which she went round to relight all the torches.

"The one I was to serve . . . well, he's dead now, right enough. But there are others. The plighting vow was made for me and my descendants, I received the mark on my flesh."

The torches all were lighted now. She went to the plinth, rummaged behind it, came out with a collection of smooth sticks, and sat on the floor before the plinth.

"Slave? No, not me, nor my kind. Call us what they will, but slaves we aren't. Nor Witches, neither!"

Her hands began to assemble the sticks, locking them into place with wooden pegs, making a rectangle as long as her arm and as wide as her shoulders.

"We'll serve them as they need. There's magic in it for us, right enough."

From her pocket she took a ball of blood-red yarn.

"The Knights, they took on themselves the evil of the *balaurin* to save all the rest of us. So we must be evil as well, to be serving evil. That's what everyone else will say. Even though what the Knights did went to the good, and we're the ones who keep them safe so if the danger comes again, they'll still be here—ah, can anyone say who's good in this tangle, and who's evil? It's too complicated for the likes of me."

She bent over her loom, tying off the warp and the weft.

"Just leave us Caitiffs to our work and weaving, can't they? Slave or Witch, in the end it's all the same to us."

*   *   *

"The real trick," Vered confessed a few hours later over a late supper at the Shadowstone Inn, "was keeping exactly to the pose. And I do mean *exactly*. Up until that very moment, y'see—"

"—it was him playing the Warrior," Rauel interrupted. "Chat had to work it so that—"

"—so there wasn't a hair's difference between Vered-for-real and Vered-by-magic," said Chat. "How and where he was kneeling, his hair falling to hide his face, the angle of his shoulders—originally he wanted to be standing up, but the smaller he became with kneeling, the less I had to duplicate."

"Painful on the knees, that," Vered observed. "Crawling in silence, making sure nothing caught on a stray splinter onstage." He grinned suddenly. "In the end, I just pretended to be one of my four new little carpet beetles. They can get into and out of a room so fast that you don't even realize they've been there to steal the candies!"

"Until you hear them yarking in another part of the house," Chat reminded him, chuckling. "And here I thought six children all nicely spaced were a plague! We'll all visit Wavertree when we need reminding of the sweet orderly silence of our own homes."

"Anyway," Sakary finished, for he hated to leave a story hanging, "after all that, it was just a matter of Rauel slicing off the magical Vered's head, while hiding the real one with a shadow while he sneaked away and then came back on as the old woman."

"Simple as peeling a turtle," Cade said. He was still feverishly analyzing what he'd seen and heard and felt. For one thing, the Warrior had said that fear was almost as satisfying a sustenance as blood. After the war, Elves had been imprisoned in the dark that terrified them in order to produce the fearing fire that, captured and enclosed in glass, lit the streets of Gallybanks by night—had the Caitiffs done something like that? Or had they skipped the fear part and simply found enough people to kill so there would be enough blood?

He could easily imagine Mieka's mother-in-law in such a role. Did the girl have the mark on her flesh that Vered seemed to have found out about in his research? It wasn't as if he could ask Mieka. And what did *he* think about what was news to him: that the Caitiffs had started out as servants to the Knights? Cade couldn't ask him that, either. He wanted badly to consult with Mistress Mirdley. She was the only person he knew who knew much at all about Caitiffs.

The conversation had gone on around him. It was just the eight of them at table, the Shadowshapers and Touchstone. Mistress Luta brought in yet another platter of food and yet another brimming pitcher of ale. Perhaps the Trollwife could enlighten him about Caitiffs—

"What about rain?" he heard himself ask suddenly.

Rauel's look of puzzlement was worn in varying degrees by everyone else at the table except Vered.

"I thought about putting it in," he said. "But it didn't quite work."

"Rain?" Rafe asked.

"The tradition has it," Vered explained, "that rain—pure water—is poison to a Caitiff's skin. Except that it isn't, really. There was a whole long passage in one of the books I slogged through—no gratitude to you, Cayden Silversun!—that dealt with standing naked in the rain and speaking the right magic to wash away the mark, so that nobody could tell a Caitiff by looking. But the bespelling and the rain also washes away the magic. I can't see anybody giving up magic, can you?"

Cade nodded. "I see now. And mayhap because they didn't want to lose the magic, the spell was deliberately forgotten and the whole thing turned into a belief that rainwater is poisonous to a Caitiff."

"That was my thinking as well," Vered agreed. "And besides, I didn't want to give the Caitiffs an escape. Everybody's trapped, y'see. The Warrior, the Wizard, the old woman—they used evil to defeat evil, and then they were all stuck with the evil."

Jeska stirred uneasily in his chair. "So at some point the Caitiffs were rounded up and taken to the Durkah Isle?" His gaze slanted ever-so-briefly towards Mieka. Cade saw it; so did the Elf. Before either of them could say anything, Jeska went on. "If that's what happened, who took care of the Knights?"

"No one." Vered shook his head to another glass of ale, and Sakary set down the pitcher. "My sense of it is that most of them died, without someone to provide them with fear and blood. The ones who weren't quite so evil, anyways. As for the rest . . . it seems to me that they were the truly evil ones, because they held their own lives so dear. They killed in order to survive. When they were killing the enemy, that was one thing. But then they started killing the people they were created to protect. My sense is that they felt all that blood was owed them."

There was a small silence. Then Rafe cleared his throat and said, "The fear, that I understand. Lord and Lady can witness that we've all had audiences that slurp up the emotions in a piece like hogs at a trough. But is it only the blood of living people the Knights can feed on? Could they get by with—I dunno—cattle? Horses?"

Vered gave a snort. "We could always go Vampire hunting on the Continent, and when we find one, we could ask."

"Armed with garlic, silver, wood, and a nice, long, sharp sword," Chat said. "You're welcome to go try, mate. Let me know how it works out."

"Talking of swords," Cade said, "now that I think on it, why was it so necessary to remove Vered from the area before Rauel did the execution? It isn't as if he was holding a real sword. It was just magic."

"Because," Sakary explained patiently, "clever as he is, it's not possible for Vered to actually, y'know, *lose* his head."

"Except over his wife," Mieka teased.

"And talking of wives," Rauel began, but at that exact moment four young men oozed into the taproom and one of them called out, "All hail the Shadowshapers! We've come to join the celebrations!"

Cayden would have sworn he'd never, ever be grateful for the existence of Black Lightning. Rauel had been about to mention Mieka's former wife; he could feel it. He stopped being grateful less than one minute later.

"Don't recall inviting you," Vered said calmly enough, but with a sharpness to his voice like the hackling spines on a dragon's neck. "Did we invite them, Rauel?"

"Not that I remember."

"Chat?"

"Not me, neither."

"Sakary?"

"None of us has the bad taste to suggest it," the fettler said, blue eyes narrowed. "Sod off, Knottinger. You're not welcome here."

"Oh, the insult! The anguish of it!" He pulled a chair from another table, turned it round, and straddled it, laughing all the while. "How will we ever recover?"

Cade saw Mieka's fingers twitch, and knew he was longing for the knives he kept in his boots, replacements for the ones lost. He owed Knottinger for Great Welkin. Jeska shifted his weight, ready to leap up at an instant's notice with fists flying. Chat and Rauel, usually men of mild temperament, pushed back their chairs and rose to their feet. Sakary had tensed every muscle to the trembling point. Even Rafe looked prepared for a fight. The rest of Black Lightning—Herris Crowkeeper, Pirro Spangler, and Kaj Seamark—seemed eager to give him one.

Vered tilted his head to one side, smiling slightly. "Now, as I see it, we've quite the dilemma here. If we were all of highborn blood, with titles to our names, we'd go about this all civilized-like. Challenges and seconds and swords at dawn and so forth. But we're none of us nobles—except Cayden, of course, and I'd make a guess that challenging the likes of you four would be beneath him. Am I right, Cade?"

"Irrefutably." He had no idea where Vered was going with this, but was willing to play along.

"Too big a word for them," Mieka chided, and, turning to Thierin, added helpfully, "He means yes."

"Beholden, Mieka," said Vered. "On another hand, if we were ordinary folk, not a word would be traded amongst us before we set at each other. The result would be broken jaws, busted ribs, and a few teeth skittering into dark corners to startle the girl when she sweeps tomorrow morning."

"Is there a third hand?" Rafe asked, politely interested.

"Always," Chat said ruefully. "Always."

"The third hand," Vered went on, "is the way they used to do it in the old days. What Fliting Hall is named for, in fact. Poetry and more poetry, back and forth like a game of battledore, until somebody delivers the sockdolager and a winner is declared."

The flicker of annoyance on Knottinger's face plainly indicated that he had no idea what in all Hells a *sockdolager* was. Cade glanced over at Mieka, brows arching. The Elf inclined his head in a gracious nod; he knew the term; either it was one of Uncle Breedbate's words, or else he'd actually been listening to his glisking master regarding the history of the theater, which Knottinger obviously had not. Mieka opened his mouth to clarify the matter when Pirro—who had studied under the same master—spoke up.

"The lines that knock everyone to the floor," he told Thierin, "ending the argument."

"Ending it," Mieka added, "with a verbal flourish so brilliant that nobody else can think of two words to put together for at least an hour afterwards." He turned to Vered. "I don't think that applies here, somehow. Like trying to bail a boat with a sieve."

"I agree." Vered gave a sad, sad sigh.

Thierin, overmatched and aware of it, smiled sweetly. "Is there a fourth hand?"

"Oh, yes." Vered laced his fingers behind his nape, elbows spread wide. "The hand nobody sees until it appears right before your eyes."

A shining globe of blue Wizardfire appeared about a foot away from Knottinger's face. He lurched back, fell off the chair, and scrambled away. "You—how *dare* you?" he shrieked. "Using magic like that—off a stage—I'll have the law on you—"

"I'm thinking not," said Mistress Luta from the kitchen door. She stumped around the bar, wagging a finger at Vered. "A shaming be on you, boy, for loosing your magic in my house! Don't you know that *I'm* the only one as is allowed magic in here?"

And with that she spread her hands wide, and a curtain of shimmering, shivering, opalescent fire appeared around Black Lightning. It expanded to encase them, from Thierin over on the floor to Herris beside a potted tree.

"Out with you now," the Trollwife said. The magic, not touching them, herded them along to the entryway. When the door had shut behind them, she turned to Vered. "No, I will *not* teach you how to do that. Finish your dinners and drink up, and go get some sleep."

When she was gone, Vered breathed again. "Great galloping Gods. Did you ever see—"

"Never even suspected," Cade managed. "And I was *raised* by a Trollwife."

They all sat back down at the table and followed orders. They finished their dinners and their drinks, and the only thing anybody said before they all went up to their rooms was when Vered remarked, "Well, at least now we know what color to make the Troll magic!"

Upstairs, Mieka went at once to his bed, sat down, and pulled off his boots. He'd been uncharacteristically subdued all evening. Cade knew very well why. He also knew that there were questions coming, and he'd better have good answers.

"Caitiffs," Mieka said at last.

"Yeh."

"You knew all along."

"It was years before Mistress Mirdley said anything." Which was true. He just wasn't specific about how many years. It was this next part that was a bit dodgy, so he pulled his nightshirt over his head while speaking, to hide his face and his eyes from Mieka's all-too-discerning gaze. "They weren't using any magic that Mistress Mirdley could tell, and she just figured what everybody else did who knew what the name meant—that it had come from a grandfather or great-grandfather or something, like all last names do."

"What made her talk to you about it?"

He resisted a sigh of relief. He'd got away with the lies. The Troll-wife had known all along exactly what the girl was and exactly what she'd done to captivate Mieka. "It was that counterpane. My Naming-day present. Remember? She put it through a cleansing. Not that she was sure it was bespelled." Cade extinguished the candle and got into his bed. There was a lot to think about—too much to think about in any coherent fashion. He was trying to get it all organized when Mieka spoke in the darkness.

"Remember when Jez hurt his leg? Jindra sewed him a pillow. Or maybe helped sew it, with her mother doing most of the work, I don't know. But he said that it helped the pain."

"Mieka, that's—"

"Every shirt she ever made me. Every pair of trousers." His voice was calm, almost meditative. "Every scarf and—and that neck-cloth, the very first thing she ever . . ." He stopped.

"Mieka," Cade said again, hurting for him.

"Was any of it real? Did she ever love me? Did I ever love her? Was it all just—just spells stitched into the seams of a shirt? Was *all* of it a lie?"

"She did love you," Cade replied slowly. "She could have used it on anybody, but she chose you. She wanted you and she meant to have you."

"You're not denying it, Quill. You're not saying she isn't a Caitiff, with a Caitiff's weaving magic."

Caught. He squeezed his eyes shut and said nothing.

"Stupid to keep the name."

"Most people don't recognize it. What it really means."

After a time, Mieka spoke again. "Quill? Is Vered right? About where they came from, and who they served?"

"I've heard enough and read enough to believe that there's a basis in fact, but—it's only a play, after all. Not really real."

"In the best plays, there's more *real* than in so-called *real* life. But only the best plays."

"Only the best plays," he echoed helplessly. "Go to sleep, Elfling."

Chapter 24

Every time Touchstone returned to Gallantrybanks from Seekhaven, Blye presented them with glass boxes to keep their Trials medals in. This year, presenting them on the fly while everyone scurried about preparing for the Royal Circuit or preparing to move house, she grumped that she was running out of ideas. A dragon etched into each had been easy and obvious, that first year. She'd referenced each play of the Thirteen Perils that had secured them their places (for the Third, a single foot in a laced boot beside a knight in full armor who was only as tall as the Giant's ankle). If there was a repeat, she decorated the boxes using symbols for their last names, a clutch of fanned-out withies, or an array of glass baskets. This year she confessed herself flummoxed by how to commemorate the first part of *Window Wall*, and instead depicted their wagon with TOUCHSTONE on the side and Derien's map.

"Another reason for striking out on our own," Mieka remarked. "Blye's convenience!"

She had come to tea to give him and Cayden their glass boxes. It was a rare afternoon of quiet at Redpebble Square. There'd been no time for lunching with the Princess this year after Trials, no time for visiting friends—unless those friends happened to drop by, in which case they were given a crate and directed to pack something in it. This was true of all four members of Touchstone. Jeska, due to become a father again by Wintering, had found a larger house into which his growing family would move while he was away. Rafe, Crisiant, and little Bram were changing residence as well—though in their case it was only around the corner from his parents' bakery. Cade, Derien,

Mieka, and Mistress Mirdley were in the midst of moving to the new house on the river; Jed, Blye, Jez, and Eirenn would transfer to Number Eight; Rikka Ashbottle and her husband, Parlen Cropready, would take over the lodgings above the glassworks. It seemed to Mieka that almost everybody he knew was moving almost everything they owned that spring—except for Jindra, who would stay at Wistly Hall with her doting grandparents until his return from the Royal this autumn. He had the occasional attack of nervous worry, wondering how she would adjust. But surely it was better for her to grow up in a home full of people who adored her. He knew bloody good and well that anything was better than growing up around her grandmother.

The problem of Derien and the journey to the Continent had worked itself out, no credit going to Cade. The boy had indeed won the competition, first place in both the examination and the interviews. He reported this news about twenty seconds after Cade and Mieka walked through the front door of Redpebble Square. Cade scowled and gathered himself for an argument; Mieka rolled his eyes; Mistress Mirdley snorted; Derien said cheerily, "You'll be glad to learn I've politely declined the invitation. After all, I have family responsibilities. I'm needed here to supervise the move. Just filing all your books onto the library shelves will take weeks, after all. And as for your wardrobe—not to speak of Mieka's—!"

Mieka congratulated Derien on his triumph and his wisdom, while Cade seemed to deflate, his anger gone. The next day, however, fear replaced it, with the arrival of a sealed-and-beribboned missive written on expensive paper.

Blye had given them the boxes, which they duly and sincerely admired. They were regaling her with the tale of Vered's play when the only remaining Silversun footman entered the drawing room with a polished brass tray. Cade extended a hand, thinking the letter meant for him.

"Master Derien, sir," the boy said, and gave it over.

Mieka saw gray ribbons and orange sealing wax and almost dropped his teacup. Derien ripped the thing open and started to read. After a moment, he grimaced.

"He's asking me to reconsider. Says his wife has taken a fancy to me—I've never even met the woman! Advantages to my future career, invaluable experience, yattering on and on—"

"Mother will be thrilled," Cade observed sweetly.

"Mother's never going to know about this—not any of it," Derien warned. "I didn't tell her about the competition. She's given up Panshilara and Iamina for the Queen's circle of ladies—"

"Good Gods, can you imagine?" Blye laughed. "An afternoon with them would be like taking a nap without losing consciousness!"

"—so she probably didn't hear about it from that direction, either," Derien finished.

"Be deferential when you write your refusal," Blye advised. "And be sure to save the letter. You can laugh over it with your grandchildren someday. Cade, I want to hear the rest of what happened. In case you've lost your place, Black Lightning had just arrived in the taproom. Say on, O Great Tregetour, say on!" She grinned at him. "But don't let me forget to brag about our own news. Windthistle Brothers has the contract to build the Princess's new sanatorium!"

Mieka laughed. "Sudden large donation, was there?"

"Very large, and very sudden. I think they're naming the gardens for the donor, but, d'you know, I can't quite recall who it is."

"That's a shame," Dery said with every evidence of sincerity. "And talking of names, we have to decide what to call this new house of ours."

Cade groaned and fell back dramatically in his chair. "Oh, Gods—not that again!"

It had been a source of mischievous contention in the weeks before Trials. Mistress Mirdley favored "Garboil House" (even though it begged to be mispronounced), considering the uproar and disorder bound to be a daily feature of life there. Failing that, "Dringler's Rest"—for, she pointed out, there was nothing Cayden and Mieka were so good at as wasting time. Mieka had proposed "Scrivenscrime," a combination of *scrivener* (Cade) and *scrimer* (a fencer, for Mieka), though he had to admit this, too, was a silly mouthful. Cade voiced his suspicion that he'd put it forth to make his other suggestion sound better, but there was no chance that they'd called the place "Gliskering." Derien's idea was "Eyas Hall," a reference to a nesting falcon, to play off his and Cade's clan. Cayden, who one would think would have all sorts of notions, being a wordsmith and all, had not one single suggestion.

Derien now presented each name to Blye, who had a few trenchant observations about each, and offered "Silverthistle's Folly" as more appropriate. This led to possible names for Number Eight, Redpebble Square—Windthistle, Cindercliff, and Wooltangle provided fine material, especially after Cade started tossing in synonyms. Mieka didn't join in so vigorously as he might have done; his gaze kept returning to that letter, now lying on the floor. Proof positive, as if any were required, that the Archduke had something nasty in mind. All by himself in foreign lands, with only schoolboy magic to defend himself in places where even the most benign magic was looked on as evil . . . it didn't bear thinking about. Look at the trouble Touchstone had got into on that journey to fetch Miriuzca back to Albeyn, and they'd been grown men at the time. No, it was much better that Derien was staying home. His success in the competition would be remembered—and what possible diplomatic use could a boy of not quite fifteen be, other than running errands for a pair of highborn twitchies who despised anyone named Silversun in the first place?

Mieka had a few errands of his own to attend to before Touchstone set off on the Royal. He spent a day at Wistly, putting together his wardrobe for the circuit and playing with Jindra. She was six-and-a-half years old now, as full of chatter as he was, and great fun. They went swimming in the river, built a fortress of ancient tables and rickety chairs and threadbare blankets on the back lawn, and borrowed Jinsie's favorite cloaks to become dragons swooping down the stairs for Tavier to "slay" with a wooden sword. Jorie had taught her niece how to read, and at midsummer, she would start littleschool. Lord and Lady witness it, he couldn't believe she was growing up so quickly. Surely it couldn't be almost seven years since he'd come back from the Continent to find her mother pregnant. . . .

Her mother was a subject not discussed. By anyone. Mieka had shied back a little at spending a night at Wistly in the room he'd once shared with his wife, scared of an assault by memories. He'd worried for nothing. Finding a stray vial of her rose perfume in a dresser drawer was merely an annoyance, not a shock. He wasn't even tempted to open the vial and inhale of her scent. He threw it into the trash and considered himself cured.

All the same, he made a brief trip to Hilldrop Crescent. He told no one but his mother where he was going, and didn't bother to lie about it. He only mentioned that some of his clothes were still there, to which she replied mildly that she would've thought his closet at Wistly held enough shirts, trousers, vests, jackets, boots, and suchlike for him to be adequately clothed during the Royal. She said this while looking at him with her usual shrewdness, but didn't comment further. He knew very well that she knew very well that he looked on it as a sort of final test. If he could enter that house and remember without too much regret the years he'd lived in it, then he could judge himself truly free. If not . . . well, nobody would see him fall to pieces. Yazz, Robel, and their children were away at her parents' dwelling, so both the house and the converted barn were empty. Mieka's former wife was now living with her new Ripplewater relations; he had no idea where her mother was, and didn't care.

He spent a rewarding afternoon, returning just before dinner with two satchels full of clothes and the last of the three-branched candle-flats Blye had made for his eighteenth Namingday. Jinsie, on the look-out for him, opened the front door of Wistly Hall as he was paying off the hack driver.

"Quite the expensive journey," she observed, taking one of the satchels.

"There was a bit of a bother," he answered easily. "Nothing dreadful, but I owed him a nice tip."

The man glared down at him, muttered something about his horse never being the same again, and drove off.

Jinsie didn't seem to notice. She had something to tell him. She had been singularly irritating the last few days, with her lists of private performances while on the Circuit and her admonitions to keep an eye on the man she and Kazie had hired to take Yazz's place on the coachman's bench (Rist being unavailable). Although Nevin Tranterly was big enough and brawny enough to control the horses—borrowed yet again from Romuald Needler's growing herd, for not even Jinsie could coax an actual sale out of the Shadowshapers' manager—he had never been more than twenty miles from Gallantrybanks and might not be able to read the maps clearly.

Mieka turned resolutely for the stairs. "Whatever it is," he said over his shoulder, "you can tell me while I pack."

"All right."

He paused on the third step. "I'm not going to like this, am I?"

The rest of Touchstone didn't like it, either. Their final gigging before the Royal was that night at the Kiral Kellari, and after "Dragon" and "Dwarmy Day" had been performed and they were having a drink in the tiring room, Mieka told them what Jinsie had said.

"Books?" Cade stared at him. "Real leather-covered books? Is she joking? Who's the publisher?"

"Damn it!" Rafe said. "I had this idea years ago, for 'Bewilderland'!"

"How did Bexan come up with it, anyways?" Jeska asked.

"Who cares?" Cade snarled. "As if anybody, especially Vered, is going to let anyone see his performance notes!"

"That's just the point," Mieka said. "It's the script that will be printed, with a few descriptions of the scenery and some stage directions for the masquer, but no notes. Not the color-coding for the withies—not that anybody could make much sense of that kind of thing—or any fettler's cues regarding where more control is needed, or anything that has to do with the actual performance. It's just the words."

"Bexan is one smart little Piksey," Rafe mused. "All attention is on the Shadowshapers these days, wondering where and if they'll perform together again, and that's not even considering the chavishing going on about *Blood Plight*. Anybody who's anybody will want copies to read for themselves."

"I still want to know why she's doing it," Jeska insisted.

"She's got four children to feed and clothe and educate," Rafe pointed out. "And I think she knows that sooner or later Vered and Rauel will be at each other's throats again."

Mieka nodded. "There won't be any income from the Shadowshapers because there won't be any Shadowshapers to generate income. Jinsie thinks so, too."

"But—but it's giving away their secrets!" Cade drained his glass of beer down his throat and looked for a moment as if he wanted to throw it against a wall. "Not to people who just want to read the plays and who don't have any magic or at least don't have any ambitions for the stage—I'm talking about other groups! Any glisker worth his withies would be able to tell what kind of magic is needed for this or that effect—masquers and fettlers would see the cues without anybody having to show exactly where they are!"

"I knew we should've followed up on 'Bewilderland' years ago," Rafe said with a sigh. "But in a way this is good. She can take all the risks. If it turns out well, we can follow her lead."

"'Follow'—are you insane?" Cade surged to his feet and started pacing. "Don't you see it? Anybody—*anybody*—could take the script for 'Dragon' and do it exactly the way we do it—"

Mieka led the hoots of laughter. "Now who's joking? Nobody could do it the way we do!"

"And anyways," Jeska said, "isn't the play already out there for anybody to see? In its original form, I mean. One of the Thirteen Perils. They're all of them in books, and most of the other old ones are printed someplace."

"What about our originals?" Cade smiled thinly as the laughter faded. "Doing up 'Bewilderland' with illustrations as a children's book might be all very well, but what about *Window Wall*? Do you really want anybody and everybody taking our script, our work, and doing it themselves? If they're good with it, they're getting a reputation based on *our* work. And if they're lousy, the reputation of *our* play suffers." He paused for breath. "And there's something else. Had any of you considered that any idiot with money enough to pay for the printing— talent or not, magic or not—can have his scribbles published? Did Bexan think of that? I doubt it!"

Mieka almost didn't tell them the rest of it. Cade was furious enough right now; the remainder of Jinsie's news would be adding black powder to the fire and produce a serious explosion. But he had to tell them.

"There's another thing. The Master of the King's Revelries heard about this—don't ask how, Jinsie doesn't know—and he'll probably decide that his office gets to inspect and approve plays for publication." When Cade drew breath to roar, Mieka held up a staying hand. "The naughtier plays—'Troll and Trull,' f'r instance—not suitable for ladies and children to read."

They were still discussing it—at a much lower volume—weeks later when a letter from Jinsie was delivered by a special messenger who galloped up to the wagon on the road to Dolven Wold. They invited the man to share their dinner, especially when he pointed out that he'd had to ride fifteen miles out of his way because they were on the long road to Dolven Wold, not the shorter one. Jinsie, it seemed, had been correct about the new driver's proficiency with maps. While he and the messenger were feeding and watering the horses, Mieka handed the letter to Cade, who read it aloud.

The Master of the King's Revelries has (so they say) been talking with the Archduke. The decision comes in two parts.

First, any play first performed at Trials or on any of the Circuits can be published only if the Crown gets a portion of the proceeds. They're talking 60 percent, but that will probably be lowered to 50 for the more successful groups, whose plays will be in greater demand.

Second, old plays—all of the Perils, for instance—will have to be substantially different in the new versions, or the group publishing it can't get more than 15 percent of the profits, even if they're the ones paying for publication. The Master of So-forth-and-so-on will, naturally, be the one to determine the meaning of "substantially."

Thus Bexan can only publish original plays that the Shadowshapers never first performed either at Trials or on a Circuit. She's not happy.

I can't imagine that Cayden will be, either. Kazie has, however, made an interesting point. The regulations say "at Trials," not "at Seekhaven"—so a case could be made for any play first performed at the Pavilion or on the final night being exempt. I'll have a talk with Master Burningcrag and get his opinion.

By the by, other rumors have it that Princess Miriuzca is supporting this plan because a percentage of the Crown's percentage will go to supporting her new sanatorium. Blye, Kazie, Crisiant, and I are lunching with Lady Vren and Lady Megs next week, and will take the opportunity to explain our point of view.

Before I forget, Yazz wants to know what if anything you want done about rebuilding. I told him I'd ask.

Seeing Cade's confused frown, Mieka knew he'd made a mistake by not reading the letter aloud himself and skipping that last bit. Well, how was he to know? Though it was addressed to him, the first few sentences had been for all of Touchstone, not just him.

Rafe was gnawing on his mustache. "We'll have to send a letter back."

"Obviously," Cade snapped.

"You write it," Mieka said quickly to the fettler. "Nobody, not even my own twin sister, can read my handwriting." Which wasn't precisely true, but anyway was beside the point, and the point was that Cayden was so furious that he was more likely to use his pen to stab the paper instead of write with it.

Thus, after dinner Rafe scrawled a letter to Jinsie asking her to ask her artist friends to submit sketches for an illustrated book to be titled *Bewilderland*. That and "Turn Aback" were the only two of Touchstone's works that were both original and first performed elsewhere than at Seekhaven. Rafe didn't mention that play, and neither did anybody else. Mieka was relieved. Ever since its failure, Cade had either flinched or got all defensive about the thing. Nobody needed to point out that of all their plays, that one was the most likely to sell two or three copies.

But those were the only two plays they had. Jinsie might be right about the wording of the regulations, or she might not. Until this was cleared up, Touchstone had no desire to see a huge slice of the profits of everything from "Dragon" to *Window Wall* go to the Crown.

"Although," Cade mused the next morning after they'd seen the rider off back to Gallybanks (he'd pointed them to the easiest road to Dolven Wold before leaving), "I suppose *Window Wall* wouldn't count. We've never done both parts together."

"You just keep on unpicking all the stitches, Cade," Jeska told him. "You're good at that."

Later that day—a lovely sunny afternoon with a gentle breeze—Cade suggested that Mieka join him in stretching his legs. It was more like an order, actually. And Mieka knew exactly what he wanted to talk about.

"Rebuild *what*, exactly?"

"The house."

"Your house? I mean, Jindra's house."

"Not anymore." He'd been rehearsing his answer in his mind since he'd done it. "When I walked in, there were all new cushions and sheets and pillows and pretty much anything that could be woven or sewn. One of the neighbor ladies saw me drive up, and came by to say that packages had come the week before, with instructions to put the new things in place, and that I'd pay her for the work when next I came by. I paid, and she left."

"Mieka, what did you *do*?"

"There were a couple of new shirts as well. I didn't recognize them.

I've never worn them. And I'm not fool enough to've touched them—or anything else."

"If you don't tell me right now—"

"I blew it up, all right? I got my stash from under a floorboard and I blew the whole fucking house sky-high!"

Cade seemed to be speechless.

Mieka took advantage of it, knowing it wouldn't last. "Scared the shit out of the hack driver—and his horse—and people came running from all over the village. I said that there was so much rot in the wood and the cracks in the masonry were so bad that my brothers the Master Builders said just to get rid of the whole thing and start from scratch. I don't know if they believed me, and I don't care."

After a couple of false starts and a throat-clearing, Cade managed, "But—but it was Jindra's inheritance from you. Her property."

Mieka stopped walking and grabbed Cade's arm, glaring up into his face. "D'you think I'd leave that place standing for Jindra to come to and find who knows what waiting for her in the pillows and counterpanes? They did all of it just on the *chance* that I'd go there within a month—can you imagine what they'd do if they knew Jindra was going to live there or even visit for a couple of weeks with Jinsie and Mum?"

"So you blew it up."

"Every stick, stitch, and stone of it. Especially the stitches."

Cade squinted into the sunshine, then nodded. "Wish I'd been there. Sounds like fun."

"Oh, it was, Quill, it really was! Used up every damned bit of my black powder, though."

"Well, look at it this way. You started out by obliterating a bathroom. Now you've blown up a whole house. How could you ever top that?"

Mieka laughed. "You don't really want me to try, do you?"

Chapter 25

Scornful, willful, and even gleeful as that act of destruction had been, it turned out to be unnecessary.

It was full summer, and Touchstone was halfway through the Royal Circuit, and had earned their week at Castle Eyot. Warm days lazing in the sun or swimming in the river; soft beds and good food; nothing to do but let the tension unwind.

Jinsie was waiting for them. More specifically, for Mieka.

"Are you *sure* Yazz isn't well enough to come be our coachman again?" he was whining as the four of them entered the upstairs drawing room—five hours later than expected—where refreshments awaited while their bags were taken to their rooms. "If we get lost one more time on this trip—"

He broke off at the sight of his twin, who rose from a chair and started across the room to him. Her pale eyes were solemn in her dark face. She wore a plain brown dress that became her in neither color nor style.

"What is it?" he asked. "What's wrong."

"Mieka . . ."

He panicked. "Jindra? Something's happened to Jindra—"

"No! Oh, Gods no, I'm sorry—I really am sorry, brother." She stood before him, taking his hands. "It's not Jindra. She's fine. It's—it's Lord and Lady Ripplewater."

For a moment he had no idea whom she was talking about. And then he knew. He knew.

"A carriage accident," she went on. "It was a few days ago. They were on their way to his family's seaside cottage. They—" She gulped and shook her head. "The constable's messenger said it happened instantly. They didn't suffer." Her fingers spasmed in his. Helplessly, she finished, "Mieka, I'm so sorry—"

He bent his forehead to hers, a gesture from their childhood. "Beholden for coming yourself to tell me," he whispered.

"D'you think I'd send a stranger, or a letter?" She freed her hands and wrapped her arms around him.

He didn't quite know how he ended up in a bedchamber upstairs, seated in a soft chair with a half-empty glass of whiskey in his hand. Considerable time had gone by; afternoon shadows spread across the bright flowered rugs.

"More?"

Cayden. Of course. He shook his head and looked up. Cade sat across from him, the bottle by his feet, holding an empty glass. There was a faraway look in his gray eyes that Mieka had never seen there before. In the years since instinct and brash confidence and a fair measure of terror had sent him to Gowerion to claim a place in a group that didn't even have a name, he'd seen Cade's eyes somber, infuriated, contemptuous, frightened; glazed with pain, dancing with laughter, blazing with creative fire, soft with tenderness—but he'd never seen this aloof, meditative sadness.

"His family will make the arrangements, of course," Cade said. "Their ancestral manor and . . . and burying ground—it's about a day and a half from here. Will you go? Should I come with you?"

"Yes. And no."

"I think I ought to."

"Beholden, but no. Jinsie and I will be there." He shifted his gaze to the dark golden liquid in his glass, not even tempted to finish the drink. The taste in his mouth told him he'd had a few swallows. He didn't want any more. "That'll be quite enough hypocrisy, don't you think?"

"Mieka—"

"I hope he made her happy. I never really did. I never could have."

"Touchstone was in the way."

"*You* were in the way," Mieka corrected. How clear it all was now. The life he shared with Cayden—and Rafe and Jeska—was the life he needed and wanted. His life with her had always been an afterthought, an accessory—like a neck-cloth or an earring or a pair of gloves to put on and admire, then take off again and abandon when it was time to get back to his *real* life. He remembered how heavy those silver brace-lets had been, purposely heavy, so that he could never quite forget her even while performing. Especially while performing.

"Mieka . . ."

"All I can remember is that last night. I can't see her like she was when we got married, nor when we went to Hilldrop the first time, nor even the very first time I ever saw her. It's that last night, Quill. When I left her. I never told you about it, did I?"

"You don't have to, Mieka."

"I wasn't going to. It's just . . . I *saw* her, as if I'd never seen her be-fore. She was so beautiful . . . the most beautiful thing I've ever seen. . . ." Lifting the glass, he stared at it for a moment and then set it on the table beside him. "Gods, how I wish I wanted to get drunk."

There was a silence while the shadows crawled an inch or so across the rug.

"Don't start blaming yourself."

"Start?" Mieka echoed incredulously. "Are you serious?"

"Never more so. Most of it was false from the beginning. You know that. I told you what her mother said. Her grandmother, I mean." He paused to pour himself more whiskey. "And then with Touchstone pulling you in one direction and her in the other—and all the lies—"

"I wanted all of it, Quill. I wanted everything."

"You had no idea what the fuck you wanted."

"But I *did* know. Exactly what every man is supposed to want. I wanted Touchstone and her and for everything to be perfect." He heard the bitterness in his voice and couldn't stop it. "I'm Mieka Windthistle of Touchstone, right? Rich and famous and funny and clever and gor-geous and—and—I thought I could take what I wanted and have every-thing, and it would all be just like it's s'posed to be."

Cade gulped down his drink and bent to put the glass onto the floor. Mieka suspected this movement was to hide his face, but he didn't speak until he straightened up, and when he did, he looked Mieka di-rectly in the eyes.

"I know you'll never see it the way I do—and I never claimed to be impartial when it came to her. But she was trying to change every-thing about you that didn't fit her idea—hers and that old woman's—of who and what you ought to be. I know, I know, you went along with it so it was partly your fault, and it was my fault, too, because I let them get away with it for so long. But you never saw her clear, Mieka—not until that night, I guess. I never blamed her for wanting you. What I can't forgive her for is not understanding the first thing about you, for trying to make you different and—and *less* than you are."

Mieka watched the anger fade from Cade's face until there was nothing but the sadness. "That time you took me to Ginnel House . . . you showed me a way to change, but you left it to me to make the choice. I never understood that about you before. The Elsewhens—is that how you figured out that you can't *make* people decide what's right? That it's their choice to go one way instead of another—but, Quill, when you see the Elsewhens, at least you know that you have to *think* about the consequences! You should've told me what you'd seen."

"You never would have believed me."

"No," he admitted. "But it would've been there inside my head, and I would've had to think about it, and—"

"I couldn't. I didn't want to lose you."

He almost laughed. "Quill! How could that ever happen? You're the only one who looks at me and *sees* me, just like I am." When Cade shook his head, Mieka leaned forward in his chair and persisted, "You *know* me. With you, I never have to be anything but myself." Gray eyes clouded for a moment, and Mieka knew he was seeing a flash of an Elsewhen. But he didn't ask. Instead, he smiled slightly, and when it was clear that Cade was back, he said, "O' course, that means I can't get away with much. Which is, if I may say so, my dear old Quill, irksome as seventeen different Hells." He pushed himself to his feet and stretched. "Gods and Angels, I'm tired. Let me have a lie-down for a bit, all right?"

"All right."

He didn't sleep. He lay on the bed, watching the afternoon become evening, wondering—without much curiosity—why he didn't feel a deeper and more personal grief. He hurt for Jindra's sake, and even for the old woman's. He was angry, in a detached way, that her new life with her new husband had been cut so tragically short; he pitied the Ripplewater family the loss of their son. But for himself . . . there wasn't much in him but a feeling of suddenly being rather old.

And he liked it not at all.

He was coming up on twenty-six—if he lived as long as most people did who had substantial Elfen ancestry, he had at least thrice that number of years ahead of him.

What in all Hells was he going to do with them, anyway?

Theater was, as he had himself arrogantly stated many a time, a young man's game. Anybody older than thirty was a graybeard, and an object of contempt. Chat Czillag was older than that, of course, but Chat was a special case . . . or was he? A group as brilliant as the Shadowshapers—or Touchstone, damn it!—didn't come along all that often. The Shadowshapers could break whatever rules they pleased, especially now that they played only where and when and as they liked. Currently they were meandering throughout Albeyn on a sort of working holiday, with two carriages each for family and servants (except for Vered, who brought only Bexan; the babies, too young for such lengthy travel, were at Wavertree with Bexan's mother and all those nurses). When they approached a town of any decent size, a rider was sent ahead to ask if the Shadowshapers might have the privilege of playing for them a night or two hence. Some of the shows were outside; some were given inside the local landowner's biggest barn or whatever hall was used by the magistrate. If there was a castle nearby, its courtyard became the theater. People got their money's worth and more: three plays were done at each show, something short and light and funny, and then the two parts of *Blood Plight*. By now, in high summer, a fair portion of the citizens of Albeyn knew the whole story, either by direct experience or through hearing the raptures of their friends and neighbors.

Even if they never played anything else besides their current folio, the Shadowshapers could go on being the Shadowshapers pretty much until they dropped dead of old age. Why couldn't Touchstone do the same? Mieka almost laughed, reminding himself of that Elsewhen of Cade's, the party on his forty-fifth Namingday—they'd just got home from a gigging, so obviously Touchstone was going strong. There was no reason why Mieka wouldn't be dancing behind Blye's beautiful glass baskets well into his forties, his fifties . . .

She would never see twenty-five.

She was dead, the woman who had been his wife. Jindra's mother. A Caitiff, whose powers had been dedicated—or so legend and Vered Goldbraider had it—to the service of the Knights of the Balaur Tsepesh.

But why not call them what they were? Everyone in Albeyn must be calling them by their right name by now.

Vampires.

Half of Jindra's heritage came from the Caitiffs who had provided the Knights with what they needed. Might as well call that by its right name, too.

Blood.

But the other half was his, with all the Dark Elf and Light Elf, Wizard and Piksey and Sprite and Human and Fae—half of her was his. In looks she was almost entirely his: eyes, cheekbones, the shape of her ears, the thick black hair. But especially his were her hands, small and fine-boned, with the ring fingers and little fingers almost the same length. Quick, clever hands. Magic was in them, surely, but of what kind? Would it be the "golden threads and silver needles" of that horrible chanting song?

Her mother would never know.

Mieka curled onto his side, squeezing his eyes shut and his hands into fists. He'd lied to Cayden about not wanting to get drunk. There was a whole cellar full of liquor and a cabinet full of thorn here at Lord Piercehand's pretty castle. Easiest thing in the world to ring for a servant and order up whatever he fancied.

He told himself he wouldn't. He swore that he absolutely would *not* find the bellpull and—

"Mieka? Are you awake?"

Jinsie would never know how acutely he loathed her at that moment—or how heart-deep grateful he was.

She came in, sat in the chair Cade had been in a few hours ago, and regarded him with a mixture of curiosity and determination that made him nervous.

"What?" he demanded, sitting up on the bed.

"Are you going to feel guilty about this?"

"About taking a nap?"

"Don't be a quat. You know what I mean. It wasn't your fault. You two were so wrong for each other that everybody who looked at you saw it. All the while you were married, Mum and Fa worried every single day."

"*What?*"

"You never could see much that wasn't the size of a dragon and shoved right under your nose. I used to hear them talking late at night, and it was always the same things. You were too young, both of you. She wasn't the kind who could be left on her own for half the year— she needed attention and she'd get it wherever she could. You were drinking too much and pricking too much thorn. You didn't even laugh the same way. They were starting not to recognize their own son. You were turning nasty and mean and you didn't even realize it."

He heard this catalog of his sins and acknowledged them all.

"I remember watching a show last autumn—you weren't playing for the joy of it like you used to. It was more like you were shattering the withies because you wanted to *hurt* them. And that's not how you were meant to play. You weren't our Mieka anymore. She was trying to make you nothing but hers, and that meant taking you away from the rest of us."

Cayden had said much the same thing. Why was it that these two people who loved him and knew him had never said anything to the point? Jinsie's next words gave him the inevitable, inarguable answer.

"But you wouldn't listen."

"No," he murmured. "I wouldn't listen."

"And still, out of all of it, somehow there's Jindra. And Touchstone, where you're supposed to be. Two incredible *rights* out of all that *wrongness*."

"Are you saying you think it balances out? The things that happen are *supposed* to happen?"

"You don't agree?"

"I can't agree. I've heard about too many of Cade's Elsewhens."

The reminder that the future was in fact unfixed only made her shrug. "They're just *versions* of what has to happen. But maybe I used the wrong word. Maybe it's not balance, but payment for what we take."

He'd done a lot of taking. More than his share. He'd reached out and grabbed with both greedy hands. Money, acclaim, girls, thorn, liquor, things that pleased him and a life that excited him . . . and he had possessed in marriage the most beautiful thing he'd ever seen.

Lord and Lady and Angels and Gods, how he wanted a drink.

"Jinsie . . . how does her being dead pay for what *I've* done?"

"What *you've* done?" she cried. "Haven't you been listening? It was her paying up for what she'd done to you!"

He knew that if he said anything to the contrary, he'd be treated to another hour or so of her emphatic opinions—all of them in his favor. Well, she was his sister. At least Cade could admit that he wasn't exactly objective and detached. Jinsie knew what she knew, and Gods help anybody who tried to convince her otherwise. Just like Mieka.

"All right," he said. "I understand. Not stupid, y'know—just lacking in education. And hungry."

"If you want to stop talking about this, you don't have to be so obvious." But she got to her feet and turned for the door, saying, "I drove here in that purple contraption of yours, with a hired horse and driver. It's light enough to make good time, but we'd best leave at dawn tomorrow if we're to get there for the service."

"Jinsie—wait. Mum and Fa won't come, will they? Nor Jindra? It's no place for a little girl."

Hand on the doorknob, she faced him again. "Jindra is very happy exploring her new home. Derien and Blye are taking her to spend a few nights there, with Cilka and Tavier and probably Jorie, with Mistress Mirdley to look after them all. Mum will tell Jindra about her mother when she thinks it's right. And Mum *always* knows what's right."

"She does, doesn't she? I wonder if it ever gets boring, being right all the time."

"Well, *you'll* never know, that's for certain sure! Wash your face and come down for some dinner."

He nodded, and she left the room. He could guess at his mother's reasoning. The house at Hilldrop Crescent, Jindra's home, was a pile of rubble. She hadn't seen her mother in months. Give her time to learn and like the new house, where she would live with her father but not her mother, before telling her that she would never see her mother again. Give her a place to think of as home, where family and friends and father would be. Give her something real and secure.

She would have that. So, he realized with a start, would he. A house that was really his—not the place where his wife lived, not the place where his parents and siblings lived, but a home that belonged to *him* as surely as his magic and his withies and his work.

But before that happened, there was the rest of the Royal Circuit to be finished. And before *that*, he would travel to an unfamiliar house and sit in a chair beside his sister, unwelcome, while the most beautiful thing he'd ever seen burned to ashes.

Chapter 26

Predicting that Mieka would be gone for roughly five days (two going, two returning, one in between) seemed fairly safe. Cade figured he'd spend the days as he always did at Castle Eyot, reading, relaxing, taking long walks and hot baths, joining Jeska for afternoon rides, catching up on letters. He was engaged in that last activity when Rafe entered his room without knocking and told him to take a look down at the bridge.

"Has it crumbled into the river so we're trapped for the next week?" Cade glanced over his shoulder at his fettler, much annoyed. He was right in the middle of an amusing passage to his brother and Mistress Mirdley about the driver's unexpected detours, none of which had been funny at the time, and the interruption had broken his rhythm.

"Just look," Rafe insisted.

He did. That nonsensical purple rig of Mieka's was crossing the bridge to Castle Eyot's little island.

"They only left day before yesterday," Rafe said.

"And they didn't even use our driver," Cade added sourly.

He and Rafe and Jeska went down to the courtyard, full of questions that, after one look at Mieka's stormy face, they didn't ask.

"They oughta fucking mend their fucking bridges," Mieka griped when he slumped out of the carriage. "I'm full-fucking knackered, and I'm going to bed."

Rafe murmured, "My, but he's eloquent when he's tired, isn't he?" But he waited until Mieka had gone inside to say it.

Jinsie—who had been jounced and rattled from Gallybanks to Castle Eyot and then halfway to Ripplewater Tower and back—moved as if her bones had aged a hundred or so years. Cade offered her an arm as she got out of the rig. She accepted it and limped up the steps.

"We had to turn back," she explained wearily. "The manor is up in the hills, and their poxy river floods every spring. It's all put right by early summer, but last week there was a thunderstorm high in the Pennynines that washed two villages downstream and took out five bridges. Every road was just simply hopeless. So here we are."

"They were too cheap to hire weathering witches?" Rafe asked.

"That's the other thing."

They reached the entry hall, and Jinsie sighed at the welcome coolness. That was the problem with courtyards: no trees, no shade, nothing but heat radiating off stone.

"What other thing?"

"The weathering witches are doing a down-tools until they get their own Guild."

"Tools?" Jeska asked, bewildered. "What tools? I didn't know they—"

"It's an expression," Jinsie explained. "The tilers and thatchers got together after the wind did all that damage to the Tincted Downs a few years ago, remember? Only I guess you were out on the Royal and didn't follow the news. Anyway, they put down their tools and refused to work until the Crown granted them a Guild charter."

"And now the weathering witches are doing the same? Interesting," Cade mused. "I have the feeling it's going to be a miserable wet winter in Gallybanks this year."

"And a lousy harvest this autumn," Jinsie said. "Nobody ever thinks about weathering witches in the city unless they're late clearing the snow off the streets. But farmers need them, and badly."

"So they applied for a charter," Rafe guessed, "and when they were refused, let the rain fall so long and hard that it flooded out villages? *That's* not going to go over very well."

"It's the only weapon they have," Jinsie said.

"What I meant was that anybody going to Ripplewater Tower for the service won't be at all happy."

"And that's the *other* thing. Nobody can get there who isn't already there—and that includes the dead." She winced a little. "I mean, the deceased. The bodies. Oh, you know what I mean. I'm so tired that my brains are rattling around inside my skull. Can I *please* go upstairs and rest now?"

They stood watching her climb the stairs, and Jeska said quietly, "It's about bloody time. My mum was a weathering witch. She had to work every single day she could, to keep us with food and a roof. It broke her in the end. It even broke her magic."

Cade had forgotten that. Impulsively, he put one arm around his masquer's shoulders and hugged tight. "We can send them the proceeds from our gigging at Lord Mindrising's next week. They can distribute it amongst themselves, and hold out longer for their Guild charter."

Jeska nodded his gratitude. Rafe frowned thoughtfully at Jinsie's disappearing figure up the stairs.

"Mayhap we ought to follow their example. Mayhap players need a Guild as well."

Cade felt his eyebrows attempt to hide in his hair. "I thought you were all for making this our last Royal, and going out on our own like the Shadowshapers did."

"I'll have to think on it some more. And have a talk with Jinsie. She and Kazie do our planning, after all."

Jeska regarded him, lips pursed. "Y'know, now that you mention it, Jinsie would make an excellent Guildmistress. My wife can handle Touchstone's business on her own . . . or hire whomever she needs."

Gaze flickering from one to the other of them, Cade asked, "You've been thinking about all this? And never told me?"

"It's been in the back of my mind, yeh," Rafe said. "Out on our own would be no use to the other players who have to put up with whatever the Master of the King's Revelries negotiates for circuit performances. But if every single one of us on all three circuits did a down-tools . . ."

"There are plenty of groups who don't get invited to Trials who'd be thrilled to take our places."

Rafe snorted his opinion of these upstarts. "And how much money d'you think the Crown would make off 'em?"

"Point taken. We'd all have to agree on what exactly it is we want—a guaranteed fee for each performance, no matter if anybody shows up or not, and a bigger cut of the profits."

"As for asks," Jeska laughed, "I'm sure Jinsie's got a whole long list!"

Cade was still considering it a couple of hours later when he knocked gently on Mieka's door. Thinking about something suppositional was infinitely preferable to thinking about the something definite he had

to tell the Elf. But telling him was obligatory, so when the light voice
called for him to enter, he took a deep breath and went in.

"Jinsie told you," Mieka said.

"Floods, bridges, and a down-tools by the weathering witches," Cade
summarized. He chose a chair by the window, with the afternoon sun
behind him. It was just possible that without a clear view of his face,
and especially his eyes, Mieka wouldn't notice any little . . . prevari-
cations. "I asked them to bring you up something to eat."

"Beholden." Mieka punched pillows against the headboard and sank
into them. "So what is it that you just can't wait to tell me? I know
that look, Quill."

So much for shadowing his face. "One of the Princess's men arrived
yesterday. One of her guards, the sort that don't look it. He wasn't in
her livery."

"She wouldn't send somebody anonymous to bring condolences."

"No. He was here—" Breaking off as someone knocked at the door,
he waited until the servant placed a tray of cold beef, cheese, bread,
and dill sauce on a table. The man finished arranging the meal, then
took up a large earthenware pitcher and poured out two tall glasses of
something that wasn't beer or ale. As had become his practice at all
their stops, Cade had privately asked whoever was in charge of the
kitchen to serve alcohol only if Mieka asked for it specifically. But he
had no idea what this drink was. A cautious sip revealed it to be cold
cinnamon tea with a little honey.

"Excellent," Mieka announced. "Ever tried chilled mocah?"

"I'll inform the cook, y'r honor," said the servant, and bowed his
way out.

"We should open a shop in Gallybanks," Cade said. "Mistress
Mirdley's blends of tea over ice, and various kinds of mocah, Threadchaser baked goods—open only in the summer because who wants a
cold drink in winter?" Cade knew he was babbling, and shut his mouth.

"So tell me," Mieka invited. "What did the Princess's messenger have
to say?"

He plunged in. "It was a warning. What happened wasn't an accident, any more than what happened to Yazz was an accident." He spoke
quickly, like ripping a bandage off a wound. Only this would be a new
wounding. "Their regular driver wasn't with them. They found him
at the bottom of a cliff, with a broken whiskey bottle nearby, as if he'd

got drunk and fallen to his death. But he was murdered. And so were they. The driver they had that night survived, and was questioned and released. And vanished."

He could see Mieka struggling with it, fists clenched and lips bitten. "Why them?" he demanded at last. "What did she and Ripplewater ever do—"

"It was naught to do with them, except that they're to do with us. We're being warned, Mieka. He's put us on notice. He's willing to go this far, to have them killed just to make clear to us—"

"Make *what* clear?"

"I don't know! But whatever it is, he's serious about it. This is a warning that if we do anything at all to try to stop him—"

"No. It's got to be wrong. None of us ever even *met* Ripplewater—"

"The usual coachman turns up broken at the foot of a cliff, his replacement gives the constables a sad little story and then disappears—"

"No, Cade, it can't be that way. I won't have it be that way."

"What you will or won't have has nothing to do with anything. The Princess's man showed me a copy of the crowner's report. They both had gashes across their throats along with all the other bruises and broken bones that would happen in a smash-up like that—Mieka, I'm sorry, but you have to hear this. The only explanation is that somebody took a knife to their throats. They were dead before the—"

"Or they survived the crash and the driver made sure after. And *not* because he didn't want them to suffer."

He'd been hoping Mieka wouldn't realize that. "The coachman said maybe it was shattered window glass, and the crowner accepted it—was paid to accept it, like as not. I'm sorry, I'm so sorry, Mieka."

Mieka drew his knees up to his chest and wrapped his arms around them. "Because of me. They're dead because of me."

This was what Cade had been most afraid of: guilt. "No," he insisted. "They're dead because the Archduke ordered them killed."

Mieka rested his forehead to his knees and tried not to be sick. Cade respected the silence for a time, but when he couldn't stand it anymore, he spoke Mieka's name.

Those eyes were staring at him, their different colors glinting angrily. "Why didn't you know? You with your 'gift'—why the fuck didn't you know?"

"It doesn't work that way. You know it doesn't work that way."

"Oh, that's right—it's only the *important* things, the things that affect *you*! She never meant anything, she wasn't worth much, whether she lived or died didn't matter—not to you!"

Very softly, Cade said, "I never saw *you*. Not once."

"What?"

"I never had an Elsewhen about you. Not until after you showed up that night in Gowerion. I can't control it, Mieka, even with thorn, I've never been able to control what comes to me, waking or sleeping—but one thing I can tell you, I saw her before I ever saw you in an Elsewhen. I don't remember exactly what it was—I got rid of it, the way I got rid of so many Elsewhens—but I do remember that I saw her. And when she showed up at Rafe and Crisiant's wedding—"

"So that's why," Mieka whispered. "I never did understand the look on your face. You never told me. Why didn't you ever tell me?"

"There are some things that aren't mine to tell. I can't make the choices. I'm not supposed to decide. If you could've been happy with her, it wasn't anything to do with me. And anyway, I knew you'd never believe me."

Mieka had the decency not to argue with him again over that. "You never saw me? Not even once?"

"Meeting you was the most important thing that ever happened to me, and I never saw it coming. I think it has to do with how much choice I have, how much influence. *You* were the one who decided to come to Gowerion that night. But with her—maybe what I saw was a warning not to intervene, or maybe it was to let me know what was coming so I could work out what to do, how to make it different—Mieka, I just don't *know*!"

"So you couldn't have seen this . . . you didn't have any choices to make. It was all someone else." He sounded even more exhausted than when he'd arrived. "Forgive me, Quill. All these years, I should be able to understand by now. I forget how helpless you must feel."

Cade was astonished to find his hands were shaking. He set down the glass and pushed himself to his feet. "I should let you rest."

"Wait—please, Quill. If they were murdered, and the Archduke is responsible—what's he warning us about? What does he get from killing her?"

"You loved her," Cade replied gently. "Perhaps he thought that this would send you over the edge. He can't know that you've already looked over and seen what's down there, and turned and walked away. You *chose*, Mieka. You saw the truth—"

Mieka shook his head. "What I finally saw was all the lies."

"This wasn't your fault, Mieka. What happened to them wasn't your fault."

"That's what Jinsie kept saying."

"It's the truth."

Whatever Mieka might have said in the next few moments was lost to Cade. It was another voice he heard, harsh with sorrow.

{ "Only tell me what I must do," she pleaded. "My girl, my beautiful girl—she's dead, and I want him as dead as she is!"

"Not dead. Not just yet. I still need him."

"You have Black Lightning."

"I do. But unless you can guarantee that they will overtake both Touchstone and the Shadowshapers as the most revered and admired group in Albeyn, they will never be of as much use to me as—"

"The Shadowshapers are easy," she interrupted. "Only wait for the two tregetours to quarrel again. They'll not last together past this Wintering. As for Touchstone . . ." She brushed a hand through the air. "They'll never be yours. You ought to have known that long since."

"I find it amusing," he remarked, wiping sweat from his brow and squinting across the river to the South Keep, sunripples glinting off the water in between, "to be told what I know and don't know by someone who knows exactly nothing."

"I know this," she countered. "There are hundreds, mayhap thousands, of purebred Caitiffs on the Durkah Isle. Women, Your Grace, not the men who live in Albeyn and keep the *name* alive here but never the *magic*."

"And are they ready, all these women, to renew the old vows?"

"Yes." She repeated it, sunlight cruel on her grief-lined face. "Yes!"

"To serve as your kind were sworn—no, let's use the term that white-haired bastard used in his pathetic play—*plighted* to serve in whatever shall be required?"

"Yes. I ask in return only *his* death."

"You have no right to ask anything, Caitiff! How little you understand. How stupid you are—what is it you wanted from me before? Riches, position, favor—banal ambitions for a banal mind. And now you want a death."

"Only the one. Vengeance for my girl."

"As it happens, death is a more worthy ambition . . . so long as life comes

of it. Very well. I require an understanding with all Caitiffs that their service is again expected. **Commanded.** Will you do this? Renew the ancient
alliance on behalf of all your kind? Will you go to the Isle and make sure
they're ready when called? If you do, you will have the death you seek."

"I plight myself and my kind—" }

He came back to himself still standing—barely, with one arm slung
over Mieka's shoulders. The Elf was speaking softly, giving him something to concentrate on, anchor himself to in real and not future reality.

". . . nervous when you go away like that and you're upright—but
this didn't last long, barely enough time for me to get over to you and
hold you up if you needed it. Back now, are you? No, don't say anything. Let's get you sat down again, eh? That's it. Have some tea."

He swallowed the cold liquid that was held to his lips and looked
up at Mieka. "She doesn't know," he heard himself say.

"Who doesn't?"

"Her grandmother. She doesn't know it was the Archduke. She's all
ready and eager to serve him—she thinks she has a better chance to
get at you if she's working for him."

"At *me*? Huh! I'd like to see her try!"

Cade would have argued, but it struck him as it had undoubtedly
occurred to Mieka that the only one of her plans that had succeeded
was the one that ended in the marriage. Everything after that—the
things they knew about or could guess at, anyway—had failed. And
now that they were on their guard . . .

He felt a smile tug the corners of his mouth. "Might be entertaining," he agreed laconically.

"That's me Quill!"

Mieka danced lightly over to the tray and snatched up a knife.
Wielding it like a sword, he advanced on an imaginary opponent, and
did it with a great deal of expertise, Cade noted.

"You and me, Quill, with swords and magic and swords that *are*
magic! That flea-bitten old crambazzle of a Witch doesn't stand a
chance!"

It didn't take the magic of a withie to supply the scene as Mieka
battered his opponent to his knees. He dug his fingers into the man's
hair and swung the sword down and across to lop off his head. Cade
could damned near *see* the grisly trophy held up high and dripping
blood, and the face was a familiar face. Before Cade could react, Mieka

tossed the invisible head aside, wiped the knife on his shirt, and flourished it several times in a low bow.

He applauded and smiled because he was expected to. And he mostly meant it. But there was something both childlike and frightening about Mieka's pantomime—and, worse, the face that Cade's own imagination had drawn, slack-jawed and empty-eyed in death.

Chapter 27

It was a long, joyless slog through the remainder of the Royal Circuit. Only one other piece of news had the power to astonish, and it came to Touchstone rather tardily. After Nevin Tranterly took them on an unplanned side trip to a town in the wrong direction for Lilyleaf, they rolled in to Croodle's well after midnight, tired, hungry, annoyed. Croodle was unsympathetic, saying that they ought to know every rock in every road of the Royal by now and if they got lost it was their own silly fault for not paying attention. But she said it while carving up a roast kept hot for them, and in between slices called out to the maids to make sure the sheets were fresh and scented in their rooms upstairs.

"You'll have missed the latest broadsheets, being on the road," she said as they began plowing through beef and bread and glazed carrots. "I've letters for you, of course, but they've been here a few days and this new thing only just happened—or at least we've just got word of it."

"And that might be?" Rafe asked.

"Not even a rumor was heard of it—not until the Palace announced it the other day, and then the broadsheets published it, to be spread all the way to Scatterseed by next week."

"Whatever it is, who'd it happen to?" asked Mieka.

"Princess Iamina and the Archduchess."

Jeska sighed. "You're better at drawing out a story than anyone but a tregetour ought to be."

"You'll never guess," Croodle told them.

"I'll bet I can." Cade stuck his fork into a carrot. "They're dead."

Croodle was vastly put out. "How did you know?"

"I've been waiting for it." When he reached for another hunk of bread, she snatched the plate up and glared. "Croodle, it was obvious. The Archduchess ruined herself with what happened at Great Welkin last year. He must've been furious with her for plotting behind his back."

"She must've thought it would please him," Rafe said with a glance at Mieka.

"That's as may be. When he sent her away for the summer, and Iamina with her, she probably thought she'd come back to Albeyn and all would be forgiven and forgotten."

"Ah," Croodle murmured, her voice soft but a dangerous glint in her eyes. "By making herself useful in the only way that counts with a man like that, she made herself useless."

"Exactly," Cade said. "She's the mother of a daughter who's supposed to marry the little Prince, and a son who'll be the next Archduke. Meddling the way she did, she made herself into a liability. I was surprised when they got safely to the Continent, and I thought I might be wrong, and he was only banishing her. But it appears I was right after all."

"If you're so bloody brilliant," Croodle challenged, "tell me how they died."

He hesitated a moment, not looking at Mieka. "Well . . . my first guess was a shipwreck." The Archduke had done it before, to Miriuzca's brother. Croodle wasn't privy to that information. "However, they arrived in the appropriate number of pieces, so . . ." It was just too appealing, and he knew it to be a flaw in his character, but he couldn't resist showing off that he had figured out what was a total mystery to everyone else. "It was a carriage accident, wasn't it? Somewhere along the coast, or a road above a river gorge, someplace like that."

"How in the name of everything holy—? Cayden Silversun, you're either too clever by half, or the luckiest guesser I've ever met—in which case, I'm taking you to the new gaming club on the south side of town!"

"Neither one, Croodle, me love," Mieka said. "It's just that he's the sneakiest and twisty-turniest cullion in Albeyn—second only to me own sneaky self, of course!"

Later, upstairs and in private, Mieka simply turned and looked at him.

Cade rummaged for his nightshirt. "I didn't see it in an Elsewhen. But, really—it's obvious, innit?"

"What's obvious to me," Mieka said quietly, "is that he felt he needed a rehearsal. What's her grandmother going to do when she finds out?"

"She'll be on the Isle by now, rallying Caitiffs to the cause. Mayhap she won't hear for a while—and it's possible she won't make the connection."

Mieka washed his face and hands in the basin like a good little Elf. "The Archduke promised to make me dead, and she wants me dead so much, she'll be blind to everything else."

"There is that," Cade acknowledged.

"It's touching, the faith some people put in other people's promises."

Cade tossed him a towel. "I know one thing for certain sure. I'm going to Chapel tomorrow. Derien's safe."

"I been thinking about that." He disappeared behind the towel for a moment, then emerged, pink-cheeked, and said, "And what I'm thinking is that you don't have to worry about not seeing him in any Elsewhens. He can make his own decisions and take care of himself."

As he settled in for the night, Cade reflected that Mieka was correct about promises: little if any faith should be put in them. Cade trusted more to patterns. *Meaning* was something that religion assured believers they could discern if they had faith enough, could subsume their own individual wants and needs and bend their heads to the divinities and trust to them for some kind of purpose to their lives. He wondered if Panshilara and Iamina, had they been told in advance that they were about to die at the Archduke's bidding, would have considered it all a part of a greater plan. Was anyone's faith in the Lord and the Lady deep enough, unquestioning enough? The only "greater plan" that Cade could see was manifestly not that of any divinity. What the Archduke meant to achieve was clear enough. How he meant to get it was still murky.

But if there was in fact a supreme plan, a divine logic, what right did he have to meddle in response to Elsewhens he didn't happen to like? Or was his gift of prescience an integral part of it all? Had all his diverse bloodlines come together to some deity's purpose? When he did change things—fumblingly, uncertainly, anxiously—should he simply have faith that whatever he did had some preordained meaning in a greater scheme?

Cade had never been much for faith. If he believed in anything, it was in his magic and his art. He had faith in himself—in his ability to create meaningful work—and in Touchstone, for being the instrument of expressing that meaning.

As for the rest of it . . . he turned onto his side so he could see Mieka—a lump of pale sheets in the nearby bed, a dark head on the pillow. Oddly enough, he had a remarkable degree of trust in Mieka's promise to forswear thorn and almost all liquor. Not because the Elf had promised Cade, but because he'd promised *himself.* Cade was just the visual reminder. Why this should be so wasn't entirely clear to him, but he wasn't about to argue with it, either. He had faith in Mieka— and this thought put a smile onto his face, for if anyone had told him when he'd first met this wild, capricious, mad little Elf that he'd end up trusting him, he would have marked that person down as tragically delusional.

It so happened that their path crossed the Shadowshapers' for a few days in Lilyleaf. Two of the Shadowshapers, anyway, which suited Touchstone: no competition for audiences.

Vered and Bexan showed up first, then Chat and Deshananda and their tribe of offspring. Sakary and Chirene had lingered for a few days at her grandparents' home in the country. Rauel and his wife, Breckyn, might be in Lilyleaf within the week, and then again they might not. One of their daughters was feeling a bit poorly, so their travel had slowed.

"It's a right mess, trying to plan anything," Chat confided cheerfully on the night he arrived. "But it's really like a goodly long holiday. We play when and where we like, and if we don't feel like it, we don't." He slid an arm around Deshananda. "And having our families with us is—"

"—a rare blessing and a total disaster," she finished for him. "Four girls, two boys, all betwixt the ages of three and eleven, one nursemaid, one governess, one footman, three coaches and three coachmen— they have to play as often as possible to pay for it all. As for keeping everyone housed and fed, and gathered up with their things packed and ready to go when it's time to leave—" She shuddered. "Never again, precious husband, never again!"

They were lazing around after an early dinner in Croodle's back garden. Vered and Chat were treating their wives to a night out at Touchstone's performance that evening. Jeska was moping, picturing himself with his own wife and sighing for her absence. He'd hoped that Kazie would be at Lilyleaf to visit with her cousin Croodle for a week or two while Touchstone was there, but instead a letter had been waiting for him saying that the children were in the process of passing a summer cold back and forth. When Kasslie had the sniffles, her brother, Jeccan, had the cough. A few days later, the symptoms would be reversed. Listening to the parents in the group—all of them, except for him—discuss child-rearing had Cayden congratulating himself once again on being childless.

Once the obvious subject of Archduchess Panshilara's and Princess Iamina's demise was discussed—with Cade and Mieka studiously avoiding each other's eyes and hoping nobody else recognized how similar the circumstances were to the deaths of Lord and Lady Ripplewater—talk moved to the even more obvious subject of theater. Black Lightning was creating almost as much chavishing as the Shadowshapers' return to performing, with a new play that seemed to be effectively plotless. And *effective* it most certainly was.

"Nearly as I can figure," Vered said, "there's a sequence of scenes, each one to demonstrate a particular emotion. Happiness, rage, something funny and then something sad, and so forth. They do the setup with a minimum of words, and then drown the audience in what it feels like."

"Never the same series or situations twice," Chat said, "so people keep coming back a second or third time. Rather like your 'Doorways' for that, and full apologies for the comparison, so don't thump me. There's nothing subtle about any of it. There's one—or so I've heard—as has a man come home to find another man's socks under his pillow. Now, why they should be under his pillow, of all places, nobody says."

"I always leave mine on the bedposts," Mieka said. "That way, I see them and don't forget them when I leave."

"I didn't hear that," said the glisker, whose wife mimed throwing a bread roll at him. "Anyways, in the play—if you can call it that, which I wouldn't—first there's shock, and then there's furiousness. Which he takes out on his wife."

"Beating her," Bexan said tightly. "Nothing spoken but words like *slut* and *whore* and *bitch*—while he takes his fists to her and beats her bloody as she screams for mercy."

It was out of their power to shock Cade with this. "I read an interview Thierin Knottinger gave to the *Blazon*'s theater writer. He said— if you can believe it—that they let the audience feel such things on purpose, so they can get out all those emotions and don't act on them in their daily lives."

"Doing everybody a favor," Rafe muttered. "Isn't that sweet of them."

"Exposing and then draining away the dark and violent emotions," Cade went on, "purging them, if you will. He also said that they do gentler things—like a girl getting a proposal of marriage, for instance, that lets the 'less fortunate'—that's how he phrased it—experience such things for probably the only time in their lives."

Jeska drew expanding circles in a puddle of condensation left by the beer pitcher. "But isn't that what we all do, in a way? Think about people's faces when they come into the theater. They're hoping we're going to take them someplace other than their own lives. Cade did a piece about it. 'The Avowal'—where we promise them that there, in the theater with us, it's safe to feel."

Bexan fairly turned on him, dark eyes snapping with anger. "You're supposed to *evoke* emotions, not batter people with them! You're supposed to give them a story that leads into feeling what the characters are feeling! A masquer uses his skills to persuade, and a glisker enhances what they're already feeling because of the words the tregetour has written—"

"And the fettler," said Rafe, "keeps it all under control. I think Jeska's right, dear lady. And I think you're right, too. What Cade wrote about coming to the theater to experience things they wouldn't ordinarily experience—or that they're too scared of the consequences to let themselves feel—they *are* safe with us. They trust us to make it meaningful and yet keep it from overwhelming them. And that's where Black Lightning—and I do beg your pardon, ladies—can give you a guided tour of all the many shits they do not give. They *want* to drown their audiences."

"Something else Cade said once," Mieka offered. "That they're a group for addicts. Like thorn-thrall, or not being able to face the day without half a bottle of brandy at breakfast."

"The question is," Cade mused, "are they the future of theater? Will we all end up—"

The howls and growls of protest that interrupted him made him smile.

When the din died down, he said, "Well, then, we'll just have to keep showing them that it's more satisfying in the long view to see a play with an actual plot, and characters, and good writing, and masquers who know their craft, gliskers of skill and subtlety, and fettlers who make sure everybody's not wrung out like an old washcloth by the end of the evening."

That night Touchstone did "The Avowal" just for Vered and Chat and their wives. Standing at his lectern, Cade hid another smile when he saw the two men nodding quietly to themselves. Curious to think that the whole piece had come to him in an Elsewhen. . . .

Chat escorted the ladies back to their inn, for Vered had something he wanted to discuss with Cayden. For a time Bexan looked as if she might insist on staying, but Vered gave her a soft kiss and a softer smile and told her he'd be back soon. He and Cayden walked slowly to Croodle's, talking.

"Two years ago," Vered confided, "I would've told my wife to shut her trap and do as she was told. A year ago, I would've said it was men's business, and given her a slap on the rump by way of farewell."

"You've learned wisdom in your old age," Cade teased.

"I learned because I got *schooled*, boy, and no two ways about it. I wasn't there, y'see, when my other children were born. When I saw what Bexan went through . . . four babies, Cade. *Four!*" He shook his head, marveling. "I miss the little bantlings, though I have to say it's nice to sleep the night through. Anyway, there were a couple of things I wanted to get your opinion about."

"First tell me why you didn't use the name you know for certain sure to be one of the original Knights."

"Oh, that. Well, I thought about it. And when I do the third play in the cycle—"

"Three? All in one night?"

"With a break between the second and third. As it stands, the Knights look like heroes, yeh? Noble sacrifice and all like that. Would we want such a thing attributed to that name? We would not. But once

I show audiences exactly what they became . . ." He finished with a grin, teeth white against his dark skin in the lamplight.

Cade considered. "Just don't tell anybody about it before you present it for the first time. Talking of which, Bexan might want to have a talk with Jinsie Windthistle when you get back to Gallybanks—about publishing the plays, and who has the rights to them."

"They've been corresponding all through this trip!" Vered laughed. "All right, then. First thing is, don't you think it's odd that magical folk on the Continent were eventually all thrown out? I mean, they gave the Knights all those spells and suchlike for battle, and ended up saving everybody. Were the Knights and their Caitiffs so evil that everybody just decided to have done with magic completely?"

"Maybe the tale got warped in the centuries between. That often happens. If it twisted round so that people thought the Wizards and so on created the Knights apurpose, to terrorize and control the population . . ."

"Hmm. Yeh, I've been leaning in that direction meself. You see the same thing in the Perils—what happened according to the standard scripts isn't what *really* happened, historically speaking. But even if that's the explanation, it doesn't prevent the people on the Continent from using magical folk when it suits them."

"They're incredibly suspicious, though." About to cross a street, Cade held Vered's elbow to keep him in place as a carriage passed at reckless speed. "Lady Vrennerie told me that Miriuzca's mother was stripped naked and inspected before the wedding. Looking for the Caitiff mark, I guess. Did you ever figure out what that is?"

Vered shrugged. "Just a sop to the common folk, I think. If there's no way to recognize a Caitiff, then *anybody* could be one. So they made something up as a comfort and a reassurance."

"I think—" Cade paused, turning slightly as somebody yelped up ahead. Cursing ensued, but no shouts for help. "I think you're wrong. Mistress Mirdley said once that Trolls look for the mark before testing a Caitiff in a river after it's rained. Pure water is supposed to be poisonous to them."

"I thought we settled that."

"Yeh. But if a bespellment involving rainwater to wash away the mark and the magic got turned into an antipathy to pure water so that no Caitiff would *want* to work that spell—oy, I'm getting confused!"

"Life," Vered announced, "is so much easier when you leave the research to the Royal Archivists. But that remembers me of something. Did Mieka's wife—the Lady aid her soul," he interjected piously, "did she or her mother ever go walking in the rain?"

"No idea." Cade hid the annoyance this question caused him. "You could ask Mistress Luta about rainwater in Seekhaven, if you're touring past there this summer."

"I'll wait and talk to your Mistress Mirdley. She's the only Troll-wife who doesn't completely terrify me. And I'll tell you why they scare me silly, and I'll wager you that your Mistress Mirdley never told you *this*. Trolls have the watchkeeping of Caitiffs because on the Continent, Trolls didn't just live under bridges, but in mountain caverns, too. They like to be beneath things like soil and rock, like that. The Knights being what they became, they sought the deepest darknesses they could find during the daylight hours. Caitiffs used their weaving magic to evict Trolls from hundreds of caves."

No, he hadn't heard this before. "Didn't the Trolls fight back?"

Vered nodded. "In a small but intense magical war that involved just them and the Caitiffs. Nobody won. But I'm thinking it was one of those happenings that increased fear of magical folk in general over there."

"Where'd you learn all this?"

"Bexan's great-grandmother. The old woman—and, Gods in Glory, I do mean *old*! The only thing as has more wrinkles is a ten-pound bag of prunes! She's descended from some Piksey bloodline or other that keeps the racial records. Not in charge herself, nor anybody she knew personally, but there were family stories. There was one about a Troll having a slight difference of opinion with a dragon over the same cavern, the argument settled by the Pikseys doing something deviously Pikseyish, that would make a great comedy."

"You can ask Mistress Mirdley about that, too—if you dare!"

To Cade's surprise, Mieka was still awake. Or, rather, he explained he'd been mostly asleep and then something had occurred to him, and he'd been waiting *hours* for Cade to stop gwicking beer and come upstairs.

"We didn't touch a drop when we got back, not even tea," Cade replied. "You know Vered doesn't drink much these days. And for your information, I do not *gwick*, and never have. Neither have I swilled or bloddered, though I may have swigged on occasion and even gulped at times, and I have, perhaps once or twice, guzzled, but only when I was very thirsty."

"Yeh, yeh, whatever," Mieka said impatiently. He sat up in bed, arms crossed atop his knees. "Are you gonna keep your tongue from flapping for a while so I can talk?" When Cade gave him a brief bow and a flourish of the hand that invited him to speak, Mieka made a face at him. "Muchly beholden, O Great Tregetour. When we were doing 'Dragon' tonight, did it strike you that the dragon in 'Dragon' might not really be a dragon? What I mean is, what if it's not a dragon, but one of the Knights? Their symbol was a dragon. Drevan told you so, right? Seeing as how they were what they were—and why doesn't anybody use the word?—anyways, caves would've been perfect to spend the daylight in. As for guarding hoards of riches, though this really doesn't matter much, they'd have to pay the Caitiffs somehow, wouldn't they, for doing whatever dreadful things they did for them, like bring them living people—a princess, for preference—so the blood is fresh and warm—"

At this point Mieka was pretty much compelled to take in a good long breath. All Cade could think was that he had to have eavesdropped on the conversation with Vered tonight.

"I've been worryin' this inside me head, Quill, ever since we first saw *Blood Plight*, and we just did 'Dragon' again tonight and maybe Vered and Chat being here started me puzzling it all out again, but right in the middle, it just sort of hit me that it would kind of fit, wouldn't it? We could do it that way, now that people have seen Vered's plays—and we changed 'Dragon' the very first time we ever did it, so who cares for the standard scripts and precedents anyways? The prince goes after the princess because one of the Knights with a dragon on his shield is about to have her for dinner and he's got to save her, and her lines have to be really terrified this time because she knows what's about to happen to her—it'd be *wicked* scary, Quill, because we'd have to show the blood-drained corpses in the cavern waiting for the Caitiffs to carry them out and bury them, and we'd also have to do a real Vampire—there, I said it!"

Again the tumble of words stopped while he drew breath. Cade would never understand how he could talk so much and breathe so seldom.

"But should we do what Vered does, and have the prince slice its head off, or use one of the other methods? A wooden stake would at least be different from the Shadowshapers, though not half so flashy— no, I think we have to use a sword for the death sequence. What d'you think, Quill?"

"I think," he said slowly, tying the laces of his nightshirt, "that we'll have the Vampire wear orange and gray."

Mieka bounced excitedly on the mattress. "Then you don't hate it? You want to see if we can do it?"

"Oh, I'm sure we can do it."

Vered Goldbraider's third play to show what the Knights had become would take him months and months to write and even more months to perfect, what with the contentiousness of the Shadowshapers' rehearsals. Cade felt sure that he could write this variation on "Dragon" in a fortnight, and have it ready to perform this winter in Gallybanks.

Mieka was watching him narrowly as he got into bed. "Even showing people exactly who the Knight's family is?"

He stretched luxuriously under clean, sweet-scented sheets. "Mieka, we're not just going to show them. We're going to use the *name*, spoken right out loud."

"And Jeska can kill him?"

"Oh, yes. As disgustingly as possible. Maybe with a half-blocked sword to the neck, that only gouges him some, and he loses the sword and has to use something made of wood—" Something occurred to him. "Do they bleed, Vampires? There has to be *something* running through their veins. Do you know?"

"It's *our* play and this one can bleed lemon custard if we want him to! Ha! Glorious! Beholden, Quill! I can't wait!"

Mieka flopped back onto his pillows, chuckling. It was good to see him happy, though Cade had to admit that it was also a somewhat ghoulish joy. But one thing was for certain sure: Both of them fell asleep without one single thought for the comforts of whiskey or thorn.

Chapter 28

Despite how inspired and even brilliant his idea seemed at the time, Mieka had second thoughts about it first thing the next morning. By the time they were back in Gallybanks, the wagon rolling slowly through the early-morning tangle of traffic towards Wistly Hall, he calculated that he was, roughly speaking, on his thousandth or so thought about it. And every single one of those thoughts indicated that changing "Dragon" was a very bad idea.

He was grateful that Cayden hadn't brought it up again. Probably he had been having the same thoughts. Possibly they were even worse. Satisfying as revenging himself on the Archduke would be, changing the dragon in the cavern to a Knight bearing the name Henick was a thing so dangerous that not even reminding himself that the man was responsible for the death of Jindra's mother could keep him from the sort of cold, hollow fear that in times past had sent him to the thorn-roll. There were families to think about, and friends. The sight of Jindra running down the stairs to greet him when he walked in the front door at Wistly made his heart cringe so painfully that the wince almost showed on his face.

After a nap in a bed that didn't swing or sway, he bounded down Wistly's stairs to find everybody else ready for lunching on the river lawn. Cade took him aside afterwards and showed him a letter from Drevan Wordturner that had been awaiting him; the essence was a desperate plea to persuade Vered Goldbraider to forget his name and indeed his very existence. The questions Vered had been sending from all over Albeyn were not of the sort that could be answered without personal risk, and Drevan would like his various internal organs to stay right where they belonged.

"I've been thinking about 'Dragon,'" Cade began.

Mieka interrupted. "So've I. We can't. It's lovely to think about, but we really can't, Quill. Not *that* way, at least."

"I know." A quiet sigh, a shrug. "I'll have more than enough to do at the new house, anyways. No time to write anything."

It was as good an excuse as any. Mieka knew it was cowardice, but if being a coward kept him and his safe, a coward he'd gladly be. The Archduke had gifted Touchstone with enough attention; they didn't have to deliberately poke him in the eye with a sharp stick. Let the Shadowshapers occupy him for a while.

To Cayden he said, "Vered had better find something else to busy himself, too. Drevan sounds frantic. You said Vered really didn't tell you much, but I can guess what kind of questions he's asking."

"Me, I don't *want* to guess."

Jindra ran up to them then, demanding to know when they would go home. Mieka swung her up into his arms and traded a look with Cayden as he again realized his mother's wisdom. Having the child stay at the new house a few nights at a time throughout the summer had not just accustomed her to the idea of living there. She now thought of it as *home.*

So, to his surprise, did Mieka.

They moved in the day after returning from the Royal. Yazz was there to help—his left arm useless, but a one-armed part-Giant was still worth three or four ordinary men. Mishia used her hover-spell to excellent effect and forbade Mieka on pain of pain he couldn't even imagine not to attempt the same. Almost all the heavier furniture from the house at Redpebble Square had already been distributed throughout the new house (which still didn't have a name), but there was a lot of rearranging to be done and Mistress Mirdley's kitchen and still-room to be organized with things that couldn't be moved until the last minute. Once Yazz had repositioned beds and standing wardrobes, couches and cabinets, he was detailed to hang herbs from the stillroom ceiling and arrange pots and pans in upper shelves so Mistress Mirdley didn't have to climb up and down the stepladder a dozen times. She allowed no one else into the kitchen for several hours, in fact, and

Mieka was devoured by both hunger and curiosity when Yazz finally emerged, grinning, to announce that lunching would be at the next chime.

Jindra spent half the morning dragging Mieka and Cayden by the hand through every room at least twice. She gave them the tour as if she not only owned the place but also designed which rooms would be used for what and chosen every piece of furniture and decoration. This was her *home*. Mieka learned during the explorations that she had been told, and believed, that Mummy had gone to live with the Angels and wouldn't be able to visit because it was so very far away. This made her sad, she confided, but Mummy must be very happy where she was. This was a good thing, because Mummy used to cry a lot and now she never would again.

Mieka hid a grimace and avoided Cade's eyes.

Back in Cade's drawing room, pleasantly weary and waiting for someone to direct him to food, Mieka held his daughter in his lap and decided that this afternoon her naptime would be his naptime, too. Their side of the house was on the west, Cade's and Derien's on the east. The ground floor of each half of the archway was divided into a drawing room (with small garderobes) fronting the river, and, facing the back garden, the dining room and Mistress Mirdley's kitchen and stillroom on Cade's side and her living quarters on Mieka's. The next floor ran the width of the building above the arch, with bedrooms and sitting rooms and bathrooms. The uppermost story held Cade's library and writing room, and a long, narrow hall floored in polished oak that puzzled Mieka until his daughter announced that this was his "sword boards"—his practice room for fencing. Jinsie's idea, Mistress Mirdley later told him, so that he wouldn't be waving lethal blades about to the detriment of the drawing room curtains. There were windows all along the riverside wall and the opposite wall was decorated with all Touchstone's placards in frames and Trials medals in glass boxes on shelves. Behind this wall were two long, narrow rooms overlooking the garden. These were for any footmen and maids they decided to hire—which, considering the size of the house, was likely to happen sooner rather than later. On Mieka's side of the building, a match to Cade's library but smaller, was a study for Derien and Jindra.

She was dozing against his shoulder, trusting and comfortable. It gave him a sensation compounded of feeling protective and feeling safe, strange but welcome. He startled himself a little when it occurred to him to be glad that he was sober and clear-headed and could appreciate it.

Cade lazed near the windows in a big, comfortable armchair, long legs sprawled, looking with a whimsical bemusement at one corner of the room where a huge standing vase of dark blue ceramic contained the array of peacock feathers Mieka had given him on his twenty-fourth Namingday. Mieka had assumed that when Cade was thrown out of his flat later that year for not paying the rent, the feathers had somehow got lost. But here they were, a malevolent beauty as far as theater folk were concerned: Mieka's defiant answer to superstition. He was about to make a comment to that effect when he saw Cade's gray eyes go all unfocused. He waited out the Elsewhen, hoping it would be a good one. And it was. When it ended, Cade was smiling.

"Well?" Mieka asked softly.

"I just realized something."

"And that might be?"

His laugh was pure mischief—a sound Mieka had rarely heard before. "The Elsewhens aren't just a warning to change something or really bad stuff will happen. They're a warning that I'd better not fuck up, or I'll miss out on the good stuff!"

Mieka couldn't help laughing, which woke Jindra, which turned out to be all right because just then the village Minster chimed the hour. Yazz appeared in the doorway, carrying a large table aloft by its leg, one-handed. Mistress Mirdley was behind him with the lunching tray: bread, cheese, fresh fruit salad, pickles, carrots, mocah-almond cakes, and cinnamon tea over ice. Yazz set up the table, Mieka and Cade pulled chairs around, and they all pounced.

Later, when they'd taken Jindra up to her room for her nap and Mieka was about to announce himself intent on doing the same, Cade pulled him into the hallway and half-closed Jindra's door.

"I saw her," Cade said, low-voiced. "She was sixteen, maybe seventeen—Mieka, she just *whirled* into the room downstairs saying that somebody had accepted her—I'm not sure who or for what, but she was completely happy. Probably something to do with school. And she was so beautiful!"

"Just do me one tiny little favor, eh? You always get all compulsive and worryful about what you might or might not have to do to change the bad things. *Please*, for the love of anything holy, don't get the same way about being careful not to fuck it all up!"

Cade nudged him playfully with an elbow as they headed for the hallway leading to their own bedchambers. "Oh, but that's just it. I have this feeling that everything has come right. That being here, in this house—" He stopped, made a sound of frustration. "In stories and plots for plays, just when things are going well, *that's* when the wheels come off the wagon. It has to be that way, that the characters are at odds over something or other, so that a crisis brings them back together in spite of themselves, and they learn—the audience learns—that working together is much better than struggling on alone."

"But being here doesn't feel like that?"

"No. If this were a play, full-blown Elsewhens of total disaster should be giving me nervous fits. Warning me against even the slightest sensation of complacency. But what I saw today—it's *right*, Mieka. Doing this is *right*."

"This isn't a play, old thing," Mieka reminded him, amused. "This is life. Our life. I'm not stupid enough to think we're owed this, or we've earned it, or even that we deserve it. But I'm not gonna complain about it, either!"

"I'm not complaining! I'm just trying to say that it seems like my whole life I've done the things that felt right at the time, but this—" He waved a hand to indicate everything: the house, Derien, Jindra, Mieka, Mistress Mirdley, himself, *everything*. "This feels like it's going to be right for the rest of my life. This is where I'm supposed to be, and I've never felt that except when I'm onstage."

Mieka surprised himself again. "Me, too. It's—" He groped for a word, then realized he'd had it all along. "It's home." Out of everything that had happened, out of all the hurts and angers and mistakes and misunderstandings, somehow this good thing had come. And Cade was right: they'd be fools to fuck it up.

"And just so you know," Cade said as Mieka opened his own bedchamber door, "Mistress Mirdley and Derien and I—not to speak of your parents and Jinsie—have come to a decision. Nobody cares what you do on the Royal or in Gallybanks or when Jindra's visiting at Wistly Hall. But the first time you bring a woman here while Jindra's within a mile of this house . . ." He smiled with devastating charm. "Let's just say the first time will be your last. Ever."

"Quill!" Mieka exclaimed, outraged that Cade could think for an instant that he'd do something so vulgar.

"And I do mean *ever.* As in losing the wherewithal for any little adventures of that sort for the rest of your life." He paused, still smiling, but with a warning glitter in his gray eyes. "I take it you understand? Excellent. I knew you were a bright lad underneath all that deliberate stupidity. Dinner's at seven, as usual. Don't be late."

He pushed Mieka into the room and shut the door in his face.

*   *   *

Their naps weren't long ones. Mieka, whose bedchamber was at the back of the house, heard a mild commotion in the garden just as he was dropping into a real sleep. After dragging himself off the bed, he looked down from the window but could see nothing and no one, though the voices told him the visitors were his brothers and their wives.

He hauled his trousers on and went barefoot downstairs. Whatever they'd been doing at the back doors, they were now outside in the archway, where a door led into each drawing room. He joined Cayden in watching as Jed drilled a single hole in the thick oaken door and Blye inserted something, whereupon Eirenn—tall, chestnut-haired, dark-skinned, very pregnant, and taking the three descending steps very carefully—went back outside.

"What are they doing?" Mieka asked.

Cade answered with a bewildered shrug.

Blye tiptoed to peer through whatever she had placed in the hole. Eirenn called out, "Is it working?"

"Gorgeously! Now the other one."

Jez began filling the edges of the hole with something or other, while the other three crossed the cobbles to Cade's drawing room door and repeated the process. Mieka and Cade followed, still confused. Jindra had joined them, and Derien and Mistress Mirdley. At length, after Eirenn had once again asked her baffling question and Blye replied just as happily, they all gathered round the open door.

"Home-cozying presents," Jez explained with a grin as he finished the seal around what looked like a length of glass circled by polished brass. "Eirenn, dear heart, one more time?" She nodded, and he shut the door. "Want to give it a try, Miek?"

He didn't quite have to stand on tiptoe. Squinting through the glass, for a moment all he saw was Eirenn. Then he yelped and jumped back as the glass suddenly glowed crimson round the edges. "What the—? What is this, Jez?"

"Just a little something my brilliant bride dreamed up. Take a look, Cade."

He did, and reacted with a start. "It shows if the person outside is using magic!"

"It won't tell you what kind of magic," Blye said, "or whether it's for good or ill, but at least it's a bit of a warning."

"Do we need warning?" Cade asked, bemused.

"We think you do," said Eirenn, and lowered herself into a chair. "We've done the same for the front and back doors of all the Shadowshapers' houses."

"Especially Vered's," Blye added grimly. "I'd put them into every ground-floor window, too, if I could."

"Beholden," Mieka said. "Lovely idea, if not a particularly lovely thought behind it. I assume you're all here for dinner? Do we have enough food, Mistress Mirdley, or shall I nip down to the local shops?"

"All those months at Redpebble," she asked tartly, "and have you ever known me *not* able to feed however many showed up in the dining room? Cade, this is *your* drawing room, welcome your guests and see them comfortable in chairs while Derien and I fetch cold drinks." She left with the grinning Derien, muttering, "When I think of the work I went to, trying to learn that boy some manners—!"

Mieka had the feeling that Cade's drawing room would become their usual gathering place, and wondered briefly what would be done with his own. But someone else was knocking at the door, and he remembered to peer through the peephole—no red glow—before opening it gladly to Rafe and Crisiant.

If they'd wanted a quiet first night in the new house, it wasn't going to happen. It seemed they were throwing a party. Jeska and Kazie arrived, and Mieka's parents and the rest of his siblings, and for the first time in his life, Mieka really did worry that there wouldn't be enough to feed them all. He didn't dare insult Mistress Mirdley by asking again, but he did remind himself to do some shopping tomorrow.

And these thoughts told him that this truly was *his* home.

This was emphasized at Wintering, which he organized himself with Jinsie's help. A real Elfen celebration, with tables groaning under huge platters of food and drink, and singing and dancing with music provided by a longtime customer of Hadden Windthistle's named Garef Bendering. (Mieka had tried to get Alaen Blackpath, but he was already engaged by the Archduke for a whole week; something about a gathering at one of His Grace's country holdings.) Bendering was mostly Human from the same Islands as Kazie and Croodle, with a touch of Troll in his gait and a hint of Wizard in the long fingers that danced over the strings of his lute. No magic in his music that Mieka could detect, but that didn't mean the music didn't have a magic all its own.

The old year was banished and the lights went out one by one (courtesy Derien). Then Jindra came in, dressed as Spring with flowers woven through her thick black hair, wearing a charmingly antiquated Elfen costume of bright red blouse and bright green dagged-hem skirt that she had sewn herself with some help from Mistress Mirdley. She was as yet too young for full Caitiff magic—though her gift of a pillow for her uncle Jez's wounded leg a few years ago had the sweetness of her love and concern for him in every stitch. The lights came up again, the music started anew, and Cilka and Petrinka went round to give everyone a flower in a small, thin vase crafted by Blye. The guests would take these home and Cilka, who was very good at such things, would visit next week to read the fall of petals that would foretell the events of the coming year.

It was well past midnight before everyone left and they had the house to themselves. Mieka, who had stretched out a single beer (a rather large one, admittedly) through half the evening and then switched to icy tea that was the same color as good whiskey, climbed the stairs to the bedchamber floor, then reconsidered and kept going. Past the sword boards, more formally known as his fencing studio, where a rack of variously sized practice blades shone by moonlight through the riverside windows; down the hallway to a steep, narrow staircase that led to the roof. Flat and broad, with a four-foot wall all round (Mieka wanted to have it crenellated, like a castle), next summer it would have potted trees and troughs of herb beds, comfortable chairs and tables. For now, a visit by a weathering witch had melted all the snow, making it safe to walk across. The witch had been well paid for his work. The prospect of floods or droughts ruining the harvest had motivated country folk, and everyone knew that every city in Albeyn would come to a standstill this winter without the weathering witches to clear the snow, so King Meredan had given in to Princess Miriuzca's pleas and granted them a Guild with a Royal Charter.

That it had been Miriuzca to take up their cause impressed Derien, who had explained to them her political maneuvering. Not just the witches but everyone who depended on them—which *was* pretty much everyone—adored her even more deeply than before. There was, of course, the possible exception of the more tightfisted amongst the landowners who had to pay more for rain and sunshine at the appropriate intervals, and the more miserly amongst the city-dwellers who had to pay more to have streets and sidewalks cleared of snow. But the specter of a bad harvest and subsequent privation had scared everybody, and Miriuzca was seen as a heroine by everyone from the lowliest peasant to the King himself, who was rumored to have remarked that one did appreciate a bit of rain now and then in the hot summer months, and some sunshine every so often in winter.

"The broadsheets," Derien said, "are reporting—unofficially, of course—that she told the King about a withered harvest in her homeland one year when she was a little girl, and how much the people suffered. What they aren't reporting is that what moved her father to action was having to sell off the best studs in the royal stables to buy grain from other countries."

"And that's what convinced King Meredan?" Mieka asked.

"All very secret," he said with a knowing grin.

"Then how did you find out about it?"

"Books," he replied blithely. "For one thing, it didn't happen during Miriuzca's childhood. It was a generation or so earlier. She knows that the King isn't one for reading history, except the history of Albeyn, and then it's only what impacts him personally. And it wasn't the crown's horses, it was the crown jewels. She also knows that Meredan isn't much for shiny rocks, but he does love his horses. She's a very clever woman, our Miriuzca," he finished with an appreciative nod. Mieka, trading glances with Cade, knew that they were thinking exactly the same thing: *Future government minister sitting right here at our dinner table.*

Mieka smiled now at the memory, standing at the parapet, looking down at the snow-swathed garden. Cilka and Petrinka viewed the roughly three acres as an opportunity for agricultural experiments in shaped hedges and exotic plants. Mistress Mirdley had claimed a section for vegetables. Mieka wanted a maze, and if nobody agreed with him, then he'd buy up some of the land next door and build it himself. He rather hoped so; demolishing the wall would provide some lovely fun.

That thought led to a stifled snigger as he recalled an incident of that autumn when both he and Cayden forgot their keys to the garden gate. It happened after a gigging at the Keymarker. Mieka and Cade had both found congenial company afterwards, and just before dawn, with the mist drifting across the river, Mieka had caught Cade (though Cade insisted that he had been the one to catch Mieka) skulking round to the river side of the house at an exceedingly unrighteous hour of the morning. They'd nearly suffocated themselves trying not to laugh, fearful of waking everybody in the house.

Repairing to the kitchen for a snack, they compared notes on the difficulties of enjoying their status as celebrated theater players now that taking a girl home wasn't possible. Sometimes the chosen companion of the night had her own flat, but mostly not. Sneaking about somebody's parents' house was, they agreed, something they had outgrown long since. Mieka had found an amiable tavern keeper who, for a price, let him have an upstairs bedroom for a few hours. Cade had an old school friend who occasionally obliged by vacating his premises in favor of a night with his own girlfriend. Getting laid was getting to be unmanageable, and the only thing either of them could think of was renting a small flat in town and keeping to a schedule for its use.

Which both of them thought rather tawdry. Still, what else could they do? They were young, sought after, unattached, and well off again. It would be criminal not to take advantage of circumstances that most men would gladly give a testicle to experience.

"You're on the wrong side of the roof," Cade said softly behind him, and Mieka spun round. "Didn't mean to startle you. I thought those Elfen ears of yours caught everything in a half-mile range."

"Only when I'm paying attention. Why is this the wrong side of the roof?"

Cade ignored the question and came to stand beside him, looking out at the garden. "I'm glad we did this tonight. I'm beholden to you,

Mieka. I never had many good Winterings to remember in place of that one with Iamina and the Woodwose. I was thinking about it tonight, but in a remote sort of way. As if it all happened to somebody else."

Mieka nodded. "We can do this every year, if you like."

"I would. Come over here for a moment, will you?"

He followed Cade to the river side of the roof, and caught his breath. There below him, stretching the length of the Gally until it curved southward, was a moonglade.

"You're always asking me to make you a moonglade onstage. How about one you can live in? What d'you say we call the house that? Moonglade Reach."

"Perfect!"

And it was. There was the real wonder of it: that something, *any-thing*, in life could really be perfect. Not just the *right* thing, but the *perfect* thing.

Chapter 29

Enjoying themselves with dawdling and detouring, it had taken the Shadowshapers all summer and part of autumn to make a leisurely tour of Albeyn, sticking to the more populous middle and west of the Kingdom. As Cade understood it, they would settle at a congenial inn (or two, considering the size of the four family parties), relax, play a show if they felt like it, appreciate the weather and the sights and each other's company, then move on. Touchstone, on the Royal Circuit schedule that summer, had encountered them only once, in Lilyleaf, though they barely missed each other at Frimham.

Cade would have welcomed the distraction: Mieka thought nobody knew that he'd gone to a certain house and stood there staring at it, then walked aimlessly along the beach for hours. Cade was more relieved than he could put into words that Mieka's reaction to the pain of separation, the bitterness of divorce, and the shock of her appalling death hadn't been a months-long binge of thorn and liquor and women and sorrow. He was ashamed of himself for his impatience with this one small indulgence in Frimham—surely Mieka deserved a few brief hours to be alone with his grief. Yet when he'd returned, solemn and dispirited, Cade had been on the edge of snapping at him. It was over, she was dead, let that be an end to it. Cold of him, he knew, and lacking in compassion. But something Mieka said that night had grated on his nerves all the way back home to Gallybanks.

"You never even asked her name."

Startled, he'd turned in bed to stare across the room. "No," he said at last. "I didn't want to know it. I don't now."

"Because she never mattered to you."

"She was Jindra's mother. Of course she mattered."

An impatient sigh. "What I'm saying, in case you'd care to listen, is that *she* never mattered. As herself. As a person. Not to you."

He couldn't deny it. Neither could he explain that she had had meaning only as the source of his own anxiety and Mieka's pain, nor say out loud that he was just as glad she was gone forever. Not glad that she was dead—he wasn't a monster—but that she would never trouble their lives again.

He couldn't say he was sorry, either. He wasn't. And Mieka knew it.

The bustle and excitement of moving into the new house had pushed the subject out of his mind, until one day, a few weeks after Wintering when they'd decided that Mieka's largely unused drawing room would do much better as a sort of private tavern tap-room and dining room, he came in one afternoon to find Mieka and Jindra placing framed drawings and imagings on the wall behind the bar. Family, friends, places they'd played, Yazz standing with the horses and the wagon—all these were fine with Cade. But one of the imagings was of Jindra and her mother.

He provided the expected praise and made suggestions for other scenes and people that could be included. All during dinner his gaze kept straying to that wall. A sweet-enough portrait, a beautiful child seated on her beautiful mother's lap in a garden setting, all smiles. Mieka caught him looking. He said that he didn't understand how the imager had persuaded Jindra to sit still long enough. She was, after all, her father's daughter.

The next day, that imaging was gone. He later learned that it had been transferred to Jindra's room upstairs. Nobody ever said anything more about it.

Everybody was saying plenty about *Blood Plight*. The two plays shocked audiences wherever it was performed. *Wait'll they see the third one*, Cade thought to himself, with the feeling that in years to come, people who hadn't seen it on this particular tour would claim that they had—except those who lived on the Archduke's father's old domains. The Shadowshapers didn't set foot in those.

Interestingly, some people were saying that they'd be proud to have an ancestor who'd given his life to save the whole Continent. There'd been a long series of letters in *The Nayword* on the subject. Cade strongly suspected that "noble self-sacrifice" and "true to their vows" and suchlike had been disseminated by the Archduke himself and his cronies.

Now the Shadowshapers were back in Gallantrybanks, waiting for Vered to finish that final play, the one that would openly state the name *Henick* for all the Kingdom to hear. He was still making Drevan Wordturner's life a burden to him, and once Cayden had arranged all his books, especially his grandfather the fettler's library on theater, Vered came by to borrow whatever might be useful.

Truth to tell, he had all the material he needed. Rauel told Cade this after an afternoon Touchstone gigging at the Sailors Guildhall: a performance of "Bewilderland" to which he'd brought his wife and children. It disturbed Cade to talk about such dark things (low-voiced in a back office, to be sure) after the pure joy of children's laughter.

"There's no problem with the plot," Rauel said, frowning. "And that's what scares me. Are you *sure* this information is accurate?"

Cade nodded unhappily. He'd vacillated back and forth for a long time, and finally done what he'd known he would do all along: told Vered everything he knew.

"I'm trying to get him to tone it down some—concentrate on the emotional story rather than the political one."

"Political?"

"We've been having quite the row over it," he admitted. "Chat and I take turns not speaking to him, and Sakary says he's tired of keeping track so he doesn't speak to any of us. There's a lot about controlling magical folk, and planning to exile them if they're uncooperative. Vered says the Knights wanted dominion over the whole of the Continent, to bring order and organize society for enduring stability." He made a sour face. "From an audience's point of view, *boring.*"

"From the Archduke's, dangerous. But that won't stop Vered."

"I don't think there's anything *could.*"

Again Cade nodded. "Unfortunately, you're probably right."

They were both wrong. Something did stop Vered, about a fortnight after Wintering.

It was late at night when one of Princess Miriuzca's guards knocked on the door of Moonglade Reach. They were all accustomed by now to squinting through Blye's cunning little spyglasses, if only to see who it might be without having to pull curtains aside and peer rudely through a window. Especially did Cade take a look that night, when it was past curfew and the Minster chimes had recently struck eleven.

No magic crimson glow; just a tall, dark-haired, square-jawed young man who would have looked military even without the livery that amounted to a uniform. The brown of his tunic was dark on the shoulders and sleeves with rain. Cade opened the door.

"Master Silversun? Her Royal Highness's compliments, sir," the man said before Cade could do more than open his mouth, and extended a meaty hand clasping a folded and sealed page. Not Miriuzca's writing, which he would have recognized from graceful little notes asking them to lunching or tea. As he broke the seal and unfolded the paper, he glanced at the signature. Megs? Of course—her thin, sprawling scrawl had been on one or two letters for him in the past couple of years, not so familiar as Miriuzca's or Vrennerie's writing, but recognizable now that he'd seen the signature. What was she doing sending him a note at this time of night? And by one of the Princess's own guard?

"Invite the poor man in out of the rain," Mieka scolded from behind him.

Cade hardly heard. He'd read the letter. His free hand groped back towards Mieka's voice and he felt his shaking fingers connect with a solid arm. "Oh dear Gods," he whispered.

"I'm beholden to you, Master Windthistle," said the guard, "but my orders are to stand watch with my fellows outside your house until tomorrow morning, when others of the Princess's household will take our places. For the foreseeable future," he added.

"What the—? Cade? What is it?"

"Vered," he managed, digging his fingers into Mieka's wrist. "He's dead."

Mieka grabbed his shoulder and turned him, almost shook him. "That's—he can't—I don't—" Unable to finish a sentence—Cade knew exactly how he felt—he simply stated, "No—" and "No!" again.

Cade read aloud Megs's curt few sentences.

"'We've just had word that Vered Goldbraider was knifed to death outside Rauel Kevelock's house tonight. The murderer is unknown and uncaught. The Princess begs you to stay in your home and rely on her guards, whose orders are to protect you and yours as they would her. I'm so sorry, Cayden. He was a remarkable man.'"

The guard had meantime directed seven other liveried young men—tall like Wizards and shouldered like Giants—to the back doors, the front of the house, and the garden gate. He would patrol the whole property himself on horseback.

"Similar arrangements," he finished, "have been made for the other members of the Shadowshapers, Touchstone, the Crystal Sparks, Black Lightning, and Hawk's Claw." He snapped to attention, gave them a crisp nod, and departed.

Mieka shut the door behind him. "No," he said once more, but without hope. "It's not true. Not Vered."

"I never thought he'd go this far," Cade murmured.

"It has to be a mistake. Somebody's fucking with us."

"Megs's handwriting. The Princess's seal. Her own *guards*, for the love of—Mieka, it's true. Nobody could magick up all that. Nobody. And why would they? Just to scare us? It isn't Touchstone that's a fortnight away from performing a new play at the Palace theater."

Mieka didn't seem to be listening. "What did that guardsman say? Did he say Black Lightning?"

"All three parts of *Blood Plight*," Cade said numbly. "And this last one, this new one that Vered just finished, he's heard about it somehow, he knows what Vered plans to—*planned*—"

"Quill!" Mieka shouted. "Black fucking Lightning! Why would the Princess want to protect *them*?"

"She wouldn't, if she knew. I don't think she does." He gulped and started for a chair, his knees wobbly, his thoughts skittering. "Mieka—he's dead. Bexan . . . their children . . . his boys . . . what was he doing at Rauel's? Are we really in danger? No, I don't think we are. He got what he wanted. The Shadowshapers won't ever do that play—"

All at once there was a teacup in front of his face, brim-filled. "Drink," Mieka commanded, and he drank, spluttered, drank some more. The whiskey went down him as if he'd swallowed molten glass.

"Quill, listen to me." Mieka was crouching before him now, those eyes staring up into his, gone all dark and shadowy. "There's no point in trying to figure it out tonight. Megs will send to us tomorrow with whatever she learns. Everybody else is being guarded. We're all safe. I think you're right, and the only danger was to him—" Tears welled and were knuckled away. "Ah, damn it," he muttered.

They stayed downstairs, mostly silent, with lamps burning until dawn. By then news had spread throughout Gallantrybanks and was well on its way through the rest of Albeyn. Megs justified Mieka's prediction by sending another letter with the replacement guards just after Derien and Jindra had been told and Mistress Mirdley had cleared away a mostly uneaten breakfast.

> It's just dawn, but there are flowers and ever-flame candles outside the Kevelock house and the gates of Wavertree. Miriuzca has official and unofficial questions being asked. I'll write with whatever answers seem true later today.
>
> All we know right now for certain is what the hire-hack driver said: He was driving off when he heard someone cry out, and by the time he'd turned the horse, Vered was lying on the front steps. A maidservant opened the door and screamed. Rauel came out, saw Vered, and yelled at the driver to get a physicker and the constables. Which he did, but of course by then it was far too late.
>
> Preliminary word is that a group subscribing to Iamina's religious views has decided to attack all players. The King's Guard and Ashgar's Regiment are guarding everyone on the Circuits. Miri's people—her best and most trusted—are guarding the Shadowshapers and Touchstone. She insisted.
>
> Keep the children home from school and please don't even try to go anywhere for the next few days.
>
> More when I know it. Have a care to yourself, you and Mieka.

Mistress Mirdley was going round to each ground-floor window of the house, locking locks and drawing curtains shut. There seemed to be a dozen guards now. Cade knew they were unnecessary, just as he knew that the religious angle was nonsense. A deliberate deception.

Jindra had known Vered as a nice man who came to the house every so often and had wonderful white-gold hair and a kind smile, and once had brought her a lovely porcelain doll. She had been gently told that he had gone away and would not be coming back. She thought this over, then asked if he had gone to visit Mummy, and if so, she hoped he would be as happy there as she knew Mummy was. Derien, of course, knew what Vered's death meant. During the months of the Shadowshapers' rehearsals at Redpebble Square, he had got to know each of them better, and to see the boy bite both lips and look away when told what had happened clenched at Cade's heart. After he had read Megs's letter—Cade had given it to Mieka and then to Dery, not wanting to read it aloud where Jindra could hear—he took the little girl upstairs to her room to play.

"Don't leave the house for the next three days?" Mieka asked once they were gone. "Fuck *that*."

"Mieka," Cade began, but he was already up and heading for the back hallway. He returned with hooded cloaks, gloves, and boots.

"Get dressed," he said. "We'll take one of the guard with us if you like, but you know and I know and everybody who knows anything about the Archduke knows that we won't need him. You had the right of it last night. The Shadowshapers won't ever be doing that play. Might be none of *Blood Plight* won't ever be performed again, anywhere. But I'll bet you my half of this house that Bexan publishes it just as soon as she can get a clean copy put together."

"Who'd take the risk of printing it?"

Mieka snorted. "There's a small fortune to be made. They'll be lined up for a mile to print it. C'mon, put your boots on. We'll find a hack and go over to Rauel's. If we go in the back way, maybe nobody will see us." He wrapped himself in his oldest cloak, woven with a dark green warp and a black weft with crosswise threads of blue. Cade remembered when that cloak was new. The "gold" threads had tarnished years ago.

"What are you going to tell our guard?"

"That he's welcome to escort us if he likes, but we'd rather he stayed here to protect Jindra and Derien. As if anyone taking one look at Mistress Mirdley would think she's in need of any help protecting them!"

The guard captain assigned one of his underlings to accompany them—the price of allowing them to go at all. The burly young man rode up top with the hack driver, who wasn't pleased but didn't dare complain. They were, to say the least, conspicuous on the streets of Gallantrybanks. They reached Rauel's five-story town house without incident, and, driving past on their way to the back alley, they saw that Megs had been right. There were several gardens' worth of wet, bedraggled flowers on the steps, and dozens of ever-flame candles in glass containers. These wouldn't burn infinitely, but they would last at least a week—by which time Vered himself would have been consigned to the flames. Cade reminded himself to send a note to Blye to make the urn, and in the next instant heard Mieka's voice inside his head, and Mieka's face—older, wearier, framed in silvering hair—was clear before his eyes.

{ "Don't let people turn the steps into the Royal Botanical Garden. Send all the flowers to the Princess's Sanatorium for the patients there. And *don't* let 'em burn down the house, neither, with candles! I don't trust some of those ever-flame crafters."

"All right," he replied quietly. "But don't ask me to get rid of the letters they'll send, Mieka. They'll want to express how much you mean to them."

He looked startled. "Will they?"

"Of course they will."

"Oh. Well . . . do as you like. Just don't get all maudlin and mawky when you read them, right? I mean it, Quill. This is gonna be bad enough without all that kind of thing."

He made himself remember how to smile. From the expression in those eyes, the attempt wasn't entirely successful. So he said, "I promise that if I get weepy, I'll go into the garden and remember that time you got lost in your own maze. Will that do?"

The smile was the same smile, wide and whimsical and full of mischief, in a face that was thin and pain-weary and still beautiful. "I *still* say you had Petrinka change the layout one night when I wasn't looking."

"And then regrow all the hedges six feet tall by dawn?" he scoffed. "Your little sisters are good, Elfling, but nobody's *that* good!" }

Lost in his own garden maze . . . yes, that would be entirely like Mieka.

"Quill? We're here."

Mieka hadn't noticed the Elsewhen. Cade took a moment to praise the Lord and Lady and Angels and Old Gods. If Mieka hadn't seen it on his face, Cade wouldn't have to lie about it. And not succeed. And have to admit that he'd seen Mieka old and frail and silver-haired and dying.

Two men in the Princess's livery waited outside the back door of Rauel's house in Peasmarsh Square. Their own guardsman established their identities and they went inside, relinquished their coats, and sought out Rauel in the sitting room.

He sat there alone, staring at nothing. The big blue eyes barely glanced up as they entered. The boyish face looked twenty years older. The manservant who had escorted them paused to collect an untouched breakfast tray. Cade asked quietly if a fresh pot of tea could be readied; the man looked grateful for something to do.

Mieka, with a practical understanding of the circumstances that was more than Cade could summon at the moment, stirred up the feeble fire and loaded it with fresh logs. Only then did Cade realize how cold the room was. The Elf made sure the fire was drawing properly, then produced a distinctive long-necked bottle from his jacket pocket. When tea arrived, he dosed Rauel's and Cade's with Colvado brandy. Rauel gulped noisily, coughed, gulped again. Nobody said anything until all at once he looked up.

"We had another row yesterday. I don't even remember what we said."

"One row, counted against all those years together?" Mieka shook his head and passed him the bottle. "All the plays, all the performances—"

Cade took up the cause. "All the nights in all those flea-bitten inns—"

"All the days rattling your bones to bits in that wagon," Mieka finished. "He wouldn't be grateful to you for being so stupid. You'd've worked it out. You always did."

All at once Sakary was there, his narrow ashen face framed in red hair soaked from the rain, as if he'd walked all the way from his house. "It's true? Is it true? How can it be?"

Mieka stood, went to him, put an arm round his shoulders. "C'mon, mate. Time to have a drink."

"Why did they kill him?"

"Couldn't say," Mieka lied, coaxing him gently along, over to Rauel, who looked up with anguished eyes and got clumsily to his feet. Cade saw Mieka nudge Sakary slightly off-balance, so that he had to reach out. Rauel caught him. Mieka backed off, turning to Cade. The Elf's determined self-possession cracked for an instant, tears glittering in those eyes. But then he raked the hair out of his face and dragged a knitted blanket off a chair to drape over Sakary's shoulders.

The morning wore on, drear and dreadful. Chat arrived, to be left alone with Sakary and Rauel in the drawing room. Mieka shut the carved double doors behind him and Cade, then headed for the kitchen.

The manservant who'd shown them in was slumped at the worktable. The cook, an elderly woman with gorgeous silver-white hair, was patting his shoulder as he mumbled, "Known them both from mere puppies, both of 'em, from when they first played their first plays at my uncle's tavern—"

Mieka cleared his throat. "Could you have somebody stand at the drawing room doors and see that they're not disturbed? More tea would probably be a good thing as well. And lunching, eventually—if you can get them to eat it."

"I know all their favorites," the cook said, polishing her hands on her apron. She set to work with a look of grim determination, snapping orders at the kitchen maid.

The manservant straightened up. "Begging your pardon, sirs," he said. "I've not attended to my duties. There'll be two boys on those drawing room doors, and I'll see to the front door myself."

"You won't be able to turn everybody away, much as we'd all like to," Mieka said. "P'rhaps there's another room where Master Silversun and I could receive them, keep them occupied?"

"I'd be more than grateful to you, sir."

Cade spoke up. "There might be a letter coming for me. From the North Keep."

"I'll tell the Princess's men outside to keep watch for her messengers."

They spent the rest of the morning and some of the afternoon in a front parlor, furnished in a more formal style than the drawing room—a more public place, for show, not for everyday family living. Cade had rarely met Rauel's wife, Breckyn, but observed that she had exquisite taste. Striped wallpaper and plain curtains, a huge flowered rug, nubby silk upholstery, all in soothing colors of buff and sage and the same blue as Rauel's eyes, with accents of silver. The glass lampshades he recognized at once as Blye's work. Breckyn was at their country home with the children for a few weeks after the family Wintering celebration; Mieka made sure that someone had sent her a letter with the news.

Mieka was, in fact, a complete surprise all through the day. Cade knew he shouldn't have been amazed by the Elf's gentleness and compassion, but he was. When other friends began to arrive, he saw that everyone had tea or something stronger if desired, made sure the hearth fire was kept good and warm for the comfort of all, sat quietly and listened to those who needed to talk. The only person allowed past the front room was Romuald Needler, whose eyes were so swollen with weeping that Cade had to take his arm and guide him to the drawing room door.

In the hallway, the manservant approached to tell him that messages had begun to arrive—none from the North Keep yet—and there were certain individuals who were insisting on seeing the remaining Shadowshapers. Cade became positively ambassadorial. Derien would be proud of him. He stood beside a small table just inside the front door and sorted messages into piles in between expertly deterring people nobody wanted to talk to but couldn't simply be told to fuck off. He had a horrible moment when he first looked out the door, his gaze going to the rows of candles on either side of the steps. Last night Vered had died there. Right there.

After more than two hours, and something close to two hundred notes and letters categorized as best he could, yet another visitor arrived—some self-important nobody that Cade didn't recognize and the manservant frowned upon seeing. While expressing gratitude for the visit and explaining for approximately the thousandth time that Master Kevelock was too distraught to receive anyone—while keeping one foot firmly planted behind the half-open door—he caught sight of the same guards captain Miriuzca had sent last night to Moonglade Reach shouldering his way through the crowd.

"Beholden to you," Cade babbled to the affronted visitor, "I know they're all very much beholden for your concern, please do excuse me, message from Princess Miriuzca—"

Her name appeared to be magic. A path was instantly cleared for the captain, and he picked his way carefully through the inundation of flowers and candles. Within moments the manservant had shut the door behind him. Cade's fingers were shaking again as he ripped open the letter. Not a note or scribble message, but pages and pages of a letter.

We hear you've been naughty. Not that anybody could blame you. Mieka's doing, I suppose.

   There isn't much more to tell about what happened. The broadsheets have most of it—special editions this evening. What they don't have, because an assistant chief constable, brother of one of Miri's guards, whose sisters are amongst her maids—aren't these family connections useful?—anyway, he took charge of the knife when it was found a few blocks away. It's one of Mieka's,

"Holy fuck," Cade blurted.

*presumably lost two Winterings ago at Great Welkin. The constable
who found it recognized the maker, because he bought his own knives
(which constables aren't supposed to carry, but there it is) from the
same man. They're quite costly and not the sort that a street ruffian
would carry (unless he stole it). So the constable described the blade to
his superior, who described it to his brother (the guard), and that's
who surmised that the thistle etching might mean it belonged to
Mieka. He told Miri, and she told them to substitute another knife
and bring that one to her.*

Cade groped his way to a chair and sat down. The manservant asked
if he wanted a drink. He shook his head, then changed his mind.
"Whiskey." He considered. "Not too much. I haven't eaten today that
I recall."

*Now, trying to place the blame on Mieka for this is beyond ludicrous.
So why use his knife? Vren thinks—and I hope I get this in some sort
of logical order—that, firstly, it would have been easy to confirm it
as Mieka's by asking the maker. Secondly, because it went missing
at Great Welkin, it could have been found by anybody there. Thirdly,
this anybody could have been a servant or a guard employed by the
Archduke, or it could have been one of the crowd—who could have
sold it on in Gallybanks, to be sold again, and so on from there.*
    *Miri, on hearing this, suggested that somebody in the
Constabulary or Judiciary connected to the Archduke will put forth
the former possibility, and here's why. When everybody at Great
Welkin is questioned, there will be countless witnesses to the fact that
everyone was snug in bed or on duty or otherwise accounted for as
being exactly where they all belonged. What Miri missed is this: By
requiring his household to be questioned, not only does he clear all of
them but he makes it publicly known how loyal and devoted they are,
because even though the suggestion was made that one of them could
be so infuriated by rumors about a play that he'd do such a thing, all
of them will say that those rumors are utterly ridiculous and the
Archduke is the finest man and the best master who ever lived.*

Cade's brain was whirling—even more so after he took a large swallow of whiskey. Convolutions and complications in abundance, and those three women had figured all of it out in a few hours. They could have had careers writing for the stage.

And yet they weren't done.

About two minutes after I pointed this out, Miri said this: that she wouldn't put it past him to sacrifice one of his own people in order to provide a culprit. How much better a demonstration of their zeal to protect him and his interests than that one of them should kill Vered for daring even to hint at what the rumors hint—and how appalled he would be, how sickened, how penitent that any of his servants would dare. Not to speak of how quick he would be to hand that person over.

Part of him admired the Princess's thinking; part of him sorrowed that she had learned to think that way; most of him was infuriated that they lived in a world where such thinking was not just possible but necessary. More strongly than the need had come to him in a very long time, he wanted to hit something. He wanted to mark a wall, a window, a face with his grief and rage, do visible damage, leave evidence of what he was feeling. It scared him, this ravening impulse to violence. He'd thought he'd outgrown it—or at least learned to overcome it.

However, because the knife isn't available to serve as a prop in this little farce, we'll be spared the spectacle (reported lavishly in all the broadsheets, of course) of the Archduke's people adoring him. The authorities will pull in some random lout off the street. People must have someone to blame for the death of this beloved man. Therefore someone will be found. Miri will try to do what she can for whomever they end up arresting. But unless the real murderer is discovered—and there's no hope that he will be—some poor innocent fool will end on the gallows.

Wavertree, like Kevelock's house, is said to be hip-deep in candles, flowers, and grieving strangers. Miri and Vren send their love to all, and their sorrow. So do I. They also say to go home and get some sleep. So do I.

Chapter 30

Rauel, Chat, and Sakary didn't emerge from the drawing room all day. Cade eventually explained his sorting system to the manservant, collected Mieka, and left the way they'd come. It was nearly dinnertime when they finally got home. Once everyone—Mistress Mirdley, Derien, Jindra, and the guards captain—had been reassured that they were just fine, Cade guided Mieka into the dining room and shut the door.

"Your turn now," he said. "You've been taking care of everyone else. Now it's your turn."

All the way back to Moonglade Reach, he'd felt how tense Mieka was. Now he stiffened even further, if that were possible, as if holding himself tight so he wouldn't disintegrate. When Mieka spoke, Cade knew he'd guessed correctly.

"I wasn't doing it for any of them. I was doing it for me. So I didn't have to think."

"What didn't you want to think about?" But he knew this, too.

"It could've been you, Quill."

"He wants everyone to think it could've been any of us."

"Religious fanatics?" Mieka was still standing in the middle of the rug, seeming to move only when he breathed and spoke. "That's shit and we all know it. I can't lose you, Cayden."

"You won't. Go on up to bed. I'll have Mistress Mirdley bring you some dinner."

Mieka didn't seem to have heard him. "If it had been you—it could've been, you know it could." All at once he began to tremble. "Gods, Quill, what if it *had* been you?"

"Mieka, stop it." Crossing the room, he took the slight shoulders in his hands. Nightmares haunted those eyes, and bleak unreasoning terror. He understood. He knew those things himself, in excruciating Elsewhen detail. "That's not what he wants."

Mieka looked up at him, frowning. "What d'you mean?"

"With Vered gone, the Shadowshapers will never perform that play." Suddenly Cade caught his breath, needing no Elsewhen to know what Mieka was about to say before he said it. "We can't," he blurted. "Mieka, we *can't!*"

"We've done it before. Us and what's left of the Shadowshapers, the Sparks and Hawk's Claw if they want to join us—we *can*, Quill. We owe it to him."

"The Archduke, or Vered?"

A grim little smile touched the corners of his mouth. "Both."

Mistress Mirdley brought in a large dinner tray and stood there, arms folded, until they sat down and began to eat. Derien and Jindra joined them, but only to deliver an armful of broadsheets; they'd already had dinner in the kitchen. Once they were alone again, they took turns reading aloud. Most simply reported the few facts known. The more sensationalist papers speculated without evidence about Vered's personal enemies, bemoaned violent crime in Gallybanks, and featured lurid drawings of what the attack might have looked like. *The Nayword* confined itself to reviewing Vered's life and career, with a short, heartfelt essay by Tobalt Fluter mourning the uniquely creative artist who had been lost.

The gist of it all was that the previous night—had it really been only last night?—Vered had stepped out of a hire-hack in front of Rauel's house in Peasmarsh Square. The hack driver swore that there was no one in the street; the assumption was that the assailant had been hiding in the bushes of the central garden, and run across to the house behind the hack as it left. Vered was attacked at the steps and died instantly, his heart pierced by a knife which had been found discarded one street over and was of no distinctive type or manufacture.

Cade kept his voice steady as he read this part, and didn't look at Mieka. He hadn't yet shared Lady Megs's latest letter, and mayhap he never would.

The hack driver, hearing someone cry out—almost certainly Vered—turned his vehicle around but saw no one. At this point, a maid opened the door and began to scream. Rauel was there a moment later, yelling for a physicker and a constable.

"I wonder," Cade mused, setting aside the terse summary in *The Nayword*, "who they'll find to stitch up as guilty. They'll have to blame it on somebody," he added when Mieka glanced up from picking at his dinner. "Megs said as much, and she's right."

"They'll never find who really did it, you mean? Well, what would you expect?" He waved his fork at the other broadsheets. "That's why all the articles about thievings and murderings. It's preparing everybody to accept whatever hapless geck they choose to play the role of guilty party. What else did Megs say?"

"Not much," he lied, reaching into his jacket pocket for the letter.

"Quill."

He ought to have known he couldn't get away with it. "Miriuzca has someone of her own in the investigation—brother of one of her guards, if I understand it aright. So she's getting accurate information. Here—she agrees with you," he said, and read out the last paragraphs, leaving out everything regarding Mieka's knife.

"Sends her love, eh?" But his heart wasn't in the teasing, and Cade escaped by shrugging it all off. "I'm thinking," Mieka went on, "that Mistress Mirdley put something sleepy into the pudding. I'm for me bed. Don't sit up too late brooding, old dear. The next couple of weeks are gonna be brutal. After all," he said, getting to his feet and starting for the door, "we have a *very* long performance to rehearse."

He was gone before Cayden could observe that the play had got Vered Goldbraider killed, and what made him think the Archduke would stop there?

His fist crumpled Megs's letter. The Archduke. What gave him the right to take Vered's life? How did he justify depriving Bexan of her husband, his children of their father, his friends of his company, all the Kingdom of his brilliance?

The rage returned, more powerful than before. He felt as if his body wanted to run in twenty directions at once. Pacing—table to windows to door to the bar—didn't work. He had to do something, *hurt* something, or go mad. Some lingering remnant of sanity told him, *Outside—you can't do as much damage outside—*

Rumble appeared out of nowhere, startling him, staggering him back against the bar. The cat froze, arched, glared up at him as a glass dislodged by his elbow shattered onto the floor. He turned, seeing the shelves with all the resplendent glassware that had been Blye's home-cozying gift. Yes, that would hurt. He took the single step separating him from those shelves with their serried ranks of blue and green and yellow glasses of varying sizes and shapes and swirling patterns, no two alike, each made with love and skill and Blye's cunning magic. He drew his arm back, ready to sweep them all into splintered oblivion.

"If you do," said Mistress Mirdley from the doorway, "you'll pick up every shard with your bare hands."

Flinching, he stumbled against one of the tall stools and managed to sit down before he fell down. "I could have stopped it. I could have changed it."

"I doubt that. Nobody I've ever heard of could keep Vered Gold-braider from doing exactly as he pleased exactly when and as it pleased him to do so. But I'm willing to listen if you have a different notion."

"The first time I saw it, Bexan was screaming. Minster bells were ringing—I don't know, I didn't follow it, because it was the night at Great Welkin and I saw Mieka and Yazz—"

"And so you followed that one instead. I see. If there was a first, there was a second."

"Bexan wasn't there this time. It was just a voice. I couldn't see anything. Somebody in the darkness, a man saying that it wasn't—that the drinking didn't make them what they are, but what they are made the drinking necessary, and he was wrong—and someone else saying 'Do it, do it'—oh Gods, I don't know, I didn't stay with that one, either, because I'd just seen the Archduke and the gold, Kearney Fairwalk's gold, and—and that was more important." He stood up, paced to the dining table, to a cabinet, to a pair of soft chairs by the windows. "More important!"

"Are you sure it was Vered the man spoke to?"

"The night felt the same. The darkness had the same feeling to it as the one where Bexan was screaming. It was—it was *evil*."

She was quiet for a time. "Cayden," she said at last, "it was blood this man spoke of. Surely you guessed that." When he shook his head, she sighed. "Drinking the blood of man or animal isn't what makes the Knights what they are. It's *sharing* the blood of one already a Knight. And it doesn't happen all at once. But after they become what they become, drinking blood is necessary to keep them alive." She paused, looking far beyond him into an unimaginable distance—the past? "They crave blood that is drenched in fear. Survival is possible with cold, stale blood. Better that it comes warm from the veins of a dying, frightened animal. But best of all, hot and pulsing from the throat of a terrified man who knows full well that he is about to die."

"You're talking about them as if—you keep saying they *are*, not they *were*."

"Yes."

"You were quoting someone."

"Yes." She came closer. "You've said that you see only things you can change. Very well. Let's agree for the moment that this is *always* true."

"Those Elsewhens came because I could have stopped what happened. He's dead and it's my fault. I didn't look. I wouldn't see." Rumble leaped into his lap, startling him again. "How did you know why I see the Elsewhens?"

She gave a complex snort. "I've known you since I first swaddled you. And it happens I don't agree with your 'why.' What about Alaen and Briuly Blackpath? You can't tell me there's anything in the whole wide world you could have done to warn them. So what does this do to this idea of yours that you see only things you can change?"

"I think there's more than one kind of Elsewhen," he admitted. "But most of them—I didn't see anything more because it was too late. If only I'd looked and seen and understood—"

"And done what, exactly? Taken away all his pens and paper? A tregetour with an idea and the sheer stubborn grit to carry it through—there's nothing more dangerous in the world." She lowered herself into a chair and leaned back into its velvet-upholstered depths. "Something did change. In the second, his wife wasn't with him. You didn't hear the chimes. Can you think of anything that you did to influence whether she was with him or not?"

He thought back over the last few days. No, further back than that—anything he could have done between the night before Wintering two years ago and the Elsewhen about the gold.

He had sent the babies a collection of cuddle-toys for their Naming-day present. From his grandfather's library, he'd given Vered and Bexan a very old book of Piksey rhymes, charmingly illustrated. He'd spoken with Vered any number of times, and with Bexan, written a

few letters, sent the footman over to Wavertree with a jar of Mistress
Mirdley's special remedy for colic. . . .

Hopeless. Tracking down what he might have done—or might
not have done, and there was the real prospect for insanity—was utterly hopeless.

"So," Mistress Mirdley said in a satisfied way. "You don't know.
You'll never know." She was silent for a few moments, and when she
spoke again her voice had softened. "Am I afraid for you, boy? That's
what you want to know. Yes, I am. I'm not about to tell you how long
I've served the Silversun family. You and Derien, you're the last. At
least one of you had better marry and have sons, that's what I say.
Looks as if it'll be Derien. But it would be nice to have you alive long
enough to make the choice if you want. And with *him* slithering
about . . ." She ended with a shrug.

"It's not me he's after." But he would be, if Touchstone and the remaining Shadowshapers did what Cade and Mieka thought they ought
to do. What they must do.

Still . . . once the third play was out there, what could Henick do?
Another death? Unlikely. In a way, performing that play in public
would keep all the rest of them safe. He wouldn't dare another murder, not with Princess Miriuzca keeping ostentatious watch.

Then he remembered the gold coins. The ones that now would
never be struck—or at least would not come from Fairwalk's cellar of
gold. Whatever plot would have produced them for a preposterous rate
of exchange with the old ones, it would culminate in Cyed Henick's
making himself King. How could Touchstone possibly be important
enough to endanger a scheme that huge? True enough, they'd had
some small successes in confronting him. But they were players, theater people, not powerful nobles or politicians. Whatever victories
they'd known were private, personal. Nothing to shake a nation.

Once he was King, he could rid himself of Touchstone whenever
he liked.

Which led to a question. Two questions.

"Why Vered? Why now?" He turned in his chair, sat straighter. "It
was just a play. Insulting, yeh, but Cyed Henick's been squinted at
sideways all his life. His father was a traitor who started a war."

"And lost it."

"I know," he said impatiently. "And I'm sure that rankles, just as I'm sure he wants all the power his father was unable to grab. But how could a *play*—" He broke off and shrank back into the cushions as if the Archduke stood before him now. "It's the end of the Shadow-shapers as a viable entity. Everyone saw after they broke up that they weren't anywhere near as good without each other as with each other. Together, they had influence. Power. The best and most popular group in Albeyn—everybody wanting to see them, brag that they'd seen the latest play ten times, read every interview to find out what they'd do next, and now they're poring over the published plays—"

He looked around distractedly, but they were in the dining room, Mieka's side of the house, not the drawing room where there were shelves with a tasteful display of books of general interest. One of them was a signed collection of the Shadowshapers' original works, sent by Vered and Bexan as a homecozying gift. He knew from an article in *The Nayword* that there had been three print-runs so far—and now, after Vered's murder, there would be a dozen more.

No magic, no voices, no scenery. No sounds or sensations.

Words.

Power.

Whether read in books or performed on stages, words had power. The Archduke knew it. The magic had nothing to do with it.

It was the *words*.

Mistress Mirdley levered herself to her feet. "I'll bring up a pot of tea every couple of hours," she said.

He almost laughed. He must look like a hunting hound straining at the lead. He barely paused to hug her on his way out the door and up the stairs. A hurried gesture lighted two lamps, one on each side of his desk. Paper. Ink. Pens.

For Rauel, words existed to tell stories that evoked emotion. For Vered, they goaded people to think. When woven together, Rauel's stories in the service of Vered's ideas, the Shadowshapers had been unbeatable.

Cayden's approach was different. He had begun his career using standard, well-known stories to explore and examine ideas. It had been the addition of Mieka's uninhibited performances that had pushed Ca-de's work to another level. In addition to writing for Jeska's massive talent and trusting to Rafe's subtle and solid control, he had begun to write for Mieka. In doing so, he discovered that at his best, he was writing for himself, for the things in his partners that he knew and understood and trusted with his visions and, most important, his words. It didn't surprise him to realize that he trusted them more than he trusted himself.

He had let them down, he knew. "Turn Aback" had been a mess because he hadn't understood what the thing was really about. He'd written it, and he didn't understand it. But now he knew. All his philosophical maunderings—nonsense. It had been about the dangers of looking. Of *seeing*. He'd got it wrong in that play. But *Window Wall* . . .

He knew it still wasn't quite right. He began correcting his mistake. He was vaguely aware of a pot of tea and a mug appearing at his elbow, and he supposed he drank every so often. At some point, a different pot replaced the first, piping hot and fragrant with herbs. All the while he was marveling in a corner of his mind that he could have written all this, so many words, without knowing what these plays were really about.

They weren't about a boy imprisoned in a room, denied the world outside and his own magic by a frightened and embittered father, his life spent looking through a wall of glass. It was about *seeing* what was beyond that wall, and wanting to touch it, *be* in it, even though so often it was naught but suffering and sorrow. And fear—Gods, the fear. That was the worst, Cade thought over and over again as he wrote. Hatred stunted the soul; jealousy was poison; envy warped the heart; anger destroyed more than angry fists could break. But fear paralyzed. All those things would the boy encounter beyond the glass window.

Yet there would be love as well, and compassion and friendship, and a million different kinds of joy.

It wasn't for the girl, that supremely beautiful girl, that he would break that glass. It was for himself.

Chapter 31

Before Touchstone could do anything about the Shadowshapers' long-scheduled performance at the Palace's theater for King Meredan's Namingday, they had to get hold of all three scripts. The first two were in the possession of the surviving Shadowshapers. But the third presented a bit of a difficulty.

Mieka and Jeska put on their most somber clothing and took a hire-hack to Wavertree. The crowds of mourners outside the house were gone. So was the lake of flowers. The ever-flame candles, though, were still glowing. They were arranged on the front steps, so many of them that there was barely room to pass between the ranks of glass containers, blue and yellow and red and orange and green and purple and every color in between.

"Still burning?" Jeska whispered. "I thought they sputtered out after a week or so."

"The cheap ones do. The cheaper ones have a tendency to crack the glass. And the cheapest have been known to blow up." Mieka lifted his hand to the door knocker, sadly noting the little glass eye so recently installed. Blye had done her best. Not her fault—any more than it was Cayden's—that Vered was dead.

The Princess's Guards were gone, too. A couple of them still walked the grounds of Moonglade Reach, and lingered outside Rafe's and Jeska's homes, wearing civilian clothes in an attempt not to be obvious. There had been a contingent of them in full uniform as an honor guard at Vered's burning last week. Bexan had not been present, still too overcome with grief to appear in public. Mieka didn't blame her; the crowds outside the Kilnminster, where such things took place, had been huge despite a hammering rain.

Before he could touch the brass knocker, the door opened. A maidservant, swathed in solid black, invited them in, her voice hushed. The staircase banister was wrapped in black silk. In the entry hall, a black glass vase on a table shrouded in black held a huge bunch of blue flowers: forget-me-nevers. Beside it, stark white on black cloth, was a piece of parchment with blue and brown seal ribbons. Framing the three doorways down the hall, more black silk was gathered and draped and swagged like theater curtains. Upstairs an infant began to wail, the sound quickly muffled by a door that was not quite slammed shut. Otherwise, the house was silent. Mieka found himself placing each foot very carefully on the wooden floor, lest his bootheels make an unseemly noise.

He and Jeska were led down a passage to Bexan's drawing room. Although Cade had warned them about the black decorations, it was rather a shock. The only light came from sliver rifts between drawn black curtains, a thin gray light from the rainy day in the garden outside.

In all this darkness, Bexan's face was luminously pale. Mieka went to where she sat and took the hand she extended, pressing his lips to her wrist where a bracelet of woven gold proclaimed her marriage. She had not yet had the right one removed by a Good Sister for transfer to her left wrist, in the manner of widows.

Jeska, too, bent over her hand.

She waved them to a nearby couch. "It was kind of you to come."

Jeska said, "We thought we'd wait until—"

"Until everyone else had abandoned me?"

Mieka hid a flinch. This was going to be more difficult than anticipated. Cade had declined to join them, saying that it was entirely possible that Bexan would blame him for putting Vered in touch with people who had assisted his researches into the plays that had cost him his life. When Mieka asked how she could possibly have guessed, Cade just arched a brow. No, Bexan was not a stupid woman.

"They kept coming for over a week," she went on. "Flowers. Candles. Standing outside my house, trying to get into my garden. Reciting speeches from his plays, sometimes well into the night. They can have no idea how painful it was for me, how deeply it hurt me, hearing his words just outside my windows."

"They valued him," Jeska murmured. "They loved him. We all did."

"And now they are gone. He's dead and burned, and they'll forget him. As they have all deliberately forgotten me. Do you know the words they recited most often? Nothing that was his alone. Nothing that he read first to me, seeking my judgment and my help. No, they spoke over and over again—chanted it, like a hymn in High Chapel—" She broke off.

Mieka could guess. "The part of 'Life in a Day' about not knowing what would happen, and how much had been left undone and unsaid."

"It was what he wanted them to think about," Jeska assured her. "What he reminded them to do in their own lives. And they learned. Those lines mean that they learned what he was trying to teach. I think he would have been proud of that."

"How would *you* know?" she snapped, dark eyes glaring at him. "I knew him better than anyone! I birthed his children! How dare you presume to tell me what he would have felt? I am his wife!"

"And for that reason," Mieka said with gentle sympathy, "we've come to you."

No, it wasn't easy—but neither was it impossible. They left an hour later with Vered's own copy of *Blood Plight*, all three plays, wrapped in a shroud of black velvet.

"I don't want to do anything like that ever again," Mieka told Cayden when he and Jeska arrived back at Moonglade Reach. "You shoulda seen the place. Wasn't just her room that's black, like you told us. It's all over the house. Like walking into a cavern and the candle going out—or falling into a pot of tea that's been brewing for a fortnight."

"And gone very, very cold," Jeska added. "There were hothouse flowers from the Princess. In a black vase, with the letter right beside it, in case anybody missed the point of the forget-me-nevers."

"Sounds charming." Cade ushered them into the drawing room, where Mistress Mirdley had provided tea. Cade and Rafe hadn't waited. Mieka and Jeska fell on the food, talking all the while.

"We had to lay it on with a shovel," Mieka said around a mouthful of peach muffin.

"Both at the same time, and as fast as we could," Jeska agreed. "From the start it was clear that talking of Vered's legacy wouldn't work."

"Nor an appeal to let the Kingdom know exactly what he'd written that led to his death, neither. Oh yeh, you were right. She knows.

It's a good thing you stopped at home, Quill. She's not what I'd call—how shall I put this?—*fond* of you right now."

"How'd you get her to hand this over?" Rafe fingered the black velvet.

"Agree to give her credit for coauthorship?" Cade asked, arching a cynical brow.

"She'll do that when she has it published," Mieka said. "No, it was a combination of reminding everybody what she's lost, and her courage in working on this with us—"

"What!" Cade exclaimed.

"—and courage in attending the performance at the Palace, *and* that everybody will say afterwards that it was good, even brilliant, but nowhere near as brilliant as if Vered had been there to perform it himself."

"And," Jeska finished, "telling her that only *she* can give us permission, and how much people will love her—"

"Wait for it," Mieka advised when Cade opened his mouth again.

"—for her *courage*, that she overcame her grief to give Vered's last play to the people of Albeyn."

"Have some more tea," Rafe said, pouring from the earthenware pot, "and get the taste out of your mouth."

"Work with us?" Cade demanded.

"Settle down," Jeska advised. "It won't kill us to have her at a couple of rehearsals."

"If she starts meddling," he warned, "I won't be responsible."

"All we have to do is tell her that we swear to be utterly faithful to Vered's original script, right down to the last *a*, *and*, and *the*."

Mieka nodded agreement. "If it needs any work, we just won't tell her. She can't quibble once it's been performed. We had a look at it in the hack coming home. There's not much to be done to it, honest. Just cues and things, getting the look right for Jeska when he plays the Warrior."

"Will it have the Archduke shitting bricks?" Rafe wanted to know.

"Enough to build a twelve-room addition to Great Welkin." Mieka leaned back in his chair and stretched lingering tension from his shoulders. "Y'know, she said something really strange. People were outside the house for at least a week, giving mass recitals of Vered's work until all hours of the night, and she told us how painful it was for her. I mean, I understand that, and of course it was painful—but doesn't any pain count except hers? What about his sons? And those four babies who'll grow up without their father? What about everybody else who loved him? And those people holding vigil outside Wavertree—weren't they in pain, too? They were showing how much they loved him, and maybe easing their own grief with his words, and thinking they might be easing hers. But she doesn't see that."

"People say odd things when they're grieving," Rafe said. "We can't hold it against her."

"I don't. I just think it was weird. Like you said that time, Cade—that she's not looking *into* you but looking right through you, as if you aren't even there and don't matter to her at all."

Cade nodded. "I guess the only person she ever really saw was Vered."

"Let's just hope she doesn't make a career out of being his widow," Jeska said. "Like old Queen What's-her-nose, who shut herself up in the South Keep for fifty years."

"And came out only once a year," Mieka added. "On his death date she'd drive through Gallybanks in an open carriage with his urn in her lap." Unsuccessfully repressing a snigger, he finished, "Until one year the carriage made a sudden stop to keep from running over some children, and she dropped the urn. There being a westerly wind at the time, the ashes blew all the way to the Flood!"

"You *would* remember that part of your history lessons," Cade remarked.

"Only the stuff that was gruesome or funny—or both!" He waggled a finger at his tregetour. "And don't pretend you didn't listen with both ears instead of only one to such things. After all, you remember it, too!"

Jeska cleared his throat. "That's as may be, but what do we do if Bexan arches her back over the play?"

"As long as we can ready it in time for Meredan's Namingday, I can't say that I really much care what Bexan does." Cade shrugged. "If that's cold, too bad. There's something more important here than her."

"And her *courage*," Mieka said irrepressibly.

If the Shadowshapers' rehearsals last spring in the undercroft of Redpebble Square had been known only to a few, the meetings in Mieka's sword boards were so secret that, except for Bexan, not even wives knew about them. Rauel, Chat, and Sakary took three hacks in three directions to get to Moonglade, always arriving separately and at widely spaced times. Rafe and Jeska used no such maneuverings, for Crisiant and Kazie expected them to go to rehearsals. Bexan almost blew the gaff one sunny afternoon, arriving in an open carriage; people along the main street recognized her. Mieka had to put it about the next morning—ever-so-casually, while buying spices that Mistress Mirdley didn't need—that it was an unlooked-for politeness, to have her return their condolence call on her, and they'd tried very hard to give her a distraction from her grief during a lengthy tea. It was Jindra (who had long since charmed the locals with her Elfen beauty and ready laughter, poor little motherless mite) who had been most successful, he confided with a smile, knowing the news would be talked of in every house within two miles by lunching, and be all over Gallantry-banks by dinner. He finished with, "Y'know, we've all got to admire Mistress Goldbraider's courage through her sorrow, don't you think?"

It wasn't courage that prompted Rauel, Chat, and Sakary to agree to the plan. It was anger and shock and a crippling burden of grief. During a fortnight of rehearsals, each of them broke down in tears at different times, each of them saying the same thing: *I can't believe he's gone.* Bexan's presence at three rehearsals—once at the beginning, once at the middle, and once a mere two days before the scheduled performance—was much less intrusive than everyone had feared. The first two plays were, after all, done and dusted, with Jeska having to learn Vered's part (including that heart-stopping decapitation scene) and nothing at all for Cade, Mieka, or Rafe to do. Thus Bexan's attendance at the start of rehearsals yielded only a single piece of advice, and this from Vered himself.

"He said he had to duck down as fast as he could. It may all be done with magic, but you'll scare yourself half to death and give yourself nightmares otherwise." She made a little gesture, both gold bracelets now gleaming from her left wrist. "I can vouch for the nightmares."

"He never said anything about that to us," Sakary protested, then supplied his own answer. "Well, he wouldn't. He wrote the thing to do himself."

During the second visit, Blye and Jinsie were most conveniently there to provide distraction. They'd shown up just before tea, giving Derien a ride home from the King's College in the hire-hack and picking up Jindra from littleschool down the road. Both women knew something was up; neither could contain her curiosity an instant longer. They hadn't even manufactured an excuse for coming by. They sat with Bexan at one end of the long, wooden-floored room and watched Touchstone and the remaining Shadowshapers grind out ideas for staging the final play, and were quiet through all of it.

After Bexan returned home to her children, however, Blye presented Cade with a sheet of paper, closely written on both sides.

"Her notes. She didn't want to say much while she was here. I think that was nice of her, don't you?"

The challenge in her eyes for anyone to say anything about Bexan's meddling made them all feel like shits.

"And generous as well," Jinsie added, "not to embarrass you with the obvious. That last bit, for instance—even I could tell nobody's comfortable with it. The audience has already seen a throat ripped out. This time it ought to be just as sudden but not so gory—something people can imagine happening to themselves, if they ever ran across a Vampire."

They all of them flinched, the three Shadowshapers and the four members of Touchstone. Mieka realized that they'd never yet used that word amongst themselves. They knew what the Knights had become. They just never called it that. Cade was right: words *were* power. To think that this one word had such horror attached to it that they shied back from using it for what was so damned obvious—that was scary, and that, too, was power.

He had something more personal to discuss with Jinsie, though. He'd heard from her namesake, who'd heard her grandfather and grandmother talking about it, that Jinsie had turned down yet another suitor. She'd been seeing this one—whose name Mieka didn't even know—for more than a year. He wanted marriage, a home, and a family. She wanted marriage, a home, a family, and her work with Kazie managing Touchstone. It never did any good to approach things all roundabout with his twin, and he'd known her way too long to bother being polite. He asked her flat out what was wrong with *this* one.

"The fourth, isn't it? Or maybe the fifth?"

"Seventh," she replied coolly. "There was nothing wrong with him at all. I was quite fond of him, actually. But he did something I didn't much like. He hid the shears until I *was* quite fond of him."

"I don't understand."

"You're a man. You wouldn't."

"Jinsie," he warned.

"The shears. As if I were one of Petrinka's hedges to be trimmed to the proper shape." She allowed him to help her on with her coat. "As far as I can tell, Miek, there are two ways for a marriage to work. The first is to know and understand pretty much everything about each other, and love each other in spite of it. The second is to know as little as possible and not bother trying to understand, and just blindly love each other—and not complain when something comes up that you've got no idea what it means or what he's thinking. Either you marry somebody who knows you inside out so that you very rarely have to explain yourself, somebody who's glad to let you be exactly who and what you are, or somebody who doesn't know you much at all *and* won't interfere or try to control you, so you can have some privacy. You can have understanding or you can have mystery, but you can't have both."

There was something wrong with that. He was certain sure there was something wrong with that, though he couldn't quite put his finger on it. "I'm the very last person to lecture anybody on married life, but—"

She laughed and patted his cheek. "Don't worry about it, old dear. If I find someone, I find someone. If I don't, I don't. We can't all be Jed and Blye, or Jez and Eirenn."

Back inside, what Cade, Rauel, Chat, and Sakary were trying to understand involved Mieka and Rafe only peripherally. The three who had known Vered best had plenty to say about the way certain lines were read. Jeska was content to wait until they came up with directions for him to follow, and meantime occupied himself by teaching Derien card tricks (after a stern admonition that he was never to use them in a serious game or they'd kick him out of the diplomatic service before he'd even been awarded his colors). Mieka watched for a while, learned nothing new, then wandered over to a table where Vered's own folio lay. The code used by the Shadowshapers was different from the one Mieka and Cade had worked out, but he could more or less follow the changes—when to take up a new withie, what color it should be, how intensely to use it, and so forth.

Vered's style of writing was different, too. Doubtless Cayden and every other tregetour worth his magic could point out subtleties of phrasing and how the choice of what scene to include influenced the whole. For Mieka, it was much more basic. Vered's plays and performances had always been more about Vered than anything else. In them he deigned to give others a glimpse into his soul. *This is what I think, this is what I feel. I'll show it to you and if you find something to think about or react to, great. But expressing what I think and feel is more important. Yes, I'm letting you take a look into my soul. Seeing into yours doesn't much interest me.*

Rauel, on the other hand, did a lot of hiding. He presented things that would engage the audience's emotions, and to that end he told his stories. Making people react the way he wanted them to was the most important thing. *Don't ever think that somehow through these stories you can catch even the briefest glimpse of my soul. They're only stories. I create them to make you feel. I create them to touch your soul. But I'm not them and they're not me, and to convince yourself otherwise is sheer folly.*

As for Cayden . . . Mieka smiled as he set aside the folio. He knew exactly what Quill would say. *This is what I think and feel, and this is what I think you ought to think and feel about it. To that end, I'll leave enough space for you to inhabit a character, find your way inside, discover things that are similar to and even exactly like you. But don't ever think that because you've slid inside a character of mine that somehow you've also slipped inside me. My soul is my own, and I'll let you see of it only what I wish you to see.*

And that ain't much, Mieka thought. He'd walked past butcher's shop windows any number of times, and if the brains of people were anything like the brains of calves and sheep to look at, Cade's brain must be thrice as convoluted.

Only two people witnessed the full rehearsal: Derien and Mistress Mirdley. By the end, Dery was limp in his chair, staring wide-eyed from one to the next of them, ending with his brother.

"It's . . ." He spread both hands helplessly.

"Yes," said Mistress Mirdley. "It is. Now, if you're quite finished for the evening, there's dinner about to burn in the oven." She stood, making for the stairs, then hesitated and turned round. "I can't decide if it's more bravery or foolishness to present these plays, but people will be talking about them for a hundred years after we're all burned and urned." Then she smiled. She actually smiled. "I'm proud of you all. Now, wash up and come downstairs."

Chapter 32

Every morning for many weeks, Cayden woke with an unfamiliar and mildly bemusing sense of peace. Not of tranquility; instantaneous recollection of Vered's death and recognition of the work to be done tensed his muscles and impelled him out of bed almost the moment his eyes opened. Yet there was within him a deep certainty that *this* was what he was supposed to be doing, in the place he was supposed to be doing it. The work wasn't so much an anodyne to grief as a defiant answer to the man he knew had caused it. Let the Archduke exert his power in stealth, in darkness, in silence. Cade had power, too, and of the kind that stood proudly in the light.

Moonglade Reach had much to do with his mood. This house on this land next to the river was his. In a way, it had been ever since the first time he'd seen that Elsewhen of his own forty-fifth Namingday. How often had he gone this far and farther up the Gally River on boat or barge or just for a walk, and not noticed this peculiar building? It had been waiting to be seen until he was ready to see it.

Now he had, and it was his. His and Mieka's. And that was how things were supposed to be. And so he woke in the mornings rested in body and at rest in soul, feeling ready for anything.

Three days before the King's Namingday, Cayden woke with an Elsewhen in his head.

{ The red glow, a dark and sinister blood-circle round the view of the splendid sunny day outside, warned him that magic stood on his doorstep. Because he'd never known this woman to use magic in front of anyone, he suspected that it had something to do with the wrapped package cradled like an infant child. Something for Jindra, no doubt. Something stitched with Witching spells.

He opened the door. "What are *you* doing here?"

"I've come to see my granddaughter."

"She's dead."

"My great-granddaughter, then," she said through tight lips. "I've a right."

He stepped outside and pulled the door shut, leaning back against it. "Your granddaughter is dead, and all your hopes of power and fortune with her. Unless you count all those weeks on the Durkah Isle, gathering influence for the Archduke."

She looked startled for an instant. "Your foresight, I suppose. What I did or didn't do is no concern of yours. I want to see Jindra."

"That won't happen."

"Refuse me now, I'll only keep coming back," she warned. "I'll appeal to the Archduke and demand my rights."

"You fool," he murmured. "Who do you think gave the order that led to her death?"

She laughed.

"Panshilara tried and failed to destroy Mieka. She paid for her presumption. Your granddaughter's death was the rehearsal."

"Liar. Liar!"

"Didn't you notice the similarities? The overturned coach, only the coachman surviving—the fatal wounds caused by 'broken glass'? I never knew a shard of glass to slice itself neatly across anyone's throat. And I've shattered quite a lot of glass in my time."

Her face crumpled. She swayed on her feet. He made no move to help her, keep her upright. He watched the destruction he was causing and if he wasn't quite rejoicing, he certainly saw it without compassion.

"No—an accident—he wouldn't—not my girl!"

"The two coachmen were cousins. Did you know that? No, I don't think anybody knows except the Princess, and whichever smart constable or courtier bothered to match up the names. Blackslash and Shiverwing are both Raven Clan."

"You don't know that. You can't possibly—"

He stared down at her. Merciless. She had had no mercy for anyone else, not for Mieka or for him or even her own granddaughter with her plots and weavings and manipulations. Why should he have any for her? "I know a great many things. I know that there's useful knowledge, and useless knowledge, and knowledge that's dangerous. Knowledge like Vered's, about Knights and Caitiffs, that he put into his plays. And died for it."

"Whatever he wrote, he got it wrong." Something had changed in her eyes, the same iris-blue eyes that she had bequeathed to her granddaughter, eyes that had bewitched Mieka at first glancing. No sorrow, no outrage, not even anger anymore—instead, a fervid passion that burned like ice. "Slaves they made of us—despised by all other magical races, regretting that they'd ever made the Knights at all. As for the Humans—the blind and stupid and gift-less Humans hated and feared us."

"With reason," Cade said. "Once the *balaurin* were defeated, and there was no more need—"

She kept on talking. Lessoning him again. Speaking quickly, her arms clutching the parcel to her chest. "The Elves went first. Visible, with those ears. Easy to capture, with their terror of the dark." She didn't look at him. He didn't think she was looking at anything in the real world. "Giants. Gnomes. Goblins. Wizards lasted longest, being most like Humans to look at. *They* cared for nothing but their feeding. We were exiled, sent to that miserable island—and there we learned to weave our weavings for ourselves, not in slavery to our masters. *Our* magic!" She pulled in a wheezing breath. "But *they* knew by then that they could survive without us. Without tasting fresh blood more than a few times a year. Fear and turmoil—violence, hatred—"

Fascinated, the rapacious curiosity of the writer crowded out all other thought. "Why not just let them die?"

"They don't die. Hadn't you guessed that by now? They grow weak, they languish beneath the shrouds we wove for them, they sleep beneath the castle—neither alive nor dead—"

"Until somebody cuts their heads off."

She looked up at him then. "A silver sword is best. Remember that. Nothing does the work as well."

"Remember it?"

"You'll have need, when you defeat him."

"What castle?"

"Theirs, you fool! His! Do it, you must do it for her," she urged. "For my girl, my beautiful girl—" A small, tortured moan escaped her. "Don't bother with wood. Don't let them feed. They grow strong from the magic, wrench it from you, all the fear—all the pain—" Another moan rose from her very bones. "My girl—my beautiful girl—" }

When he'd caught his breath, he lunged for the pen and ink and paper on his bedside table. He had to make a record of what he'd learned. He scrawled the words so swiftly that no one but he would ever be able to read them. And when he finished, he fell back into the pillows and shut his eyes tight.

"Vered was wrong," he told Mieka as they went downstairs for breakfast.

"How do you—? Oh. Elsewhen."

He nodded. "It's even worse than what he wrote. Send notes round to everyone. We have to do it all over."

"Quill," he began in a whiny voice, then stopped. In a completely different tone he said, "Not all of it, surely. Just the third play, right?"

"Yeh." At the bottom of the stairs, he walked into a flood of sunlight through an east-facing window and flinched. "Wh—when did that happen?" he asked stupidly.

"Sunrise? Happens every morning, Quill. Granted, neither of us is awake to see it, usually, and with all this rain one begins to forget what it looks like. Don't forget we're lunching with the Princess today—" Again he stopped, and again his voice became softer, deeper. "Will your Elsewhen happen today?"

"I don't know. Could be. Do we have any guards left?"

"A couple. They're not yet back from taking Dery and Jindra to school. Miriuzca's sending a carriage for us. Will the Elsewhen happen soon?"

"I think so. I'm not sure. But I saw the damned thing once, I don't want to live through it for real." Was the light the same intensity? The same angle? Was there the same taste to the air, and the smell of carrot muffins from the kitchen? As far as he could tell . . . *yes.* "I know what I need to know."

"Tell me how it happened. We'll change it together."

Oddly enough, the sensation of peace returned. Yes; this was what they were supposed to be doing. This was where they were supposed to be. There was nothing he couldn't do, no puzzle he couldn't solve, and no difficulty he couldn't overcome.

Except one thing. Mieka saw it first. Cade took some convincing.

"We can't do it. Not at the Namingday."

"We have to."

"*Not* at the Namingday." Mieka set aside his teacup and turned slightly in his chair to face Cayden. "In the first place, the old man wouldn't understand the half of it. I know exactly what he'll look like—all confused at first and then impatient and then angry that he doesn't understand, and resenting all that grim and grue on what's s'posed to be a celebration night."

"Who cares? He's not the one we're playing to."

"Well, it's his Namingday, poor old codger," Mieka observed mildly. "And in the second place, you're good, Quill—we all are, the best there is or ever will be—but not even we can put together the writing and staging and rehearsal of something this important in two days."

"Three."

"Two. If we slog away at it for three solid days, we'd be too knackered to perform. And it wouldn't be *right* yet, you know it wouldn't. And don't you go locking yourself in your library all day and all night trying to get it written. Let it steep in your head for a while. I know you, old dear. I know how you work."

"But the whole Court—Hells, the whole Kingdom!—expects something new and brilliant and—"

"So we'll give them *Window Wall*."

"Mieka, it has to be Vered's play. All three plays. I want to see the Archduke's face when we—"

"Oh, you'll see it, right enough. When we do it at Seekhaven."

"At the opening of his new theater?" Cade snorted.

"No, as the very last final-night performance given at Fliting Hall."

"But it won't *be* the final night of Trials. This new theater's supposed to be the setting for that performance from this year on. Everybody's doing something new for it. I wanted to save *Window Wall* for that night."

Mistress Mirdley came in to remove the breakfast dishes. The two of them stared silently at each other the whole time she was there. She seemed not to notice their tension, merely poured more tea into their cups and left with the tray of used crockery. But Cade was certain sure he'd seen a smile twitch the corners of her mouth.

"*Window Wall* is too long," Mieka said as if there'd been no interruption at all. "There's four or five groups performing that night. We're the best, so we'll be on last—and by then it'll be getting late. Do you really think they'll pay attention for another whole hour?"

It had been understood, ever since the opening of the Archduke's new theater (years in the building; everyone wondered what had taken so long) was announced at the beginning of the year, that the Shadowshapers would be the final act that night. After Vered's death, Cade had assumed that Rauel, Chat, and Sakary would want to keep that position and do *Blood Plight*. But they were adamant: There would be only one performance of all three plays. At the Palace theater. On the King's Namingday.

Mieka was right, and Cade knew it. He couldn't rewrite it as it demanded to be written, and the rest of them couldn't plan out the staging as it demanded to be staged, in three days.

"I thought you were going to send letters to everybody, telling them the new plan," he grumbled.

"The plan to do *Window Wall* at the Palace, and save *Blood Plight* for when it's ready?"

"Yeh."

Mieka stood, reaching over to pat Cade's shoulder. "Stop scowling like that. It'll get done. The play, I mean. As for the letters telling everyone . . ."

"All right, all right, I'll do them!"

He could have done the play. All it would take would be some thorn to keep him awake and sharp. But there was none in the house. Not a single twist of paper with powder in it, not a single glass thorn, nothing. Well, except for a tiny stash of blockweed deep in a drawer in his bedchamber. Just in case he had trouble sleeping—which, he realized with some surprise, he hadn't since his very first night here.

Mieka was moving towards the riverside door. Cade gave a start. "Where are you going?"

"Somebody's come. Didn't you hear the knocker?" He spun suspiciously on one heel. "Is that how the Elsewhen started?"

"I don't want to see her. I already know what she's going to say. Let Mistress Mirdley answer it. Tell her to send the old bitch away."

After a brief hesitation, Mieka nodded and started for the door to the kitchen. The knocker sounded again—Cade could see it in his mind, the polished steel made by Rikka Ashbottle's uncle, the ironcrafter. A beautiful thing, the background a sunburst, the knocker a thistle. He could see it vanish under the woman's fingers as she lifted it and let it fall. Her other hand would be clutching the package, whatever bespelled dress or shirt or coverlet she'd stitched for Jindra. The source, undoubtedly, of the magic to turn the edges of the glass red.

She didn't know. For Cyed Henick she had gone to the Durkah Isle to call the Caitiffs to their traditional service. Unsuccessfully; he gathered that, not content with their lot but unwilling to resume slavery, they had declined.

She didn't know. Not knowing, what else would she be willing to do for him? For the heirs of the Knights of the Balaur Tsepesh? For the man whose ancestral castle had become their refuge?

Moving very deliberately, Cade walked to the door. He didn't bother to look through curtained windows or the peephole. He knew what he'd see. He opened the door and there she was, exactly as in the Elsewhen.

"I know why you're here. You won't be seeing Jindra. Not now, not ever. You have no rights where she's concerned."

She looked up, offered the package. "You won't even give her—"

"She'll touch nothing made by you."

"It's only a skirt. Just a simple skirt. Pretty, with violets embroidered at the hem—"

"There's something you ought to know."

He told her. She said almost what she'd said in the Elsewhen. He listened, and it was as if he heard her voice in that moment and in the Elsewhen, an inexact echoing, as if the lines spoken by a masquer had been changed and he hadn't quite got the newer version right.

{ **"Liar. Liar!"** }

"That's a lie!"

{ **"You don't know that—"** }

"How could you know that?"

{ **"No—an accident—"** }

"No! Not my girl!"

But it was true, and she knew it. He saw her face age a hundred years and knew what was coming next.

It didn't.

No anger. No words about the Knights, the Caitiffs, the expulsion of magical folk from the Continent. Instead, she clutched the package to her breast like a suckling child and curled around her grief.

"My girl . . . my perfect, beautiful girl . . ."

"I'm sorry," he heard himself say. Some small fragment of him truly was sorry. How odd.

"You!" She glared up at him. "*You're* sorry! It was coming out perfect—even though she first chose that stupid little Elf! She became a titled Lady, just as she deserved! But *you*—he's obsessed with you—your foreseeings and your arrogance—and the Elf, always that bed-amned Elf! I could have made it perfect there, too, only *you* were there. He was never truly hers. No matter what we tried, the pair of us—but he ruined everything and now she's dead. It's your fault, it's *you* who should be dead, not her! Not my beautiful girl—"

His fault? How could it be *his* fault? Cade took a step back, as he had not done in the Elsewhen. Her frenzy had been directed against the Archduke then; now she spat her rage at *him*. He wondered what had changed.

"What is *that* doing here?" Mistress Mirdley snapped, shouldering him aside. "Begone with you, Caitiff! Take your weavings and stitchings and get yourself gone from this house. We want none of your kind here."

Spent, hollow-eyed with suffering, she whispered, "Yes, gone."

Cade watched over Mistress Mirdley's head as the Caitiff turned and walked down to the narrow cobbled road between the house and the river. She turned right, moving with slow, stumbling steps upstream.

"Good riddance," Mistress Mirdley growled.

"I had to tell her. She had to know." He heard himself babbling and couldn't stop. "Otherwise, she would have done other things for him—helped him—I couldn't let her do that. I had to tell her." He hauled in a long breath to clear his head. The Elsewhen and the reality backed away down some side road in his mind.

He thought Mistress Mirdley would leave the doorway, come back inside the house. She was still watching the Caitiff, who had passed the brick wall that marked Moonglade Reach's land. He squinted, try-ing to see. Just walking, only walking, her gait more certain now, and she got to the steps carved into the grassy riverbank.

Too late, he realized what she was about to do. He started forward.

The Trollwife seized his arm in a grip like stone. "No. She has noth-ing left. You just made certain of that."

There was no blame in her voice. He heard Mieka's light footstep behind him, the soft gasp as the Caitiff walked purposefully into the water.

Someone in a sailboat called out a warning. Mistress Mirdley hung on to Cade's arm, and in his turn, he hung on to Mieka's shoulder.

"No," he whispered. "She's right. There's nothing left for her."

They watched as sodden skirts dragged her down and washed her into the current. If she cried out in pain as the water took her—clean, pure, new water swelling the river after so many days of rain, water that was poison to a Caitiff—if she screamed, he didn't hear.

Perhaps Mieka did. Perhaps those elegant, sensitive Elfen ears heard her agony. *"My girl . . . my perfect, beautiful girl . . ."*

Mieka stood beside him, trembling but not flinching; if he did hear, he gave no sign. The muscles of his shoulder shifted as he tensed, strong with his almost daily practice with sword and knife. He wasn't a boy anymore. He was a man full-grown. When Cade turned his head from the scene of people vainly trying to save the Caitiff from the river, he saw a face just as beautiful, but older. It had been happening for months now, without his consciously noticing it. His capricious, sweetly outrageous, mad little Elfling had grown up.

He didn't know whether to rejoice or mourn.

Mayhap a little of both.

Chapter 33

"Honest," Jeska said, returning to the tiring room after getting a peek at the audience, "Yazz and Rist and all their uncles and cousins shoving together couldn't cram more people in."

Cade really hadn't needed confirmation that the Palace theater was packed. He'd taken a look himself earlier, and seen them squeezed in everywhere, even behind the last row of seats—the space where, Vered had told Cade, the Old Gods lingered, invisible, more judgmental than any Steward. *"Amateurs play to the front row, because that's where their friends sit. So-called professionals, they aim for the middle, thinking that the front will take care of itself and the back doesn't matter that much. But those of us who really understand . . . we play to the Gods."* There would be scant room for the Gods tonight, Cade thought wryly.

Everyone who had paid any attention to the broadsheets, and *The Nayword* in particular, expected the surviving Shadowshapers and *Blood Plight.* Of course the place was crammed to bursting. Throats encircled with diamonds or sapphires or spectacularly knotted silk scarves craned to get a glimpse of Rauel, Chat, Sakary, even of Romuald Needler, their manager. All four were here tonight, drifting aimlessly about the artists' tiring room, forlorn and trying not to look it. Cade guessed that it had finally struck each of them that there would be no more Shadowshaper performances—not in the way there had been for so many years. He'd had a frightful time convincing them that the plays had to wait for Seekhaven. What they would do after that, with no prospect at all of standing on a stage together again *as* the Shadowshapers, he didn't want to guess. During the two years or so they'd spent apart, Sakary had begun tutoring aspiring fettlers. Chat had given Master classes to those gliskers who belonged to groups but wanted to hone their skills. Rauel had written a couple of plays for others to perform. Cade, glancing at Mieka, didn't let himself wonder what might have happened to him and Jeska and Rafe if they had indeed lost their Elf, as so many Elsewhens had shown him. He didn't worry about that anymore. He'd realized that the peace he felt at Moonglade Reach was founded on something that it had taken him months to understand: safety. He and Mieka were safe there. Never again would he hear in an Elsewhen the words that terrified him: *"When Touchstone lost their Elf, they lost their soul."*

A few months ago, just before Wintering, they'd played the Downstreet (three nights, two shows each night, and still people had had to be turned away), and Mieka had impishly changed one of the "Doorways" to a view of Moonglade Reach. Just for a moment; just a glimpse for the audience as the scene moved to a prospect of the Gally River's green, tree-lined banks and blue water with the city rising in the background. *"This life, and none other."* Cade had hidden laughter behind an exasperated glare. Mieka just laughed.

As Touchstone took the stage, this sureness of safety allowed Cayden to see with perfect composure the Archduke's smug face there in the front row. He was more certain than ever that this man had been the second member of the audience during their final gigging at that creepy mansion outside New Halt. It made no sense, of course. Cyed Henick walked about in daylight just like anyone else. He couldn't possibly be what Cade suspected him of being. And as for the other man—or woman, there'd been no way to tell, what with all the disguising cloaks and enshrouding blankets—Cade hadn't a clue. He only knew that both of them had fed off the emotions Touchstone's magic had provided that night, and Touchstone had emerged from that cellar staggering with exhaustion.

No such possibility tonight. Just a regular audience—well, an audience made up of regular people, some having bits of magic and others not, but all of them rich enough or important enough to be invited to the King's Namingday. He remembered something else Vered had said once, that when an audience such as this one applauded, it was difficult to hear the handclaps over the rattling of jewels.

The Archduke wasn't looking well. His color was bad, his hairline receding, his fingers swollen around his rings. He sat next to Prince

Ashgar, whose good looks were fading. Cade, whose father had died in the Prince's service (more or less), could make a pretty good guess about the activities wearing down his health.

Maybe, he thought as *Window Wall* progressed onstage near him, maybe the pair of them would do everybody a favor and drop dead. Then, when King Meredan finally died, Princess Miriuzca could act as regent while Prince Roshlin grew into the kingship.

"Magic!" Jeska exclaimed, and Cade nearly jumped. The Father in the piece was well into his ranting. "Magic and the war fought because of it took my wife from me. Very well, then. Magic will keep my son safe from the world and all its hurts—especially those wrought by magic."

The staging of *Window Wall* had cost Touchstone day after day of perplexity and the occasional shouting match. It had been maddening, figuring out how to show both the inside and the outside of the room where the Boy lived his isolated life. The first section of the first play was the easy part. The Father's arrival home from the war to find his wife dying of an enemy spell; their infant son whimpering in his crib; the promise to protect the child at all costs from the magic that had destroyed thousands of lives. Cayden watched closely as the wall was built, the room stocked with furniture and books and toys and a lute, a glowing hearth over to one side and no door. As he worked, the Father kept talking, mumbling to himself about what the Boy would need as he grew older. Food, and a bowl and a spoon and a knife to eat it with—skirting the issue of where the food would come from. It was a play, it was magic, why waste time on trivialities? Or so Rafe had convinced him, slicing out the parts of the speech that dealt with some friend delivering food and so forth. "Boring. Get rid of it. And the lines about the piss pot and bathtub and fresh water. Nobody cares. None of that is the point of the play."

"But it's supposed to be real!"

"You think we can't convince them that it *is* real?"

Rafe, he'd had to admit, had a point.

As the bricks rose to knee-height and glass began to fill the space—a glistening sheer curtain of magically conjured glass—the sound of the Father's voice and the urgency of his emotions were gradually blocked from the audience. Cade grimaced as he noted that Mieka had once more done what the rest of them had decided was unnecessary: included a loaf of fresh bread on the table and a cauldron of simmering

soup on the hearth, using the scents and their slow fading to emphasize the barrier of the glass. Perhaps it was best, for King Meredan
wasn't the shiniest withie in the basket.

Now came the tricky part. The entire scene ebbed into shadows,
and when the room reappeared it had rotated a quarter-turn, angled
so that the room and the glass window were on two-thirds of the stage,
towards the back, and the outside world took up the rest. People and
horses, flower-sellers and sausage carts, clatter and laughter and shouting and songs—the tumult of sensation washed over the audience
until the Boy entered the room. And then all sound and scent, the
brush of the breeze against a cheek, the warmth of the sunny day and
the cheerful bustle of a Gallybanks street were gone. The people were
still there, beyond the window; shoppers strolled, carriages passed,
children chased a ball. But it was all as silent as a magical stained-glass
window in a wealthy Minster.

The Boy was nearly grown. The Father lay in bed, dying.

"I've done all I could do," he grated, coughing, and Cade hid a smile,
knowing it was anybody's guess as to which figure was Jeska and which
was wholly made of magic. Damn, but he and Mieka were good! "You're
safe from the world, my son. Nothing can hurt you. Should you ever
doubt the wisdom of what I've done, watch through the window and
see how they suffer and grieve and weep and hate! You're well out of it.
Safe. Protected. Alone."

There was a death rattle, and the Father fell back into the pillows.
The Boy rose to his feet, feeling nothing. Surprise and discomfort rip-
pled through the audience. Shouldn't he be feeling *something?* The
only person he'd ever spoken with was dead.

In rehearsal, Mieka had wailed, "What in all Hells am I to do with
the body?"

Rafe again, confident in his judgments: "Just let it fade out. They'll
be watching the Boy move towards the window. I'll make sure they're
concentrating on that. The body can just disappear."

And it did. The Boy shifted a chair to face the window, and settled
down with an expression of remote interest to watch life happen a finger's touch away.

Outside, two men got into a fistfight. A nimble child picked pockets.
A girl pettishly turned her face from her lover's kiss. A carriage rolled
by and crushed an old man beneath its wheels.

"Alone," said the Boy, well-satisfied. And the silence and his emptiness filled the theater.

Thus ended the first play. The stage faded into darkness, and one or two people in the audience clapped half-heartedly.

"That's the finish of it, then?" the baffled King was heard to say, and someone tittered, swiftly hushed.

"There's another play coming after this one, Your Majesty," Miriuzca told him, just loudly enough for Cayden to hear. "Look—it's starting."

The scene flickered into being again, this time with the room crowded into the front third of the stage, the window wall angled towards the space halfway between Mieka and Rafe. The audience was now looking through the glass just as the Boy was doing, seeing Elf-light kindle in the streetlamps, shadows deepen beneath trees, traffic slow and finally cease, a cat prowl delicately across the cobbles. No scents this time, no sounds, no warmth from the hearth fire, no sensation of footfalls as the Boy paced back and forth, back and forth, older now, a man grown.

"Safe from magic—protected from all hurts—did he understand what he did to me? No heartache, no pain, no fear, no grief, no wickedness. Yes, I've seen those things. I watched through my window. But I've also seen love and delight, joy and pleasure, and goodness." He paused in his pacing. "At least, I *think* I've seen those things. I don't know. I can't tell. I've never felt any of them—not the bitter, not the sweet. I've read all these hundreds of books, and the stories and poetry are about love and pain and evil and good and they're naught but words to me! I don't know what any of it *means*!"

In a fit of rage, he began pulling books from the shelves, flinging them wide, gasping for breath.

"What is it like to be happy? What is it like to feel sunlight on my face? I've seen the rain fall from the sky—is it cold? What does it *taste* like? How does it *feel* to laugh or to cry?"

He grabbed a thick volume and hurled it against the window. In the instant before it hit the glass, the book turned into a bird the same green as the leather binding, pages fluttering into wings. The bird flew around the room, increasingly frantic, then slammed into the window, broke its neck, and fell dead to the floor.

On the other side of the window, a girl came into view. Graceful, furtive, cloaked in wool the color of midnight, she paused before the window and pulled her hood back to study her reflection. She was as beautiful as the morning, as the starry night sky. The Boy stumbled to the glass, looking at the girl, who could not look at him.

She tucked a wayward golden curl behind her ear. She adjusted the glowing white pearls at her throat. She ran the back of her finger along the delicate line of her jaw, and smiled. She was the kind of woman who couldn't pass a reflective surface without admiring her own perfections. The audience knew it; the Boy did not. Love awakened in him and spread through the theater: helplessly enthralled, desperately craving.

In Cade's original version, she had been sweetness personified, kind and gentle and good. In the revision, the audience knew her to be vain, shallow, thoughtless. The Boy didn't see that, of course. He saw only her beauty. She didn't see him at all. And that was the beginning of the point Cade was making: no matter how it might hurt in the end, and sometimes it could seem as if life were one long series of hurts, one had to see other people as they were, clearly and without—

"Wha's all this, then?" a man's voice bawled from the side aisle. "Call this a play, do you?"

Mieka pulled back the magic slowly, carefully. Rafe smoothed it like the fur on a cat's arching spine. They kept the audience safe as always.

"Seen better'n this in village taverns! Don't tell me the Crown is *paying* for such chankings!"

Lord Rolon Piercehand, large, loud, resplendent in a dark red silk suit, and very drunk, shoved his way through to the front row. The erstwhile favorite of all the Queen's ladies had used up his considerable good looks in the pursuit of whiskey, thorn, and women, though he seemed to believe he was as winsomely handsome as ever. He bowed to Queen Roshian, straightened up, bowed again to Princess Miriuzca, and nearly toppled into her lap.

"Dreadfully sorry—just got off a ship, don't you know, the legs aren't yet what they should be on dry land!"

Cayden saw King Meredan frown. But it was the Queen—the plump, motherly, completely uninspiring little Queen—who, glancing round and finding her confused husband on one side and her ineffectual son on the other, fixed a glare on Cade himself. "Remove this man at once!"

He started forward from his lectern before he could even think about it, astonished that this unassuming woman could command and he would instinctively obey—or did she have some droplet of magic in her veins that compelled him? Lord Piercehand was staggering about between the front row and the stage, waving cheerily at all his friends (who were busy making believe they'd never seen him before and didn't see him now), laughing riotously as he tripped over his own feet. Righting himself by grabbing the lip of the stage, he looked up and blinked at the players and the fading scenery.

"Oy, look at all those books! Oh—no, they've gone—by all the Gods, the whole *room's* gone! How'd they do that, eh?"

He clambered up onto the stage before Cade and two members of His Majesty's Household Guard could converge on him. He stood swaying, as if still on the deck of a ship, peering about him. "Never knew what a *view* one gets from up here! 'Strord'nary, ain't it?"

Cade gripped his arm, abruptly furious. How dared this drunken quat destroy a Touchstone performance?

Piercehand pulled away and wagged a teasing finger. "Now, now, lad, don't crease the silk!" He bestowed a smile on everyone that was a parody of the endearing charm that had captivated the Queen and her ladies thirty years ago. In the next instant, his eyes went out of focus and he stumbled back, eluding the two guards. "Wha's you doin'?" He waved his arms wide, spittle flying from his lips. "D'you know who the fuck I am?"

"Yes, Your Lordship," said Jeska, "everyone is very much aware of who you are."

Piercehand swung about to face him in a staggering, drunken whirl that added to the impact of the masquer's experienced fist. His Lordship's head snapped back and to the side, and he went down like a felled tree.

"Nice one, Jeska!" Mieka called out as several people in the audience began to applaud.

The guards picked up an arm each and lowered Piercehand over the edge of the stage with a notable lack of tenderness. He collapsed in a red silk heap. They jumped down and hauled him more or less upright again. It was the King's bad luck that His Lordship roused just as the guards dragged him past His Majesty. A groan, a curse, a convulsive cough—and he yarked, colorfully and thoroughly, right into the King's lap.

The guards lugged him hastily away. More guards attended the King out of the theater, and then the Queen and the senior members of Court.

"That coulda been me," murmured a soft, light voice at Cade's side.

He glanced down at the unsmiling face. "You? Never."

"Me, absolutely. And we both know it."

The sudden ringing of a handful of coins onto the stage startled them both. Cyed Henick walked past, glancing up with a shrewd smile as he tucked his purse back into his pocket.

Into the sudden deathly silence left behind, Lady Megueris Mindrising said mildly, "Well, I don't know about the rest of you, but I could use a drink."

*   *   *

At the awkward reception that followed, Jeska was the hero of the evening. Cade quickly lost track of him in a crowd of appreciative admirers. Where Rafe and Mieka had got to, he'd no idea. He politely accepted his share of congratulations qualified by pity and even some indignation—though he couldn't tell whether the resentment was on his behalf or their own, for not being able to see the entire play. Never mind; they'd have a much better story to tell their envious friends.

"Not what you had in mind, I gather." Lady Megs signaled a passing servant and snagged another glass of bubbly white wine, handing it to Cayden. "Here. If anybody deserves to get good and drunk tonight, it's you."

"I don't want to get drunk." Contradicting his own words, he tossed back the entire contents of the glass in one swallow.

"If not drunk, then . . . ?" She arched a pale eyebrow.

He had put his guts into *Window Wall*, worked on it for years, argued about it and rewritten it and agonized over it, and that stupid fucking drunkard of a nobleman had wrecked its first performance. "I want to beat him so bloody that even people who *look* like him will bleed."

Megs gave him her own glass of wine. "If there's anything left once the guards are through with him, you'd have to compete with Her Majesty for the privilege. And it's my opinion that you'd lose. So drink up."

He did as ordered, Kearney Fairwalk's admonition echoing in his head: *"You are appreciating a fine wine, not filling a bucket!"* There was somebody else he'd like to take apart piece by lying, cheating, thieving, worthless piece. He looked into the empty glass, then at her. "Lady Megueris, are you trying to get me drunk?"

"So I can have my way with you?" She laughed up at him, green eyes dancing. "I must say, Master Silversun, you're much better when you have the use of both your hands. But no, sorry to disappoint—if you *are* disappointed, that is, and I'm trusting that you're too much of a gentleman to admit if you're not. I'm in attendance on the Princess tonight. And she'll be wondering where I've gone. I promised a full report on the party."

"She's not missing much." He looked around the grand reception room—garlanded with flowers, candles twinkling everywhere, food on silver plates and drink in crystal decanters displayed on tables lining one wall. Eight young boys in green and brown outfits sang complicated harmonies at the far end of the room. The guests milled about, attempting to impress each other, but not so avidly as they would have had the personages they truly wanted to impress been present.

"Actually," Cade confessed, "now that I think on it, I feel sorrier for the King than for myself. Poor old duffer. We can always do *Window Wall* again. He'll never get the stink out of that jacket."

"He can afford a new one." She looked him down and up. "Talking of which, all of you look quite splendid tonight. Harmonizing but not identical. Which is always just too precious for words."

He received the compliment graciously. Jinsie had insisted on new clothing for tonight's performance, in shades of dark blue with black accents. Jeska got the trousers, Rafe wore the jacket, Mieka had the shirt, and Cade the longvest.

"These days we get frustled up for a gigging only when Royalty will be in the audience." He chuckled, beginning to feel the wine. "Mieka finds this rather vexing. Silly little peacock."

"Well?"

"Well what?"

"According to the rules, at this point you're supposed to say something nice about my gown. Or my jewels. Or my hair. A compliment to a lady never goes amiss."

His turn to survey her. She wore a plum-colored silk bodice and overskirt swagged up to her knees, showing the white lace underskirt beneath, and a necklace of alternating pearls and amethysts in silver.

Her dark blonde hair was swept smoothly up and back, secured with pearl-headed pins. "No turquoise. I approve."

"Surely a tregetour can do better than that."

"Surely you can find a dozen or more men who'll tell you all the pretty things you can stand to hear."

"Yes, and every word they speak is actually in praise of my money." She smiled and sipped wine, then said, "I'm glad the rumors weren't true."

"What rumors?" The sudden shift in subject confused him. Was this his third glass, or his fourth?

"That you'd be doing Vered Goldbraider's final play, you and the remaining Shadowshapers. Are you about to ask how I knew?" She gave him the sort of patient, indulgent look that one would give an otherwise reasonably bright child who didn't quite understand that two and two really did add up to four. "Once a week we go out for drinks. Miriuzca joins us when she can get away."

"Who's 'we'?"

"Jinsie, Blye, Vrennerie, when she and her husband are in Gallybanks. Kazie and Deshananda and Breckyn when they're not exhausted by their children. Mishia's joined us a few times. So has Crisiant, though she's not much of a drinker and usually has apple juice. What we don't know about what *all* you boys are up to isn't worth the knowing."

"Drinks?" he echoed foolishly. And then, as it finally hit him: "Did you say *Princess Miriuzca?*"

"I did." She was laughing at him again. "You really don't understand much about women, do you? Anyway, as I was saying, it's a good thing you didn't do Vered's plays."

"Umm . . . yeh." He wanted very much to ask which taverns they met at, and whether the Princess went disguised, and why he'd never heard even a breath of rumor about these little excursions. What sort of ungrateful friend was Blye, anyways, to keep that sort of gossip from him?

"It was an interesting piece," Megs was saying. "I hope I get the chance to see the rest of it."

"What did you think of what you saw?"

She considered. "I liked it very much, based on what we didn't get to see."

"How do you think it ends?"

"I'm assuming that the point you wanted to make *isn't* that one shouldn't read books." Seeing his bewilderment, she elaborated. "Well, look at where reading got him. Everything he said about love and pleasure and hate and so forth—he didn't know what any of those really felt like, did he? He knew only what the books had told him. Until he saw the girl."

He nearly groaned aloud. Was that what people would take away from this truncated version of *Window Wall*?

"But I think you were also saying something you and I can agree on."

"And that might be?"

"You can't see someone's soul in her face. Physical beauty is so often a lie, isn't it? Please tell me he doesn't break the glass and escape that horrible room just for the wanting of the girl."

"Good guess."

"I wouldn't expect you to do something so . . . expected."

"Much beholden." As he looked around for someone to take his drained glass (and *not* supply him with a fresh one; it was pathetic, the amount he couldn't drink anymore; he must be getting old), his gaze lit on the Archduke and Prince Ashgar. The latter, he could understand—he was the kind of man who never missed a party if he could help it, even if someone had just vomited on his father. But the Archduke? What was Henick doing here?

Oh. Of course. He'd come to gloat. And smirk. Cade saw it as their gazes met. It wasn't just that Henick thought they hadn't dared do *Blood Plight*. It was seeing Touchstone's humiliation at an interrupted, unfinished performance. Add to these the insult of coins tossed onto the stage as if they were piddling amateurs in some drab little provincial tavern, and his enjoyment of the evening was complete.

Rage stirred once more. Then Cade recalled that it wasn't so many months until Trials. Touchstone would do *Window Wall*—the whole of both plays, damn it—and Touchstone plus the remaining Shadowshapers would do Vered's plays. The Archduke could simper all he pleased. He wouldn't be simpering for long.

Chapter 34

It was a nice tavern in a nice neighborhood, the Goldhawk. Its padded chairs and cushioned benches welcomed the prosperous posteriors of professional people—merchants, physickers, lawyers—who lived in the area and popped in for a pint or two before or after dinner. They were often joined by their womenfolk, who sipped ladylike brews of tea or fruit juices (which, on request, were spiked with alcohol). Of dockworkers, common laborers, clerks, and whores there was no sign.

No stage, either. Entertainment was provided by a pair of young lutenists trading stringed flourishes over in a corner, aided in their musical conversation by an even younger man beating his palms raw on a pair of drums and a singer who tossed his dark golden curls to emphasize words nobody was listening to. The Goldhawk had an excellent reputation and no one thought twice about the presence, unescorted, of the four young women who entered one pleasant spring night and hung their cloaks and coats on the brass stand beside a round table.

Sparkling glasses, beer in a pitcher, and red wine in a decanter were soon brought without their having to order. This told Mieka, quietly watching from the doorway, that these ladies were known here. The question was, were they actually *known* here?

There were no furtive glances, no looks of surprise or muffled exclamations of recognition. Granted, only one of them was in any way famous. But surely someone must suspect that the beautiful girl with laughing blue eyes was accustomed to costlier clothing than a plain black woolen skirt, white blouse, and short red jacket, and that her wheaten hair was not usually in a single braid down her back but dressed in curls and studded with gems.

Observing their laughter and easy conversation, Mieka realized that if they *were* regulars here, not only would the usual patrons be accustomed to them by now but willing to show them the courtesy of not openly recognizing them. Indeed, lack of reaction would signify a certain refinement, as if everybody here bumped elbows with Princesses in taverns all the time.

Eh, what did it matter? He grinned to himself and waved to a party of gentlemen who raised their glasses in salute. They might or might not know Miriuzca for who she really was, but they certainly knew Touchstone.

Sauntering over to their table, he doffed his cap and greeted the startled ladies with a bow. "May a lowly player, a clumsy wielder of withies, naught more than a freckle on the cheek of Albeyn, make so bold as to offer the comeliest women in Gallantrybanks a drink?"

"No," said Megs.

Jinsie seconded, "I don't believe we've been introduced, and of course it would be unthinkable to be seen drinking with a *strange* man."

He clapped a hand to his heart, staggering back. Miriuzca giggled.

"Ladies!" Vrennerie chided. "How often do we get the chance to treat such a pretty gentleman to a beer?"

"I still say he's *strange*," Jinsie said, but made room for him on the bench.

Mieka made himself comfortable and raised a finger to summon the serving girl. "One more glass, if you please, darlin', and another pitcher when this one's empty. Beholden." To his sister: "I wonder if Nahael Silkspin will be around here tonight. That's his name, innit?" When she gave him innocent stare for innocent stare, he persisted, "I'd like to meet him."

"A very nice young man," said Megs. "But not, I think, a prospective husband. Not for Jinsie, at any rate."

Jinsie took a swallow of beer, then said serenely, "I think it has more to do with whether or not I'm a prospective wife. I can't seem to find anyone who wants the same kind of marriage I do."

"And which kind is that?" Mieka asked, remembering her words about either knowing everything or knowing nothing about the person one spent one's life with.

"In my experience," Vrennerie said, "the best marriages are the ones that are causing each to be better people. More deserving of that person's love."

Miriuzca made a rueful face. Vrennerie, realizing what she'd said, blushed crimson. It wasn't exactly a description of the Princess's marriage; she did strive to become a better person, but not for Ashgar. For Albeyn.

Quickly, Mieka said to Vrennerie, "That's easy enough for you to say—you and your husband both started out perfect!" All of them laughed, and the moment was saved. He went on more seriously, "I think there are as many kinds of marriage as there are marriages."

"You may be right," said Jinsie, much to his surprise. "But I didn't much like the sort that Nahael seemed to have in mind for us. Too many compromises—and all of them *mine!*"

"But isn't marriage a series of compromises?" Vrennerie asked. "I don't mean arguments when one or the other just gives in."

"Ah, but it's usually the woman who does the giving in." Megs grimaced.

"Still want to be a Steward, do you?" Mieka asked, smiling.

"And why shouldn't she?" Jinsie demanded.

Vrennerie said, "She has the right sort of magic and knows how to use it."

"Indeed," said Miriuzca. "From all my talking with the Stewards, I'm not seeing any reason why a woman should not become one of them."

He held up both hands. "Ladies! Please! I give in!"

More laughter, and his twin muttering, "You wouldn't know a compromise if it bit you on the nose," and the arrival of another pitcher. Mieka drank sparingly, and Jinsie noticed it. He received from her the kindest and most compassionate look he'd ever seen. She had overheard their father on the night he'd presented two choices.

"The drink and the thorn, or your profession. Give up one or the other, Mieka, because you can't have both."

Never again devour the energy that was enough for two shows in one day and two girls right after? Never again watch bejeweled mists trail from every mote of plain dust, never again sense his body floating on a river of white fleece that tasted of apples and spices? Never down whiskey after whiskey, laughing, relaxed, instantly ready with the mockery and silliness that everyone expected from him? Never again sleep the long, deep, dreamless sleep that redthorn always provided?

If he kept on with it, he might as well ready himself for the longest, deepest sleep of all. That was what had been in his father's eyes.

"Face it, my son. Make your decision."

Never again hear the tumult of welcoming, excited applause as Touchstone took the stage. Never again dance his way through "Dragon," "Doorways," "Bewilderland," plucking withies from the glass baskets and feeling Cayden's magic within them—feeling Cayden himself, all his brilliance and intensity ready for Mieka to release in service to their art. Never again leap over the glass baskets and join his partners to take their bows, tired and exhilarated and laughing, while shouts and cheers washed over them like waves in the Ocean Sea. Never again exult in the certainty that he was good, that Touchstone was beyond good, that no one, not even the Shadowshapers, could give an audience what they did.

The choice became difficult sometimes—like tonight, in a tavern where everyone drank their fill while he dawdled over a single beer. Perhaps he wasn't so funny these days; perhaps the jokes didn't come so quickly or get told so elaborately. But he didn't black out anymore, either. He didn't wake in some girl's bed wondering how in all Hells he'd got there. He didn't have to ask Rafe or Jeska or Cade the next morning if there was anyone he should apologize to.

As for thorn . . . some nights it was damned near impossible to get to sleep. Some days it was damned near irresistible, the thought of sneaking off to Master Bellgloss (Auntie Brishen had been forbidden by her sister from providing Mieka with anything but medicinals) for a little something to make all his worries disappear, or give him that extra punch when a tough performance was coming up.

"The drink and the thorn, or your profession. Give up one or the other, Mieka, because you can't have both."

He'd made his choice. He had no regrets—but Gods how he missed it sometimes.

Besides, there was nothing to prevent him from drinking himself stuporous every night or using thorn until his arms bled, once Touchstone had shattered their last withie. Something to look forward to in his old age.

The drummer and one of the lutenists came by the table, looking for praise and, Mieka supposed, trimmings. Miriuzca smiled and produced a gold royal—much too much, but Royals never carried money and perhaps she wasn't all that certain about which coins were which. He saw the Elfen-eared drummer eye Miriuzca with an invitation all over his face. To judge by the glint in his dark eyes, he recognized her.

Mieka tugged on his sleeve, and when he leaned down, whispered, "Forget it, lad. You can't afford her."

"Ah, but you're assuming that *she* can afford *me*!"

When Mieka glowered, he laughed.

When Mieka's boot-knife suddenly appeared three inches from his nose, he backed away hastily and went to bother someone else.

"It's a truth generally acknowledged," said Mieka, sticking the knife back into his boot, "that whatever can be accomplished with a smile can be accomplished much more quickly with a smile and a sharp blade. Now," he went on, turning to address Megs and Vrennerie, "I'll tell you why I'm here. And by the by, Jinsie, if you want to keep these little crawls to yourself, you'll have to learn how to sneak out of Wistly in secret, not stroll out the front door. I followed you tonight because Cayden wants to be kept up to date on what Touchstone is doing. I'm told you know everything there is to know."

"Oh, very funny," Jinsie observed. "It's not as if you rehearsed in secret."

"If you knew," he pointed out, "then so did others. And that's why I'm thinking that Piercehand would've done what he did no matter which play we performed that night."

"You mean that he was prepared and at the ready to stagger in and make a fool of himself?" Megs shook her head. "He's not that stupid."

"He's not that sober these days, either," Vrennerie said.

"You may be right, Mieka," said Miriuzca. "I'm seeing that it would be easy to provide enough whiskey and then point him in the right direction." She poured herself more beer. Mieka knew he should have been amazed by the sight of the Princess serving herself, but he couldn't think of her as *the Princess* in these surroundings. "The Archduke did not wish the Shadowshapers' play to be performed. He couldn't know you'd changed your minds."

"He got a good giggle out of it anyway," Megs observed acidly. "I wanted to smack him."

Vrennerie nodded agreement. "Let's hope the man either was paid enough to compensate for publicly disgracing himself, or that the liquor was the best in the Archduke's cellars."

Mieka blinked. They knew not just about the play but also about the Archduke. He wanted badly to know exactly what they knew, but instead remarked, "He's at that stage of whiskey-thrall where he'd down a bottle of cheap scent for the alcohol in it, then belch behind his hand and ask for more."

Jinsie was looking at him again, and he knew what she was thinking: exactly what he'd told Cayden that night. *It could have been him.*

Conversation turned to the publication of *Bewilderland* the previous week, with congratulations on the transfer of a stage show to the printed page, aided by whimsical illustrations. Touchstone was the first to employ an artist in this fashion, but surely not the last. Jinsie had already been contacted by the Crystal Sparks and Hawk's Claw, for she was the one who had selected the *Bewilderland* artist from the students and graduates she knew at Stiddolfe and Shollop.

"I'm thinking about starting up a Guild for illustrators. None of the people who do woodcuts and pen drawings for the broadsheets have any representation."

Mieka waggled a finger at her. "Don't you go neglecting *us* for your new project!"

Ignoring him, she went on, "And I'd like to talk to the imagers as well. All of them seem to be at the mercy of whoever hires them, with no set fees or system of apprenticeship or anything."

"It wouldn't help, I suppose," said Miriuzca, "to have them be doing a tools-down, the way the weather witches did. People can live without pictures."

"And plays," Megs put in impudently, winking at Mieka.

"Gracious Gods," he drawled, "is this really what you women talk about behind men's backs?"

"Not always," Vrennerie replied sweetly. "Usually we discuss how adept men are—or aren't!—in bed."

"And," Megs added in the same tone, "what we can do to help them improve."

The evening was still young by Mieka's former standards when Vrennerie regretfully reminded Miriuzca that they had an early morning ahead of them.

"An emissary from the Grand Something of Somewhere wants to

plant some exotic sort of flower in the Palace gardens," she said as Mieka gallantly helped the ladies into their cloaks and coats. "Beholden, kind sir. His personal fortune-teller insisted that tomorrow morning is the absolutely perfect time to plant the thing, so . . . ." She finished with a shrug.

"They are seeming to be great believers in oracles and such to see the future," Miriuzca said. "Every important person in his country employs someone—Oh, Megs, remind me to look up what his land is called and practice how to pronounce it!"

"I predict," said Mieka, "that you'll say it perfectly on your very first try."

"Hmm." Vrennerie looked at him sidewise. "If you're so good at predictions, why didn't you know about Lord Piercehand?"

Aware that this turn of the conversation was dangerous, he smiled sweetly and opened his mouth to reply he knew not what. Megs beat him to it.

"The lore in Albeyn is that only the Fae can see the future—and they tell only the good things, never the drunk and disgusting."

"How very considerate of them," said Miriuzca.

"Not at all," Jinsie told her. "It's just that they hate all the fuss and bother the rest of us make if the news isn't good. Mieka, walk me home, yeh?"

They said good night out in the street, where a nondescript carriage was waiting to take Miriuzca, Megs, and Vrennerie back to the Palace. The Goldhawk wasn't so far from Wistly Hall that it would be dangerous for a man and woman to walk the well-lit pavement—especially if the man was carrying one knife behind his back and another pair in his boots and knew how to use them. Not that he'd ever actually fought anyone with the blades. It was all speculative. But he wasn't about to tell Jinsie that.

"You could've just asked to come along, you know," she said all at once.

"More fun to sneak after you." He let another half block of shuttered shops go by before he said, "I forgot to ask Lady Megs—how's her little brother?"

"How much do you know?"

Were Jinsie and Megs close enough friends to share this sort of thing? "How much *is* there to know?" he parried.

She stopped under an Elf-light streetlamp and searched his face. He saw the quick calculation in her eyes and tried to look both innocent and knowledgeable at the same time.

"I don't know why her father didn't marry again years ago, if he wanted a son so much."

Which told him exactly nothing about how much she knew. He placed a hand beneath her elbow to urge her along. "So Megs is disinherited. She doesn't seem all that broken up about it."

"She's bloody thrilled, if you want the truth. Lord Mindrising settled an allowance on her, more than enough to live very well in Gallybanks—more than more than enough, actually. As a lady-in-waiting, she takes all her meals with the Princess and has private chambers at the Palace."

"Mm." Of this he was well aware, for a couple of years ago, he'd found Cade not just in Megs's bedchamber but in Megs's bed.

Jinsie linked her arm with his as they walked. "There's nothing in her way now except those smarmy old Stewards and their obsolete rules."

"I haven't noticed many of them being smarmy. Senile, yeh, but—"

"Oh, you know what I mean. Every time she talks with one of them, they pat her on the head and tell her to be a good little girl and run along and play. How can she prove herself when they won't even let her try?"

"I'm sure she'll figure something out. She's good at that—figuring things out, I mean."

So was he. None of his business, of course . . . except that the boy was Cayden's son. And Cayden didn't know. And would never know, if Megs had her way. During the rest of the walk back to Wistly Hall, he debated the wisdom of telling him (thereby bringing Megs's wrath down on his own head) or waiting for Megs to decide to tell him herself (thereby provoking Cade's much scarier wrath if he found out that Mieka had known all along and never said a word). It was the lady's secret to tell or not tell, of course. Mieka kept other people's secrets.

He stayed the night at Wistly, breakfasted with those of his family still living at home who rose at the same late hour he did, then took a hire-hack out to Moonglade Reach at around noon. He could have lingered in town the rest of the day, for Touchstone had a gigging that night at a private party, but he missed home. Strange and actually quite lovely to realize that this was indeed *home*. As the hack pulled through the open gate (the guards had been called off long since) and down the short drive, he smiled to think that it was odder still that he'd so quickly come to treasure the peace and quiet.

A nice, calm, lazy day. Lunching with Cayden and Mistress Mirdley in the kitchen. Receiving the woodcrafter sent by Jed and Jez to finish off a few things in the house and check the banisters on the stairs to the roof. A short nap followed by sword practice and a long, hot bath. Listening to Jindra recite the poems she'd been set to learn at littleschool. Dining early, while discussing what they'd do at tonight's gigging. Gathering glass baskets and primed withies for the ride in a hire-hack back into the city. A successful show for an obscenely rich and very generous silversmith (whose younger son was one of Jinsie's artistic friends) and his two hundred guests. Driving home just as the Minsters were ringing ten.

"Y'know," Cade said in the tone of voice that meant he'd been pondering the issue for a while, "it's probably good that *Window Wall* got interrupted."

Mieka didn't ask how he figured that; Cade would eventually tell him. He just enjoyed being asked.

"What I mean is, everybody will be expecting it at Seekhaven. If nobody tattles, then when we all walk onstage to do *Blood Plight*, it'll be a total surprise."

"Mm." Mieka looked out the window at the dark street.

"Don't you think so?"

"I think we can't hold any rehearsals here at all. And no more than two run-throughs of the whole thing. We can't trust people not to notice, and we can't trust them to hold their tongues." He snorted. "I just spent an evening with the ladies, after all."

"They'd keep it quiet if we asked."

"I'd rather not have to ask. Why not send everybody the script, with notes, and—I know! We can rehearse at Hilldrop! Yazz and Robel won't mind. It'd be perfect."

The barn—untouched by black powder—had been renovated to hold Touchstone's wagon, with room for a couple of horses when and if Romuald Needler could be persuaded to sell. At Mieka's request and at his expense, Windthistle Brothers were rebuilding the cottage to Giant specifications—twenty-foot ceilings, twelve-foot doorways, everything wondrously outsized and comfortable for Yazz and Robel. Mieka owed it to them. Yazz could move his arm at the shoulder, but hooves and the carriage wheel had broken too many bones and damaged too many muscles. He could still drive, having proved it on short trips starting this past winter. He had yet to join them on the Royal Circuit. Mieka was hoping that overseeing construction of his new home would keep him from the coachman's bench one more year, so he could heal completely.

Cade stretched and resettled his long limbs in the stiffly uncomfortable seat. "Hilldrop. Yeh, I think that would work. If we don't all arrive and leave at the same time, nobody will think much of it. But let's make our visits on days when the workmen aren't there, all right?"

"Good thought."

Mieka loved returning to Moonglade Reach after a gigging. As the hack rattled up the street of shuttered shops and Elf-light lamps spaced well apart, the house could not be seen for the wall and the row of trees on the adjoining property. And then the wall and the trees ended, the hack turned in at the gate, left open on nights when they performed in town, and there was the house: the peculiar, top-heavy, inverted U, its central tunnel lit on either side with blue Wizardfire by Derien to welcome them home. Nobody, not his mother or father or siblings or even his wife, had ever thought to leave lights on for him.

Mistress Mirdley had prepared a snack, as usual: fruit, muffins with butter, hot tea. They ate in the kitchen where it was warm, seated on tall stools at the central worktable, the evening broadsheets spread all around them.

"Review of the *Bewilderland* book in the *Blazon*," Cade said. "They like the illustrations. 'Best cherished as a keepsake after seeing the play onstage.'" He snorted. "Hasn't anybody realized yet that if you get children interested in the pictures, they'll want to read the book themselves, and—"

"—and go to see the play, which will set them on the road to being theater-mad their whole lives," Mieka finished for him. "Mayhap the reviewer for the *Blazon* is too pure-minded for any thoughts so rancid as those about money." He paused for a sip of tea. "Here's a good one—letters from adoring populace about recently published plays. Quill, guess who they're talking about." He read aloud. "'A swift and absorbing hour's read. I had the great privilege of experiencing this in person, and even on the page it summons memories of the most exciting night I ever spent at the theater.'"

"Well, if he got through it so fast, it can't be us or the Shadowshapers. Or Hawk's Claw." He considered. "Not the Sparks, either—they haven't published anything yet. They're having trouble finding something that's a drastic enough rework of the old standards to get them the majority of the money. Who's this man writing about?"

"Black Lightning."

Cade grimaced sourly. "Should've guessed. How about us?"

Grinning, Mieka declaimed, "'I read the first ten pages and gave up. This is a terrible play, with no action, no plot, strange words, unsatisfying characters, and a sloppily described backdrop.'"

Bristling, Cade demanded, "Which play was that?"

"Does it matter? From the sound of it, whoever this is has a real problem paying attention for more than a couple of minutes. Who cares what somebody like that thinks? If you can call it 'thinking.'"

"He probably eats his dinner in two minutes flat."

"And spends the same amount of time making love." He laughed aloud. "Master of the Two-Minute Fuck! How many lovers d'you think his wife has?"

"None." Cade laughed, too, good humor restored. Mieka could always do that for him. "Any woman who marries a cullion like that doesn't deserve any fun in bed."

"Talking of cullions," Mieka said, "it says here that Fairwalk is selling the ancestral barracks."

"Not surprising," Cade replied, "when you consider all the gold he brought back that somehow didn't find its way into his bank account."

Mieka raised his teacup. "To Derien."

"Derien," Cade agreed. "Who d'you think will buy it?"

"Not a clue—but we should send Lady Vrennerie and Lady Megs to talk to him. Five minutes with them, and he'll be donating Fairwalk Manor to the People of Albeyn!"

"I've been there," Cade said. "It'd make a spectacular holiday camp."

"Let's do it! Only we'd have to find him first. Jinsie says nobody's heard anything of him. Seems he doesn't go to *those* taverns anymore—but word is Bellgloss makes up a special velvet pouch just for him every week, lined in silk and stitched with his initials."

Cade winced.

Seeing it, Mieka went on, "I'd be lying if I said I cared. And so would you. Slimy git, he was and is and always will be."

"He helped give us our start," Cade said softly.

"And bloody damned near finished us!"

Unfolding *The Nayword*, Cade shook out the page. "Lord Rolon Piercehand is holed up at Castle Eyot, writing his reminiscences."

Mieka was willing to be distracted from the subject of Kearney Fairwalk, though Piercehand was an equally unwelcome name. "First of all, I didn't know he could read, leave alone write."

"All those books—" Cade began.

"It took Drevan Wordturner to figure out what they were," Mieka reminded him. "Second, he never even went on his so-called voyages."

"Which is why," Cade informed him with a grin, "he's advertising for all the sailors and scholars and imagers to get in touch with him. 'An all-inclusive record of exploration and adventure,' he calls it. A week or so at Castle Eyot, reminiscing—which is code, I suppose, for 'Please come tell me what happened while I spent four months lying on a beach in Yzpaniole.'"

"Actually," Mieka said, "he might be just lonely. He had to slink out of town after what happened at the King's Namingday. Nobody will go near him. So he has to advertise for somebody to come keep him company."

"Hmm. You're probably right." He squinted at another article. "Tobalt is at it again."

"*Another* review of us? Jinsie and Kazie will have to put him on our payroll. Not but that some people think he's there already." A thought hit him, and he asked quickly, "It isn't *Window Wall*, is it? He couldn't have been at the Palace that night, could he?"

"No, it's not *Window Wall*. It's not even of Touchstone. Just you."

"Me?" He set down his teacup.

Cade's turn to read aloud. "'The wild, barely controlled energy of those first few years has given way to a crisper, more professional style. Whereas at the beginning, he was eager to share everything he had, he has learned to modulate and discipline the shadings of his performance. Subtlety, hitherto unknown to him, has become a hallmark. Easing delicately from one aspect to another, in complete control of everything the withies can give, Windthistle has lost none of his enthusiasm but

has gained insight that makes his style the most compelling and polished on the Kingdom's stages.'"

"'Discipline'?" Mieka exclaimed. "What a frightful word! *Discipline*
is forcing yourself to do what you don't want to do. Doesn't take any
discipline to be doing what you love!"

"And we even get paid for it!" Cade laughed. "Maybe even enough
to pay for replacing that bit of wall upstairs that you used for knife-
throwing practice."

Mieka shrugged. "So get me a proper target. The Archduke's about
the right size."

Cade wasn't listening. He was reading. And if his expression was
any indication, he wasn't much liking what he read.

Mieka leaned over and snatched the broadsheet from his hands. Ignoring Cade's protest, he skimmed over the headlines until he saw
what had put the glistening fury into those gray eyes.

DOES *WINDOW WALL* EVEN EXIST?

Silversun has teased us for what now seems like years about
this two-play work. Many people are beginning to believe that
it doesn't in fact exist. Touchstone has been doing the same
old standards for a very long time now, and word has it from
informed sources that Silversun has simply written himself out.
Other sources indicate that he never actually intended to finish the plays. Chaverish about them has, after all, kept his name
and Touchstone's before the public eye. It's not outrageous to
assert that he owes the public these plays—or a really good explanation for why nobody has seen them yet.

"Don't do it, Quill."

"How do you know what I want to do?"

He waved that question away as the absurd irrelevancy it was. "You
can't write a reply."

"Why the fuck not?"

"Don't put yourself on this cogger's level. He didn't even sign the
article—that tells you what kind of balls he's got: none. You don't owe
anybody anything but the best work you can give. If they don't or
can't or won't understand that, there's not a damned thing you can

say otherwise." Pausing for a sip of tea, and to judge how successful he was at tamping down Cade's temper, he finished, "Besides, once you get down in the dirt and roll about in their shit, it's gonna be really, really hard for me to drag you back out and rinse you off. And even after I do, you'll still stink for days."

There followed a few tense moments while Cade visibly decided whether or not to start shouting. At last, with a very sour smile, he said, "I'm sure Mistress Mirdley has a bespellment that would help. Pass the peach preserves."

Chapter 35

Never less than vigilant about the workings of his own or anyone else's plays, Cayden had spent the last ten years or so picking up various tricks of his trade. For instance, he'd learned long since to speak dialogue out loud before presenting it to Jeska. It wasn't that the masquer's glib and nimble tongue couldn't render comprehensible even the most impenetrable speeches. It was just that Cade didn't like to see a particular look on Jeska's face—and on Rafe's and Mieka's as well—that clearly said, *You don't* seriously *think that anybody talks like that, do you?* or, worse: *You can* write *this shit, Cayden, but you sure as Hells can't* say *it.*

On their first night at Seekhaven, alone in the bedchamber of the Shadowstone Inn that he always shared with Mieka, he was reading aloud to himself when the Elf strode in, bored. Cade knew he was bored because he said as much, as if it were Cade's fault.

In no mood to indulge him, Cade snapped, "Gods, you're in a foul temper tonight. Why don't you go out and find something to fuck?"

For just a moment, Mieka looked as if he might rearrange Cade's teeth with his fist. Then he suddenly roared with laughter and flung himself flat on his bed.

"I knew it! I knew it! You're as skittish about this as the rest of us!"

He didn't like having to admit it. Two rehearsals at Hilldrop, in as strict a secrecy as they could manage, had smoothed out most of the problems of performance, though everyone was shocked by the changes to the final play. Cade's reassurances that his own research had produced the new emphasis were accepted by Rafe and Jeska. They knew about the Elsewhens, and rightly assumed this was the "research" to which he referred. Rauel, Chat, and Sakary were more difficult to convince. But everybody had to admit that it was even more powerful his way.

Mieka sprang off the bed, bouncing to his feet. "All in all, that was an excellent suggestion just now. Care to join me? Or are you too enchanted by the sound of your own voice?"

"Oh, get out," Cade said irritably. Mieka laughed again, and went.

Cayden had scarcely read through two sentences of the next speech and made an alteration when, after a perfunctory knock on the door, Rauel came in.

"Worried, I take it," Cade said tiredly.

"We need more rehearsal."

"Everybody's got their work down cold."

"I'd like to run through it one more time."

"Fine. Go out and find us a venue where we won't attract any attention, staffed by people who won't say a word."

"I just want it to be perfect." Rauel used his big, soulful eyes in much the same way Mieka often did. Cade was impervious to it by now. Besides, Mieka was much better at it; something to do with the eyelashes.

Still, his voice was softer as he said, "I know. For Vered's sake."

Rauel nodded miserably. "Months now, and I still can't believe he's gone. Bexan's coming, did I tell you?"

Cade frowned. The instant she walked into Fliting Hall, everyone would know that *this* would be the performance of Vered's last plays. Hells, the instant somebody recognized her on the streets of Seekhaven, they'd know. He'd been counting on the audience's ignorance until the seven of them stepped onstage.

"We can't let her miss the one and only time this will ever be played," Rauel went on.

Well, no. They couldn't rightly do that. "Can you ask her to arrive that same afternoon, or at least not advertise her presence in town, and not come into the hall until just before we start?"

Rauel shrugged. "Nobody tells her what to do. I don't know but that Vered ever bothered to try."

"She'll have plenty of time to enjoy her bereavement afterwards. I'm sorry, that was a shitty thing to say."

"Ever noticed how the shittiest things people say are sometimes the truest?" With a sigh, he turned for the door. "I'll let you be getting on with it, then. Can I send up some tea, or a pitcher?"

"Beholden. Some of Mistress Luta's special blend tea wouldn't go amiss."

Another six sentences, and Chat arrived with teapot and mug. *Three down, three to go,* Cade told himself, wishing mightily for his library at home, where everybody knew not to bother him unless, say, the Gally River had risen to the front steps and, moreover, caught fire.

"I know you know what you're doing," Chat said. "I'd like to know why you're so determined to do it."

He could have given a million answers, starting with owing it to Vered, and most of them would be true. The real reason? That was vague in his mind, manifesting itself only as a gut-certain knowledge unsupported by much evidence that the Archduke had to be exposed for what he was, and soon, or it would be too late. Not even an Else-when to bolster this feeling, no real facts to point to—but he *knew* it.

"The final last-night performance at Fliting Hall," Chat mused, pacing idly about the room from desk to bed, window to door, and back towards the desk again. "We shoulda been the ones to do it. Everybody knows that."

"And the first to initiate the new theater," Cade agreed amiably. "Do they have the order for the program yet?"

He spread his hands wide, then tucked them into his trousers pockets. "Five groups, short plays from each. That's all I know."

"It should have been Black Lightning, Hawk's Claw, Crystal Sparks, us, and then you."

"Yeh. Been to look at the place yet?"

"Somebody showed me a plan. The biggest open-air theater ever constructed. Not quite in-the-round, but as close to as makes it tough on everybody."

"Now, there's a thing I don't envy any of you."

But Chat did envy them the performing. He knew as well as the rest of Albeyn did that as individuals, the Shadowshapers could never be better than they'd been together. And, having been the best for so many years, working with lesser talents could only emphasize their loss.

It was one of the reasons Chat and Sakary and Rauel were doing this: It would be their final performance together. One last night of being where they'd been born to be, doing what they'd been born to do. They were all in their thirties now—in fact, Chat must be nearing forty. Cade never thought much about Touchstone's future. He'd seen his forty-fifth Namingday. But what would the three surviving Shadowshapers do with the rest of their lives?

There wasn't much of a pattern for how to age gracefully after having been a player. You could keep on for much too long and become an object of derision. Or you could quit and become an irrelevancy, referred to as history and not very interesting history at that. Or you could set oneself up as a Master and teach, and thereby expose yourself to the constant anguish of remembering how it had been.

Or you could die.

How long would Touchstone last, beyond Cade's forty-fifth year? He hoped they'd all know when to stop. He was terrified of becoming irrelevant. He didn't think he could find much satisfaction in teaching. And he most certainly didn't want to die.

"Gettin' late," Chat said at last. "I should let you work."

"Beholden for the tea."

"Anytime, mate." A smile, always so funnily endearing but somehow a little sad as well, crossed his slightly lopsided face, and he left.

Cade returned to the script, making a wager with himself about who would be the next to interrupt him. He was right; it was Jeska; but not for the reason Cade had guessed.

"A messenger just arrived," said his masquer, not bothering to knock. He shook the letter in his hand as if it were a squirrel he was trying to strangle, exactly as he would have in a play. "They're coming, all of them!"

"All of whom?"

Jeska didn't seem to have heard. "Cilka and Petrinka volunteered to watch the children—the Lord and Lady help anyone still at Wistly Hall. They're coming by barge and post coach, with Derien—Derien!—as escort. He's only fourteen—"

"Sixteen this summer."

Once more he was ignored. "Kazie waited until I was well away before making the arrangements, and when she found out that Bexan would be here, they all of them got together to rent the barge and make a holiday of it. A *holiday*!"

"Oh. I see." Bexan, Kazie, Jinsie, probably Crisiant . . . Mishia Windthistle, if the two younger girls would be taking care of the offspring . . . perhaps Chat's wife, Deshananda, and Sakary's wife, Chirene, as well. That was a lot of children to keep track of.

"And now *of course* it's too late to send the messenger back to stop them! They'll be on the river by now and here in four days!"

Quite the contingent of ladies they'd be playing to at Trials. Megs and Vrennerie would be here with Princess Miriuzca, and that would almost certainly mean that their annual lunching at the Castle would be completely overrun by women.

Curious, Cade asked, "Do you really think you or anybody could stop any of them?"

Jeska deflated like an empty wineskin. "I just—I dunno, Cade, this play . . . it's not like anything we've ever done. I don't want our women-folk anyplace near here, if the Archduke decides to take offense."

"He could get to them anywhere. They'd be no safer in Gallybanks. Maybe safer here, in fact, with the Princess nearby and watchful." He paused a moment. "Do you want to cancel?"

"Fuck no!" Jeska exclaimed, outraged.

Cade smiled. "Then tell Mistress Luta that there'll be more rooms needed, not to mention more baths."

"I should do that, shouldn't I." Sighing, he waved the letter one more time, but his heart wasn't in it. "I blame Mieka for this. Women attending theater—damn it!"

He left, and Cade sat back in his chair, amused by his masquer's instinct for an exit line. They were all anxious about *Blood Plight*. Not about the performance, for despite Rauel's frettings, they had the thing as near to perfect as it would get. Vered would approve. It was what might happen *after* the play that put them all on edge. And now the women would be there to see it, too.

Over an hour later—part of it spent waiting for Sakary and Rafe to show up, and puzzled when they didn't—Cade was tired but satisfied. He'd gone through every line of all three plays and changed a few words here and there, but it really was damned near perfect.

Then Mieka strolled in, purring.

And drunk.

All these months—over a *year* now—of sobriety—or at least of limiting his drinking to a beer with lunching and a glass of wine with dinner and maybe another beer to relax after a gigging—and here he was. Sloshed. Luffed. Paved. Sozzled. Swaying slightly on his feet, a foolish grin distorting his face, a flush on his cheeks. Drunk.

"You stupid, *stupid* little fuck," Cade breathed.

The Elf tightened his grip on the door handle, steadying himself. The grin faded, leaving him with a big-eyed look of betrayal that infuriated Cade so deeply that he could find no more words.

"What's it t'you, then?" he slurred, pushing away from the door, slamming it behind him.

That he had chosen anger as a defense was the final outrage. Before Cayden knew it, he was on his feet and one hand was bunched in Mieka's shirt and the other was raised to beat all Hells out of him.

"Go on! Y'always wanted to! G'on, Cade! Do it!"

It was what the second man in the shadows had said. *"Do it!"* he'd said, and Vered had died.

Cold seeped through his veins like thorn. He shoved Mieka stumbling onto the floor. "Why?" he demanded. "Why now?"

"Because I'm fuckin' *terrified* and if you had the sense the Gods gave a goat, you would be, too!" He propped himself on an elbow, glaring up at Cayden, looking and sounding abruptly sober. "This ain't some little play we're doing for shits and giggles! This is as much as accusing that slimy git of being a fucking Vampire!"

"'As much as'? I thought we were pointing all our fingers at him outright!"

"I've gone along with it—Hells, I've aided and abetted! I'm not saying we should back down. But I'm scared, Quill, we're all scared—why aren't you?"

Because it had to be done. Because they owed it to Vered. Because *Blood Plight* was too good never to be performed. Because he wanted to show Bexan that no matter what she might think, he and Touchstone and the remaining Shadowshapers could do justice and more to Vered's work. Because the Archduke needed to know that even if they didn't know what his means and methods would be, they knew his goal.

"Because I saw us," he said softly. "We've just come home from a gigging, and you're giving me a party for my forty-fifth Namingday."

"Ahh . . . *shit*." Mieka sat upright, arms wreathing his knees. "Mighta known. You and your fuckin' Elsewhens. You're insane, Quill. You know that, right?"

"And you're drunk. Go to bed."

When he'd closed the light and they were both beneath sheets and blankets, for there was a chill in the night breeze, Cade turned to look over at Mieka's bed.

"I'm sorry."

"Huh? Oh. Yeh. Me, too."

*   *   *

The next morning when Mieka woke, Cade was waiting with a pot of hot tea brewed strong enough to strip the hide off a wyvern. The hangover remedy Brishen Staindrop had concocted for him years ago didn't work for Mieka. And even if there'd been something readily to hand that worked, Cade wouldn't have given it to him.

The Elf moaned and squinted, rolled onto his side, and pulled the sheet up around his head. Muffled within this cocoon, he said, "I feel like twelve different Hells—and in ten of them, I'm about to die."

"Good."

"In the other two, I'm scared I *won't* die."

"Even better."

"Have a heart, Quill."

"Have some tea."

Cade left for the bathroom and twisted the tub spigot. A short time later, Mieka wandered in—awake enough now to see that no steam rose and the water was icy cold.

"Quat," he accused. "Rantallion. Son of a diseased one-horned goat and a five-clawed Harpy."

Rantallion? That was a new one. Or else a very old one, something Uncle Breedbate had dug up. The old buzzard had refused to vacate Clinquant House after however-many-greats-grandmother died; the last time Cade heard, he'd barricaded himself with a score of other Windthistle connections in a tower with river access, where Hadden Windthistle was content to let them flourish or rot as they so chose. Ah, yes, that was where he'd heard *rantallion* before: one of the insults Barsabian had included in a defiant letter that Hadden had read aloud at dinner to the hilarity of all present. But he couldn't recall just what it meant. In no mood to admit his ignorance, he replied instead to Mieka's closing observation. "As it happens, that's a fairly accurate description of my parents. See you downstairs. The draw's today."

Trials continued much as usual. The following afternoon as they rehearsed, he reflected that it might be a good thing to remind people of the real perils attendant on mucking about with things that belonged to the Fae. For he'd learned, quite by chance, that the Archduke's new theater had been constructed on what some suspected to be an ancient Dancing Ground.

"No bounce off the ceiling, because there isn't any ceiling," Rafe mused as the four of them joined Hawk's Claw and the Crystal Sparks in pacing off the open-air theater's dimensions. Black Lightning was not present. They'd helped design the theater; presumably they had seen it many times before its completion. Cade thought it odd that Thierin Knottinger wasn't here to gloat.

"Have to be careful with that marble wall at the top, behind the seats," Rafe went on. "What is it, four feet high? But I think that's the only potential problem."

"Those seats look bloody uncomfortable," Mieka said. "Quill, should we make them feel nice and soft, as if they're sitting on a pillow? And then whisk it away when they least expect it?"

The seats—stone benches, really, with slight depressions carved out to fit an average-sized bottom—were arranged in three sections with stepped aisles in between. At sixty rows to each section, fifty seats across, the theater held three thousand people. Front row center, a two-foot marble wall partitioned off six carved stone chairs where the Royals would sit, presumably in well-cushioned comfort. The ranks of seats rose at the perfect angle to allow everyone to see everything, and for a fettler to modulate the magic without concerns such as wooden beams or stone pillars. Flanking the seats were grassy hillsides topped with flowering trees.

"Not much comfort in what passes for a tiring room, either," Mieka added. "I'll be generous and assume they'll bring in chairs on performance days. But, really, it ain't nothin' more than the space between a few walls."

Cade stood center stage to survey the seats from one side of the theater to the other. "It's more than half a circle," he told Jeska. "You'll have to make your turns broader, play to the sides more."

The masquer nodded. "It isn't in-the-round, praise all the Gods. I won't have to play with my back turned to half the audience half the time."

Mieka and the gliskers for Hawk's Claw and the Sparks had gathered on the slightly raised platform provided for benches and glass baskets, farther back from the lip of the stage than usual, nestled close to the back wall. This was paneled in polished fine-grained wood, supported at regular intervals by stout round beams. Cade watched for a moment as three Master Gliskers discussed the technical aspects of their profession, and rejoiced in the serious, absorbed expression on Mieka's face. The hangover was forgotten—and the reason that had prompted the acquisition of that hangover. He wasn't scared anymore. Now that his wife was gone, there wasn't much that could hurt him enough to seek alcohol or thorn. And it wasn't danger to himself that had frightened him last night; it was what might threaten those he loved.

It was odd, really, that he hadn't fallen into a whiskey bottle and never come out after his wife left him. Cade supposed she'd told one lie too many. Considering how many times Mieka had lied to her about other women, it was two-faced and despicable to use her lies as reason to leave her. But Cade thought he understood that, too. Mieka's betrayals were of the flesh, and bad enough; hers were of honor, which he saw as infinitely worse. Cade wasn't sure that Mieka wasn't right about that.

When he married her, Mieka had promised faithfulness, and broken his promise more times than anybody could count. He'd lied to her about other women and would have continued to get away with it if he hadn't contracted the pox. Cade didn't know whether or not he'd once more sworn fidelity after that, but he did know that the dalliances hadn't ceased—though he'd been much more careful about his supply of sheaths. There was nothing excusable in his conduct or in his lies. But were his worse than hers?

Cade wasn't exactly impartial. One of her betrayals had been of Cade himself, telling her mother about Mieka's drunken revelation of the Elsewhens. True honor would have kept that knowledge between husband and wife. Instead, she had shared it with the person she honored more than she did Mieka. Certainly she valued herself more highly than she did him—witness the lies she'd told about that night at Great Welkin, endangering Mieka's freedom and even his life. Mieka had understood why she'd done it, and possibly forgiven her. Cade had never asked. What Mieka couldn't forgive was that she hadn't trusted him, relied on him to help her. He might have sacrificed himself for her sake, loving her, if only she had told him the truth.

In the past now, Cade told himself firmly. He watched his glisker for a few moments more, satisfied that Mieka was now where he'd been born to be. He might find another woman someday, someone to marry. Cade hoped he would—for one thing, it would cut down on their ridiculous early-morning encounters, returning to Moonglade Reach after a night in town.

Jeska and Rafe were still pacing off the dimensions of the stage. Cade stood where he would place his lectern, scanning the seats, thinking it would take a bit of doing to monitor everyone in this vast theater when it was full. Scant wonder it had taken so long to build: the hillside to be dug out and reshaped, the stone quarried and moved, set in place, carved, the pathway laid out and flagstoned, and all of it—entrance to pathway to theater and the grassy verges on either side—landscaped. Cilka and Petrinka would have done interesting things with trees and flowers, Cade mused. The Archduke's gardeners had planted unimaginatively: all the trees had flower beds in a circle beneath, with thick bushes forming a kind of backdrop. It must have taken a while to coax all that transplanted greenery to grow. Likewise the dozens of ornate bronze torch stands rising from the back wall and placed at intervals along the pathway and down the aisle steps hadn't been finished in a fortnight.

The theater was only a mile or so from Seekhaven Castle, the last quarter of it done on foot along the pathway; carriages were not allowed. Refreshments were obviously not allowed either. Cade had seen no provision for booths selling drinks or nibbles—and, more important, there were no garderobes. All these people in one place for hours, and nowhere to piss?

"I don't like it," said a voice beside him, and he turned to see Trenal Longbranch, Tregetour for Hawk's Claw, beside him. The boy had grown into a man these last couple of years, long-locked and handsome, sure of himself and his talents, confident that he and his group were in the company of equals. It pleased Cayden to see it, for of course Trenal was right.

"It's big," Cade conceded. "But it won't be that much of a strain." *Except to three thousand bladders.*

"I don't mean the size of this place." He pointed round the curve of the seating, blue eyes narrowed in the afternoon sunlight. "You'll all tell me I'm insane, I know, but I can't help it."

"Help what?"

"Don't you see it? Turn all the way round. No, stand center stage, just here, and turn a circle."

Cade did, and faced front again. His imagination suddenly gave him the feeling that the seats extended in a full circle, a gigantic stone bowl with the stage at the center, each aisle a groove cut into the hollow as if to drain liquid smoothly down to the stage.

It reminded him of something. He wasn't sure what. Something he'd seen or read about? One of the Elsewhens he'd deliberately forgotten?

"It's a Fae Dancing Ground," Trenal said at last. "There are circles like this all over the place, where I grew up. Made of stones, some of them—just a circle of rocks—but some of them are outlined by trees or bushes, and all of them have a kind of focus in the middle. A place where all the magic converges—at least, that's how my granny used to tell it. The Shadowshapers got that play wrong, you know. The one they used to do about the Prince on his way to his wedding, and meeting the Fae Queen. There was no convergence in the Dancing Ground."

"Or drainage."

Longbranch looked startled, then nodded. "If there *was* a drain, like at Rose Court, I'd tend to agree with you. But this is different."

That was it—Rose Court, the outdoor theater with the blood trickling through to sate the hungry ones below . . .

"How is it different?"

"No drain," Trenal replied impatiently. "Whoever stands in the exact center, that's the focal point of all the magic."

"But this hasn't been built as a complete circle."

"Mayhap not. But I'd swear on my daughter's life that a long time ago, this was a Dancing Ground." He raked both hands back through straight brown hair. "And did you get a look at the carvings atop those support struts?" He pointed to the wall behind the stage.

Cade peered upwards—he admitted, but only to himself, that one of these days he'd need spectacles like some tottering old man—and could just make out the features of the middle two. Well, they *were* thirty feet high, those beams, and the tall, handsome Wizards in long flowing robes took up only the last five feet or so. The next supports were shorter, each featuring a beautiful Elf in full traditional Elfen regalia of dagged-hem tunic and trousers bloused over pointy boots.

The rest of the beams descended to a height of about fifteen feet, with matched figures of other magical races staring out at the audience.

"The expressions on the faces of the Pikseys and Giants are bad enough," Trenal went on. "But the Trolls and Gnomes and especially the Goblins look like pure evil."

Evidently the artist who had repainted part of the Kiral Kellari's wall—and been sacked by Master Warringheath—had a friend who worked in wood. The figures were exquisitely carved and grotesquely offensive.

"Cade! Cayden!"

He turned at Rafe's bellow of his name. "Be there in a tick!" Then, to Trenal: "Is there a way to, I dunno, test for it or something? Just to make sure it *was* a Dancing Ground?"

"Wizard, Elf, Goblin, Human—and a bit of Piksey—I am. Fae, I am not."

But Cade was. And Mieka. He tried to feel something, sense something, but all this was to him was a vast half bowl of stone edged by grass and trees, with six seats for Royal backsides and a raised platform for gliskers. He'd ask Mieka.

"Ask around," he told Longbranch. "I'll talk to the Trollwife at the Shadowstone, see if she knows the history of the place."

The younger man nodded, and Cade went to consult with Rafe on whatever he needed to be consulted about.

Mistress Luta, when asked, shook her head. "Not to my knowing. But I wouldn't be surprised."

"Why's that?"

She folded her arms and frowned, then seemed to decide in favor of providing information. "When that man first plotted out his theater, it was on the other side of the river. Bought up the land, started digging. Then he brought in those boys who're so reckless with their magic—"

"Black f—Black Lightning," he supplied.

"As you say," she agreed, her eyes telling him she'd heard what he hadn't said. "Seems they told him that wasn't the right place. Tromping all over Seekhaven and miles into the countryside, they were, until the location was settled. Him having no magic and them having not as much of it as they'd like to think."

"They felt something there? In that exact place? Did it used to be a Fae Dancing Ground?"

"One thing, lad, that I know for certain, and it's this." She looked up at him almost resentfully with her gorgeous lavender eyes. "With suchlike as the Fae, there's no such thing as 'used to be.'" She nodded once, portentously, and returned to her kitchen.

Cayden had no more time to pursue the subject, because a couple of days later, the ladies arrived, and then Touchstone won First Flight on the Royal (again), and suddenly they had only two days before the last time Fliting Hall would be used for the final night's performance. Touchstone would have a busy time of it, doing *Blood Plight* there and then *Window Wall* at the new theater. Cade was just as glad that Mieka had drunk the drunk out of his system. Cade needed everyone awake, aware, sober, and more brilliant than even Touchstone had ever been.

Chapter 36

Dismayed, yes; daunted, never; but for the first time in a very long time, Mieka felt sick to his stomach at the idea of being onstage. Cade trusted implicitly in that Elsewhen of a forty-fifth Namingday party; why couldn't he?

It wasn't Cade who had damned near been brought up before the justiciars for attempted murder, now, was it? And it hadn't been Cade's former wife that the Archduke had ordered killed. But it *was* Cade who could change enough things to make that Elsewhen of eighteen years hence impossible. That was how it worked, wasn't it? Or had he seen it in the future because something he'd already done had brought that future about? Was it something that might happen because of something he would or wouldn't do, or had he already done whatever it was that was necessary to make that future inescapable?

It gave Mieka a headache to add to his grumbling stomach.

Three afternoons before the one-time-only performance of *Blood Plight*, they all gathered for one last rehearsal. Their Steward friend of the last few years, Baltryn Knolltread, stood watch outside the hall with a friend he swore he could trust. "Mainly," he'd grinned, "because he's married to my favorite sister, and if he tells anything, she can make his life more of a misery than I ever could!"

Up in Mieka's sword boards, they'd run through the final play for Derien and Mistress Mirdley, but that had been more than a fortnight ago. The three Shadowshapers seemed to have spent the time thinking up questions for which, Mieka thought grimly, Cade had better have all the answers. Impatient with the waste of time they should have spent on the play, nonetheless Mieka kept his mouth shut. It would be as well to go over it all one last time.

"I still don't quite understand how we can be sure of the way they . . . feed, for want of a better word," said Rauel.

Mieka saw Cade repress a sigh. He was as weary of these justifications as Mieka was of listening to them. But with quiet certainty he began again.

"You remember that gruesome old place outside New Halt. The one where we were paid a small fortune to play to one person in a cellar. Whoever it was, he was wrapped up as if it were winter."

Sakary said, "Nobody ever found out who we were playing to. I mean, who cared, as long as the money was that good?"

"Our first year," Rafe said, "we'd've done all Thirteen Perils stark naked in a snowstorm for that kind of money."

"Ugh!" Rauel grimaced, trying to lighten the atmosphere. "I'll need a while to wash that image out of my poor, innocent brain."

Cade went on, "Eventually we all decided that the money wasn't worth it. Remember what it felt like?"

"Too right, I remember!" Sakary said. "We couldn't hardly walk, we were that exhausted."

"It wasn't just physical, though," Rafe reminded him. "It was as if every emotion had been yanked out of you and you'd never feel anything ever again."

"Yeh," Rauel said, frowning now. "But—no, that can't be."

"Explain it some other way," Cade invited. "We were playing to a Vampire who'd learned how to feed off emotions to sustain himself between blood feasts."

When Chat took up the persuasion, Cade looked simultaneously irked and grateful. "After they weren't needed to defend the Continent anymore, they became outcasts. Having them around was just fine when they were doing battle, and feeding off the blood and terror of the enemy. But once the war was over—"

"That's why there are so many legends," Sakary said. "They starting hunting regular people. It took a while to figure out how to ward them off and how to kill them. Silver and garlic and wooden stakes—"

"Why," Cade challenged, "do all those old stories specifically talk about how the corpses were found not just drained of blood, but with faces frozen in terror?"

Rauel was still resisting. "It'd be pretty scary, having something like that pounce on you—"

"The fear was part of the feast." Chat met his tregetour's eyes squarely. "You forget, I'm *from* that part of the world."

Rauel shook his head vehemently, long dark hair flying. "Don't you realize what you're saying? And if it's true, if that person at New Halt *was* a Vampire, why haven't there been any tales in Albeyn about blood-drained corpses?"

"Because," Cade told him, still patiently, "they can live off emotion and off other kinds of blood than what's in here." He raised his arm and pointed to his wrist. "But the emotions have to be powerful, and who better to give that than players like us?"

"I can tell you who better than us," Mieka said. "Black fucking Lightning. And the Archduke owns them."

"The Archduke?" Rauel laughed, though a bit nervously. Full marks for stubbornness, if not insight. "Last time I saw him, he was inspecting horses at last autumn's fair in full daylight! Next you're going to say he doesn't have a heartbeat!"

"Do I look like an authority on Vampires?" Cade snapped. "All I know is what Vered found out and what I found out—and it's going into this play, Rauel. If you don't want to participate, tell me now, so I can learn your part."

Oh, clever Quill! Mieka hid a grin. No better or swifter way to shut Rauel up and gain his total cooperation than to threaten his last great role.

"You? Play the Wizard?"

Chat faced him again. "If you don't, he will. I mean it, Rauel. If you want out, say so right now."

He scratched his jaw, shook his head, and capitulated. "All right. In spite of what I've been saying, this feels right. That's why we all need to be sure. We can't prove it because we've got no real proof. All we can do is convince everyone else the way we're convinced. And that means onstage."

"Are you convinced?" Sakary challenged.

"Yeh. I don't like it—Hells, I *hate* it—but I believe it." Running both hands back through his hair—Mieka saw that since Vered's death, or perhaps because of it, there was a gray streak—he suddenly laughed, reminding everyone of how charming and boyish he could be. "Ah, bugger it! Can't wait to see the look on his face, can you?"

*   *   *

Bexan was waiting for them back at the Shadowstone Inn. She was not happy. The ladies had all arrived days ago, and Cade, overruling everyone else's objections, had left a copy of the rewritten play in her room this morning.

Rauel escaped upstairs with his wife, Breckyn; Chat suddenly remembered that he'd promised to bring his children some sweets, and vanished; Sakary was left to greet Bexan. She looked right through him, her eyes fixed on Cayden.

"You changed it. Without my permission, without telling me—you *changed* it!"

Mieka rolled his eyes at Rafe behind Cade's back. They went to the bar and asked for a pitcher—make that two pitchers—of ale. "How much does it take to get a Piksey dead drunk?" he whispered to Rafe.

"Dunno. She's little, but she's tough."

"Poor Quill."

"His own fault, for giving her a copy."

They took the pitchers and glassware over to the table where Bexan was favoring Cade with quite the lecture. But it wasn't to do with having treacherously changed Vered's immortal words. She was furious that now she'd have to call back the final version of the plays from the printer's and rework them so the text fit what would be presented onstage.

Mieka poured Cade a drink and put it at his elbow. He was listening to Bexan's tirade, staring down at his hands. At length she was done. Mieka didn't think he even tasted the ale he swallowed before speaking.

"Sorry."

She waited.

But that was it. Mieka bit his lips against laughter.

"One thing more," she warned.

She glared at Cayden, who didn't look up. Mieka noted that a flush of color on her pallid, ever-so-slightly blue-tinted cheeks produced a unique shade of lavender. No, more like mauve. He liked to remember little details like that. It was part of his job.

"None of you—not you, not Rauel, not anybody—will claim a single rewritten line as your own. Not a single *word*!"

"Fine." Cade drained his glass and stood. "Is that all?"

Mieka opened his mouth to say something—anything—when Chirene Grainer made her elegant, exquisite way into the bar. "Bexan!" she exclaimed happily. "Here you are! I've found the most wonderful silk—exactly your color! Hurry, come with me right this minute or somebody else will have bought it!"

Mieka knew full well that Chirene was of the opinion that the wares in every shop in Seekhaven were overpriced and underwhelming. As she urged Bexan towards the door, she cast an exasperated glance at her husband, who raised both hands in innocent disclaimer of all responsibility for anything—except, Mieka thought with a hidden grin, the resulting bill from the silk merchant's.

Mistress Luta ambled out from the kitchen with a folded parchment note, which she handed to Cayden, and a small package wrapped in burlap. This she gave to Mieka.

"Don't ask, because I don't know who sent it," she said. "I didn't see the messenger, nor did anybody. Waiting on the hall table, it was, and no note."

As Mieka picked at the twine knot, Cade said, "They've set the order of performance for the new theater. By popular vote, or so Megs says." He snorted. "It's certainly not by merit! Hawk's Claw, the Sparks, Black Lightning, Touchstone. Oh, and opening night will be free to anyone who doesn't actually have an invitation—which means about a thousand seats for the general public. The rest are the King's personal guests, a dozen ambassadors and their aides, justiciars, nobles, ministers of the Crown who aren't in Gallybanks running the country. Megs says her father will be there—we'll have to remember to find him before the show and offer our compliments."

"You *do* have an interesting and useful correspondence with the lady," Jeska teased.

Mieka barely heard. The twine and burlap had been wrapped around a knife. *His* knife, six inches of steel with a silver thistle and leaves inlaid in the blade and a big dark amethyst at the tip. The knife he'd lost at Great Welkin. He pretended to drop the burlap onto the floor, and bent down to slip the knife into his boot before anyone else saw it.

"She'll be here tonight," Cade went on. "The ladies are all dining together, which means we men have to find someplace else to eat. What was your present, Mieka?"

"Hmm? Oh. New buckle for that red belt." He wadded up the burlap, not looking at Cade. "It's hideous. Nothing like what I ordered. I'm returning it." Which got him to wondering who had sent it. He'd thought it lost forever, that night before Wintering. Well, it had been found again.

"Where shall we have dinner?" Rafe wanted to know.

"Did you say Megs was coming tonight?" Mieka asked. "Did her father bring the child along?"

"She doesn't say anything about her stepmother, so I assume not."

This proved to be the case. The men got back from a tavern on the other side of Seekhaven—not a patch on the food at the Shadowstone—just as the ladies were finishing up, and joined them for a drink. Mieka bustled about, making sure everyone had a whiskey or wine or a cordial (except him; mocah over ice) and then made sure he was sitting next to Megs.

"How's your little brother?"

"Fine."

"Are we ever going to see him?" Meaning, of course, was Cayden ever going to see his son.

"When he's older."

And that was the end of his questions, which had gained him no information at all. He had a lot he wanted to say, of course, but he couldn't say it here. So when everyone rose to go up to bed or, in Vrennerie's and Megs's case, return to the Castle, he made sure he was the one to help Megs on with her lightweight tan velvet cloak.

"You ought to visit us at Moonglade more often. And bring your nephew."

"Now, why would I want to expose the poor child to Cade's endless wittering about snags in his writing?" She spoke lightly, but there were sparks in her green eyes.

"Oh, but with Quill, that's half the fun! Getting him to laugh himself out of his sulks—he *can* be a lot of fun, y'know."

"Aren't you the one who spent half an hour one time regaling me with the—what was it? The invisible play?"

He couldn't help making a face. Back in the awful months when they'd taken any gigging offered so they could pay off their debts, Cade had been drinking a lot of brandy and pricking a lot of thorn. Well, they all had. As their tregetour, however, Cade was responsible for coming up with something new for their performances (which was why any snide remarks about "the same old plays" still stung him right where he lived). One of his ideas had been for the main character, a young girl, to be invisible.

Jeska had wanted to know how he was expected to play somebody invisible. Cade told him that he would instead be all the people she interacted with. Jeska asked, What sort of interactions? Rather unwisely—he'd been either drunk or thorned, he couldn't recall and in those days it hadn't mattered—Mieka had suggested that they should make her a prostitute: Disappearing Diella, Albeyn's Only Invisible Fuck. Jeska would have no problem being the customer, except that Touchstone would get quodded for obscenity.

Cade had exploded. What was *obscene*, he snarled, was the way women were ignored in society. It was criminal. It was wrong. It was—

Rafe had quietly pointed out that making the girl the center of the play wasn't exactly making the point about invisibility. And that perhaps it wasn't the girl's being invisible that was the point here; perhaps it was the *tregetour*.

Cade had used it, of course, in the way tregetours had of slicing out bits and pieces of one play and grafting them onto another. For this had been part of the key to *Window Wall:* that everybody wanted desperately to be visible to *someone*.

Now, looking into Megs's sardonic face, Mieka said defensively, and without thinking too much about it, "He was pretty drunk at the time. And that wasn't anything compared to—"

"Compared to what?"

Caught, he decided he might as well tell it. "There was another idea of his."

"Drunk or thorned? Or both?"

"No idea," Mieka lied. He knew very well it had come from an hallucination Cade experienced while reacting with predictable unpredictability to a new kind of thorn. "Anyways, he wanted to make words real. To have Jeska speak the words and me turn the words into what they were—what the words meant, I mean."

"Sounds . . . bizarre," she finally said. "If Jeska said 'dragon'—"

He nodded. "What Quill was going for—I *think*—was that words are symbols for things, whether they're spoken aloud or written down or you read them. And if the symbols become the actual things they symbolize, we'd all be a lot more careful about how we use words. Treat them with more respect."

"Oh." She considered for a moment, frowning. Then she asked, "But is that your job? To make symbols or force people to understand the relationship of words to images, or—or whatever it was he wanted to do? Isn't it your job to entertain?"

"That's just about what Rafe said."

"You alter perceptions," Megs said musingly. "While you're onstage, you change the way people see or hear things. Mieka . . . what if you could do it so it's permanent? What if you could change their perceptions—"

He hitched a shoulder uncomfortably. "I'm sure it's been tried. The fact that we don't do it has to mean nobody succeeded, right?" The underhanded practice of planting a thirst in the patrons of a tavern didn't count. Did it? On their brief tour of the Continent, had Black fucking Lightning really managed to increase the demand for rumbullion? "Giving them something to perceive isn't the same as telling them how to perceive it."

"What did you and Rafe and Jeska do about the play?"

"Told him it was shit," he replied bluntly. "And that we wouldn't do it." He paused a moment, reminiscing. "You've never lived until you've been on the wrong side of those gray eyes when he's like that. Knives, swords, and bright sharp shiny three-inch nails are nothing compared to Cayden Silversun in a temper."

"I'll bet that when he sobered up, though, he agreed with you. One thing I'll say for him, he's reasonable, once things are explained to his satisfaction."

"There's one thing," he said quietly, "that I wish you'd explain to my own satisfaction. I don't promise to be reasonable. I'd just like to know."

"I can guess. Shall I?" Annoyed, she faced him squarely and lowered her voice. "Here's what I see. All of you—Touchstone, the Shadowshapers, Hawk's Claw, any group that's been together for years—you're married to each other. You live in each other's pockets on the Circuits. You put up with each other's moods—or, as you say, laugh each other out of them. You work together, eat together, travel together, get drunk together—and when one of you is lost, as Vered was, the grief is . . ." She broke off, bit her lips together, then continued, "I've seen enough of players to know that it takes an exceptional sort of woman to be married to any of you. The theater fascinates me. It always has. As exciting as it would be to live with a man whose whole life is the theater, that's exactly the point. I want to live *my* life."

He really couldn't argue with that. "You're always welcome at Moonglade Reach, y'know. No invitation ever necessary."

She gave him a smile—and from her, he realized such things really were a gift. It wasn't the bright social smile Court ladies seemed to wear all the time or the tight, narrow-eyed baring of a few teeth that was a warning a blind man would recognize. This was a warm, humorous, whimsical, confiding smile. The kind one shared with a friend.

"I'm beholden to you, Mieka. And one day, when he's older . . ."

He nodded, and Vrennerie approached, and he handed the ladies into a hire-hack for the drive back to the Castle. He stared down the street for a time, thinking that he'd lost his chance to tell Cade what he knew. He'd said nothing for so many months—no, longer than that, for Mieka had known Megs was pregnant, the way he always knew somehow, whether a woman was far enough along to show or not—that to speak now would be to bring forth a storm of angry betrayal from which neither of them would emerge intact.

Later, once he and Cayden were in their beds, he said, "That package I got tonight—somebody sent my knife back. The one I lost at Great Welkin. Somebody there must've found it." When Cade seemed disinclined to reply, he went on. "Why send it now, unless to warn us against doing the play?"

"Mieka! Can you think of anybody who believes a warning would put us off? Go to sleep."

Chapter 37

Blinded by tears, the Wizard lopped off the Warrior's head. The old woman began her weaving. The scene faded into shadows, leaving the audience to its own thoughts and feelings.

Then there was bright sunlight, dazzling, almost painful. A town street empty of people, though sharp chimes rang out midday. A man ran into view, gasping, hurling himself into the shadow of a doorway. He tried the shop door; locked. The sunlight moved gently, slowly, touching his cloaked arm. He huddled into the shade, whimpering.

An old woman—not the one from the cavern—hobbled along the street, hunched in an intricately woven shawl. The man cried out incoherently. She sped up her pace a little, and he reached to haul her into the shadows, moaning as the sunlight fell on his hand. Once more he shrank back, cradling the hand to his chest.

"Here, now, my fine Lordship," the woman scolded, "and now you see the folly of leaving it too late to find the safe, quiet dark!"

"Get me out of here! It's your sworn duty to help me! Take me out of this damned sun!"

The light shifted again. Soon the sun would find him. He yanked again at the shop door, panicking.

She regarded him sardonically, enjoying his predicament, seeing it as vengeance for a thousand thoughtless slights. "How many times have I warned you? But it never sinks in, not until the sun catches you—and you're about to be well and truly caught. Do you understand that you can't go hunting on your own? They know enough now to seal themselves inside their homes and not go outside after dark. And when you're caught outside, as you are caught today, they lock their doors against you. Soon enough word will spread and they'll come for you."

He drew as far back into a corner of the doorway as he could. "We *saved* them! If not for us, they'd have no homes to cower in nor doors to shut!"

She shrugged. "The sun shines, and people forget."

"Damn you, take me somewhere safe!"

"Come along now, put on your gloves, pull up your hood, hide your face from the light. That's right. This way."

The scene changed, became a cellar. The old woman went around lighting candles. Some were in elegant filigreed holders; others were stuck into empty bottles; still more were snugged into guttered wax on coffers and cabinets, shelves and wine racks. As the cellar slowly filled with light, the man flung back his hood, peeled off his gloves, winced as his injured hand was scraped by leather. He paced, muttering, while she unpacked the bag that had been slung over her arm.

"Is it so much to ask?" he demanded suddenly. "All the lives we saved—is it so much to ask in payment?"

"You refused the last one I brought you," she reminded him tartly.

"Old! He was old! Old, feeble, unafraid! He *welcomed* death!"

She shrugged. "Blood's blood."

"That's all *you* know." He moved towards her, his eyes glinting red. In spite of herself, she shrank back. He laughed. "Fear me, woman—tremble, and remember how long I can make linger the deaths of those on whom I feed."

"You don't dare kill me," she spat, facing up to him. "You need me."

"And you have not provided. Tonight I did not feed. I hunger and thirst and I must feed." He paced the confines of a cellar not even big enough to bring a swirl to his cloak. "Bring me an Elf. Make it a woman. And bring her to me in the dark. They fear the dark as they fear nothing else. There's exquisite sport to be had with an Elfen woman."

"I would," she retorted, "if it hadn't just happened this last fortnight that every Point-ear was gathered up and thrown out! But you don't pay any attention to such things, do you? As long as there's blood enough and fear enough, you don't care what happens!"

"Gone? They can't be."

"The Elves will only be the first. They look different. They're easy to spot. Taken away by night they were, by moonless clouded night when Elves are most afraid, from every city and village and crofter's cottage, by every soldier these many lands command! Loaded into carts and wagons with only what they could carry, driven to the borders of every country in a thousand miles, told never to return on pain of death! That frightened sweet Elfen blood you crave isn't to be had!"

He was genuinely bewildered. "But what had they done?"

"They're magical folk. That was offense enough. You don't understand what's happened out in the world. Everything we are, everything we can do, all the advantages we bring, the help we give them—they don't want magic anymore. It's wicked. Evil. That's what their religion tells them. And do you know why they think so? Because of *you*! Your stupid greedy kind, killing as you wish, making no effort to mask what you've done, no shame or remorse for doing it—"

"We are *owed* this!" he thundered. "Of the thousands—millions!—we saved, one life each month!"

"Whose life shall it be? Do you choose the criminals amongst them? The murderers? The ones who rape? The ones who would take the last warm blanket from the backs of their own grandmothers and leave their own children to starve?"

He waved a dismissive hand. "There is no fear to be had from such offal."

"Oh, of course not," she sneered. "You want the *good*, the *kind*, the gentle of heart. The ones who can't believe anything terrible could ever happen to them—when it does, their terror is all the greater! Well, my Lord, these good, kind people have turned their minds against all magic. Soon enough, the Goblins and the Gnomes, the Trolls and the Giants, all of them will be found and flung away!"

"But—but where shall they go?"

"How kind of you to ask! Mayhap to join the Fae in the Wester-countries across the Flood. Nobody knows. Nobody cares. But *you'll* care, you and those of your kind, once the Caitiffs, too, are banished!"

"We will protect you."

She snorted. "Aye, that's likely." She opened a large trunk and hauled out something heavy. A doe, half-grown and very dead. "Go on. Feed."

"On *that*? You expect me to live off *that*?"

"Your hand wants healing."

His lip curled, but he knelt before the broken body of the doe and bent to it. Hunger, shoved down and buried during his flight from the sun, swelled and was not sated. Eventually he stood, wiping his mouth that was smeared with blood. He looked at his hand, watching as the red blistering gradually vanished, turned to white, white skin.

"I have something for you," she said when she saw that he was finished.

"Something warm and living, I trust," he said bitterly.

"There was enough blood."

"But no terror." He kicked the limp corpse. "Lacking the taste of fear, the blood was dead."

"Later," she told him, and brought from her satchel a parcel of woven stone-gray wool. Before she could speak again, there came the sound of something heavy battering at the upper door. She hid in a shadow. He stood arrogantly in the center of the cellar, his face greedily turned to stairs.

Men appeared, four of them, six, ten, with torches that flung new shadows onto the walls. They snarled and cursed and shouted, braving a few steps down the stairs. "Vermin! Killer! We'll burn you with fire you can't hide from as you hide from the sun!"

One moment the Vampire was in the middle of the room. The next, he was halfway up the stairs. He grabbed one man, pitched him over the railing. The next two he took, one in each hand, and dragged them downwards, laughing. At the bottom of the stairs, he threw one of them to the floor and the other across the room to slam into a rack of wine bottles, toppling it, shattering glass, red wine running in the seams between the stones like blood-thick veins.

The remaining men were shrieking now. One, brandishing a torch, stalked down the last few steps. For his bravery, he had his throat ripped out.

Darkness again, but with the scents of trees and grass and running water. Murky light slowly illuminated a woodland road that curved into the distance. Far away was a craggy mountain, and to its side clung a castle: turreted and towered, crenellated and merloned, impossible to breach with anything less than a Wizard's most lethal magic.

The Caitiff was seated on a tree stump, breathing hard. "I'd hoped we'd be at the castle by now. Dawn soon."

"It's been days since the village." He paced nearby, wrapped in the gray cloak. "Bring me something on which I may feed. Bring me a man. Living."

"Only another few miles, my Lord. You can last that long."

"Do it! Now!"

All at once she surged to her feet, furious. "I've done enough! I'm finished!"

"You swore! You vowed!" Pausing, his hands fretful, he insisted, "It's too far. I won't make it unless I feed."

"And I say feed yourself!"

He loomed over her, terrible in his rage and hunger. "I've tongued the blood of dumb beasts and it's not enough! I need creatures with *minds* that can imagine death, and imagine escape from it, and know with absolute certainty that everything they think and imagine and hope for is useless. *Then* their fear is complete, *then* I can feed—"

"Gorge yourself, you mean. I saw you, my Lord, back in that cellar, glutted on blood and terror. It's *people* you crave, people who have imaginations to foresee the kind of death you glory in. As for your scorn of the animals I've brought you—they kept you alive. Had you killed, you would have been tracked, traced by your litter of corpses. My way, there were no drained bodies abandoned beside the road for others to find."

"I need more!"

She glared up at him for a moment, then turned and walked a little ways from him. Swinging back around, she said, "There are Caitiffs awaiting you. They serve several of your kind. They will see to it that you survive. But heed me. There will not be a life each month. There will be blood, but not from men or women. One, perhaps two, each year—"

"That's not enough!"

"There will be animals and blood enough. But not men and women. Not to kill. Feed off their fear, but not from their blood. Leave them their lives. Or they will surely take yours."

Quietly, menacingly: "How dare you leave me. How dare you dictate to me what I shall and shall not do."

"I tell you I am through with this! The Wizards will be next expelled, there is already talk of Caitiffs—"

"You dare to value your pitiful little life higher than mine?"

"The time when you and your kind saved whole countries is long since gone. You're worthless now. Can't you understand? They don't need you anymore. Be prudent, and survive—or continue in your arrogance, and die. I'm finished and done." She gestured to the cloth. "The colors of your benefactor and your ally, the man who owns the castle. Though you arrive in daylight, still they will know you by his colors." She smiled a little, and shrugged. "Gray for the stone caverns that are your safest refuge—and one of the colors of flame, the only light that you can bear without pain. Go swiftly, my Lord."

He wrapped the cloak more tightly around himself and pulled up the hood.

She nodded, and turned to take a few steps back down the road she had come.

But suddenly he was there, catching her by the shoulders, held fast in his arms, and her face contorted with terror and knowledge as he stood behind her and sank his teeth into the exposed veins of her neck and ripped them from her flesh, and fed.

When he was finished, he let her body crumple to the dusty road. Turning to look at the castle, he resettled the cloak around him, swirling it, showing the lining: orange, a color of flame, within the stone-gray wool of a Caitiff's weaving.

"Your service," he said, glancing down at the dead woman, "is no longer required."

*   *   *

"Stunning. Never to be forgotten."

"You must be so proud, to have done such perfect justice to Vered Goldbraider's final work."

Mieka nodded tiredly. The smile pasted on his face was starting to come unglued. More than an hour of this—Sir Thises and Lady Thats, rich merchants, Ministers of the Crown, Lords and Stewards and, oh Hells, pretty much all six hundred or so people who had witnessed the one and only performance of *Blood Plight*, fighting a path to the seven performers to tell them how wonderful and marvelous and thrilling it had been. He could have dealt with it had there been a succession of drinks in his hand, or if he'd pricked bluethorn before the show. He could have been cheerful and charming, with a merry quip for everyone. As it was, all he really wanted was to find a quiet corner somewhere and sleep for a week.

"Spectacular, Master Windthistle. Simply spectacular!"

It was no help that the others were as knackered as he. They were all getting old, Mieka decided glumly and resentfully. Gods alone knew how the Shadowshapers, even at full strength with Vered instead of Jeska playing the old woman, would have accomplished this on their own. He intended to make it excruciatingly clear to Cayden that if he had any more productions of this size and complexity in mind, he could go find himself another glisker, and best of luck to it.

"I was weeping by the end! I'm weeping still, and it's all your fault, you naughty thing!"

Chat looked close to collapse, which wasn't surprising considering some of the tricky stuff he and Mieka had pulled off. Changing, for instance, from Chat handling the real Rauel in the cellar and making him vanish to Mieka creating an illusory Rauel at precisely the same time halfway across the stage, ripping out an equally illusory throat. The only way they'd been able to do it was by hiding Jeska as the Caitiff over in a shadow so they didn't have to do his character and costume, too.

"And frightened—! That ending—! I nearly brought blood to my palms, clenching my fists—see?"

That had been tricky, as well. Choosing exactly when to switch from the woman's angry contempt to the Knight's rage and hunger, then back to the Caitiff for the sheer sudden terror when he grabbed her—and then . . . nothing. They'd argued quite a bit over this, but Cade and Sakary had persuaded them against Rauel's insistence that the final emotions be those of the Vampire: sated, scornful, with the taste of blood on his lips and the cloak of Henick's colors on his back. Better, Sakary had said, and Cade had agreed with him, to leave the audience frightened out of its collective wits, with the sight of the red-streaked chin and the sound of his arrogant dismissal.

"I don't know how you do it, really I don't!"

When the stage had at last faded into shadows again, and they gathered at the front, all seven of them, to take their bows, it was anybody's guess as to whether Mieka was holding Chat upright or Chat was holding him on the way from the glisker's bench. Then Cade's arm had gone around his back, and Jeska's shoulder nudged up under his own shoulder, and Rauel and Sakary supported their own glisker. Mieka had gulped in air and barely heard as applause began—slowly, a few people here and there, everyone within Fliting Hall so staggered that it took a while for them to realize that the play was in fact over. The ensuing roar still vibrated in Mieka's ears.

"A brilliant performance. People will be talking about it for years. Forever!"

They had not gone to the tiring room after. They had been swept like last autumn's brown leaves to the main hall of Seekhaven Castle, instantly separated and individually surrounded by a shifting, prattling mass of people. Everybody had drinks. Everybody but Touchstone and the Shadowshapers.

"Better than anything I ever saw either of you do—and I've seen nearly everything, for years now. Why, I remember a performance up in Scatterseed—"

"Master Windthistle?"

He looked dully at a man in Princess Miriuzca's blue-and-brown livery. "Yeh?"

"—or mayhap New Halt—anyway, that's not the point. What I mean to say—"

"Her Royal Highness's compliments, and would you do her the honor of waiting on her? May I guide you?"

"—just splendid, it was, and so real! Like tonight, when I thought the wine on the cellar floor would run right off the stage into the King's lap!"

"I'm beholden to Her Royal Highness," Mieka said with feeling, and the young man visibly repressed a smile. "Lead on."

Many jostled, elbowed minutes later, they were in a hallway empty of all but a brace of guards. At the end of the hallway was a large room, where Touchstone and the Shadowshapers were sprawled in various attitudes of exhaustion on sofas, and a select group of friends were providing drinks and food while teasing them about being tired old men who needed to be tucked up in bed before the Minster chimes struck nine.

Blye caught sight of Mieka, swaying in the doorway, and hurried over. She helped him to a chair and asked sweetly, "How about a nice, lukewarm cup of weak tea?"

"How about I tell me brother the truth about you," he growled.

"He'd never believe it."

"I deserve a whiskey, but I'll settle for a beer. Cold. *Please.*"

"Whiskey would only put you to sleep, crambazzle," she chuckled, and went off to fetch something from the drinks table by the windows.

A few deep swallows reminded him that he'd given in to his nerves and found a garderobe to yark into before performing. Even something as innocuous as beer was going straight from his empty stomach to his suddenly spinning head. His sister-in-law had also brought a plate of food, bless her. He scraped the icing off the cake and shoved the whole slice into his mouth, willing his insides to stay put. A near thing, but within a few minutes he felt well enough to take another swallow of beer. Had she brought him whiskey, he would have yarked up his guts again. He *was* getting old.

Somewhat revived, he shamelessly began listening to the conversation of the three ladies seated on another couch at right angles to his. Miriuzca and Vrennerie were congratulating Bexan, who as far as he knew had never met either of them before. She showed no shyness, no hesitation; well, she wouldn't.

". . . many ways an answer to that horrible play Black Lightning does about separating the races. Do you know it, Your Highness?"

"I've never seen it performed. I've heard of it. I agree, a dreadful piece."

"Vered, my husband, loathed it. To imply that none but Wizards and Elves were clean of taint—!"

"I appreciated the last play tonight especially," said Vrennerie. "It explained so much about why magical folk are feared on the Continent."

"Oh, that's right—you both come from there," Bexan said. "Do you miss your home?"

"Albeyn is home now," Vren said gently. "And has been these many years. But please do tell us more of your husband's thoughts. We never get to hear about the work that goes into a play."

Mieka blinked. That was a flat-out lie, and he was surprised at her. She had been present at any number of lunchings with the Princess where Cade sometimes went on for hours, chavishing about historical research and plot points and pacing, about leaving enough room for the audience to inhabit a character and the communal experience of theater and a dozen other things until Mieka wanted to stuff the nearest loaf of bread down his throat to shut him up.

Then he realized that it must be different for them to hear about someone else's artistic process—and to hear about it from a woman into the bargain.

"My husband wished to show, in the first play, that all the magical races could work together, share their gifts to defeat a common enemy."

"Everyone is having—*has*—something unique to give." Miriuzca sighed a little. "All these years, and I'm still making mistakes!"

"But it was no mistake in the plays, was it, the colors of the Knights' benefactor?" Vrennerie asked smoothly.

"No mistake at all. During rehearsals . . ." She glanced round and Mieka tried to be inconspicuous. The next instant he wanted to wring her neck, for, lowering her voice, she went on, "The cloak was my suggestion. Gray for the stone caves and cellars that were their refuge, orange for—"

"—for the fire that is the only light they can bear without pain," Miriuzca finished excitedly. "I thought those lines beautifully poetic. And frightening at the same time."

Bexan's annoyance at being interrupted—even by a Princess—vanished at the praise. "I am beholden to you on my husband's behalf. The colors of the cloak were in his mind—he just hadn't written it all down yet when . . . when I lost him."

"When Albeyn lost him," Vrennerie said warmly, and pressed her hand to Bexan's arm. "Everyone grieves for him."

Blye returned and sat down beside Mieka with another plate, this time of little slices of bread smeared with various things: butter and jam, meat paste, savory mashed greens. He chose the most innocuous looking and bit tentatively into it. His stomach didn't revolt, so he chomped it down and had another.

"You haven't noticed the glassware."

He pretended to examine his beer glass. "It's hollow, it has a hole at the top, and it doesn't leak. So far, it has that much in common with all your finest work."

She smacked him one on the arm.

"What I was about to say, before you started knocking me about—which isn't fair, because I've not got but two hands and both of 'em occupied—anyway, it's very pretty, the way you put a forget-me-never at the bottom of the glass. True of all of them, yeh?"

"For the stemmed glasses, the flower's in the foot. Took me bloody forever, I don't mind saying. Rikka did the bowls while I did the flowers. But there's something else. First time I've used it."

"Used what?"

She took the beer from his hand and drained it down her own throat, then turned the glass over and showed him. He forgot to protest this loss of his only drink of the night when he saw the hallmark—*the hallmark!*—stamped into the bottom of the glass.

"A thistle! Blye, it's beautiful! But I thought with the Gifting of the Gloves and all, you didn't need a hallmark."

"I don't. But I wanted to do it properly, so I applied to the Glasscrafters Guild with this design. And it's only right that the first set of anything with my hallmark ought to go to the Princess."

"Did she notice?"

Blye nodded happily. "First glassware with the first hallmark ever granted to a woman glasscrafter. She told me she felt like issuing a proclamation or suchlike to celebrate."

"At the very least." He leaned over to kiss her cheek, then sat back, frowning. "Does this mean your prices will go up like a maid-of-honor's skirts on Wintering Night?"

"Mind your language," Cade scolded, and Mieka looked up. "And finish your food. I'm just about able to climb into a hack, climb the stairs of the Shadowstone, and fall onto my bed. And I warn everyone, another half hour and somebody will have to carry me." Cade wore a lazy-eyed half-smile that was no disguise at all for the triumph glittering in his gray eyes.

Mieka rejoiced to see it. After all they'd been through . . . "I'm sure the Princess has a spare guardsman or three she'll lend us to the purpose."

"Three?" Blye scoffed. "A pocket-sized Piksey with bad knees could pick you up and toss you off the nearest bridge without breaking a sweat. Cade, do you *ever* eat?"

A little while later, Touchstone had taken their leave of the Princess and were seated, all four of them, in one of her carriages. The womenfolk—Kazie, Crisiant, Jinsie, and Blye—had accepted Miriuzca's invitation to stay up very late at the Castle gossiping and then spend the night.

Mieka dozed with his head against the padded brown suede window frame, kept awake only by the uneven jouncing of the wheels on cobblestones, until something occurred to him.

"Damn it!" he exclaimed, and his partners actually jumped. "I forgot!"

"Oh, Gods," Jeska moaned.

"No," Cade said firmly, "you are *not* going back to shatter Blye's new glassware!"

"I didn't mean that." He peered at the three of them in the dimness. "Did anybody think to keep an eye on the Archduke's face?"

No one had.

"Damn it," Rafe echoed wearily.

"Our only chance," Jeska mourned.

"I wouldn't worry," Cade advised. "I'm sure we'll find out sooner or later what he thought of it."

Chapter 38

Long-boned, rail-thin, spindle-shanked, and with a nose that sometimes seemed to take up most of his face, the one thing Cade had always been grateful for about his physical self was his height. Even as
a lanky child whose limbs didn't seem to be acquainted with one another, he'd been able to see over everyone's heads. He used his height
now to make a final count of players in what passed for the artists'
tiring room of Archduke Cyed Henick's gorgeous new theater. Hawk's
Claw, the Crystal Sparks, Black Lightning, Touchstone. Cade strode
to the stage entry, lit by torches on either side, and held up a hand for
quiet. To his private amazement, they all obeyed. Even Thierin Knottinger.

He sought out Trenal Longbranch with his gaze, and called out, "Before you go on, all of us should go onstage—"

"To introduce ourselves?" Pirro Spangler, Black Lightning's glisker,
laughed a high, nervous laugh. "I thought there were Stewards to do
that!"

"Don't be silly," Thierin—of course it would be Thierin—chided.
"It'll give the rest of them a chance to hear some applause before we
snatch it all."

Cade smiled amiably. "Some of you may know that my grandsire
was a fettler who left me a lot of books. One of them described an old
custom. I'd like to reinstate it here, at this new theater. Nothing
fancy—just a few words to the King."

"Any objections?" Rafe drawled in a tone that indicated there
wouldn't be.

A couple of minutes later, they had all filed onto the stage. Even with sixteen men spread out along its width, it was quite dauntingly huge.

Mieka was evidently having the same thought. He nudged Cayden with a shoulder and said, "Shame we're not doing 'Dragon' tonight—I could send it right up into the clouds!"

"But think how much fun you'll have at the end of *Window Wall*," Cade replied. "All that room to play in."

Somebody in the back began to clap as all four groups assembled onstage. Applause was tentative, then enthusiastic. Cade took center stage and once again held up a hand for quiet. It was barely dark of a fine summery evening, the sky a deep purple-black, the stars just beginning to shine, the air green-scented and silken on the skin. A perfect evening.

"In times long past," he began, and hid a start of surprise as he learned for himself just how good the acoustics were, how well the theater had been designed. Black Lightning, it seemed, was good for something after all. His voice—never quite good enough for the stage—not only reached easily to the upper rows but also didn't bounce back at him. He knew because the whole theater hushed by the time he'd got the third syllable out. "In times long past," he said again, "it was customary to bring all the players onstage and to ask of the audience, 'How may we please you?' The most noble prince present would then reply, 'Please us as you believe right and fitting.' Tonight, for this new theater, we revive this venerable custom. And so we humbly ask of Your Majesty—How may we please you?"

King Meredan stood at his velvet-cushioned seat. He had either forgotten the replying words, despite having heard them not three seconds ago, or had decided to add his own little embellishment. "Please us as you always do, good Masters—always right and fitting!"

The audience laughed and applauded. The King turned and waved, and looked very happy. Cayden and all the assembled players swept His Majesty low, flourishing bows, withies twinkling in the hands of the gliskers. The King sat down again beside Queen Roshien, Miriuzca on his left, Lady Megs next to her. Beside the Queen was Prince Ashgar, and next to him was the Archduke. He was talking to a man seated on the other side of the little stone barrier, someone Cade didn't recognize, who wore a wide purple sash crossing his chest from right shoulder to left hip, a mark of some sort of exalted station. Possibly he was the senior ambassador present. There were a dozen of them here with their retinues, plus Albeyn's Lords, Ladies, Knights, Ministers of the Crown, Good Brothers and Good Sisters, justiciars—in brief, everyone who wasn't back in Gallantrybanks keeping an eye on the country and making sure nobody broke it.

Trenal Longbranch and Gorant Pennywhistle, the tregetour and masquer of Hawk's Claw, had several days before made a startling request of Touchstone: that Touchstone open as well as close the night's show. Further, they had a piece in mind. Touchstone had talked it over, and agreed. Thus it was that, to the surprise of everyone else, Jeska, Cade, Rafe, and Mieka stayed onstage.

They were all of them in white and black: crisp shirts unbuttoned at the throat, lightweight woolen trousers, suede boots. The only difference was in their jewelry. Rafe wore the copper bracelets Crisiant had given him before they were married, and a silver wedding necklace. Jeska's necklace matched that of his wife: gold, with a ruby pendant in the shape of a heart. Mieka had long since had his marriage bracelets unsealed and removed. He wore tiny diamond studs in the lobe and the tip of his right ear, and a large, dark amethyst ring on his left little finger. Cade had on the silver falcon pin his brother had given him years ago. Derien had surprised him again this afternoon with an austerely beautiful silver ring set with a sea-green beryl, worn on his right middle finger. Cade had put it on to admire it before Dery said, a bit defensively, "It was Father's. I'm wearing the sapphire one," and held up his hand. As Cade frowned, Dery added, "They weren't really his. A description of his assets says they belonged to our grandfather." This, Cade decided, made it all right. So he wore it.

Thus torchlight struck glints off silver and gold and deep red and purple and green, and sharp, shining white diamonds. Touchstone finally looked what they were: the most successful theater players in Albeyn.

There was no magic in the air, no shimmer of power. There were only the four men, and the audience was as silent as if every one of the three thousand seats had been empty. Jeska spoke the words Cayden had first heard in an Elsewhen, and then written down for Touchstone. That night, he was speaking for every player who would take the stage.

"We *will* get to you. We'll make you feel. That's what you've come here for, that's what you want. We're that good. And you need us that much."

Cade had shortened it, adapted it some. It was no longer the defiant answer to those who claimed they'd been tricked into feeling. But it was a reminder to the audience of why they were there, and why players were needed.

"We will give you excuses to weep and reasons to laugh. Within the safety of this theater, you can fall helplessly, wondrously in love. You can hate without reservation, cower without shame, or want desperately to ease someone's suffering. You can laugh at the ludicrous, rage at injustice, pity the afflicted, sneer at folly. You can want and need and desire, all without fear.

"You're safe here. You can lick at sentimental tears and crunch on the bones of your enemies, sink your teeth into fury, taste pleasure or merely lust, swallow drunken draughts of joy. You can feel these things without shame or remorse. Because here, you are safe. You will feel all the things that frighten you, elude you, compel you, seduce you, exalt you. Things you cannot allow yourself to feel in their entirety, in their reality, in their mad intense awful purity for fear that they will overwhelm you.

"Here, within the theater, there is no need to be afraid of what you feel and how deeply you feel. Here, you are safe.

"Look around you at the thousands here tonight. Some you know, others you recognize, but most are strangers to you. And yet . . ." Jeska took a small step forward, speaking more intimately now. "Yet when you walk out of this theater tonight, every one of you will have experienced the same happinesses and sorrows, the same tears and merriments, the same excitements and amazements and wonders. What we will do tonight is something you will share, every one of you. And this, too, is something that you need.

"You need us. You may trust us. You will be safe.

"And we *will* provide."

Listening to the words he'd written, Cade had a moment of dread, realizing that something else shared was what Touchstone and the Shadowshapers and so many other groups had done at that mansion outside New Halt, what Black Lightning presumably still did. *Provide.* Sensation; emotion. Sustenance.

He scarcely heard the applause as he joined Jeska, Rafe, and Mieka center stage and bowed. He was trying to calm himself down from sudden panic. There was no one here tonight to feed off what tregetours, masquers, gliskers, and fettlers provided. The players were as safe as the audience.

As Hawk's Claw left the wings for the stage, Jeska pulled Cayden to one side. "Listen," he said urgently, low-voiced. "Thierin was talking to Pirro earlier, trying to soothe his nerves—"

"Thorned." Cade delivered the verdict as scornfully as if he'd never gone onstage with a skinful of liquor or an armful of thorn.

"No, *listen*. What he said was that they had nothing to worry about. No Shadowshapers."

"Conceited snarge, ain't he?"

"And then he said, 'If it had been them going on last, I'd be worried, too. But it's not. It's just Touchstone.'"

"So?"

"Pirro said something like, 'It should've been us, we planned it to be us.'" Jeska pulled him farther into a corner of the tiring room. "And then Pirro asked if he could do it—Thierin, I mean."

"Can't wait to hear the reply."

"Direct quote: 'With both eyes closed and a girl on my cock.'"

"To which Pirro said . . . ?" Cade didn't really care, but his masquer was insisting.

"That everything depended on it." Jeska shook Cade's arm impatiently. "Forget the arrogance. We're all used to that. Why would the Shadowshapers worry him when Touchstone doesn't? What's the *everything* that depends on tonight? And why would Black Lightning *plan* on performing last?"

"I haven't the first clue," Cade said. "Settle down, Jeska. Leave it be. It's just them being them. Be glad we're us."

Disgruntled, Jeska moved off. Cade returned to the wings, wanting to catch a glimpse of what Hawk's Claw had put together for tonight.

They were a few minutes into their tale of a boy on the verge of manhood, surrounded by a large, squabbling family that paid no attention to him, especially when he cried out that he wanted to *do* something, *be* someone. Parents, sisters, and brothers hooted with laughter, and then a baby started to howl and the boy was forgotten again, shunted aside. The whole scene was composed in dreary shades of brown— unpainted wooden walls, table, and chairs, dun-colored clothing, beige curtains, tan rugs—and all the faces except the boy's were blank and featureless below thatches of brown hair. Interesting effect, Cade thought as the boy stormed out the door and the stage went dark.

The next scene was the one Cayden had heard about. He watched with interest as the boy wandered around a dull, nondescript street. Light began to glimmer in a storefront window. Intrigued and uneasy as the light glowed more strongly and sparked with color, he was drawn closer and closer. In a burst of tense courage, he entered the shop. After a few moments, cascading from the open door and into the character-less street came amazement and joy and the feeling of something cool and smooth in the right hand. The scene gained color—shop signs were brightly painted, trees turned green, the insipid gray sky changed to vibrant blue. The boy walked out of the shop—twice. One of him, dressed in black and red and yellow, held a shining glass withie. A second version, wearing black and purple and blue, held a sword.

Thus was the story split into two equal halves, one on each side of the stage. Cade found it impossible to tell which was the real Gorant Pennywhistle. Rather than have two masquers onstage, the glisker, Tolz Flintsmithing, had brilliantly doubled him: identical faces, clothing, gestures, everything. Cade didn't like to think how much rehearsal it had taken and what kind of precision had been demanded of Long-branch in priming the withies as two versions of the same boy, who danced gleefully into a wooded glen, intent on practicing with his new possession.

The withie created magical things. Birds with long multi-colored tails sang in harmony with each other. The forest floor burst into life with a million flowers that turned into chiming butterflies. Acorns popped off the oak trees, dipping and twirling in time with the wild sweet music. The sword made different noises, cutting through bushes, hacking at tree limbs, hissing through the air to attack imaginary foes. Though the sounds and images were all different, the gestures were identical. So were the emotions.

Two little girls scampered into each glade. Their voices rose, shrill and demanding, as they pestered each young man to show them what he could do. On one side of the stage, the withie conjured up a swirl of colors that resolved into a dance of whirring dragonflies. The children giggled with delight. At the same time, on the other side of the stage, the flaunted sword caught a girl in the shoulder. She burst into tears and she and her sister ran away, leaving one youth standing alone in the leafy hollow, guilt and unhappiness swiftly subsumed in defiance. He began hewing tree branches again, every swing of the sword stronger and more vicious.

Now the stage held two different scenes. In the first, the young man was in a gilt-and-brocade drawing room, performing his whimsical magic for a crowned king and queen who laughed and applauded and showered him with gold coins. The other half of the stage was a battle-field. The boy swung his sword desperately in the thick of the fight, kill-ing and maiming, dust and blood clogging his breath, fear shuddering through his veins.

Almost anyone else would have ended the play there. Hawk's Claw weren't finished. In the grand drawing room, a Wizard took the young man aside and offered to make him famous and powerful beyond his wildest dreamings. A nod, an eager smile—and the two scenes became one. The boy wielding the sword spared not a glance for his double, who cringed and shook and finally, frantically, gripped the withie in both hands and flung it at the advancing enemy. It exploded in a flare of light and fear and shattering glass.

The stage went dark. The audience, unnerved, took many long sec-onds to begin their applause. Hawk's Claw stood at the front of the stage, bowed in unison, and strode off.

The glisker and fettler looked exhausted. Longbranch caught Cayden's eye, tilting his head in a silent question. Cade nodded slowly, knowing his approval wasn't needed. It was welcome all the same.

Crystal Sparks were next, and when Cade saw that they were doing one of their older pieces, a crowd favorite called "The Glass Glove," he returned to the tiring room to find Mieka.

Seated neatly on the ground, carefully polishing withies, the Elf looked up with raised eyebrows. "I'd started to wonder if you were intending me to prime these things myself."

"Sorry. I wanted to see Hawk's Claw."

"Any good? The audience sounded a bit vague."

"Once they think about it for a while, they'll like it." Something occurred to him. "Didn't you sense any of it back here?"

"Not a flicker. Now that I think on it, that's quite an accomplish-ment for the first time on a stage this big, with this many seats. Keeping all the magic where it ought to be, I mean."

"Oh, be sure to mention that to Rafe." Cade grinned, sitting down beside Mieka. "He'll just love it."

He spent the next fifteen minutes at work, giving Mieka the magic necessary for *Window Wall*. So what if it was a long play? This was opening night of the grand new theater. Touchstone would give them something to remember. When he got to the last withie, a new one, dark blue with Blye's thistle hallmark at the crimp, he lingered over the priming. Years ago, he'd promised Mieka this particular scene. They'd not used it at the King's Namingday. Rolon Piercehand had ruined the play long before its ending. Tonight he wanted it to be extra special.

Rafe and Jeska came over, pulling the two of them to their feet. "Black fucking Lightning's doing their horrible 'Lost Ones,'" Jeska said, disgusted.

"And you can feel it all the way back here," added Rafe. "When is that no-talent Crowkeeper going to learn his job? Lady Megs is ten times the fettler he is."

Cade opened his mouth, intending to reply that they lived in an age of wonders, indeed, when Rafe said such about a woman in theater. In the next instant, the words flew right out of his head. Replacing all thought, all feeling, was a self-loathing he'd felt only once before. *Troll*, something inside him accused, repelled by the very word. *Goblin. Fae. Mongrel*—

Shame for what he had been born squirmed in his guts. Wizard and Elf he might also be, but those things could not cancel out or even mitigate the filth that ran through his veins. He wanted to fall to his knees and sob with the grief of being what he was. What he could never atone for being—

"Cade. Cayden!"

Somebody was shaking him. Rafe. Large, powerful hands on his shoulders. The mortifying self-hatred was gone. No, not completely gone . . . hovering out there, perhaps an arm's length from where he stood. He took an involuntary step back. He didn't want to feel that again, not ever again.

"Good. You're back." Rafe didn't explain this. He let go of Cade and turned to Mieka, then to Jeska. Their faces showed what Cade suspected his own must show: lingering humiliation, confusion, fear.

"They had all of you for a minute," Rafe said. "But not me. You're protected now. I've got you. What worries me is what's going on out there in the audience. Who's protecting *them*?"

"Rafe?" Mieka asked in a voice that didn't quite tremble. "Why didn't you—?"

"Wizard," Cade managed. Rafe nodded. "We three are other things besides Wizard or Elf." And Rafe was shielding them from Pirro Spangler's vile magic just as he would an especially sensitive person in an audience.

Jeska was looking round at the other players backstage, alarmed. "Sweet Lord and Lady, look at their faces!"

"They look the way I felt," Mieka rasped. "Worse. They look as if they want to kill themselves."

Hawk's Claw. Crystal Sparks. The Stewards hanging about backstage. Magical folk, all of them. Magical things other than Wizard or Elf. Despising themselves for being what they were.

Cade whispered, "They look as if they'd give anything to be free of this."

"What about the audience?" Rafe said again. "There's three thousand people out there. The King and Queen—Miriuzca—she's got no magical blood, but what happens to those who do?"

Mieka jumped in place to see over Gorant Pennywhistle's shoulder. The masquer looked stricken to the soul. "Oy! Baltryn! Over here!"

The young Steward seemed to shake himself, and looked around, utterly bewildered by the blank, staring faces all round him. He hurried to where Touchstone stood. "What in all Hells is going on?"

"Black *fucking* Lightning," Rafe growled. "Can you wrap some magic around a few of your friends? Like you're protecting them from a careless fettler."

Baltryn nodded. "I'm pretty good at that, though I say it myself."

Cade had guessed Rafe's idea. "Do it, and when they're themselves again, tell them to do the same to as many people in the audience as they can reach. Keep Black Lightning's magic from touching them."

"It won't be easy," Mieka warned. "Rafe's protecting us—all right, fine. But I can still feel what Pirro wants me to feel. He's working with more than withies up there. I'd bet anything that Thierin and Kaj are joining in."

"Why is almost everyone else affected," Baltryn asked, "but not you and not me?"

"You're Human and Wizard and Elf—and nothing but," Cade said quickly. "It'd take too long to explain. Go shake a couple of your friends awake and—"

"The King!" Jeska exclaimed. "Gold coins with the Archduke's profile on them—"

Gold Coins reminded Cade that Derien was out there in the audience. And Blye—Kazie, Jinsie, Crisiant—the other Shadowshapers and their wives—people he cared about, people who had to be protected.

"Cayden?" Baltryn was more confused than ever.

"Go. Protect as many as you can. *Now.*" Turning to Rafe, Cade asked, "Can we move around? Can you—I don't know, wrap something around us?"

The fettler nodded. "Already done. I was going to build something between Black Lightning and the audience, but Mieka's right. There's more happening than withies account for."

They started for the stage. Their first look at the audience was terrifying. Thousands of faces—some of them awake and aware and frightened, some of them blank and unseeing, some recoiling from those around them, others flinching with unendurable shame. Cade easily sorted them into categories: those who had only Wizardly or Elfen blood or a combination of the two; those who were Human with no magic at all; and magical folk with Goblin or Piksey or any number of things other than Wizard or Elf.

"Jeska—go to the Wizards and Elves and Humans. Try not to let them panic, but tell them to leave." Glancing at Rafe, he added to his masquer, "If you start to feel what Black Lightning is making everyone else feel, come back."

"I'll do my best." He ran lithely up a side aisle, rightly judging that the chaos of headlong flight might be slightly less disastrous if the top rows left the theater first. Even better, he didn't pause for a single instant. Whatever Rafe was doing, it was protecting him.

Mieka was scowling. "The pureblood Humans look confused. But they're starting to get scared."

Cade said, "There aren't many—I'd say not more than a few dozen out of three thousand, mostly among the ambassadors and their people. See their faces?"

"As if they need any more reasons to hate and fear magic," the Elf muttered. "They're safe enough. They've no magic to be exploited or warped."

Rafe looked startled. "I thought you were going to say 'victimized' or something like that. What d'you mean, 'warped'?" A sudden wince interrupted him. Cade felt the intensity of Black Lightning's magic increase for a few moments, then fade to just out of arm's reach again. "Sort it later," Rafe growled. "Right now it's the Royals who need protecting."

Mieka nodded. "Get Megs to do it. She's more than good enough."

"What can the rest of us do?" Trenal Longbranch's voice, shaking slightly, came from behind Cade. Baltryn had been at work, bless him. "All our withies are spent, but we could prime them anew, have something to work with."

That was it—the spent withies. No wonder Black Lightning had been so scared of the Shadowshapers—best in Albeyn—no wonder they'd wanted Touchstone to go on *before* them—nothing to work with, no magic stored in slender glass twigs—even if someone guessed what was happening, it would take long minutes to prime them again—

"Mieka!" Cade blurted, and the Elf flinched. "All our withies—get them, quick. Trenal, you and Mirko get yours primed, and have your gliskers ready to use them at Mieka's direction. You've got five minutes."

"But—"

He had no time for questions. He leaped down the side steps from the stage level to the seats. Striding quickly along the front row, he spared a single glance for Black Lightning up on the stage. They weren't even pretending to put on a performance. Pirro Spangler sat on the glisker's bench, a withie gripped in each hand, eyes closed, sweat gleaming on his face. As each glass twig was expended, he tossed it over his shoulder and grabbed a new one. Herris Crowkeeper clutched his lectern with both hands; his eyes, too, were shut. Kaj Seamark's and Thierin Knottinger's eyes were fully open, and they stared only at each other. Some sort of silent, invisible communication was going on there, something that brought identical smiles to their faces.

Cayden reached front row center and instantly saw four things. First, the Archduke was gone from his seat next to Prince Ashgar. Second, the Prince and his father were cringing, shoulders hunched. Third, Queen Roshien was looking at her husband of over forty years as if he had suddenly turned into a pile of wyvern shit. And lastly, Princess Miriuzca was cowering in her seat as if expecting a fist to the face, which she wholeheartedly believed she deserved.

It was this last that brought Cade up short. He hadn't expected the Archduke to stay within reach while all this was going on. Everybody knew that there were magical antecedents in King Meredan's family; that the Queen had Wizardly or Elfen blood in her and possibly both was a bit of a surprise. But—Miriuzca?

They had stripped her mother naked to examine her for signs of— oh, Hells, they probably didn't even know what. Cade guessed, Mistress Mirdley's stories notwithstanding, that Vered had been right in that the "mark" of a Caitiff was purely imaginary, something to soothe people through the idea that there was a way to identify such women. Miriuzca's mother had had no such mark; neither would she. But magical blood she most certainly did have, though what kind was unknowable.

If she did, and Ashgar did, then their son and daughter did, too.

Cade shoved the realization aside and stood in front of Megs. She was so pale that her freckles looked like spattered blotches of brown paint. That she loathed herself was clear in her eyes, in the trembling of her lips. He picked her up by the shoulders and pulled her to him, holding tight, some sort of thought in his head about bringing her inside the wrapping that Rafe had created around him, but mostly because he couldn't bear to see an expression like that on her face.

After a few moments, she sobbed once against his chest and clung to him. He held her closer, rocking her, murmuring wordlessly.

"C-Cayden?"

"Just me. It's all right." It wasn't, not yet, but it would be. "I promise it's going to be all right. Can you do something for me?"

She pulled away a little and nodded. She knuckled her eyes, wiped her nose, and looked up at him. "Tell me."

"Protect Miriuzca. You're a fettler. Shield her from the magic."

"What about the King and Queen?"

"A Steward will be here soon. Don't worry about them. Your job is to keep Miri safe from—from whatever it is they've got planned. I can't pretend it won't get nasty."

She looked beyond him to the stage. "Surely a tregetour could come up with a better word than *nasty*." Meeting his gaze again, she straightened up and said, "Go on. I'm fine now. Do what you have to."

It occurred to him that in a play, the hero at this point would have bent down to kiss her. This wasn't a play. He was no hero.

He kissed her anyway. For the space of two heartbeats she kissed him back, then shoved both hands against his chest.

"For Gods' sake!" she snapped. "Why are men so fucking *stupid*? Go!"

He went.

Chapter 39

Unusually subdued, Mieka was waiting for him. Cade had passed Baltryn and another Steward on the way, and barely kept himself from demanding that one of them find Derien and protect him. The best thing he could do for his brother—for everyone—was to stop Black Lightning. For something new had appeared on the stage: a shimmering, writhing curtain of translucent light, glistening with sparks of color that seemed to be gathering together, red with red, blue with blue, and so on, accumulating into bright globes. It was this that Mieka was watching with grave uneasiness as Cade reached him.

"I'm not sure this is what's needed," Mieka said. "The withies are primed for *Window Wall*."

Jeska fidgeted nearby. "Better it should be 'Dragon' or something else with a lot of fighting in it."

"Ours are ready for the Third and the Sixth," said Trenal.

One Peril a battle against a Giant, the other a battle against demons. For reasons he didn't understand, the whole notion troubled Cayden.

Mirko looked up from kneeling beside his glisker, Jacquan Bentbrooke. "We've put our 'Piksey A-Straying' images in these." He gestured to the single, very large glass basket of withies. "Upside down, sideways, backwards, and inside out. With some extra twists."

"Dizziness, nausea, and, if you like, actual proddings to yark all over themselves," said Jacquan with a hard little smile.

Cade nodded uncertainly. "Has anybody tried just grabbing them and hauling them offstage?"

"Can't get through that damned curtain," said Lederris Daggering. "I've a few pints of Goblin blood in me along with Wizard and Elf, and whenever I get near it, it feels like I should have bad teeth and a single eyebrow and mottled skin—and a hunger for Human flesh seethed in milk." He pushed the hair off his forehead as if to make sure he indeed had two eyebrows. "Even with Brennert protecting me, I can't walk through it, or past it, or into it—whatever that thing is."

"Anybody else try?"

Gorant Pennywhistle lifted one hand, let it fall to his side helplessly. "I'm Wizard and Human, like Rafe—but I haven't the first clue about fettling. I can't protect anybody. And our own fettler . . . well, he's so many things not even he knows, and the first wallop of this hit him pretty hard."

Mieka, his arms full of multi-colored withies, looked up at Cade. "You could. I could."

"How d'you figure?"

"Fae. Wizards and Elves are pure, according to Black Lightning, right? Rafe and Baltryn—and Gorant—are our only purebred Wizards, as far as we know. They've got other work to do. But twice I've seen this play, and twice I've felt this, and neither time has there been anything that targets the Fae. I think Black fucking Lightning is afraid of them."

"Here's something else to add to the festivities," Cade said. "The Archduke is gone."

"Good riddance." Mieka seemed unconcerned. "I bet we could get past that barrier thing, and use the Fae inside us to do it. We both know how charming the Fae can be when they really try!"

Cayden had begun shaking his head halfway through this brave and unpersuasive argument. Mirko looked from one to the other of them and observed, "Quite the imagination the lad's got, ain't it?"

"You got any better ideas?" Mieka challenged.

"What happens if we *do* get inside?" Cade asked.

The familiar wickedly gleeful grin spread across his face. "Quill! I'm surprised at you! When you don't know what the fuck you're doing, doing it becomes easy!"

"Not imaginative," Lederris corrected. "Insane."

"That, too," Mieka shot back. He wasn't smiling anymore. "Can't you feel it? It's getting stronger and it's expanding. We gotta try *something*, and soon."

Cade moved a few steps towards the stage. What he saw convinced him that they did have to do something, and right now—for that curtain, like heavy silk made of magic, now curved in a gentle arc from the wings on either side all the way to the front of the stage. He could no longer see any member of Black Lightning. Embers merged together into glowing orbs of light—and the colors were just as Vered had envisioned when the magical races had given powers to the Knights of the Balaur Tsepesh. There were dozens of these globes, green and red-gold, blue-green and reddish brown, fiery red, opalescent, even purple shot through with gold, which he hadn't seen since that night on the Vathis River when a strange old man had settled the shrieking of those hideous *vodabeists*. How had Black Lightning learned—? Ah, simple: they'd been to the Continent, and they had the Archduke to educate them.

Vered had been right about the colors, but there were three missing. The blue of Wizardfire, the yellow-gold of the Elves, and the silver that Vered had used for the Fae. Perhaps Mieka's instinct was correct, and the Fae in their blood—

"Holy fuck," Jeska whispered beside him as the globes suddenly spat out new sparks, seeking into the audience. Seeking and finding— sometimes three or four at once, converging on someone whose whole body spasmed, whose mouth opened in a silent scream.

"Mieka."

It was all he had to say. The Elf gave him a single withie, and he felt it warm and alive with magic in his hand. Mieka held one in each fist.

"Give me a couple," Jeska said. "I'm no glisker, but I can give it a try."

"Protect those people if you can," Cade replied. "Get the others working at it as well. Mieka . . . " he said again, and heard his voice shake.

"Right here, Quill."

They strode onstage, heading directly for the translucent curtain where miniature multi-colored suns spat gouts of fire into the air, seeking Trolls and Gnomes, Giants and Goblins, Caitiffs and Pikseys and whatever that old man on the Vathis River might have termed himself. Cade glanced down to the front row, astonished to see red-gold and purple sputter into lifelessness no more than a foot in front of Princess Miriuzca. Megueris, close beside her, didn't seem to notice; her eyes were dark, unseeing, her face drawn in lines of terrible intensity. Miriuzca was Caitiff, then, and—what had the old man said, gesturing at Mieka's Elfen ears? *Kin*. He had the ridiculous thought that Jindra

Windthistle was the closest thing Miriuzca had to magical kin in all of Albeyn.

And then he stepped through the curtain, and his brain caught on fire.

*   *   *

Mieka saw the glimmering lights swallow Cayden, and cried out. Every instinct told him to follow. Somehow, his brain was shrewder than his instincts. He put both withies into his left hand, extended a single finger, and poked tentatively at the magic.

What flowed invisibly up his arm and throughout his body was hatred of himself and everyone and everything in the world around him. An urge to violence seized him, violence of the kind that made wars and killed without mercy. What flooded his brain was sheer evil, the kind that clawed half-grown children from their mothers' wombs and devoured them raw and bleeding. What made his lips curl into a snarl and his fingers clench like talons was everything he was. So many sorts of magic, so many talents and gifts and perceptions and abilities—some shining and others murky, some singing and others growling, stinking or fragrant, smooth or snagged or soft or hard, tart, sour, honeyed, salty—all of them his to use or to reject. He hated them all, everything he was that did not dance with Elfen magic or laugh with Wizardly pride.

The withies dropped from his hand, one of them shattering, and he was certain sure that the sharp sound of it was what saved him. Winded as though he'd run twenty miles, over the thunder of blood in his ears he heard the screaming begin. A dozen, a score—soon there would be hundreds of people shrieking in agony. Not in pain; not with physical or emotional or mental or spiritual anguish. They were hungry, as he had just been hungry for unspeakable carnage. For fountains of blood, rivers of it.

The Fae within him evoked nothing at all. He could feel it, could recognize it as the same quiver of *something* he'd felt when confronting the Fae below the Chalk Dragon. Yet it was untouched by Black Lightning's magic. He hadn't time to wonder why.

However it was being done, whatever vicious magic was producing this, it would not have been possible if there had not been evil and violence and cruelty in each and every mind the magic touched. There was nothing in the world so inherently vile as a living, thinking mind. Mieka flinched back from knowing it, and instantly recognized himself for the coward he had always been. Hiding behind masks and laughter so that nobody would see how sniveling scared he was. He couldn't even explain the things that frightened him—or perhaps he could. Without the laughter, someone might see him as he truly was . . . and be as disgusted, as contemptuous, as Black Lightning's magic had made him see himself.

Quill sees.

He doesn't hate me.

He doesn't much like some of the things I've done, *but he's never—*

Yes, he has. The last time I got drunk.

It would have to be the last time.

He discovered that he was sprawled on the stage, not quite curled up in a ball but close to it. Unwinding his limbs, feeling a million years old, he picked up an unbroken withie. There was power in it: Cayden's magic, and Blye's. He regularly and delightedly combined their magic with his own to create wonders. It was clear to him right now that what he must do with it was destroy.

He was desperate for thorn. He needed the kick of energy. He was terrified that he wouldn't have the strength to do this. He remembered what it was like, having all that lovely hot sweet power flowing through him, heightening his senses, making his dance with the withies almost impossibly quick—like Pirro, grabbing glass twigs and spewing magic from them, uncontrolled and wild, devouring Pirro's own strength and will. Before the curtain had thickened, Mieka had sensed something muddied and foul about his former friend's magic, how the bluethorn and whitethorn and the Gods alone knew what other kinds of thorn had replaced the essence of the man, mind and heart and soul. There wasn't much left that was truly Pirro Spangler.

That could have been me. He'd said that aloud to Quill, though he couldn't quite recall the circumstances. But it was true. There was so little between him and all the evils his own nature could surrender to, given the chance. The fear was absolute, crippling—until he realized that it could have been him if not for Cayden, for Rafe, for Jeska. Mieka would crave thorn for the rest of his life, but if he gave in, he would become either the hollow shell Pirro was now, or a monster. The kind of person who could put killing magic into withies, who could plot to blow up a castle with his sister and her children inside, who could order two innocent people killed just to see if the method worked and then use it to kill his own wife.

Mieka looked at the withie he held as he would hold a throwing knife: by the crimp, elbow cocked. Shifting the glass in his hand, he held it like a sword's hilt. Better. He was about to do battle, after all. He was going to use his own magic and Cayden's and Blye's to slice holes in that curtain, and if they were tiny at first, so be it. Enough rents in the fabric, and he'd be able to tear it to shreds.

It took only a few moments of slicing at the thing to convince him that he couldn't do it alone. Flinging a glance back over his shoulder, he saw that the shooting sparks of colored light had attacked the players as they were attacking the audience. The fight was clear in all those familiar faces; Rafe seemed to be winning, and Mirko. But none of them could help him. He wanted to discard the withie and seize the slight tears in the curtain and rip them wide open. But if he touched the magic with his bare hands again, he knew he'd be lost.

How had Cayden walked through it? What was happening to him, there where Thierin and Kaj and Herris and Pirro could get at him freely? They wouldn't kill him. They probably wanted to, but they wouldn't. The Archduke wanted Cayden Silversun and his unique, priceless Elsewhens intact.

Cayden Silversun.

Mieka heard himself laugh aloud. Why hadn't anybody seen it?

Had Mieka believed that certain things were fated to be, he would have called it foretold, something they all ought to have realized long ere this. He didn't believe in iron-clad destiny—no one familiar with Cade's Elsewhens could—but he did take this as definitive proof that the Gods had a sense of humor.

Not iron or gold or bronze or brass, but *silver*: the only metal that was poison to the Knights. *Sun:* the source of light that scorched their skin and charred their bones and brought them certain death. What other name could Cayden possibly have borne?

Turning, he skimmed his gaze over the audience. No improvement, no surcease—though Jeska, before his return to the wings, seemed to have cleared hundreds of people from the upper rows. Baltryn and a friend stood guard in the side aisles; Megs was holding Miriuzca's hands in her own. Which left thousands in the theater, almost all of them helpless before the magic that slithered through the air and captured their minds. *Why not just kill them all?* Mieka wondered, then shook the thought away and ran back to the wings, where tregetours and gliskers were clumped together, back to priming withies, their fettlers once more protecting them. He didn't have to ask to know what sort of magic they were putting into the withies. Fury; outrage; hate; revulsion. But that curving curtain was woven of hate and evil; more hate and more evil could only make it stronger.

"We can't use those," he said flatly.

To a man, they stared at him.

"You just try a couple of these and find out!"

"Have you lost your fucking mind?"

"What d'you suggest we do—shatter them and throw the shards?"

"Then what *will* we use?"

Mieka smiled, a real smile this time, an expression that shocked them speechless. Rafe and Jeska returned his gaze with doubt and worry—things he'd expected, so it didn't hurt that much. What had he ever done to deserve otherwise? Yet something had to have happened over these last years—Lord and Lady alone knew what—to make them trust him, because after a moment they, too, began to smile.

Clever and mad.

"Here, I'll show you," Mieka said, and pulled the knife from its sheath at his back.

Chapter 40

Expecting pretty much anything behind that glimmering wall of magic, Cade hadn't expected to walk into his own play.

Passing through the shifting curtain of magic was the opposite of a curglaff: instead of an icy-cold shock on his skin, he'd felt a blistering heat in every corner of his mind. He would never know if the step he took out of it was a stumble or not; the important thing was that he moved beyond it and saw at once Thierin Knottinger, eyes open and laughing with scorn, the only other person on the stage. Which was impossible. But there he was: lean and dark, dressed in brown leather and red silk. Seamark, Spangler, and Crowkeeper were gone. Or hidden. Or something.

"About time you showed up. I knew you would, of course. You could never resist playing the Great Tregetour, always in control of everything."

Cade took rapid stock of himself. Whole and without wound, but in control of nothing but his temper. His brain still stung like a festering thorn-welt, and it was all he could do to stand upright.

"You recognize this, I trust?" Thierin gestured with a flourish to the hallway of doors that Cade and Mieka had created so many times. "Why he won't let us turn you at the same time as everyone else, I don't know. But for some reason he wants you . . . functional." He grinned broadly, the word obviously amusing him. "Choose a door, Cayden."

Understanding now precisely why a Wizard could place lethal magic inside a withie and hurl it at his enemies, Cade decided to ignore Thierin instead. Neither would he give the tregetour the satisfaction of asking where his partners were. Someone had made the hall and the doorways, and whatever might be within them. For whom they had been made was clear. Clear as well was the one he was intended to walk through. It was the only one slightly ajar. He strode to it, opened it with a hard kick of his boot, but did not enter.

"Oh, go on!" Knottinger taunted. "You know you want to. Or is it only your Elf who gets distracted by shiny objects?"

There were none such in the scene beyond the door. Instead, blood-soaked footprints in a flat, snowy wasteland. They did not lead into the distance, but approached—as if he had already trod a path to the doorway.

The voice that addressed him now was not Thierin's.

"You've left your mark behind you in blood, the blood of those whose deaths you might have averted, and of those who died."

The voice came from everywhere and nowhere. He didn't turn to find its owner, nor search the scene before him with his gaze. The voice was familiar, even though he hadn't heard it in more than a dozen years. He'd thought the man dead. He supposed this resurrection was meant to be a staggering shock. It wasn't. Where else would this man be other than serving Cyed Henick?

Less and less as he'd grown older had he thought of Sagemaster Emmot's lessons. He had applied them as he felt necessary to the life he was making for himself, and gradually the voice—this voice echoing all around him now—had faded inside his head. But those teachings existed; they were part of him, whether he willed it or no. Hearing this voice that had freed him from Redpebble Square, from being ordinary, that had revealed what he now realized was only as much as it took to bring forth and comprehend the Elsewhens—he was peculiarly unsurprised. What puzzled him was why, after all these years, Emmot still thought that he knew Cayden. Rather pathetic, really.

In point of fact, this image of blood-boltered footsteps could not catch at his conscience, for he had read the oldest of old plays in *Lost Withies*, which he always thought of as Mieka's book. From it he knew that in ancient days, fallow farmland was drenched with blood to make it fertile and pleasing to the Gods. Should a light, swift snow fall before the blood was plowed into the soil, walking across it would seem as if one left bloody footprints. The play itself had been about a cataclysmic social change: using the blood of animals rather than the blood of children. The footprints had been those of the Goddess of the Harvest, who had seized power from an older, crueler God, lingering after she inspected and blessed the fields.

"Nice try, old man."

"Something prettier, then? There are other doorways. There are always other doorways."

True enough. He and Mieka and Jeska and Rafe had together thought up at least thirty as the play evolved over the years. The last door chosen was always the one giving each member of an audience that which they thought they most desired. *This life, and none other.* Emmot would have to do a lot better if he wished to rattle Cayden. Moving to another door, he grasped the brass handle and opened it.

Not just a pretty scene; a perfectly beautiful one. A green and flowery meadow backed by snow-capped mountains, a stream chuckling over boulders and fallen logs and between stepping-stones. The bluest of skies, the sweetest of birdsong. Tall pines, blossom-strewn shrubbery, and millions of brilliant butterflies that drifted idly here and there, opening and closing their patterned wings. Suddenly their bodies lengthened, grew vicious stingers at the tail, wings becoming the jaws of a forester's trap, steel teeth snapping.

"I'm afraid I'm not quite understanding your symbolism here," Cade said. In truth, he understood very well, and thought it rather silly. "Are these supposed to be all the plays I've written? Pretty to look at, but with a bite to them? If so, I'm beholden to you for the compliment."

"Try another doorway."

He smiled as he turned into the hall again, knowing Emmot would see it or sense it. "Where's the one where I get the girl?"

"Perhaps you'll get something you can't admit that you desire."

Opening a sleek bronze door, he saw Blye's workshop and piles of withies—hundreds of them, each prickled with thorns and filled with liquid of a dozen different colors.

"Oh, you do enjoy your thorn, don't you? You want them. You can feel them. Magic to enhance your own magic and make you invincible."

Cade couldn't help it. He burst out laughing.

"Or mayhap to create a world and live within it, dreaming anything and everything precisely as you wish it to be."

"I like my life just as it is, though it's thoughtful of you to offer."

"So. The ugsome Troll-spawn has grown to be a man. I thought it thus, but I wanted to be sure. It will make what happens next all the more satisfying."

Another door clanged open. Cade approached warily. Inside was a plain, comfortless room paved with white marble veined in blood red. The markings looked to him like words, like lines of type ready to be printed. They wrote themselves across the white stone and began to float up into the air and began of themselves to speak their own names.

He knew these words, all of them. They were his own. From every play he had ever written or rewritten, Jeska's speeches recited themselves at him, simultaneously, overlapping, a tumult of words and words and yet more words spoken in every conceivable sort of voice, from high-pitched whine to gravelly growl. The blood-red words crowded one another in sound and sight until the turmoil became almost too much to bear.

Then the words silenced themselves and fell dead to the floor.

"You see how useless you are? Nothing but words. All you will leave when you die are piles of words."

"Well," Cade said, unimpressed, "if we're all going to die anyway, why not leave, say, 'Life in a Day' behind?" He smiled again. "Or *Blood Plight*. Not an inconsiderable life's work."

Because it wasn't just the words. It was the ideas and feelings they represented. Evoked. The words and what they meant—they would be his legacy, he knew, but they were also his weapons. His particular method of magic that didn't require much magic at all. It needed only what was inside him that thought and felt and dreamed. Mieka had told him more than once that his dreams were important. Not just for himself; for those who couldn't find words to make their dreamings come alive.

"But there could be so much more."

This time, as a new voice spoke, he did flinch. Down at the far end of the ballroom, past the heaps of fallen, silent words, Archduke Cyed Henick sat in a large, overstuffed gray chair.

"Do come in," he invited. "Yes, I've seen your 'Doorways' play. I always thought it nonsense. We are what we are because we can be nothing else. There are no choices to be made."

Cade approached, stepping carefully around the dead words. "You're wrong," he said. "We all choose. I've proof of it. Mieka *chose* to stop using thorn. I've never seen anyone who used more or loved it more than he did. But he made the choice and kept to it."

"The Elf. Always that damned little Elf."

Henick rose listlessly to his feet. Cade had noted before that he didn't look healthy; now he looked positively ill. A hand was held up, palm out, the greeting of one nobleman to another. The greeting of equals. Cayden glanced at the hand, then at the watery blue eyes. Nothing on or of or in this world could impel him to touch this man.

Henick shrugged and sat back down again. Reaching into the pocket of his dark gray jacket, he withdrew something that glittered as it dangled from his fingers. His smile was the slow unsheathing of a dagger.

The Carkanet. The Queen's Right of the Fae.

"Midwinter sunrise, the year my late unregretted wife played her trick on the Elf. By all the Old Gods, what a breathtakingly stupid woman! You can imagine how furious I was."

"I take it that you didn't go after that shiny little trinket for her sake."

"She hated you ever since the night you defended Miriuzca at the bedding ceremony. That's quite a while ago now, isn't it?"

"Did she deserve to die?"

"She shared my opinion that to destroy the Elf would be to destroy you. She tried to do so without my permission. She failed. Yes, she deserved to die."

"Then why are *you* still alive? You've failed often enough."

"You can't know how long I waited for a reason to 'learn' about your talent. I couldn't let on that I knew until somebody came and told me. How luscious that it turned out to be the Caitiff! Did you know she went to the trouble of a journey to—"

"To the Durkah Isle," Cade interrupted, bored. "That wasn't much of a success, either. You really ought to get some competent people around you, Your Grace."

"I didn't really need her. And it turns out that I don't need you, either, to accomplish what will be done tonight. Black Lightning may not be as powerful in some ways, but they are far less trouble than you would have been."

"You'll keep me alive, though." It hadn't taken Thierin Knottinger to tell him that.

"Yes. You know as well as I that you're too valuable to lose. I'll let you play your future out, pounding stages like a clown—but when I summon you, you will come. And you will tell me what the future holds."

Cade pretended to consider. "Actually, no. I won't."

"Have you ever seen the future that begins tonight? The future where I rule Albeyn? Of course you haven't. You see only things you personally can influence. The things that your actions can change. Believe me when I say this, Master Silversun: Nothing you can do will alter this future now."

Cade only smiled.

"And what of your little brother?" Henick went on, relishing the words. "Do you ever see him in all these futures? You do not. And you won't, ever."

He wasn't smiling anymore. "Harm him, and I'll—"

"Oh, please. Cut out your own tongue, kill yourself, rather than tell me anything about your visions? You don't see it yet, do you?" He leaned forward in his chair, the necklet swinging gently from his fingertips. "After tonight, you'll *want* to tell me."

It made sense then. It all made sense. Identifying each magical race. Targeting them specifically. No magic could counter or withstand what Black Lightning would do, was doing, to the King and Miriuzca and the Ministers and the justiciars and the nobles and even the purebred Human ambassadors of a dozen different countries. Had their every Royal Circuit performance prepared the rest of the Kingdom? Mayhap. But why go to all that trouble? With almost everyone of importance swayed to his side—*turned*, to use Knottinger's word—why bother with the common folk?

The Queen's Right glinted from Henick's fingers. Rather plain compared to the King's Crown, it was made of a hundred links of gold and silver, thumbnail-sized plaques without jewels. Draped on the shoulders of a Fae Queen, would it suddenly come to life?

"What do you plan to do with that?" Cade asked when he could find his voice again. "It would look nice on Miriuzca."

"If not her, under my control, it can be a goad to the Fae."

He glanced around the white marble room, with all those blood-red words piled on the floor. "You do realize that we're in the middle of a Dancing Ground?"

Another smile.

Cade gathered his thoughts. "It's always struck me as thoroughly unoriginal, having the villain explain himself towards the end of the play. But as long as you're talking, you might as well tell me—"

"Villain? I'm not the villain!" He seemed genuinely shocked, and deeply offended. "None of this is for myself! It was never because I want to command 'Do this' and 'Do that' and see it happen on the instant!"

"That's what they all say," Cade remarked.

Henick seemed to gather himself, settle his outrage. "I'm not telling you this because you're going to die. I'm not telling you because it's safe to explain because the knowledge will do you no good." He moved his hand slightly, to make the Carkanet sway and shimmer again at his fingertips. "I'm telling you so that you'll understand. Because you're going to live. And serve me. And like it."

"Again, no."

"This land needs stability. Continuity. No more wars, or the idiotic political maneuverings that come within a breath of war. No more risking the ascension of morons like Meredan or wastrels like Ashgar. Can you seriously see him as *King*? No more religious squabbles—surely the most asinine reason for killing ever invented. Who cares which of the Old Gods or the Lord or the Lady or any of a thousand different Angels is worshipped or not?"

"*They* might," Cade mused. "But I'm not here for a discussion on theology. What I want to know . . ." He paused as if to find the words he wanted. He knew them exactly, of course. But he wanted this insanely arrogant man to *listen*. "I want to know what gives you the right. Who pointed to you and gave you permission? Or did you just choose yourself because nobody was there to tell you different?"

"My father," said the Archduke, "was a fool. He wanted it all whilst he was still young. From my earliest childhood I was told that I would have to wait. And I was content to do so. To be patient. To watch and plan things that would take years to accomplish. Because I alone can fix it." He pooled the Carkanet in his palm. "Do you know that chamber in Castle Eyot, the one with all the timepieces?"

Cade nodded. The room that whirred and clicked and chimed and rang every hour on the hour—reminding all who heard the noise that another hour was gone, irretrievably gone.

"Piercehand has clocks . . . but I will have *time*."

Making a face of polite interest, he waited for more. If his career as a playwright had taught him anything, it was that from people like this, there was always more.

"Other men, lesser men, simply cannot wait. My father could not. 'First, win,' they told them. 'Then reap your reward.' He came close to winning, you know, and they made the mistake of giving him what he wanted. Did you ever wonder why the gyves on his wrists were made of silver?"

The question seemed to have nothing to do with anything.

Except that it had to do with everything.

"The histories say," Cade said slowly, "to show how rich the King still was, even after so many years of war."

"And no one thought to ask why, if he was so wealthy, the gyves weren't made of gold." The Archduke snorted. "As if a ruler earns the right to rule based on how large a pile of coins he can shovel together."

Cade became aware that he was hardly breathing, and consciously pulled in a lungful of air. "Your father was executed by decapitation."

Emmot's voice came from nowhere. "I told you he was a smart lad."

"If so," Henick drawled, "why is he standing here?"

Cade wanted to ask the old man how he had known about the Else-whens when Cade was still so young. He wanted to ask if Emmot had worked with Cade's grandmother, Lady Kiritin, to make withies that exploded and maimed and killed. Who was the generous donor who had paid for Cayden's education? Had Emmot always known that Cade would become a tregetour? Stupid questions, all of them, the answers mattering to no one but himself.

Emmot asked a question instead. "Tell me, Cayden, did you ever think of what you could have been?"

"Of course he didn't," the Archduke interrupted. "If I'd been born with a hundredth part of what he was born with—"

"Content, are you," the Sagemaster went on, "to fritter away all that power telling ridiculous stories and making pretty scenes, and showing people how they ought to think and feel?"

Cade addressed Henick, giving a little shrug. "It's a living."

"You never considered that you could make your stories *real*. That the scenes could be *real*. That instead of nudging an audience to feel a certain way or to think a certain thing, you could have changed the way they think and feel *permanently*. You could have created order and meaning out of the chaotic meaningless clutter all around you. And you could have changed it forever."

"You were the one who always told me I couldn't make other people's choices for them."

"I hoped that eventually you'd understand that most people are idiots who don't know what's best for them. Your Elf is a case in point. All the disasters he visited upon himself—you could have stopped them. You could have prevented them. I thought that sooner or later you would see that his emotional calamities were detrimental to Touchstone, and your pride in your work would cause you to make the decisions for him. When it became clear that you actually cared for him, I realized that because of that caring, you would do what you had to in order to save him from himself."

"That's not caring for someone. That's controlling them."

"For their own good. Precisely. As Albeyn itself will be controlled. Stability demands it."

"No," Cade said. "No. That isn't how life ought to be. People have to learn on their own—it isn't *love*, forcing someone to change into what you think he should be. You have to let people be who they are. Otherwise—it's like painting a white marble statue. It doesn't change what the statue really is. It just makes it look like something it's not."

"How many people," Emmot challenged, "make stupid decisions— like your Elf!—and disrupt the lives of all around them? Impose rational order on such persons, and everyone benefits."

"He'll not be persuaded," the Archduke said suddenly. "Why are you still trying to convince him? By tomorrow, it won't matter." The shining rivulet of silver and glass slid from hand to hand.

"Mind telling me how you managed to get the Queen's Right?" Cade asked. Then, realizing the obvious: "Master Emmot is part Fae. And related somehow to the Oakapple family."

"Perhaps you were right after all, Emmot. He does have possibilities. Perhaps, given enough time, he might even work out how we got away before the Sentinels came."

"You didn't try it on. Briuly Blackpath put the King's Right on his own head," Cade said promptly, like a schoolboy trying to impress his teachers.

"Inspired! Truly inspired!" Henick sneered. Tucking the Carkanet into a jacket pocket, he pushed himself to his feet. No, he did not look at all well. Sweat seeded his brow, and his lips were tinged blue. He didn't look anything like a man who had time.

"So what's the plan?" Cade inquired, striving for a tone of voice that expressed impersonal interest. He didn't achieve it. Henick snorted his opinion and Cade tried again, more successfully this time— although he really didn't have half a fucking clue what he was talking about. "One of your ancestors was one of the original Knights, I get that. And another of them provided a castle for them to hide in when they were no longer needed. You're not interested in having the Caitiffs resume their role of servitude." Suddenly he knew. "After all," he went on, his voice steady although his heartbeats were suddenly so quick, they almost choked him, "why bother with a few dozen slaves when you can have a whole Kingdom?"

Pale eyebrows arched in an exaggeration of surprise. "Oh, surely not a *whole* Kingdom! Just selected portions of it."

"Including most of the important government officials, a bunch of justiciars, some nobles, and the ambassadors of a dozen or so countries. *And* the King. Tell me, do you plan to make Miriuzca a widow for your own convenience?"

"That rather depends on how cooperative she's willing to be. It seems someone's protecting her. I must say, I didn't suspect her of Caitiff magic."

"How did Black Lightning find any to practice on?" Cade snapped his fingers in a deliberately overdone gesture. "Of course—a few must still linger on the Continent, to be served up for their education." He looked around, but he and the Archduke were the only ones in the room—except for Thierin, whom Cade had forgotten until now. The tregetour was looking a bit strained around the eyes. "Fun, was it?"

"Go fuck yourself."

Only the three of them. He wanted to bring the fourth out into the open, but he didn't know how. "Tell me, Emmot," he said, addressing the Sagemaster without his title for the first time in his life, "when did you get the notion of using a group of players to suborn a whole Kingdom?"

"Enough!" Henick snarled.

Cade ignored him. "Exactly how furious were you and your boy, here, when Touchstone wouldn't play along? Smarted, didn't it, when you had to settle for something considerably less than the best?"

"Go fuck yourself *sideways*, Silversun," Knottinger invited. "You're there and I'm here. That tells me who's the best."

"But Quill's the one they want to keep alive," said Mieka, and Cade spun on one heel to see his Elf standing this side of the shimmering curtain, a sword in his hand. Shining steel, inlaid with silver along the blade, with a purple amethyst in the hilt to match the jewel on his finger, he held the weapon with assurance and easy grace. "And *that* tells *me* who's the most important!"

Chapter 41

Everyone knew that Henick wanted Cayden alive. He had no fears for himself. He was safe enough. But Mieka—

Cade didn't know whether to be more proud or horrified. Trust that fool of an Elf to charge right on in without a by-your-leave, holding a withie magicked to seem every inch a real sword. It was so insanely like him, to match the amethyst in his ring to the amethysts in the hilt. Hells, he'd probably start a new fashion.

Just how real *was* this magic, anyways? Illusion only, the kind they used onstage? The clothes Mieka had worn strolling into the *Lilyleaves* office years ago—bits of feather fluff had drifted to the floor from his fan, vanishing with those ridiculous flounces. But Cade had known that if he'd put out a hand to touch, he would have *felt* silk, feathers, lace. Hawk's Claw had tonight given the audience the feel of something shiny and smooth in the hand. Combine that with the sight of a sword . . .

As with all things magical, it was *belief* that really mattered.

"Weren't you wondering when I'd show up?" Mieka went on, taking a few steps towards Cade. "I mean, you *knew* I'd be here eventually, right?" He glanced over at Thierin, who seemed to be gagging on his own tongue. "Pirro's a bit winded by now, y'know. You'd best toddle off and give him some help."

"What—how—you—"

"Were you always this articulate, or is it something they teach at tregetour school?"

"Mieka," Cade managed, then cleared his throat and tried again. "Mieka—" It came out as a warning, which made the Elf smile.

"With you in half a tick, old thing." He walked towards Knottinger, his steps more precise, his body tensing, his lips unsmiling. Those eyes were deep blue with flecks of green, with gold sparks of anger. "You're owed something for Yazz," he said quietly.

"You can fuck off, too," Thierin informed him.

"Articulate, eloquent, *and* original! How will Albeyn ever survive without you?"

As he came within sword's reach, he assumed a challenging stance. Cade recognized it, not so much from watching Mieka practice as from years of seeing Jeska's work onstage; fencing lessons were part of a masquer's training, to prevent any real swordsmen in the audience from laughing themselves silly.

Thierin Knottinger had not gone to masquer's school. He gave it a good try. The withie in his hand took on the look of a sword, two feet of gleaming steel. He knew how to do that much, at least. A tiny smile curved Mieka's lips as he advanced. A swipe to the top half of Knottinger's sword went right through it—for there was naught but illusion to slice through. Thierin stumbled back a few steps, white-faced with panic, and yelled Pirro's name. Mieka danced lightly in, the tip of his sword prodding contemptuously at Thierin's arm. He reacted as if well and truly perforated. Real or not, magic or not, he believed in that sword.

Mieka toyed with him for a moment or two, waiting for something. The sword in Thierin's hand blurred, indicating a faltering connection between the magic he was putting into the withie and the magic he was using as a glisker would to make it seem like a sword. Mieka lunged close, and in a move Cade had never seen Jeska use—and which would probably have had Master Flickerblade shrieking in outrage—swung his sword two-handed. The sword became a withie, gripped in a hand no longer attached to a wrist.

Screams were obscured by the crash of shattering glass. The room vanished, and the hallways of doors, leaving them all onstage behind the glittering curtain—which showed a long gash over to the left. Cade almost lost his balance as the floor of the white marble room disappeared beneath his feet. It hadn't been real, he *knew* it hadn't been real—but then he also knew that the sword in Mieka's hand, stained now with Thierin's blood, couldn't possibly be real, either.

Thierin believed it was real.

Sagemaster Emmot emerged from a shadow near the wooden wall at the back of the stage. He wore a neat, spotless robe of dark blue, the hem concealing his feet, the cowl up around his hairless head, the sleeves long enough to hide all of his hands but the fingertips. He looked exactly the same as when Cade had left the Academy ten years ago. Exactly the same.

"I had a feeling it would turn out to be him," Mieka said. Cade frankly gaped at him, and he explained, "Great Welkin, when you and His Grace over there had your little talk a few years ago." When Cade didn't react, he continued impatiently, "Me in the ballroom, him in the minstrels gallery, tossing spells down at me? And it was him in the cellar outside New Halt, too. Feeding off us and the Shadowshapers and everybody else." Turning to face the hooded figure, he asked, "How's it feel, knowing that you educated the man who'll destroy you?"

"That remains to be seen, little Elf."

Thierin was on his knees, clutching his arm, crying in a rhythmic whine. The Archduke snapped, "Somebody shut him up!"

"Quill, you have to do something about all this."

"Me?"

"Of course. It couldn't be any other way. I'll explain later. But it's yours to choose how you deal with it. If I may, a little advice?"

Cade waved a helpless hand, inviting him to continue.

"Well," Mieka began, but at that precise moment light and darkness coalesced and became a hideous yellow *vodabeist*, clawed hooves pawing the stage and leaving long scars in the wood.

Instinct caused Cade to grip the withie in his hand and retaliate. He conjured up two Fae hounds, huge and black and ugly. They sprang from the shadows and sank their fangs into the *vodabiest*'s throat. It shrieked and the battle was joined.

A dragon, more grotesque than any Cade and Mieka had ever conjured, formed from a million glittering lights scattered through the magic. Wings spread and head rearing back, it spewed fire up into the empty night sky—where there was no resistance, no curtain of magic, nothing but air. Cade flatly refused to believe that the fire was real— but he countered with ice anyway, sheets of it molding around the outstretched crimson wings and rearing head. It froze, toppled with a thud that shattered the ice tinkling onto the stage, and vanished. For a moment there was respite.

"This isn't how, Quill."

He was too busy to reply. Emmot gestured broadly, and sparkles of colored light slammed together. Another monster appeared, this one a massive snake, so big as it slowly reared back that it was physically sickening. Worse, it had five heads, each with malevolent red eyes and a mouth decorated with gleaming fangs as long as Cayden's arm.

Once more *Lost Withies* provided the answer. A Hydra was a huge beast, and stupid with it; after all, it wasn't as if its five brains (or more, because if you cut off one head, more grew in its place) were on speaking terms with one another. Cade didn't even have to adjust the magic in the withie very much. In *Window Wall*, one of the scenes outside the glass was of a flock of birds. He conjured them now and sent them flitting and chirping around the Hydra's heads. Thick, slimy green necks strained in all directions, jaws snapping, eyes frantic to find the sweet little singing blackbirds. It didn't take long for the Hydra to tie itself in knots and fall over, strangling to death.

As it winked out of existence, Cade heard Mieka laughing. "Where'd you get that one?"

"Your book," he said. Just for Mieka, he sent the birds hurtling around in a perfect circle. "'Sir Riddou and the Great Dizzydumb' was the name of the play. Just a description, no lines or cues or anything—"

He broke off and they both lost their grins as the blackbirds squawked, each hit by a separate bolt of black lightning. Feathers fluttered to the ground and the birds disappeared, and Master Emmot chuckled. Cade turned in time to see him tuck his thumbless hands back into his sleeves.

Mieka sighed quietly. "Nothing I'd like more than to have that sort of fun all night, Quill, but eventually he'll put together something you won't know how to counter."

Cade was about to say something snarky about how much he appreciated Mieka's faith in him when someone else laughed—Kaj Seamark, now holding a dark red withie of his own. "He couldn't keep pace even if we gave him the spells to do it with! Give it up, why don't you?"

Mieka ignored him. "All this blood and gore—it's not you, Quill. It may be Black fucking Lightning, but it's not *you*. Think, damn it! They've been bashing people witless with magic so long that they don't know how to do anything else!"

"So what d'you want me to do?" Case asked, exasperated. "Talk them to death?"

"It's an idea," Mieka retorted. "So are words."

"What?"

"Words. They're ideas, Quill, and they're powerful. They *mean* something."

There had been piles and piles of them in the white marble room. But that wasn't what Mieka meant, and Cade knew it. He couldn't think of words as physical things, like that notion for a play he'd had during those months when he was, he admitted to himself, thorned or drunk or both during at least half his waking hours. Words—ideas—thoughts—emotions—

That was what came at him all of a sudden: emotions. And somehow they *were* physical things, each one a clout in the guts. Raw, basic things: rage, hatred, pain, fear. Things with teeth and talons, monsters compacted into emotions. Subtler things: contempt, jealousy. Things of poison, bitterness distilled into seeping acid. All the emotions Black Lightning had compelled him to feel. Cade, who always held himself apart from the emotional impact of any performance, who feared his own violence, who hid behind his careful fortress of words—he felt himself splintering. He had nothing with which to combat this. Nothing.

"Cayden!"

Someone walloped him a good one in the shoulder. Real pain, real physical pain, courtesy of an Elfen fist. The withie dropped from suddenly nerveless fingers.

"You can't defeat them that way! It's all they know!"

Didn't Mieka understand? Summoning up the same things inside himself was the *only* way to fight them. If these things were all they knew, he had to counter with—

"If you do, everyone here will die! Pirro's magic is horrible enough—if you add to it, we're all going to die!"

The Lord and the Lady knew that right now he was scared enough to drown Pirro and the rest of Black Lightning and probably everyone within a mile in his own terror.

Terror such as the Balaur Tsepesh fed on. Emotion that would feed them, make them stronger.

Cade looked down into Mieka's strained, unhappy face. "I don't know what to do," he breathed. "Help me."

"I'm here. All of us are. We're here with you, Quill."

Mieka gave him the silver sword. It had to be a withie, it had to be—but when he closed his hand around the hilt, it *felt* like a sword. The heft of it and the balance were real, and the grip was warm with the warmth of Mieka's small hands.

No, the weight was wrong. Too light. He recognized it then. The knife that Mieka had worn at his back, that he had lost that night at Great Welkin. The knife returned to him here at Seekhaven—but not by the Archduke. Megueris, probably—but what did it matter? It was the knife that had slain Vered Goldbraider.

Cade stared at the length of it, the gleam of steel that looked exactly like a sword, the slightly different shine of silver inlay along the first six inches. No wonder Mieka had surged so close to Knottinger—he had to make sure the part that was real got close enough to do the cutting.

A sword—or even a knife—wasn't his sort of weapon. But words were. Words . . . ideas . . . concepts that words made into reality . . . words such as courage, and kindness, and loyalty, and devotion. Bravery was an idea expressed through deeds. Gentleness was in the eyes, the touch, the smile. Trust wasn't an emotion, it was a *knowing.*

All these things and more were naught but dim memories to the minds assaulting him now with magic that could no longer touch him. He met their anger and hate with words that meant infinitely more.

He thought of Derien, Mistress Mirdley, and Blye. Rafe and Jeska, Vered and Rauel and Sakary and Chat. Megs. Miriuzca. Everyone he loved.

But more than anyone else: Mieka.

"Here, Quill. Always here."

Not knowing whether he'd heard it with his ears or only within his mind, he focused his gaze on Sagemaster Emmot. He walked forward—not hurrying, not striding, merely moving to close the distance between them.

"What's your connection with him?" He nodded towards the Archduke, who was still just standing there, motionless, silent.

"Come now, Cayden. I expect better of you. I knew your grandmother, boy. Perhaps you've guessed—dreadful word, most unsuited to a scholar—why he still has no magic of his own, why he is unafraid of the fact that he's dying."

"He *trusts* you?" He couldn't help a snort of laughter.

"As much as you used to. Granted, his first four servants aren't doing as well as we'd hoped—"

"They were to go on last, after everyone else's withies were empty. Which is why Vered Goldbraider had to die. The Shadowshapers were too powerful. And Vered *knew*."

"Now you're seeing it. Once the work here is done—rather messily, but one can't quibble with success—he need never fear death again."

"His daughter weds Prince Roshien, his son weds Princess Levenie—but none of *them* gets to live forever."

"He will rule as King for enough years to create order in Albeyn, and then do as we have all done through the centuries."

"Pretend to die," Cade said, "and go on ruling all the same. Are there more of you, waiting to turn Albeyn into your own private feeding trough?" Cade shook his head slowly. "You've fed enough for one lifetime," he said, and plunged forward, stabbing the knife to the hilt into the Vampire's neck.

Cade yanked the blade free. It left a hole behind that quickly, neatly sealed itself.

The Vampire began to laugh. The muscles of his throat rippling as he leaned back his head. "Cayden! Did you think any of this is *real*? That if only you believe hard enough and strong enough, what happens here will be real in the flesh-and-blood world?"

Stunned and horrified, all he could think was that Mieka had failed him. The sword was no sword; it was naught but a withie's magic cloaking a steel blade.

"*I* can smell the silver in the hilt," Emmot went on, taunting him. "Knottinger could not, with his thorn-dulled senses. But one goes to war with the army one has." A fleeting gesture, and the steel in Cade's hands flickered, shrank, magic fading away. "Foolish of you, Cayden, to fight that war with only an imaginary weapon."

Cade glanced at Thierin, whose neck had twisted so that his face was half-hidden in his shoulder. With the hand he had left he pulled his truncated wrist closer, licking at his own blood. To him, that blade had been anything but imaginary. Dreams, imagination . . . Cayden was a man whose dreams, waking or sleeping, often enough became reality.

"You can't live without dreaming, Quill."

Reality could be defined as what one could get other people to believe.

"You have to do their dreaming for them."

So one went to war with the army one had? An army composed of fear and hate, pain, unspeakable horrors, corrosive emotion, and conjured monsters. None of it was real. Not the way Cade's arsenal was real with years of knowing and caring, of shared triumphs and failures, of loyalty and of love.

He looked down at the blade. Naught but a knife again, without the withie-magic. A beautiful thing, all shiny and smooth in his hand—but still warm to the touch with Mieka's magic and with Blye's. Into it he placed all the magic at his own command. Not the sort of magic that could create forested mountains or castle battlements or dragon or Caladrius. He primed the knife—made of steel, not glass; solid, not hollowed for the insertion of magic, but absorbing his magic all the same—he felt the growing warmth of the amethyst in its hilt that had been made to Mieka's grip. The steel did not respond—mayhap its iron resisted the Fae idiosyncrasies in his magic—but the gem and the silver did.

It was magic defined by words. His feelings for his family and his friends. Their gifts, their joy in their work, their love for each other. Words and emotions that were the real magic of being alive. And somehow these things became a libation, cleansing the blade that had killed Vered Goldbraider.

Turning, tempted to laugh at the puzzled scowl that creased the Vampire's brow, he returned to where Mieka stood and extended the knife.

"Here," he said. "Use this."

Mieka looked down at it, and then those eyes met Cade's with triumph gleaming in them, gleeful and golden. "Beholden, Quill." He paused, a grin suddenly decorating his face, and made a flourishing bow to the Archduke. Then he ran back towards the curtain, and swept it aside, and disappeared.

Left alone with four men who would love to see him dead and two who wanted very much to keep him alive, Cayden gifted all of them with his happiest smile. It widened when Thierin Knottinger cried out, and Kaj Seamark clutched at his skull, and Herris Crowkeeper fell to his knees, and Pirro Spangler toppled face-forward into his glass baskets.

Mieka had made quick work of it. *That's my Elfling.*

The glittering curtain of magic was still between the audience and the stage. But no longer did it concentrate globes of colored lights and send them like malicious arrows at any of the thousands of people out there.

He looked over at the Sagemaster. "Your work?"

A nod. "What's already done will not be undone."

Cade noted that he had not said "cannot be undone." It would be easy enough to identify those affected—just ask how much they adored Cyed Henick. Maybe he'd save them all a lot of bother and just keel over. From the look of him, that was entirely possible.

"You think you've won." His voice was thready, rattling in his throat.

"Not quite yet," Cade admitted. "But I know you're going to lose."

"Can you be so sure, boy?" asked Emmot.

He turned his face up to the night sky, studded with stars. Something inside him began thrumming with power not his own. "They're not happy with you."

High overhead, a section of sky had turned blacker than the night, like a cloud of nothingness blotting out the stars. It widened, and just as huge bodies and vast wings became visible, thunderous roars split the air, akin to the terrible cries of the *vodabiests*. The Sentinel Fae, more than a dozen of them, circled their mounts directly above the ancient Dancing Ground and slid from their saddles to descend gracefully, soundlessly, to the stage.

Chapter 42

Years and years and years—Cade might be able to understand how and why he did it, if he had a hundred years or so to think about it. But the facts were that he walked right over to Henick and rummaged in the man's pocket for the Queen's Right. The theory that donning it was fatal but that he could touch it without penalty was as yet unproved. He was shaking as he went towards one of the Sentinel Fae, the one with the biggest opalescent sashes tied crosswise on his chest. He held out the Carkanet in both hands. The silver and gold plaques were set with dollops of clear glass—no, not entirely clear. Specks and shimmers of silver and gold glinted within the glass, unfaceted but sparkling with some unnerving radiance that made him wonder what it must be like when worn by the Fae Queen.

"Yours, I believe," Cade said, grateful that his voice was steady.

The Fae studied him. It wasn't like someone staring into his eyes to try to discern his thoughts; this was a scrutiny that took him apart, observed and evaluated the workings, and put him back together again. It lasted perhaps two seconds. When it ended, he was gasping.

"Our thanks," rumbled the Fae as he slid the necklace into a pouch at his hip.

Beholden implied indebtedness. That single syllable informed him that the word itself was payment enough and he was owed nothing beyond it. Cayden devoutly agreed. Even though he'd been the one to identify the place where the Rights had been hidden, and was responsible (in a way) for recovery of the Crown and now the Carkanet, he had absolutely no desire for the Fae to consider themselves obligated.

He didn't want to contemplate what their idea of recompense might be.

"This one," called another of the Sentinels, pointing at Emmot.

"And this," said a third, standing near Henick and looking as if the Archduke smelled like something he'd scrape off the soles of his boots.

There were no gestures, no spoken words, but suddenly a cage of uprights encircled both men. The bars were made of sunlight—the way sun shafted to earth through parting clouds, and had they proved to be fire taken directly from the sun itself, Cade wouldn't have been at all surprised.

The Fae who now possessed the Carkanet turned his head slightly as another asked, "What is *this* thing?" He stood beside the gleaming curtain, scowling.

"Some rather foul magic," Cade heard himself say, even as he saw that it looked dead, somehow, a thing of substance still but without essence.

At the same time, the Fae Lord (Commander? Captain? Who knew?) said, "Nothing to concern us." He tilted his head slightly to one side, as if listening. Then he said, "She comes."

The Sagemaster and the Archduke shifted within their cages of sunshafts, not liking this news at all. For himself, Cade could hardly wait. Anything they didn't like, he was bound to welcome.

He changed his mind when she arrived.

Not that he saw it. She was simply *there*, without sound or flourish, folding leathery batlike black wings and smoothing taloned fingers through sinuous snaking curls of black hair. As tall as Cade himself, and bizarrely beautiful, she fascinated and repelled at the same time. Enormous black eyes contrasted with skin as pale and luminous as moonstone. Her mouth was wide and full, lush as a ripe plum. Most of her body—a sensuous perfection of curves and suppleness—was covered to the knees with what appeared to be petal-shaped medallions of black glass that reflected no light and chimed ever-so-gently when she moved. In one long, elegant hand she held a leather scourge tipped in gold spikes.

Cade knew her to be a Harpy, and he had never seen anything so beautiful and so terrifying in his life.

A hundred flittering winged things suddenly appeared all round her. They were iridescent and every color of the rainbow and reminded him of gnats circling a corpse. One of them separated from the rest and flashed towards him, too quickly for the eye to follow. He began to lift a hand to swipe it away, and froze as his eyes focused on it. A faerie dragon—they were all faerie dragons, creatures of legend and speculation that no one had ever really seen—he raised his hand very slowly and extended a finger, and the tiny beast hovered for a moment before deciding to alight. Its claws were like fine hot needles but he brushed aside the pain as he had so often ignored the prick of thorn in his arm, and watched it fold its shimmering wings, tilt its head, seem to examine his face with big lustrous red eyes, faceted more complexly than princely rubies. Enchanted, he took mental note of its every aspect, wishing Mieka—no, Tavier—were here to see this thing that no one had ever seen before—if Cade remembered enough, he could hire an artist to draw the thing after all this was over, and Tavier would be—

Assuming Cayden survived *all this*, which was a generous assumption.

The faerie dragon evidently made up its mind—Cade wasn't very interesting after all—and flew back to its swarm. The Harpy stretched her black wings, resettled them in elegant folds down her back, and the faerie dragons withdrew to form a small, flickering cloud of color just beyond her shoulder.

"The Seemly Court have judged?" she asked in a low, honeyed voice.

"Lady, they have."

Henick looked around dully, as if wondering where this "Court" had convened.

"This one?" the Harpy asked, drifting delicately towards Cayden. He remembered to be scared again. "I can smell the Queen's Right on his fingers."

"Touched," the Sentinel Lord informed her, and gestured to the pouch at his hip. "But only to return it."

"Ah." She smiled and, feather-light, ran the back of one curved black talon down Cade's nose. His eyes nearly crossed, staring at it. "Good lad."

Breath seeped back into his lungs and his heart began to beat again as she glided off with a tinkling of glass. Her eyes weren't completely black; they were lit with crimson and green and yellow and silver sparks.

"That one, then."

"Yes, Lady."

He couldn't help but watch those long, luscious legs as she walked to where Emmot stood within a cage of sunlight. He told himself that it was because in the event of his survival, he wanted to be able to describe her so Mieka could get her exactly right onstage. Of course he knew it was really because they were the most perfect female legs he'd ever seen. He also knew that portions of his brain were nattering at each other for no other reason than that he was frightened out of his wits.

The Harpy looked the Vampire down and up. "You have been judged by the Seemly Court, and found guilty. Not since the day when we created the Plume to ward off barbarian raiders has anyone defiled this ground."

Emmot's voice dripped with sarcasm. "Were those the barbarians who put carved dragon heads on the prows of their ships? Just to remind you that it wasn't you Fae who rode the dragons, but Giants?"

The Sentinel Lord was not amused. He rasped, "Fortunate they were that we didn't transform their ships into dragons to devour them."

When Emmot laughed, the Harpy hissed and spat. Droplets sizzled against the bars of light. "You think magic is for fun, little man? For playacting? Perhaps it's safest that way, for mortals—even mortals who are our kin," she said, with a glance at Cayden.

"As am I," Emmot retorted.

This she found entertaining, and smiled, good humor restored. She leaned closer, the serpentine ropes of her hair almost touching the shafts of light, and whispered confidingly, "Not so much that anyone would notice." Then, moving away, she pointed to Henick. "And that one as well?"

"Yes, Lady."

Wafting over to him, wings folded neatly at her back, she sniffed at him. "A sickly one." She flicked a talon against the light rays. They vanished. The Archduke looked close to death. "For some," said the Harpy, "magic is a pretty toy. For others, vengeance. For me . . . it is justice."

The same finger she had used to touch Cayden now ran down the center of Henick's chest, clawing it open with a single incision. She removed his heart with a dainty pluck of one talon. He still lived; there was agony in his eyes, the torture of physical pain and the despair-

ing horror of failure. He died only when she took a tentative bite out
of his heart, dripping blood, still beating in her hand.

The faerie dragons whirred around each other in excitement, and
moved as a single bright cloud to the fallen corpse. They began to feed.

The Harpy, however, spat out the mouthful. "Diseased filth," she
snarled. Then, more swiftly than Cade could see—but with that sweet
chiming of black glass—she was in front of Emmot, flicking a talon
against his cage. It vanished.

"You don't dare!" he grated.

She took his face between her hands and used sharp white teeth to
bite off his nose. She chewed while he shrieked, then spat him out,
too, like chankings, and said, "No crunch. Not like bones. And no salt."

"No blood," the Sentinel Lord reminded her.

Still holding his face, her talons digging deep into his scalp and his
skull, she inserted her long, steaming tongue into one of his eye sock-
ets and pried out the eyeball. Something white and slithery connected
it to his head; she bit down and freed it, then swallowed the eye like
an oyster.

Cayden turned his head away. He was within a heartbeat of being
very sick indeed, and it wouldn't do to yark all over the stage, especially
not in front of . . . kin. Emmot kept on screaming, the sound of it going
gurgly all of a sudden. Some strange, cold portion of Cade's mind commented that it could not be the sound of his throat filling with blood.
Vampires had no blood. The screaming stopped with the grinding
sound of bones being chewed. Cade dared look, and saw Emmot
sprawled on the wooden stage, his throat torn out, his head no longer
attached to his spine. Faerie dragons thronged about his corpse too.

With his death, the magical curtain collapsed with an almighty crash
of shattering glass. There were other screams now—weak, whimpering,
terror robbing everyone of breath as for the first time they looked on
the Sentinel Fae and the Harpy. Cade saw Mieka and Rafe and Jeska
clustered together, hanging on to each other for dear life. With them
were Derien and Blye—though how they'd escaped the magic and
gained the stage was something he didn't know, and frankly didn't
care about right now. Miriuzca and Megueris had their arms wrapped
around each other. Miriuzca's face was streaked with tears. Of the
three thousand or so others in the theater, Cade looked for only these,
to be sure they were safe.

The Harpy glanced about, delicately picking her teeth with one claw. She seemed mildly surprised by the sight of the rows upon rows of people in the audience. Then her shining gaze found Pirro and Kaj, Thierin and Herris.

"I believe," she said musingly, "I'd prefer to take them with us, if that suits the Seemly Court."

"As my Lady desires."

Unfurling her wings, she was gone as suddenly and soundlessly as she had come. The faerie dragons lingered for a moment, then collected together in a gorgeous blur and followed her.

The Sentinel Lord gestured, and the others collected Black Lightning and ascended to their mounts, still circling high above. He scanned the stage and the audience, then turned to Cayden.

"We are not the Gods," he said sternly, his voice carrying from the wooden wall at the back of the stage to the stone barrier behind the last rows of the theater. "But, like the Gods, we are always watching."

Always. Not just onstage, but always. From somewhere, Cade found breath to speak. "We'll remember."

"See that you do." Once more he fingered the pouch where the Carkanet now resided, and Cade was astonished to see him very nearly smile. And then he was gone, soared upwards, and the black horses bellowed once and galloped silently into the starry sky.

Cade's knees wobbled as if he'd drunk dry every tavern in Seekhaven. Blood roared in his ears, and his vision fogged around the edges. His brain stuttered almost to a stop. He couldn't think.

{ In the antechamber, all sea-green velvet and gilt, a small commotion was centered round a tall, good-looking blond boy who was talking with shy eagerness to Jeska and Rafe and Mieka. Cade approached in time to hear Jeska startle everyone in earshot by saying, "You're more than welcome to come along tonight to our celebration at Wistly Hall, Your Highness."

The boy, after a glance over his shoulder at his mother in the next room, as if wondering whether he mightn't get away with it, shook his head and mumbled, "Supper and King lessons tonight with Mum."

Megs came up in time to hear this, and laughed. "I hope she kept a good grip on the sword." Leaning up, she gave Cayden an affectionate kiss on the lips. "Sometimes, when she's knighting somebody wearing a uniform, there's shreds of shoulder fringe all over the carpet after."

Mieka snapped his fingers and exclaimed, "Damn! I forgot to ask when I'm gettin' a sword!"

"You're *not*," Cade said firmly.

The Prince was grinning. "I'm sure we've a few spares someplace."

Before Mieka could yelp his delight, Cade clapped a hand over his mouth and said, "Please, Your Highness, don't encourage him. He's behaving himself for now, but it won't last. He's handy enough with a knife, but what he might do with a three-foot blade just doesn't bear contemplating."

At exactly the same time, Megs and Mieka exclaimed, "You're no fun anymore!"}

Not now, he begged. *Please, not now—I don't have time for Elsewhens, no matter what they show me—*

But they were the futures that would spin from these moments, and he could not resist them. On his knees, one hand bracing himself on the smooth planks of the stage, he felt something cool against his fingertips, and closed his hand around it.

{ They walked at the head of a large group through the portrait gallery, to the newest addition: an imaging of Touchstone.

The imager had spared them nothing—not a line, not a sag, not a wrinkle, not a jowl, not a single white hair. The interesting thing about the piece was that uniting each separate portrait was a second one, from an imaging taken just after their first Winterly. Painted in gray tones, just behind the rich colors of the individual portraits, were four very young men—boys, really—unaware of the journey ahead of them but recklessly eager to get started.

The Princess Regent folded the blue velvet cloth that had covered the imaging, and winked at Cayden. Toasts were raised and drunk; the artist collected his accolades. As they walked through the gallery towards the back garden where the celebratory dinner would be served, Mieka touched Cade's elbow and slowed their pace, let the others get ahead of them.

"I'm glad we're not them anymore. In the painting behind the painting, I mean."

"Why? I am, too, but is there a specific reason?"

He hesitated, waiting until Cade met his gaze. "I'm glad I'm not him anymore, because I'm not sure I woulda made enough right decisions again. I did some horrible things—I was a right bastard—but I coulda made even worse mistakes. I can't trust that I wouldn't *really* mess things up, if I had to make those choices again."

Cade shook his head. "We'd just make different mistakes. Nothing that wouldn't lead us to right here and now anyway."

"You're saying that? *You*, with all your Elsewhens?"

Laughing softly at how incredulous he sounded, Cade nudged him with a shoulder. "I've discovered philosophy in my old age. And my philosophy is that whatever happens is what's supposed to happen. So here we are." }

Was that it? Did it really matter for nothing, all his agonizing and fear?

His hand clenched around a withie—no, a pen, and he was watching his own hand move that pen smoothly across the page of a letter.

{ *What I've finally realized is that every year refines you in some way. You become more purely yourself, and who you are inside becomes more visible outside. Like those lines framing your mouth. They mean you smile too much, you laugh too much—but how can there ever be too much of your laughter? Those lines are proof that I make you happy. Don't ever think they mean you're getting older. They mean you're mine.*

He saw his hand pause, reach over to dip the pen in more blue-black ink. He felt the smile curving his lips as he reached for yet another page to continue the love letter. }

But to whom?

He had no time to chase down the feelings or any images that might have lingered, for there was another scene, another Elsewhen, crowding into his mind.

{ It took effort these days to climb up to the rooftop garden. Twenty years ago, even ten, he could have bounded up the stairs, if no longer young then at least not yet old. His knee hurt, and his back. Limping slightly, out of breath as he reached the door, he paused to glance towards the far gate. He'd done what Mieka wanted. All the flowers went to the Princess's Sanatorium. He hadn't been sure what to do with the candles until Derien suggested lining the drive with them. Megs and Jindra and Blye and Guerys arranged them (and collected the flowers) every evening. By night, they became a double ribbon of multi-colored lights, stark emptiness between them. There were gaps where the candles had burned out. After a fortnight, very few were being left at the gate to replace them.

He went to the river side of the house, staring out over the dark water where no moonglade shone.

His fingers clenched around the withie he didn't recall bringing with him. It would make a moonglade for him, spread sparkling silver across the water if he so chose. But Mieka wasn't here to see it.

"I'm still here." How he hated those words, and their bleak truth. "Ah, damn it, Mieka—why am I still *here*?" }

Guerys? Who was Guerys?

From somewhere very far away, he heard a shattering of glass.

Chapter 43

"Easy, now. Careful, don't startle him."

He had heard glass shatter. He thought so, anyways. Had they performed *Window Wall*? Was it over?

"Stay back, Dery. We have to bring him out of it gentle-like."

There was a moonglade, stretching right in front of him in what was otherwise a frightening darkness.

"Out of what? What's wrong with him?"

A moonglade. This confused him. So they *had* performed *Window Wall*, with the Boy seeing the moonglade and shattering the glass with his fists and walking out into the world. But he couldn't remember, he didn't remember doing any of it, had somebody pricked him with some frightful new kind of thorn without his knowledge?

"It's all right, Quill. You're safe now."

He hesitated, squinting at the path of silver before him. "Did—did Jeska break the window?" But he was certain sure he'd heard it—hadn't he?

"What is he talking ab—"

Jeska interrupted smoothly, assuring him, "Shattered to a million tinkling little shards. Lovely, it was."

"Come on, Cade," said Rafe, very gently. "It's over."

The play was over. The first time it had been performed in full, and he didn't even remember it.

What he did remember was . . . was . . . a rainbow swirl of tiny dragons and Sagemaster Emmot and—

"All over," Mieka said. "It's all right. I promise."

—and a letter such as he'd never written before in his life (never thought he was capable of writing) and the Archduke with one eye ripped out and a *Harpy*, by all the Old Gods, a *Harpy*—

"Does he even hear us? Really hear, I mean, and understand? Mieka, what's wrong with him?"

—and huge hideous black horses and the Carkanet and Thierin Knottinger licking at his own blood and somebody named Guerys had gathered up the flowers and Mieka wanted a sword but he already had one he'd given it to Cade—no, not a sword, a knife, made of steel and silver and amethyst—

Black Lightning's fear and hate and horror had not been conquered with more and worse. It shamed him that he had taken so long to understand that. But Mieka wouldn't scold him. Mieka would understand. Mieka knew him. Mieka saw him with absolute clarity—arrogance and stupidity and cowardice and all—and cared about him just the same.

Cade would disappoint him sometimes, just as Mieka had disappointed him. But wasn't the whole point of it to make each other strive to be the best of themselves, *for* each other? To live as if the Gods were always watching . . . because they were.

—but he saw guttering candles from the rooftop and an imaging both filled with color and shaded in gray and no moonglade on the river no moonglade ever again because Mieka was dead—

"Mieka!"

"Right here, Quill. It's all right. You're safe."

"Moonglade—there has to be a moonglade—"

"Ah! Of course there is, Quill, don't you see it? There it is, old love. Walk the light, just like you're supposed to."

He nearly sobbed as the silvery pathway deepened, became substantial—as if light itself could be touched and held. There *was* a moonglade. Mieka was alive. They were all alive, and Emmot and the Archduke were dead.

Because he really was safe, because he trusted Mieka and Rafe and Jeska, he pushed himself to his feet and took the first step, and then the next, onto the pathway of moonlight. With each footfall, the darkness receded. His legs felt secure and strong beneath him. Within moments he had reached them and they were all holding each other up and that was exactly how it should be. He knew without having to think about it that without them, without that moonglade, he would have been lost.

The Crystal Sparks, Hawk's Claw, and the Stewards were milling about bemusedly onstage, mayhap looking for evidence that what they had just seen was real. Miriuzca and Megs were huddled over the King, the Queen, and Prince Ashgar.

"But it *did* just happen, right?" Rafe whispered.

Cade drew away and nodded. "Go take a look at Emmot and the Archduke—if you've the stomach for it."

"Holy fuck," Mieka said after a long, shocked squint. "They even took Thierin's hand with them."

"Just in case Her Ladyship the Harpy gets peckish on the way home," Cade said, unable to help himself, knowing that he was punch-drunk when he nearly choked on a slightly mad giggle.

Someone—not Miriuzca or Megs—screamed, "The King! He's dead!"

It seemed to release something in every one of the thousands left in the theater. Moans of fear, cries of loss, weeping and panicking and trying to escape—all of it quelled by Stewards who had never had to control this many people this powerfully before—

"They could probably use some help," Rafe said.

"Not my problem," Cade decided, and the murky haze overtook all his vision once again, and after Jeska and Mieka grabbed him to hold him upright, he knew nothing more.

*   *   *

". . . what that old man said—one of the cleaners, and *there's* a job I don't envy, what with those bodies onstage, and washing all those stone seats after three thousand people have been scared out of their minds—and their dinners—in one direction or the other—"

"Don't be disgusting, Mieka. What did he say?"

In a deep, gravelly voice: "'Ain't nobody dead up there what shouldn't oughta be.'"

"Hmm. Pithy, succinct—a rather fitting epitaph, I'd say."

"Probably not what the Archduke had in mind for himself."

"Where are they going to put him? Once he's burned and urned, I mean."

"They're not. Miriuzca says that both of them are going just as they are into a very deep hole in the ground. Again I quote: 'The worms can have them, though I can't but suppose that even worms have more discriminating tastes.'"

Cade gave a little snort of laughter.

"Are you awake, then? Finally?"

He opened his eyes. In point of fact, he was awake *again*—he'd stirred sometime before dawn, trying to turn over, to find Mieka curled up at the foot of the bed like a sleeping puppy. After the hazy thought that he really ought to nudge the Elf into a less awkward position or he'd wake with a Hellish cricked neck, he remembered nothing more until the sound of Mieka's voice woke him again.

Jeska sat cross-legged on the other bed, and Rafe lounged in the desk chair. Mieka was still at the foot of Cade's bed, a smile decorating his face.

"You *are* awake! Somebody yell down to Mistress Luta. She's been cooking up your favorites all day long."

Pushing himself more or less upright, he punched a couple of pillows into a backrest. "What have I missed?"

Rafe ticked off points on his fingers. "King Meredan is dead. So are nine Lordships, five Justiciars, a Minister of the Crown, three Ambassadors, and close to a hundred of the audience. Roshian hasn't left Ashgar's side. He is, shall we say, considerably muddle-headed—"

"How can they tell?" Cade asked sourly.

"—probably permanently," Rafe went on, "along with a few dozen others, including the Chief Steward, who was supposed to be shielding the King. Miriuzca was named Regent last night at midnight, there being enough of the government and nobility here to propose and agree to it."

"You're running out of fingers," Mieka observed.

Rafe extended his middle finger and grinned. "Miriuzca is stunned but also rather intrigued to find out that she has magical blood. Those of the audience who discovered the same are just plain stunned. Turns out that purebred Humans aren't that common in Albeyn. Everybody's got something of Elf or Piksey or Wizard or Gnome or whatever."

"Including," Jeska said, "the eight Good Brothers and Good Sisters who were there, several of whom were of Prince Ilesko's opinion about magic." He sniggered. "Until they found out that *they* have magic, too!"

"Derien?"

"Attending Miriuzca. Don't look so surprised!" Rafe laughed. "He's full young yet, but he and Megs between them are weeding out those she ought to see from those who just want to see her. I predict a brilliant future for him as her primary councilor of state—after he's old enough to legally buy a drink."

"Then Megs is—"

"Fine," Mieka said. "Once she was certain sure Miriuzca was all right—this is, you understand, after the curtain came crashing down with a noise like six dozen shattered window walls, and everybody saw what was up onstage, and the Fae left, and you fell over, and all that sort of thing—" Pause for breath. "—she sort of wilted. Dery sent word that she slept for ten hours and woke up good as new."

"I'm glad." Cade watched Mieka grin from ear to ear. "What?" he demanded.

"Oh, nothin'."

"All right, then." Hitching himself higher against the pillows, he asked, "What were you *thinking*, slashing through that barrier?"

Mieka didn't answer directly. "It wasn't destructive things that got poor Pirro in the end, y'know."

"I know."

"You do?"

It would sound sappy if he put words to it—but words and what they meant to him had got him out of that encounter with skin and brain intact. He could scarcely scorn them now. He took refuge in something Mieka had said last night. "All Black Lightning knew was how to evoke fear. Hate. Shame for being born anything but Wizard or Elfen. I made that mistake myself, y'know, when I countered their fire-breathing dragon by icing him up like the Pennynines in a snow-storm. That worked, but it wouldn't have for much longer. You're right, Mieka, it was the opposite of what they were spewing through the theater that defeated them."

Rafe nodded and got to his feet. "We'll go see about that lunching, shall we?" He collected Jeska with a glance, and they left the bed-chamber.

Cade had known them all long enough to know that Mieka had something he wanted to say and the other two had left so he could say it. Cayden relaxed into the pillows and arched a brow at him.

"Yeh, about Pirro . . ." He shifted uncomfortably at the foot of

Cade's bed. "I don't know what sort of thorn he was using, but—he wasn't anything I recognized. And it wasn't as if he was doing this on his own. Thierin was using him like—like he was a living, breathing withie, naught but magic that he gave him. It wasn't even his own magic. It was all Thierin's."

"Maybe it wasn't thorn," Cade mused. "Maybe that sort of magic, all that power, is a thrall in itself. And Pirro wanted more. Couldn't help himself." There would be a certain dark glory in it, he supposed.

"Maybe so. Towards the end there, I felt him reaching out. Pathetic, really. Some tiny crumb of him was still there and wanted to feel something—*anything*—other than what Thierin had put in those withies."

"And did you?"

"Did I what?"

"Provide."

One shoulder hitched in an embarrassed shrug. "Kind of. I guess. I tried to. There was an awful lot to work with, once I explained to everybody what was needed. Longbranch and everybody, they put everything they had into those withies, and then used them to back up what I was doing with the knife—How did you . . ." He searched Cade's eyes and trailed off. "Never mind. Tell me some other time. Anyways, first I concentrated on just a section of it, so I could hack my way through—"

"That sword was nicely done, by the way."

"Knottinger believed it, and that's what counted. Though I had to get in close, to make sure the sharp part caught him. I wanted to take his whole arm, but I didn't dare risk it." He pleated an edge of the blanket. "Quill . . . what *was* the point of all this?"

"To make everyone in the audience love and adore Cyed Henick." When Mieka snorted, Cade insisted, "No, think about it. Everybody who's anything other than Wizard or Elf hated themselves. They'd do anything not to feel that anymore. Black Lightning had found a way to identify all the magical races—"

"The colors!" Mieka exclaimed.

"Exactly. And once they knew who was what, there'd be a specific magic to change them—I've forgotten what word Emmot used, or maybe it was the Archduke, but it doesn't matter. The goal was to make everybody support him as King. They'd never question him. Never gainsay him. Because they'd *love* him. Everyone would obey, and willingly, because it would never occur to them to doubt him." He saw Mieka shudder. "He said that I'd do just what he wanted, tell him about the Elsewhens whenever he asked, and *like* it."

There was a small silence. Then Mieka said firmly, "Well, he's dead. Pity he took so many people with him."

"I feel sorry for King Meredan."

"Feel sorrier for the Queen. The last of her life with him, she hated him for everything he was."

"Somebody ought to tell her that wasn't her fault."

"We can talk it over with Miriuzca. Oh—almost forgot! Dery said that Megs was approached by the Stewards and I've a feeling Miri will make *her* Chief Steward so she can reorganize and retrain everybody."

Cade nodded. "She'll enjoy that! Might be a good idea to have a Steward at every performance, not just at Seekhaven, but out on the Circuits. Just to be safe. The Lord and Lady only know what Black Lightning might've got up to, these last couple of years. Experimenting on their audiences, preparing for last night."

"We can talk about that, too. Miriuzca wants to see us at the Castle tonight for dinner, if you're recovered enough."

"I'm fine. I'm not sure what happened to me just before that moonglade, though."

Mieka took a moment to consider his answer. "I've never seen anybody who looked like he was made of glass, but you did. I thought if I gave you something familiar . . ." He finished with a shrug.

It hadn't been just the sight of it that was familiar. It was the word itself. Moonglade was *home*. Where he was safe. Where he belonged.

Cade searched Mieka's face. This was not the broken man Cade had seen in the worst dreams—for even the death dreams weren't as bad as seeing Mieka destroyed. This was his lively, laughing, mad and clever little Elf, strong and confident. No, more than strong: *powerful*. He knew himself. He knew his own worth. He knew that he could face up to any fear. He would still play the jokester, and he would still drive them all to distraction with his pranks. But he was more than that, infinitely more, and he knew it. As for the magic . . . it glimmered from him, shining in his eyes, practically glowing on his skin.

Rafe and Jeska came in with trays of food and drink. After arranging one on Cade's bed and the other on the desk, chairs were dragged over and a lavish lunching began.

All at once Rafe asked, "Seen much of anything lately?"

The casual question interrupted him in mid-swallow. He coughed slightly, then said, "No. Why?"

"Well, it's just that it kind of occurred to me . . . to us, I mean . . ." He sighed, impatient with himself, and started again. "None of this showed up, did it? Nothing of what happened last night. Because you didn't have anything to do with it."

"I *beg* your pardon!"

Jeska held up a placating hand. "That's not what he meant. It took all of us, Cayden. Not just you alone. It was you and me and Rafe and Mieka, Hawk's Claw and Crystal Sparks—"

"Megs and Baltryn," Rafe contributed.

"And the Fae," Mieka finished.

"And the Harpy," Cade said.

"I swear that I'll never call your mother that again," Mieka said fervently.

"I should think not," Rafe drawled. "Lady Jaspiela likes her meat fully cooked."

Cade felt queasy. "D'you honestly think the Harpy—? I mean, did Black Lightning—?"

"—become dinner?" Mieka supplied brightly.

Jeska set down his fork and scowled. "I'll make you regret that, I swear I will."

"She spat out Cyed Henick," Cade said. "Didn't like Emmot much, either. Though the faerie dragons made a feast of them both."

Jeska pointed a long finger at him. "No. Not a word more." He turned to Mieka. "From either of you!"

Cade laughed. This, too, was where he was supposed to be. So easy, so welcome, to think of spending the rest of his life like this: laughing, sniping, discussing, arguing, traveling the Kingdom's stages, all in service to their creativity and their unequaled performances. It occurred to him then that last night they'd given perhaps their greatest performance to date, without ever formally taking the stage.

Which reminded him of something he wanted to ask Mieka. "How *did* you convince Thierin that it was a real sword?"

"Quill. Old thing." Making a face of infinite tolerance, he asked, "How long ago did I save your sorry asses that night in Gowerion?"

"Nine years, and I could quibble a bit with your interpretation, but what's that to do with—"

"Nine years. Do I really have to remind you after nine years that on that night you joined up with the best and finest and cleverest and gorgeous-est glisker in Albeyn?"

Jeska threw a buttered muffin at him. Rafe rolled his eyes. Mieka smiled sweetly. Cade looked at each of them in turn. The rest of his life, just like this . . . with grayer hair, of course, and in his case much less hair . . . he had the feeling that whatever the Elsewhens might show him from now on would have their basis in this moment. He laughed again, and poured them all another cup of tea.

AUTHOR'S NOTE

Seriously, now—how could books about theater not include a *deus ex machina?*

There is a nagging temptation when writing an Author's Note to address various things brought up by readers (*Yeah, they do cuss quite a bit. But who'd believe these guys were nineteen years old if their strongest language was, "Well, fooey"?*). For the most part, however, it is not a good idea to comment. The books ought to stand on their own—or, as Robert Redford succinctly puts it, "Do the work, and move on."

I am muchly beholden to Russ Galen, Danny Baror, Beth Meacham, Laurie Rawn, Gena Lang, Jim and Tracy Taylor, BJ Doty and Primus St. John, Rodney and Jeane Relleve Caveness, and Ellen Browning Scripps.

Please visit my website at www.melanierawn.com. Good folks there, to whom I am also beholden.

Moving on now.

DRAMATIS PERSONAE

(most of them, anyway)

BELLGLOSS, MASTER purveyor of thorn
BLACKPATH
    ALAEN lutenist
    BRIULY Alaen's cousin; lutenist
BOWBENDER
    AIRILIE Jeska's daughter
    JESCHENAR masquer, Touchstone
    KAZIE Jeska's wife
CHALLENDER, MIRKO tregetour, Crystal Sparks
COLDKETTLE, LORD Prince Ashgar's private secretary
CROWKEEPER, HERRIS fettler, Black Lightning
CZILLAG
    CHATTIM glisker, the Shadowshapers
    DESHENANDA his wife
DAGGERING, LEDERRIS masquer, Crystal Sparks
EASTKEEPING
    LORD KELINN Vrennerie's husband
    LADY VRENNERIE lady-in-waiting to Princess Miriuzca
EMMOT, SAGEMASTER Cade's teacher, now retired
FAIRWALK, LORD KEARNEY Touchstone's manager
FLUTER, TOBALT reporter, *The Nayword*
GOLDBRAIDER
    VERED tregetour and masquer, the Shadowshapers
    BEXAN Vered's wife

GRAINER
  CHIRENE Sakary's wife
  SAKARY fettler, the Shadowshapers
HENICK
  CYED Archduke
  PANSHILARA his wife, the Archduchess
HIGHCOLLAR
  LORD ISSHAK Lady Jaspiela's father
  LADY KIRITIN Lady Jaspiela's mother; born Blackswan
KEVELOCK, RAUEL tregetour and masquer, the Shadowshapers
KNOTTINGER, THIERIN tregetour, Black Lightning
LONGBRANCH, TRENAL tregetour, Hawk's Claw
MINDBENDER, MEGUERIS lady-in-waiting to Princess Miriuzca
MISTRESS CAITIFFER Mieka's mother-in-law
MISTRESS GESHA Trollwife at Shellery House
MISTRESS LUTA Trollwife in Seekhaven
MISTRESS MIRDLEY Trollwife at Redpebble Square
MISTRESS TOLA Trollwife; friend of Mistress Mirdley's
MISTRESS WINGDOVE innkeeper in Lilyleaf; "Croodle"
NEEDLER, ROMUALD the Shadowshapers' manager
OAKAPPLE, LORD distant cousin of the Blackpaths
PIERCEHAND, LORD ROLON owner of Castle Eyot, compulsive collector
ROBEL Yazz's wife, part Giant
SEAMARK, KAJ masquer, Black Lightning
SILVERSUN
  CADRIEL Zekien's father, Master Fettler
  CAYDEN tregetour, Touchstone
  DERIEN Cade's younger brother
  LADY JASPIELA Cade and Dery's mother; born Highcollar
  ZEKIEN their father
SPANGLER, PIRRO glisker, Black Lightning
STAINDROP, BRISHEN Mishia's sister
TAWNYMOOR, LORD Princess Iamina's husband
THREADCHASER
  CRISIANT Rafe's wife; born Bramblecotte
  RAFCADION fettler, Touchstone
  MISTRESS Rafe's mother
  MASTER Rafe's father; baker

WARRINGHEATH, MASTER owner of the Kiral Kellari
WINDTHISTLE
    BARSABIAS Hadden's great-uncle; "Uncle Breedbate"
    BLYE Jed's wife; born Cindercliff; glasscrafter
    CILKA Mieka's sister
    HADDEN Mieka's father
    JEDRIS Jez's twin brother
    JEZAEL Mieka's brother
    JINSIE Mieka's twin sister
    JINDRA Mieka's daughter
    JORIE Tavier's twin sister
    MIEKA glisker, Touchstone
    MISHIA Mieka's mother; born Staindrop
    MISTRESS WINDTHISTLE Mieka's wife; born Caitiffer
    PETRINKA Cilka's twin sister
    SHARADEL Hadden's great-grandmother; born Snowminder
    TAVIER Mieka's youngest brother
YAZZ Touchstone's coachman; part Giant

The Royals
ASHGAR Prince; heir to the throne
IAMINA Princess; King Meredan's younger sister
MEREDAN King of Albeyn
MIRIUZCA Princess; Ashgar's wife
ROSHIEN Queen of Albeyn

GLOSSARY

aflunters in a state of disorder; discombobulated
agroof flat on your face
backspang a tricky evasion
blodder to flow with a gurgling sound
bonce head
brach a hound bitch
breedbate someone who likes to start arguments or stir up quarrels
bully-rook a bragging cheater
caitiff witch
carkanet necklace
chavish the sound of many birds chirping or singing at once; the sound of many people chattering at once
clinquant glittering
clumperton clownish, clumsy lout
cogger false flatterer; charming trickster
Consecreations, the *consecrate* collided with *creation*; the local holy book
crambazzle worn-out, dissipated old man
cullion rude, disagreeable, mean-spirited person
fliting an exchange of invective, abuse, or mockery, especially one in verse set forth between two poets
frustle to shake out and exhibit plumage
giddiot "giddy" and "idiot"
ginnel a narrow passage between buildings
glunsh to devour food in hasty, noisy gulps; by extension, a glutton
grinagog person with a stupid, gaping grin

grouk become gradually enlivened after waking up

hindering a warding put on an individual's magic so it cannot be used

kagged mutilated Elfen ears

naffter stupid person

pantomancer person who sees omens in all events

pillicock idiot

poofter silly, effeminate man

quakebuttock (aw, come on—isn't it obvious?)

quat a pimple; used in contempt of a person

quod jail

quoob eccentric fool

stitch up frame

tiring room from *retire;* a private chamber

yark vomit

TELL THE WORLD
THIS BOOK WAS

Good	Bad	So-so